THE TWELVE LOVES OF CHRISTMAS

THE TWELVE LOVES OF CHRISTMAS

AN ADVENT ROMANCE COLLECTION

ALEXANDRIA BELLEFLEUR * ELISE BRYANT * OLIVIA DADE * ALEXIS DARIA
SARAH HOGLE * ZAKIYA N. JAMAL * REBECCA JENSHAK * JESSICA JOYCE
SUSAN LEE * JOSS RICHARD * M.A. WARDELL * REBEKAH WEATHERSPOON

SIMON & SCHUSTER

London · New York · Amsterdam/Antwerp · Sydney/Melbourne · Toronto · New Delhi

First published in Great Britain by Simon & Schuster UK Ltd, 2026

1 3 5 7 9 10 8 6 4 2

Simon & Schuster UK Ltd, 1st Floor
222 Gray's Inn Road, London WC1X 8HB

Simon & Schuster Australia, Sydney
Simon & Schuster India, New Delhi

www.simonandschuster.co.uk
www.simonandschuster.com.au
www.simonandschuster.co.in

The authorised representative in the EEA is Simon & Schuster Netherlands BV, Herculesplein 96, 3584 AA Utrecht, Netherlands. info@simonandschuster.nl

A CIP catalogue record for this book
is available from the British Library

Paperback ISBN: 978-1-3985-6706-1
eBook ISBN: 978-1-3985-6707-8
Audio ISBN: 978-1-3985-6708-5

Printed in China

FSC www.fsc.org
MIX
Paper | Supporting responsible forestry
FSC® C144853

INTRODUCTION

The Twelve Loves of Christmas includes twelve festive romances from today's bestselling authors—each one filled with swoony moments, a little heat, and heart-fluttering holiday cheer. From magical winter nights with strangers to snowed-in second chances and unexpected sparks with coworkers, these stories celebrate the joy, connection, and romance of the season.

Open one story each day as you count down to Christmas and unwrap a new happily ever after—one magical moment at a time.

1

A MERRY LITTLE CHRISTMAS

Jessica Joyce

"Are you sure your parents won't mind that I'm crashing your Christmas?"

Naomi, my twenty-six-year-old friend in body and eighty-year-old chauffeur in spirit, spares me a glance before turning back to the snow-dusted highway we're moseying along. "How many times are you planning to ask me that?"

"I don't know," I reply. "How many times are you going to play 'Have Yourself a Merry Little Christmas' before we get to Tahoe? Because I'm ready to match that just to annoy you."

I get another look for that, this one more pointed. "There are seventeen versions on this playlist, Eleanor."

Of course.

"I guess I have to up my game, then." I let her digest the full, ominous weight of that possibility. We still have an hour left of our drive up from San Francisco to Dollar Point, which sits on the northwest side of Lake Tahoe. "Out of curiosity, why do you have seventeen versions of the saddest Christmas song known to humankind on the same playlist as *NSYNC's 'Merry Christmas, Happy Holidays'?"

"It's not sad, it's cozy," she shoots back.

"Your argument would be much more compelling if you didn't just sniffle your way through Phoebe Bridgers's rendition."

"Jeez, McIntyre, for a social media manager, you're a hell of a litigator," Naomi says, then waves a lazy hand between us. "Fine, it's a touch melancholy, especially because she's singing the Judy Garland lyrics instead of the Sinatra ones." She glances over at me, the amusement in her brown eyes softening. "I, of course, love the Sinatra version."

"No surprise."

"Regardless of the version, it reminds me of staying up late on Christmas Eve when everyone else is asleep, soaking in the quiet before all the excitement and chaos starts the next morning. Knowing everyone is under the same roof for a while and that you're stuck together for a few days, minimum."

"You're a real poet, Naomi Molina," I say, ignoring the ache starting to radiate in my chest at the picture she's painted. My Christmases never looked like that growing up; I got a front-row seat to the rotating menu of yelling matches and stony silent treatment between my parents instead, whose resentment of each other—and complete disregard of me—only intensified during major holidays.

But I certainly wished for my troubles to be miles away in the years ahead, like Judy sang about so wistfully. I always hoped someday I'd have the kind of Christmas I'd seen in movies and heard my friends talking about.

In college, at least, I got a taste of it. I spent three years as a guest in a cozy Chicago home drenched with lights and laughter, which meant I got three years of just-after-midnight Christmas Days curled up in front of a tree decked in ornaments made out of Popsicle sticks and glitter that had chipped away with season after season of devoted handling. Three years of my head on a warm, hard thigh; of long, patient fingers combing through my hair; of a body pressed against mine in a childhood bed that squeaked when we breathed, let alone attempted other things. Three years of the Sinatra version of the song Naomi's been subjecting me to playing on a scratchy record player.

I'm still convinced that having to let it go hurt worse than if I'd never had it in the first place, but I can't find it in my heart to regret my time with Max Durham and his family. I only regret that it had to end.

"The answer is yes, by the way."

I look over at Naomi. "What?"

"You asked if I was sure that my family won't mind you crashing," she replies, "and the answer is yes, I'm sure. You're going to be greeted with open, probably terrifyingly enthusiastic arms."

"My dream," I say, hand over my heart. "I'll be on my best behavior for you, promise."

"El, I've been talking about you nonstop for the last seven months. They already know you're an angel. The only thing I really had to warn them about is your dangerous moves on the dance floor."

I snort out a laugh, which pulls a cackle out of her. Our meet-cute was facilitated by my enthusiasm for a Shania Twain song at a mutual friend's wedding back in May. Instead of getting mad that I'd bumped into her, Naomi turned around with a huge smile and said, "Oh, yay, my new best friend is here."

She was right; we've been inseparable ever since.

"Is a dance floor included in this weekend's festivities?" I ask.

"Anything can be a dance floor if you try hard enough," she muses. "Anyway, you're not crashing. I invited you."

I shoot her a look. She grins. *Invited* is a sanitized PR word for the campaign she launched to get me up to Tahoe when I mentioned that I never go back to Arizona for the holidays. I shook her off at first; I learned the hard way that getting attached to a temporary space I wished were permanent made me sadder than spending Christmas on my own. But Naomi refused to take no for an answer, threatening to strap me to the roof of her car like a piece of luggage every Christmas from here on out because "you are now an honorary Molina, and if you try to disagree, I'll tell Mom and Dad on you. Do you want to devastate your honorary parents by rejecting them?"

I didn't, nor did I want to reject the option of an ongoing Christmas invite, so I capitulated. Now, as we wind our way up Highway 80 toward the house Naomi's parents have rented for the holidays, the fizzy anticipation that hit me as soon as I said yes grows tenfold. It helps that we're driving through a literal winter wonderland as we climb farther into the mountains: giant trees with snow pillowed on every bough stretch as far as the eye can see, the rocky peaks in the distance are capped in white, and a caravan of cars ahead are decorated to look like reindeer, their little plastic antlers whipping jauntily around. I wouldn't be surprised if Santa himself pulled up alongside us in his sleigh.

"I will warn you that it's going to be chaotic," Naomi says, pulling my attention away from the festive scenery. "Every few years my mom, her best friends, and their families celebrate the holiday together, so we've got people descending from all over—Chicago, San Diego, etcetera. The kids—full-grown adults, by the way, but they still call us kids—are pretty chill, but the elders are always dialed up to a ten." She grimaces, glancing my way. "I probably should've told you that up front, but I didn't want you to bail on me."

"I wouldn't have bailed on you," I say, even as my heart dances at the passing mention of Chicago. I think about Max often, but there are three times a year when he's particularly top of mind: before, during, and after the texts we exchange on each of our birthdays, and especially the one he sends me every Christmas, just after midnight.

Merry Christmas, El. You have good plans today?

I always tell him yes, even though I want to write back, *Never as good as those Christmases with you*. But it would just be a temporary hit of something I can't have permanently. He's in Chicago and I'm in San Francisco, and that distance is the reason we don't spend Christmases together anymore.

I push the thought away as the opening strains of "Jingle Bell Rock" drift out of the sound system. I have a feeling this Christmas will give my favorite ones a run for their money, anyway.

"I love chaos," I assure Naomi. "Besides, I'm sure it won't be *that* chaotic."

She shakes her head, her laugh mingling with Bobby Helms's festive crooning. "You'll see."

It is unbelievably chaotic.

I'm not sure who I've hugged at this point. All I know is that everyone rushed outside when we pulled into the driveway of a gorgeous cabin-style home, that I've been pulled into more than a dozen people's arms, and that I'm *exactly* where I want to be.

"I'm so glad you're here with us," Naomi's mom says, squeezing me closer.

"Thank you so much for letting me—"

"Don't say *crash*!" Naomi interjects.

"Spend the holiday with you," I say, directing a cheeky smile at my best friend before turning my attention back to Annette, who beams. She's adorable, a bite-sized white woman with silver-laced wavy brown hair and a hilariously hideous Christmas sweater that lights up.

"We were very excited when we heard you were going to be a guest of honor," Naomi's dad, Oscar, says. He has sparkling eyes the same shade as his daughter's, and they're just as warm as he tosses me a wink. "For a minute, we thought we'd be subjected to another one of Mimi's terrible boyfriends."

"Eleanor," her brother, Cameron, calls as he runs after a tiny child making a break for the trees, "now that you're in my sister's life, please help her improve her taste in men."

Naomi holds her hands up in a T formation with a buzzing sound. "Did no one read the lengthy rules and regulations I sent the group chat two weeks ago?" She points at all the parents—I think there are three sets in total—before towing over a tall Black woman with shoulder-length curly hair and a wide, brilliant smile. If I remember correctly, she's the daughter of Annette's best friend, Toni. "Thea, you remember, right?"

"No commentary on or questioning of the single kids' love lives," Thea replies with a meaningful look at each parent. "Signed off on by *all* of the single delegation, by the way, so keep those thoughts to yourself."

A chorus of boos echo in the air.

I bite back a smile, sliding my arm through Naomi's as we move inside en masse. "I take it the elders regularly interrogate you about your love lives?"

"When they're together? Without mercy, hence the rule," she replies, rolling her eyes. "I snooped on some of the texts in their group chat"—she points to Annette, Toni, and their third best friend I met minutes ago, a Korean woman named Genevieve, who are cackling as they make their way inside—"and a solid thirty percent of it was them plotting date setups. I would've been hounded if I'd come up here alone."

I bat my lashes. "But then I swooped in and saved the day by having a shitty family."

"And thank *goodness* for that, because now I get you to myself," she replies, smacking a kiss on my cheek.

She says something else, but I'm too busy drinking in the scenery as we step into the house. It's lovely in all the obvious ways: soaring ceilings with wooden beams lining the open-concept space; the living room, dining room, and kitchen all lead into one another and there's a sprawling, wraparound deck that looks out into the woods. Just beyond it is the deep, beautiful blue stretch of Lake Tahoe.

But it's the less tangible things I really latch on to: it's warm and loud with conversation, full of bodies happy to be there, strewn with winter jackets and snow-sugared boots, and the air is thick with the scent of pine from the massive Christmas tree tucked into the corner of the living room.

Holiday grief is such a strange animal. I'm happy to be here now and so unbearably sad that the kid version of me never got it. And inevitably, I miss that Chicago house, with its similar feeling. Inevitably, I miss—

"Max?"

As soon as I hear that name, my head whips around with neck-cracking speed.

"What?" I blurt, but my question gets gobbled up in the louder conversation between Annette and Genevieve.

"She texted that he'd just picked them up from the airport six-ish hours ago," Genevieve is saying. "So, given the roads . . ."

Annette glances at her watch. "They should be here any minute."

As if on cue, the door swings open. I get the barest glimpse of a middle-aged white couple before they're immediately swarmed, blocking my view.

Naomi leans into me with a jokingly intoned, "The beloved Durhams have arrived."

"*What?*" I repeat, and this time my question doesn't get lost.

"Janey, the fourth musketeer, and her family," she says. "They flew in from Chicago with their youngest, and their older son picked them up from San Francisco because he was in town for a . . ." Her smile melts away as she searches my face. "El, are you okay? You look like you've seen a ghost."

There's no way, I think. *There's absolutely no way.*

But when I turn back to the front door, ghosts are exactly what I see. The Ghosts of Christmas Past, to be exact: Jane and Marcus Durham shrugging off their coats. Their younger son, Levi, who's blossomed from a gangly fourteen-year-old into a very tall and grown-up eighteen-year-old. God. Can that be right?

Yes. Yes, it can, because their older son is twenty-six now and he's changed too. His body, a rangy runner's build in college, has filled out, and so has his face. It's more angular now, his jaw glass-sharp. But his light brown hair is the same, cut in that perpetual '90s heartthrob style, and so are his brilliant blue eyes, framed by glasses I helped him pick out after I accidentally stepped on his old ones in the middle of the night. The smile he's always handed over so easily is there too.

And right now, it's directed at the beautiful woman holding his hand.

❄

I yank Naomi onto the deck and around the corner before anyone—Max, mainly—can see me.

"What the hell?" she exclaims, nearly taking me down with her as she slides on a patch of ice. "What is going on?"

"I—*shit*, oh my god—I need to avoid someone," I say, half ducking next to a covered hot tub. I think I'm having a heart attack.

She ducks down with me like a true friend while giving me a look that broadcasts she's questioning my sanity. "Who could you possibly need to avoid right now?"

My panting breaths burst into clouds between us. "Remember over the summer when I had that really bad date, and I came straight to your apartment afterward and we got drunk and talked for like six hours about all our relationships?"

"Yes," she says, drawing out the word, her eyes moving back and forth between mine. "That was a formative night of our friendshi . . ." She gasps. "Oh my god, is *Fish Breath* in there?"

I swallow hard. "Worse. It's Max."

"Janey's son?" Her eyebrows draw together as she mentally digs through our wine-soaked conversation, trying to draw a line between that moment and this one. Between the Max she knows and the one I told her about.

But I only ever talked about him that once, and in hindsight, did I even say his name? Or did I just say *he* and *him* and *his* and probably *mine*, because there's no one else in my romantic history who could properly fit those words, so my wasted brain thought names were unnecessary?

"My college boyfriend," I clarify. "*The* boyfriend. It's Max Durham. He's here. Now. With his *girlfriend*."

Every additional fact I tack on makes my stomach twist further, and the gravity of the situation hits me: I'm stuck in Tahoe for Christmas with the only man I've ever loved and the woman he's now dating. The person *he* might love. I'm going to have to *watch* him love someone else.

Naomi claps a hand over her mouth, her "No" muffled but suitably horrified.

"I'm going to throw up," I tell her matter-of-factly, then lift my head to peek back inside. Said girlfriend is still next to Max, her hand resting against his back. She's nearly as tall as him, maybe five-ten, with long, pin-straight brown hair, wide eyes of a light, indeterminate color, and cheekbones that defy gravity. She's lovely, and looks like the kind of person who could charm anyone into best friendship in a matter of minutes.

Naomi's eyes narrow as she reaches out to finger-comb

my auburn lob into something I hope looks simultaneously tousled and perfect, then wipes away the mascara that must've smudged under my eyes.

"Okay," she says with a confidence I don't feel. "We can totally figure this out, all right? It's going to be fine."

My gaze snags on the railing of the deck, and then on the barely visible stone path beneath it that winds around the side of the house. I turn back to Naomi, holding out my hand. "Give me your keys."

"Huh?"

"Give me your keys," I repeat. "I'm going to jump the railing and flee in your car."

Her expression turns skeptical. "Right. And what am I going to tell everyone who's already met you? That you were a figment of their imagination?"

I perk up, hopeful. "Do you think that would w—"

Just then, the sliding glass door rumbles open and a tiny voice bellows, "See, I told you Aunty Mimi was playing hide-and-seek with her friend outside!"

Fuck.

"Please tell me your adorable niece is talking to herself and there's no one else with her," I whisper, squeezing my eyes shut.

"I have bad news," Naomi whispers back.

"El?"

My heart twists at hearing Max's voice for the first time in four years. It's still so familiar, still so perfectly pitched, just deep enough that it gets a little gravelly when he's tired or turned on—

Or shocked, like he very audibly is right now.

I straighten, trying to arrange my body into nonchalance. Hard to do when just seconds ago I was hiding behind a hot tub with my best friend, but I'm attempting to hold on to *some* dignity here.

There's no dignity to be had, though, because when I turn around, everyone is lined up along the floor-to-ceiling windows on either side of the door, their faces pressed to the glass.

Max and his girlfriend, however, have stepped outside.

"Eleanor," he says, his eyes raking over me, like he's not sure I'm *not* a figment of his imagination.

See? I want to tell Naomi. *It would've worked.*

"Hey, Max! It's great to see you," Naomi chirps, winding an arm around my waist. When I don't say anything, she digs her fingers into my stomach, a very clear *Get your shit together*.

"Hi," I blurt. Brilliant. Groundbreaking.

"Hi," he breathes out, then clears his throat. "You're—hi."

His girlfriend looks back and forth between us, and I watch in real time as recognition blooms across her delicate features. She nearly yanks his hand out of hers and walks over to me and Naomi, the heels of her boots clicking against the deck.

"Are you *the* Eleanor?" she asks, something I can't quite name sparkling in her eyes. This close, I can confirm they're a lovely green, several shades paler than mine.

"Um." I glance over her shoulder at Max. I have no idea how to navigate this conversation: What does she know about me? What does Max *want* her to know about me?

Given that he's still staring, his beautiful mouth slightly parted, I'm on my own.

"I'm *an* Eleanor," I hedge.

A smile breaks out across her face, turning her incandescent. Unfair. "The only one who matters, right?"

Max's eyes widen incredulously, but she misses it. Her attention is laser focused on me.

"Oh, wow," Naomi murmurs.

"W-well, I don't—" I stammer.

"I'm Abby," she says, "and I'm *so* glad you're here. We were actually just—"

Max is at her side in two long strides. He grasps her hand again, fingers lacing through hers, his knuckles briefly blanching white. Abby releases a husky laugh while they carry out a silent conversation with widened eyes and raised eyebrows. Having front-row seats to the simple intimacy of it makes me die a little inside.

"You'll see," she murmurs when they've seemingly finished, her tone lilting.

Max ignores her, turning to me. His attention is like sparks under my skin, but then, it always was. A soft, disbelieving breath curls out of his mouth as he slides his hands into the pockets of his jeans. He's wearing a thick wool coat and a cream cable-knit sweater, not dissimilar to me. When we were together, we would've laughed about how we were turning into one of those couples who morph into each other. Now, all I can do is stare.

He takes a stuttering step, then rocks back on his heels, like he doesn't want to get too close. "What are you doing here?"

I tuck a strand of hair behind my ear with a shaky hand, forcing myself to glance at my best friend posted beside me like a bodyguard. "Naomi is my best friend. She invited me to spend Christmas with her family."

"Ah."

The sound is soft, knowing. A memory and a kindness. It pulls my eyes back to his—they're ocean blue. Sky blue. The color of the marker he used to scrawl his number across my thigh the night we met at some frat party after flirting for hours. The shade that colored my world in the months after we both got our dream jobs thousands of miles apart—him in Chicago to work on the Cubs' operations team and me in San Francisco to work on my favorite skin care company's social media team.

"Well," he says, rubbing a finger against the corner of his mouth as he continues to look at me, some emotion making that blue unfathomable, "I'm glad you're here."

Does he mean that? Our breakup wasn't acrimonious; if anything, it was the opposite. We tried long distance for months, neither of us willing to let the other give up their dream and move. The longer it went on, though, the harder it got, and the more I wanted to preserve what we had instead of letting it erode into what I'd watched with my parents my whole life. I told him that one night, sobbing, and from there it was inevitable. Agreeing that we loved each other but the timing was wrong was the kindest thing we could've done, and the fucking hardest.

Secretly I hoped that the timing would right itself at some point, that we'd find our way back to each other. I'd be lying if I said I haven't occasionally looked at job listings in Chicago, even though I love San Francisco.

Clearly, Max hasn't been doing the same, and I can't be mad about that, can I? Not rationally, anyway, so I paste on a smile I hope looks cheerful. Totally fine. "I am too."

Abby claps her hands together, looking between the two of us with a grin. "Wow. This is going to be *so* fun."

My smile drops as soon as Max turns to direct Abby back into the house with one last glance over his shoulder.

Naomi turns to me with her dark brows sky-high. "Well, that was . . . something."

"You know what? Forget fleeing in your car," I say. "Just run me over with it."

Almost immediately, I discover that there are two houses involved in this getaway, and that the Russells and Parks are staying in the rental next door for the next three days, while the Durhams will be staying here with the Molinas.

Which means Max and Abby are staying here.

But I'm *staying here and I can't handle that*, I want to wail. Instead, I smile when Annette tells the happy couple, along with Naomi and me, that the rooms downstairs belong to us.

"They only have twin beds, though," she says. "Hope that's okay."

"Totally fine," Abby says cheerfully. "Max snores. The farther away we are from each other, the better."

My gaze jumps to him. He snores? That's new.

"And Eleanor kicks," Naomi adds, slinging an arm over my shoulders.

Now it's Max's eyes that skip to me, flashing with awareness. That bedtime habit *isn't* new. I swear I see the ghost of a smile before he schools it and looks away.

"Fine with me too," he says, so neutrally that it makes me wonder if he's even ten percent as shaken over this situation as I am. It's so hard to tell. The shock that carved out his features for the first ten minutes after he showed up has settled into something else entirely.

When Naomi pulls me into the kitchen, it's a relief.

The chaos distracts me from counting the number of times I catch Max looking at me (ten) or the number of times he catches me looking at him (thirteen, ugh) or the number of times he touches Abby (two). I get folded into the Durham magic while I'm at it, and it makes me ache and glow in equal measure. Jane pours me a huge glass of wine, exclaims over my intricately designed Christmas nails, and asks a million questions about my life. Then she hands me off to Marcus, who shows me pictures of this year's tree setup, pointing out the blurry approximation of the spots where the ornaments I gifted them each year hang. I round out the tour with a lump in my throat while I chat with Levi, who tells me all the colleges he's applied to.

"I'm hoping to get into UC Berkeley," he says, glancing over at his brother, who's standing next to a stocking-draped fireplace, engaged in conversation even though his eyes are on us. "Especially if my brother—"

"Levi, c'mere," Max calls. "Toni wants to hear about how soccer is going."

Dinner comes and goes with Max on one side of Naomi and me on the other, with dessert and a teasing but nonstop interrogation of everyone's romantic life. Oscar starts to pull me into the fold, which makes me feel lovingly included and incredibly perceived, but Naomi shuts it down with a quelling look that Max catches.

Our eyes meet in the middle of the space Naomi's carved out between us. That takes our tally up to eleven. Or is it fourteen? Maybe this counts as the first time, since we looked simultaneously.

That brain-pounding math is a sign I need to take a quick breather, so when the idea of charades is introduced, I decide to make my escape. Naomi peers through her place in the middle of an enthusiastic huddle as soon as my hand touches the sliding glass door handle and mouths, *You good?* I give her a thumbs-up I hope is convincing, then slip outside.

Earlier, I overheard Jane talking about a smaller lake-front dock at the end of the backyard, so I head that way now, following the winding stone walkway lit with brushed gold path lights. Snow blankets the ground, and the sky stretches out endlessly overhead, velvety and star-sprinkled. I inhale the icy air, taking my first real breath of the night.

I'm so busy deep breathing that I don't realize someone else is on the dock until I'm at the edge of it. Two some-ones, to be exact—Max and Abby. They're faced out toward the inky lake, their elbows resting on the railing.

"All I'm saying is, I don't understand why you're waiting until you know the outcome," Abby says. "You just told me that the guy basically said it was yours, so why don't you just—"

"Abby." Even if he weren't right in front of me, I'd know Max's voice anywhere. But the tone is foreign to me: low and authoritative, a brick wall. "I love you, so don't take this the wrong way, but . . ."

"Shut up?" she deadpans, because of course he wouldn't say those words directly to her. Because that's just the kind of guy he is. Because he *loves* her.

I should turn around, but I can't. Hearing those words directed at someone else has frozen me more effectively than the nighttime air curling under my coat. After four years apart, I have zero claim to him, but it feels like losing him all over again all the same.

Max looks over at Abby. In the moonlight, I can just make out the strong line of his jaw, the curve of his cheek, the dark slash of an eyebrow. "Yes, that," he says. "I'm supposed to hear back for sure next week. I'll do it after that."

With a sharp sigh, she turns toward him and reaches up, cupping his cheek with irritation and affection carved into her expression. She gazes at him with such easy belonging, and I don't want to watch, I can't, but I also can't look away.

"You know," she says, "for such a brilliant guy, you sure are a dumbass."

His choked laugh quickly dissolves into a sigh that makes his body droop. "You don't get it."

"Please. You've been talking about it nonstop. I know you're scared of what she'll say, but—"

I don't know if I make a sound or if I move or if Abby just has the senses of a cat; whatever it is, it sends her focus bouncing from Max to me. She jerks with surprise, her hand falling from his cheek as a smile overtakes her face.

"Hey!" she exclaims.

Max looks over his shoulder absently, then double takes when he sees me frozen ten feet away. He straightens in increments, eyes on me; it reminds me of those time-lapse videos of flowers blooming.

"Sorry, I was"—*shamelessly eavesdropping, to my mental and emotional detriment*—"just getting some air. I didn't mean to interrupt."

"You're not interrupting," Abby says, already striding toward me, her hands jammed into the pockets of her long, puffy coat. "In fact, your timing is perfect. I was just telling Max a minute ago that you two should catch up. Chat about life and things."

"Oh, I'm not sure—"

"I am," she says as she passes me with a wink. Her hand

lands on my shoulder, squeezing, and then she's off, headed back toward the lit-up house.

I stare at it, trying to brace myself for being alone with Max. Trying to prepare myself for the possibility he won't be interested in catching up, that in a matter of seconds he'll be right behind Abby instead. I take in the cheerful movement across the windows on the first floor, the raucous noise that even the distance can't muffle, the Christmas lights that blink merrily on the tree inside. A jazz rendition of some holiday song I can't place curls into the air from a neighboring backyard, but otherwise the night is quiet.

Behind me, the deck creaks once. A second time. A steady third and fourth. I recognize the cadence of Max's footfalls; we had hardwood in our apartment that would groan if you looked at it wrong.

And then he's next to me. My heart dips as I turn to him. The warmth of his skin intensifies the scent of his cologne—spicy, delicious—and it drifts between us as he dips his chin to gaze down at me, his breath escaping his mouth in one long, white cloud.

"Hi again," I say, my pulse beating hard in my neck.

His mouth quirks. "Hi."

Several beats pass between us before I huff out a laugh. His comes a second later, much easier than mine.

"We're a little rusty with the conversation skills," he says ruefully, then nods toward the other end of the deck, his eyebrow lifting in a questioning, *Want to relocate?*

"In our defense," I say as we make our way over, "it's been four years since we've needed to use them with each other."

"Besides our texts three times a year," he replies, leaning

against the railing, his body angled toward mine, pink-cheeked and smiling.

"Besides that," I say, unable to hide my surprise that he keeps track of the exact number too.

He studies me, like he can see it, and the smile pulling at his mouth drifts away. Moonlight pours over him, edging him in silver. It turns his eyes electric. I should be cold—it's freezing, it's nighttime, there's a breeze coming off the lake—but the way he's looking at me makes that impossible.

Softly, he asks, "How have you been, El?"

I miss you I miss you I miss you.

"Good." *I miss you.* "Um, I just moved into a new apartment a few months ago—roommate free, no less."

He whistles through his teeth. "Making those big bucks now, huh?"

"*Raking* it in," I joke. "I did get a promotion, though, so that helped."

"Of course you did," he murmurs with a grin, his eyes roaming along my face. "They knew they had a good thing when they wooed you out of Chicago."

I don't miss the sadness that slips into his voice; it pushes its way into my chest too. I've tortured myself more than once thinking about an alternate path where I never found that job, where Max never found his.

But it always makes me sadder to think about the years we could've gotten had I stayed or he left. Now it's even worse, thinking about how it could be *us* here together celebrating Christmas. How I could so easily erase the space between us, slide my hands inside his coat, up under his sweater, step my fingers up the ladder of his ribs, press my palms against his hot skin, where the evergreen air can't bite at him. How I could kiss up his neck, his jaw, his mouth, how I could wind my tongue with his and taste him and it would be okay because there would be no Abby, no heartbreak, no distance. It's so real. I feel it inside my body, even though my hands are curled in my coat pockets, and that's a different kind of hurt. To be close enough to touch. To know I can't.

I realize belatedly that I've been staring at him. That he's been staring back, his throat working in a hard swallow. I look back out at the dark, quiet lake, my heart beating fast.

"You and Naomi seem close," he says, breaking the silence.

I nod enthusiastically, hungry for a subject change. "We really are, which is funny considering we only met in May. We just clicked right away, I guess."

"I'm not surprised," he says. "You're good at that."

"Clicking?"

He nods with a lopsided smile, and I can tell he's thinking of that party where we started talking and never stopped. It was so immediate, so easy.

Dammit. I have to stop thinking about us like that.

"How are things with you? Work is good?"

I nearly ask about Abby—how long they've been together, if *that's* good—but I don't want to know.

He nods. Opens his mouth and then closes it, his eyes scanning the shoreline like he's considering what to say.

"I actually had an interview out here a few days ago," he replies finally. When his attention returns to me, it's a weighted thing. "With the Giants."

My heart stops. The Giants are San Francisco's team. *My* San Francisco.

"Oh," I think I say.

"Oh," Max echoes, confirming I did.

There are a million things I want to say: *Did they find you, or did you apply on your own? Did you love them? Did they love you? Of course they did; you're so talented and unbelievably smart. Why would you choose a team in my city when you have Abby? Will you* bring *Abby? Will I have to share a city with you? Please don't make me share a city with you when you love someone else.*

But instead I ask, "How'd it go?"

His breath leaves him slowly, softly. His eyes don't leave mine, turning intense. "It went really well."

"Oh," I say again. For a second, it's all I can get out. I'm pretty sure he's just answered several of my questions, and I'm afraid of what that means for my heart.

The conversation he just had with Abby makes sudden sense: He wanted to wait until he heard back about the job before telling me about it, but she was pushing for him to say it now.

"Well." I swallow around the lump in my throat, around the sadness and, frankly, the anger, though I know I have no right. It's just—of *all* fucking teams. "That's amazing, Max. They'd be lucky to have you."

He doesn't respond right away. He just looks at me in the near darkness, his expression searching. After a moment, he straightens, something fortifying in his eyes.

"El—" he starts, but then Oscar's voice bellows from the house.

"Come in for charades, kids!"

I'm halfway up the path before Max has even moved. For the rest of the night, I stay the hell away from him and try not to think about what he was going to say next.

❄

I wake up on Christmas Eve with a black cloud hanging over my head.

Naomi keeps me close during our ski day at Palisades, having been privy to my meltdown the night before, when I told her about my conversation with Max by the lake. Specifically—and repeatedly—about how I overheard him telling Abby he loved her.

"It's just weird," she mused once my fifth retelling had stalled because I was falling asleep midsentence. "My mom said Max told her it wasn't serious."

That's the thing: From the outside, it doesn't *look* serious. I can count on one hand the number of times they've touched, and it's not like the contact is ever deeply affectionate. They're certainly not hanging all over each other. But I know what *I love you* means, especially from Max Durham, and in this case, the old adage *actions speak louder than words* doesn't apply.

That thought trails me up and down the mountain all day, but my spirits improve once we get back to the house. It's hard to stay despondent with holiday music piping through the sound system and all the little kids begging their grandparents to open presents and conversation flowing while snow falls gently outside. It is, in so many ways, the Christmas I always crave.

And when I catch Max looking at me an additional eleven times, when I notice the close, intense conversation he and Abby have in the kitchen while the rest of us watch *White Christmas* on the couch, when I feel an ache in my chest I can't seem to shake, I studiously ignore it all.

But I'm still awake sometime after midnight, listening

to Naomi's soft snores, my body waiting for the text message that usually comes around this time.

Eventually, I give up the fight and creep up to the living room. The tree is still lit, presents stuffed underneath, waiting with anticipation for the crack of dawn, when all the kids will no doubt be up and ready to tear into them.

For now, though, this space is mine. I curl up on the couch, drape a fuzzy blanket over my lap, and then pull up a song on my phone and press play.

The first strains of "Have Yourself a Merry Little Christmas" hit me right in the throat. All the memories I have synced to it play in my mind—the early morning Christmases with Max, every night I spent alone after them, the drive up here yesterday with Naomi—and I let them, leaning my cheek on my hand as I gaze up at the tree. I'm listening to the Judy version because that's partly how I feel: wistful that someday the fates will conspire to pull me toward the people I love most. Max, if I'm being honest. My parents, if I'm being even more honest and ten times as delusional, because that relationship will likely never change.

But I feel the Sinatra version, too, like that moment has already arrived in some ways. Like I've *made* those moments, because they matter so much to me. Like all I have to do is hold on.

Maybe that's how it's always going to feel for me: a little bit torn in two. If that's the case, I can handle it. I can love it, even.

But the ache in my chest is still there, and as the minutes pass and the text I normally get doesn't come, it starts to radiate. Logically, there's no reason Max would text me. Not when we're in the same house, and especially not when he has Abby.

I can't help wishing for it anyway.

A second later, like a little Christmas angel's bell, my phone dings. I look down, my heart in my throat, to find a text staring expectantly up at me.

Merry Christmas, El. You have good plans today?

Something dissolves inside me. Some sadness, a little bit of anger, both at him for moving on and myself for not ever telling him I couldn't. And in its place grows a tiny bit of hope, though I don't know for what.

I pick up my phone, mulling over how to reply while my heart throws itself against my ribs. I could give the standard answer, but his message doesn't feel standard, even though it's the same as last year and the three years before that. It feels like a hand reaching out, and I can't help reaching mine back, so I send a picture of the Christmas tree with a text that reads,

Currently.

And then I stare at my phone screen, waiting for his response. I stare at it so hard and with such intensity that I don't notice he's in the room until he's a foot away.

"Holy shit, you *scared* me," I gasp, pressing my hand over my heart.

The tree lights illuminate his tiny smile. "Consider it payback for the shock you gave me yesterday."

"Yeah, well, please note that you did the same to me," I reply, watching as he lowers himself onto the couch. He's wearing the threadbare sweats he should've thrown away years ago, an old Golden State Warriors shirt with a significant rip at the left shoulder seam, and his glasses. His hair is mussed like he's been running his fingers through it. He looks almost frozen in time, like the college boy I fell in love with and let take me home. It's hard to believe we've spent any time apart.

I glance at the bare space between our knees. When I look back up, Max's attention is trained there too.

"I was hoping you'd be up," he says quietly, curling his fingers into his palm. His gaze flickers up to my face, roaming for a beat before our eyes latch. "Didn't expect you to give me the exact coordinates, though."

"Why were you hoping I'd be up?"

It takes him a few seconds to reply. I always loved that about him, that he considered his answers at length, that he seemed to arrange the words in his head before letting them go, but right now I wish he'd spit it out.

"Because we didn't get to finish our conversation last night," he says finally. "And today, you were . . . pretty unavailable for a one-on-one talk."

He doesn't say *because you were avoiding me*, but it's heavily implied by the look he gives me.

I shift, caught off guard. "What else is there to say? I got the important parts: You had an interview, it went great, and you might be moving to San Francisco."

With Abby. I can't bring myself to say it out loud. I don't want it confirmed, not on Christmas.

His expression softens, even as resolve sharpens in his eyes. "Actually, I didn't get to the important part at all."

I'm shaking my head before he even finishes the sentence. "Let's just leave it for now, Max. It's Christmas, and I overheard you saying you won't hear back until next week anyway, so—"

I stutter to a stop, realizing a second too late that I'm not supposed to know that.

"How do you know that?" he echoes.

"I"—*shit*—"I heard you and Abby talking last night, before you saw me. She was encouraging you to tell me and you were saying you didn't want to before you knew for sure." I swallow hard, trying to stave off the emotion welling in every corner of my body, but it leaks out of my voice when I say, "I heard you tell her you love her."

It must show on my face, too—how hard that was to hear, how much I wish I hadn't heard it, how immensely I wish he hadn't *said* it—because understanding lights his eyes. Because he lets loose that quiet "Ah."

I focus on rearranging the blanket on my lap so I don't have to see whatever emotion comes next: pity or sympathy or some version of *Well, what did you expect? I moved on. You should too.*

But that's not what he says. This is: "I hope you know that if I'd known you were going to be here, I wouldn't have invited Abby."

My eyes fly up to meet his. *"Max—"*

He holds up a hand, scooting over until our knees are pressed together and I can feel the heat of his skin through his sweats, through my blanket. He leans closer, his eyes moving back and forth between mine. He looks so earnest, a little flushed. "And I sure as hell wouldn't have asked her to pretend to be dating me."

All I can get out is a choked "What?"

"I just . . ." He lets out a breath, his voice quieting. "Christmas has been hard for me the past few years."

A knot forms in my throat. "Yeah."

"Given the Christmas setup this year—all the families together for the first time in years—I knew there'd be questions about whether I was dating, and if I was, who? If I wasn't, why?" he says, his attention drifting to the tree. "I just didn't have the energy to deal with it, and Abby's family is in San Francisco, so she was already planning to travel here from Chicago. It was easy enough to get her on board." His eyes find mine again. "She was a great friend for agreeing to help me out, but that's all we are."

"Friends," I whisper, dazed. "You're friends. You love her like a friend."

Max nods, moving closer. "She also has a really fucking awesome girlfriend. So."

I press my hands against my hot cheeks. "So last night you weren't trying to gently break the news that you were probably going to move to San Francisco with *your* fucking awesome girlfriend?"

He laughs, a short, shocked guffaw. "No. That is not at all what I was trying to say."

"Please tell me what you were trying to say, then."

"Eleanor, I . . ." He stops, shaking his head. A muscle in his jaw jumps before he tries again. "I saw the posting for that job six weeks ago and wondered if it was a sign. And then I didn't give a shit whether it was or not, I just *wanted* it. I applied for it thinking I had maybe a ten percent chance of making it through the first round, never mind getting to the final one." He turns back to me, his eyes lit up from the reflection of twinkling lights. The color of them brings new, beautiful meaning to the idea of a blue Christmas. "There was a not-insignificant part of me that was scared of what you'd think of me even trying. I know it's been four years, and maybe you want nothing to do with me. Maybe me being anywhere near you is a nightmare, and fuck, I probably should've *asked* you all that before I applied, but I—"

"No."

Max stops, inhaling sharply. I swear I see something like hope flickering across his face. "No?"

"It wouldn't be a nightmare. It would be . . ." My breath catches on a knot of emotion in my throat. "It would actually be the opposite." *A dream.* "And since you confessed first, I'll confess now that after you told me about the interview last night, I had a meltdown thinking about you moving. Thinking about you being in San Francisco with someone you loved."

"Well"—he stops, then laughs softly as he shrugs, his expression a little helpless—"I would be."

The confession dumps adrenaline into my veins. Something warmer into my heart. I whisper, equally helpless, "Max."

A shy smile spreads across his mouth. "Since you confessed back, I'll give you another one: I did get the job."

My jaw drops. "But you told Abby—"

"That I didn't know for sure yet, yeah," he says. "She pulled me outside to badger me about telling you everything right then, but like I said, I was scared of how you'd respond, and also completely fucking turned around about seeing you." His gaze drifts over my face, resting on my mouth. "I still am."

"Terrified?"

"Turned around," he replies, catching his bottom lip with his teeth as he smiles. His eyes bounce back up to meet mine. "Was from the first second I saw you in that shitty frat basement."

Outside, snow continues to fall, but for a second it feels like that late fall night we first laid eyes on each other. "And here we are all over again."

"Exactly where I hoped we'd be," he says.

My throat tightens. "Me too."

He nods, then murmurs, "Will you come closer, El?"

I do, heart pounding and also perfectly settled, because he's pulling me into his arms and it feels like all my favorite Christmases, like coming home. I close my eyes when our bodies crush together, laugh when he pulls me sideways onto his lap, when he presses his nose into the curve of my neck. But it dissolves into a sigh when he lays a collar of soft, tender kisses across my throat, when he presses his mouth to the underside of my jaw, my cheek, and then my lips. We sigh together and I think, *Finally*, at the same time he says it out loud. The first kiss is light, a snowflake on my skin, but when he brushes his thumb along my cheek, when he angles my head to take it deeper, it turns into something else altogether.

"You're coming to San Francisco," I whisper against his lips after a few minutes of dizzying making out.

"You're going to be in San Francisco," he whispers back, wrapping his hand around my ponytail, his eyes luminescent, "with me."

We fall back into it, but eventually Max murmurs, "We have so much time, honey, let's take our time," and we fall back into something else that feels just as familiar: me with my head in his lap, him with his fingers combing through my hair, "Have Yourself a Merry Little Christmas" playing on my phone. Jane even brought one of their family's old ornaments, and it hangs next to the ornaments of the Molinas, the Russells, the Parks. I swear the glitter that coats the Popsicle sticks winks at me. We laugh about how shocked everyone—well, everyone but Abby and probably Naomi—is going to be later when the news comes out, and Max tells me his mom is going to cry, which makes *me* cry.

I'm watching the Christmas lights twinkle, trying not to fall asleep against the warmth of his thigh under my cheek, when he says, "You know, you didn't answer my question."

"What question?" I ask, rolling onto my back.

Max curls over me, cupping my chin, a soft smile playing on his lips. "If you have good plans this year."

"Oh yeah," I say just before his mouth covers mine. "The best."

2

DECKING HIS HALLS

Alexis Daria

CHAPTER ONE

On Thanksgiving, after I rant to my brother, Fernando, about my roommate telling me *two days ago* that she's not signing our lease renewal, and the impossibility of finding an apartment I can afford alone on such short notice, Nando puts a hand on my shoulder and says, "I got you, Noelia. Just stay at my place."

I've been talking a mile a minute, so it takes me a second to catch my breath. "What do you mean? You don't have an extra room."

He glances around, then beckons for me to follow him upstairs to the second floor of our parents' house. Once we're out of earshot of our nosy tías, he leans in and speaks in a hushed tone.

"Don't tell anyone, but I've been living with Iris for the past few months."

My eyes widen at the mention of his girlfriend. "You *have*?"

"Yes, and before you ask, I *am* going to propose to her. I just don't need all of them"—he gestures downstairs, encompassing our loving but overbearing Puerto Rican family—"on my ass until I've done it. I want to wait for our trip to DR in February."

I scoff. "I wasn't going to ask."

I was *totally* going to ask.

I can roll my eyes about my family's love of bochinche, but the fact is, I'm as big a gossip as any of them. Except maybe for Titi Concha, who literally keeps a set of binoculars on her windowsill.

"My furniture is still there," Nando is saying. "But I've moved out most of my stuff. I'm paying rent, so you might as well put your things in storage and use my room until you find a new place."

My heart swells with gratitude and relief. This is quite possibly the best-case scenario for my predicament.

Except for one thing.

"What about David?"

Nando's expression doesn't change. "What about him?"

I squint at my brother. "You don't think he's going to have an opinion about someone else moving in with him?"

Nando shrugs. "Why would he? It's not like you're a stranger. He's known you practically your whole life."

"That doesn't mean he'll want me in his apartment. What if he says no?"

"He won't."

There's a commotion downstairs. Someone new has arrived, and everyone's voices rise in greeting. My mother's Bronx accent cuts through the din.

"David, you made it!"

Speak of the devil.

"I'll ask him now," Nando says, and I can't ignore the dread settling in my gut.

Or the glimmer of anticipation.

I watch my brother go, his tall, lanky frame jogging down the staircase.

I'm not a coward, but I hide in one of the bedrooms for a little while.

Okay, maybe that does make me a coward.

I finally come out when my youngest cousin insists I be on her team for *Mario Kart*. When I get downstairs to the living room, my gaze immediately zeroes in on David as he exits the kitchen with a full plate of food.

Our eyes lock. The breath squeezes from my lungs.

Fuck. Me.

David Fonseca is thirty-six years old and looks like a hot Latino dad, aside from the fact that he's not married and doesn't have kids. He's got deeply tanned skin; brown hair cut short; a trim beard; straight, thick brows; and lips that I imagine are soft and kissable. His nose is a bit large for his face, but it keeps him from looking *too* handsome.

It's his eyes, though, that have always been my downfall. They're narrow, but thickly lashed, and the most stunning amber brown I've ever seen.

Those eyes keep me rooted in place, unable to look away.

After what seems like a year but is probably just a heartbeat, he gives me a barely perceptible nod.

A warm, tingling feeling washes over me, but I just press my lips together and nod back.

And that's how I end up living with my older brother's hot best friend.

CHAPTER TWO

It's probably obvious that I've harbored a massive crush on David for *years*. I hate being that much of a cliché, but here we are.

David is four years older than I am. He was the first kid in our neighborhood to grow a mustache, which meant he was the first one to be able to buy beer. Not at our local bodega—please, the owner would've called David's mom in an instant. There was another store in walking distance that didn't card, so that's where David and Nando went. Nando, who could *not* grow a mustache until maybe three years ago, would wait outside.

The whole thing made David something of a legend in our little corner of the Bronx. It wasn't like I was partaking in said beer, considering I was only in middle school at the time, but the fact that he was *my* brother's best friend and always hanging out at *my* house made me feel a little more grown-up by extension.

All that to say, David was *cool*.

He isn't that tall, maybe five-eight, but he still seemed like a giant to me. He played football in high school, which means he bulked up right around the time I started paying attention to his body.

I never made a move, though. And unsurprisingly, neither did he.

I had a prolonged awkward phase that lasted until I was seventeen, when I finally got a bra that properly fit the massive boobs that popped out of my chest overnight in eighth grade. My hair is black, and I'm the palest one in my family, with a perpetual Resting Bitch Face, an inexplicably deep voice, and overly large dark eyes. It's only natural that I was drawn to every Tim Burton–esque fashion subculture you can imagine. Goth, emo, grunge, punk . . . It's amazing my fingernails weren't permanently stained by black Sharpie.

These days, my style is what I call "cleavage-forward." I topped out at five-three, and I'm curvy and soft all over. But while I now embrace my body instead of hiding it in dark, baggy clothes, I'm still that rebellious New York City teen at heart, and to me, David is still my older brother's best friend, the unattainable hot jock.

As of today, however, he's also my annoying roommate.

❄

Exhibit A.

It's my first day in David's apartment and I'm feeling unsettled, so I decide to put up a small, fake Christmas tree in the living room to cheer myself up.

"Already?"

David's voice comes from right behind me, and I jump, nearly dropping the delicate glass bauble in my hands.

I glare at him over my shoulder. He's wearing a T-shirt and an old pair of sweatpants that somehow manage to look indecently sexy on him. A feat, considering he's got his hands planted on his hips and his upper lip is curled like I tracked dog shit across the rug.

"What's the problem?" I say it a lot nicer out loud than I do in my head.

He eyes the tree up and down like it insulted his grandmother. "Isn't it a little early?"

"For what?" I know for what, but I want to make him say it.

"For Christmas."

I give him a saccharine smile. "It's December first."

"Exactly."

I clamp my mouth shut, because I haven't even been living in this man's apartment for a full twenty-four hours, and I probably shouldn't tell him where he can shove this Christmas tree so early into our cohabitation.

Instead, I take the opposite tack, making my voice as sugary sweet as possible. "Would you like me to take it down?"

"I didn't say that."

"So what *are* you saying, David?" Okay, that didn't come out as sweetly as I'd intended.

He raises both hands and slowly backs away. "Just that it's early. Carry on."

"I will." My tone is haughty, but I watch him go, biting my lip at the way the worn cotton pants mold to his sculpted ass.

❄

Exhibit B.

The following week, I'm blasting noughties Christmas pop songs while baking coquito snickerdoodles for my school's annual teacher's cookie exchange. David comes in for his daily can of ginger ale, his only vice these days, and shoots me an exasperated look.

I turn up Britney and sing along—poorly.

He sighs.

❄

Exhibit C.

Two days later, after a tough afternoon with my kindergarten class, I pick up a wreath for the front door on my way home. It's decorated with pine cones, holly berries, and a big red bow, and it smells amazing.

David gives the smattering of needles that fall onto the welcome mat a pointed look and passes me the handheld vacuum.

Welcome, my ass.

I can't explain what comes over me, but something about David's reaction to the Christmas stuff makes me want to see how far I can push him.

I buy a bigger tree—a real one, this time—and make sure I'm in the living room when he comes home.

His response doesn't disappoint.

He's in the process of taking off his heavy down coat when he stops short.

And stares.

The star on top of the tree brushes the ceiling. This is a prewar apartment on Pelham Parkway, so the ceilings aren't low, and it wasn't easy to transport a tree this tall by myself. Thankfully, the building has an elevator.

I've covered the branches with colorful blinking lights, the most ostentatious garlands I could find, and those silvery strands of tinsel that get absolutely everywhere. I also remembered that my mom has a collection of lifelike bird decorations that were only used once because my father hated them. He said their eyes followed him around the room. Mom still has them, of course, because she never throws anything away. So I picked them up yesterday, telling her I needed them for a class project. Aside from keeping Nando's secret, I wouldn't put it past my parents, who are both Catholic in only the loosest sense, to suddenly decide I'm living in sin if they knew the truth.

Anyway, those creepy birds are now nestled throughout the gigantic tree in David's living room. And Dad was right; their beady little eyes *do* follow you. They are perfectly hideous, and I adore them.

David, on the other hand, takes one glance at the tree and sends me a pained look. "One wasn't enough?"

"Nope." I pop the *P*, just to be a brat.

He squints. "What are those in the branches?"

"Birds." I hum the opening bars of "The Twelve Days of Christmas."

His eyebrows shoot up. "Not real ones, I hope."

I let out a snort of laughter. "No, viejo. You need glasses."

He sighs and bends to untie his boots. "You're probably right."

I watch as he hangs his coat in the closet, sets his boots on the rack by the door, and strips his burgundy sweater over his head. He's only wearing a white T-shirt beneath, and the hem rises to his rib cage when he pulls off the sweater.

I fight the urge to bite my knuckle as I take in the bared expanse of skin and the shift of muscles underneath. He doesn't have the definition he had when he was younger, but he's broader now, solid and strong. I imagine he could throw me around—in a fun way.

"I made lasagna," I say abruptly, and face the TV, because I don't want him to catch me salivating. "And banana bread."

He pauses at the entrance to the hallway. "All right, I forgive you for the tree."

I hide a smirk and resume watching Christina Milian's latest Christmas rom-com. And to my surprise, David joins me on the sofa a few minutes later with a big helping of lasagna and watches the rest of the movie with me.

A week later, I'm watching *The Holiday* in the living room and waiting for David to come home from visiting his mom at an assisted living facility in Riverdale.

"Welcome back, roomie," I call out when the door opens. It takes all my self-control to keep my eyes on the TV and feign nonchalance, but at the sound of clinking glass, I whip my head around to see him with no fewer than three reusable grocery bags twined around one solid fist.

I catch the way his expression changes when he sees what I've done. Surprise turns to shock, shock to horror, and then, finally resignation. His response fills me with gleefully petty satisfaction, and I bite my cheek to hold back a grin.

His features settle into a baleful glare.

"What?" My tone is all innocence.

He gestures wildly with his free hand. "You really needed more?"

"What do you have against Christmas?" I ask primly.

"I don't have anything against *Christmas*. I just don't like *clutter*."

That, I could've guessed. This apartment is a minimalist's wet dream. Everything is dark brown and beige—*so* boring—with sharp corners just waiting to kneecap you in the dark. It does, however, make the perfect backdrop for all of my thrifted decorations. It's like the holiday aisle of a craft store exploded in here.

There are pine boughs and holly draped over the archway into the living room and above the lintels of every door in the apartment. Lights twinkle *everywhere*. A miniature Christmas village covers the top of the TV stand—his fault, for mounting the large flatscreen on the wall and leaving a completely bare surface just begging to be adorned. There's a life-sized baby reindeer made of some kind of dubious organic materials peeking around the edge of the sofa, and a plastic nativity scene sits in the center of the dining table. Gingerbread-scented candles and glittery pine cones surround the manger like a summoning circle.

I've also replaced all the charcoal-gray place mats with red-and-green ones featuring kittens and puppies in Christmas sweaters. They were the worst ones I could find, and I sort of fell in love with how unbelievably tacky they are. I am truly my mother's daughter.

I sniff. "I think it's festive."

He eyes me with suspicion. "How much more *festive* are you planning to get?"

"To quote the cinematic masterpiece *Mean Girls*, the limit does not exist."

He blinks. "Maybe we should discuss this."

"Who are you? The Grinch? Putting restrictions on Christmas cheer?" I get up and lead the way to the kitchen. "Come on. If you stop complaining about my decorations, I'll make us dinner."

"I knew there was a reason I hadn't kicked you out yet," he grumbles, but he's smiling when he says it.

I make us chicken piccata with roasted vegetables, then force him to watch *The Holiday* with me while we eat.

"Tomorrow we're watching *Die Hard*." He says it like it's

a threat. Like Nando and I didn't watch it with our father every year growing up.

Like I'm not *thrilled* by the prospect of another movie night together.

"You *would* think that's a Christmas movie," I mutter, just to get a rise out of him.

It works.

Afterward, as I'm unloading the dishwasher in the narrow galley kitchen, I catch David's eyes lingering on me whenever I bend over or reach for a high cabinet. His unexpected perusal sends a rush of heat through me, and I take every opportunity to brush against him. By the time we're done cleaning, I'm sweating, and he probably thinks I have no sense of spatial awareness.

There's no denying it: I want David Fonseca. And not just because he's great to look at. I like spending time with him—and yeah, annoying him too.

But if I throw myself at him and he turns me down, it'll make living here supremely awkward.

And if he doesn't turn me down? We'll have to deal with my brother.

It's a lose-lose situation, which means I need to keep my hands to myself.

CHAPTER THREE

Christmas is a week away and every inch of the apartment is decorated . . . except David's room.

But that's about to change.

I've been paying close attention to his schedule. He works from home as a coder, using the small third bedroom as an office, but he goes to the gym every Saturday morning and visits his mom afterward.

I'm writing lesson plans at the dining table and eavesdropping while David talks to his mother. He's speaking Spanish, and while my conversation skills are limited, I understand well enough to gauge how long he'll be gone.

I wait five minutes after he leaves, just in case he forgot something. When he doesn't reappear, I spring into action. I have about two hours, which should be more than enough to execute my scheme.

❄

Half an hour later, I'm knee-deep in tinsel when his bedroom door slams open.

"Noli, what the hell are you doing?" David snaps, making me scream and fumble the heavy vintage snow globe I was placing on his dresser. David lunges for it like it's a football, but I try to catch it too, and my foot tangles in the Christmas lights hanging over the arm of his chair. I lose my footing and crash into him. David manages to catch me *and* the snow globe, but our momentum carries us sideways. He twists at the last second, toppling us onto his bed.

We both land with a loud "Oof!"

My heart tries to pound out of my rib cage, and I can't seem to catch my breath. All I can think about is how fucking good he smells and how much I like the feel of him beneath me. I'm sprawled across him, my breasts pressed to his chest. One of his arms is banded around my waist, and that damned snow globe is cupped in his other hand, resting beside his head on the mattress.

Inside the glass orb, specks of glitter swirl before landing on a childlike angel's gilt-covered form. This snow globe belonged to my late grandmother, and I hope she's tuning in from Heaven right now, because she'd find this shit highly entertaining.

I plant my palms on David's chest and push myself into a sitting position—a mistake, because I'm now directly on his lap, and the warmth between my thighs is pressed right up against an area of his body that feels suspiciously . . . rigid.

On second thought, I hope Abuela's *not* watching.

My brain short-circuits, unable to compute the possibility that I might be straddling David's erection. It's the only excuse I have for what I say next.

"God, David. If you want to fuck me, just say so."

It's a joke. *Obviously* it's a joke. I'm smiling, half laughing, but I'm also breathless and there's a ragged edge to my words that makes the statement sound like what it is.

An invitation.

I cast about for something, *anything*, I can say to deflect, but then David pushes himself up on one arm so we're face-to-face. His jaw could be carved from granite, and when his lips part, I swear the earth shakes.

"You want me to say it? Fine. I'll say it." He cups my jaw and brings our faces even closer together. His amber eyes glint with a nearly feral intensity as he enunciates each word. "I want to fuck you, Noelia."

The smile drops from my face, and for a second, I'm sure I've misheard him. Is this a prank? Retaliation for the Christmas decorations? But there isn't a trace of humor in his expression. Only . . . *need*.

"Are you serious?" It comes out like a squeak.

He huffs, and some of the tension in him visibly eases. "You have no idea how I feel about you, do you?"

His proximity has demolished my already flimsy filter. My mouth, the thing that always gets me into trouble, opens, and I whisper, "*Show me.*"

As if he'd been waiting for permission, he pulls me into a kiss.

I'm not expecting it, and the angle is wrong. But then he tilts his head and teases his tongue along the seam of my lips, and I part them with a sigh.

From there, everything is right, right, right.

Whenever I imagined kissing David, I always thought of movie kisses where the characters crashed together, so overcome by passion that they lost their minds.

But this isn't a movie. There's no swelling music, no mood lighting, no clever camera angles. There's just me and him, lit by his standing lamp. The only sounds are my quiet intake of breath, the rustle of fabric as he shifts on the bed, and the slick glide of our lips.

We take our time, learning each other's mouths and tastes. It's good, *really* good, but I want more. I grab the hem of my low-cut tank top and peel it over my head. My hair settles around my shoulders, and I wish I could take a picture of his stunned expression as he gazes slack-jawed at my heavy tits, displayed to perfection in black lace cups.

"*Fuuuck.*" He exhales the curse like it's a prayer.

Honestly, it is the only acceptable response to my boobs, which are objectively fantastic. If he hadn't reacted like he was in the presence of divinity, I might've gotten up and left. But he looks appropriately awestruck, so I stay put and flick at his hoodie. "Your turn."

He releases my waist and holds himself in a sitting

position through core strength alone, yanking his sweatshirt and T-shirt off in one go. And then I get a close-up look at those flexing abdominal muscles, and I swallow hard on a throat that's suddenly gone dry.

"Nice." My voice sounds strained.

He quirks a brow. "Ditto."

He kisses me again, deeper this time. His hand slides up my back to unhook my bra.

I break the kiss, sucking in air. "Yes," I whimper. "Touch me."

With an appreciative groan, he pulls back a little to give the expensive undergarment space to fall away. I slide the straps down my arms and toss the bra to the side, where it lands on his rumpled comforter.

A look of wonder transforms his features as my breasts are revealed. And then, *finally*, he cups them in his big, warm hands. His thumbs tease my nipples, and the answering jolt of arousal makes me moan.

"These are the only snow globes I care about," he murmurs, squeezing gently.

A laugh bubbles out of me. "If you'd let my grandmother's snow globe break, she would've haunted you for the rest of your life."

He lowers his head, muttering, "It would've been worth it." And then his mouth closes over my nipple. The warm, wet curl of his tongue is perfection, and for once, I can't think of witty quips, because I'm too absorbed in *him*.

My fingers sink into his hair. Pleasure spirals through me, electric and all-consuming. I rock my hips, needing the friction. But it isn't enough. I push on his shoulders and we end up lying on the bed, me on my back and him leaning over me, continuing to worship my breasts. The hot suction of his mouth stokes my desire higher, and I writhe beneath him until I'm so turned on, I can't take it anymore. I undo my jeans and begin to push them down my hips.

He raises his head. His eyes are dark and lust-drunk, his lips swollen and wet, his hair in disarray. "What are you doing?"

"Getting naked. You wanted to fuck me, right?" I'm feeling vulnerable, which makes me brash and bossy. "You'd better make this good. Don't waste my time."

"You're such a brat." But he says it like it's a compliment, like he finds my brattiness delightful. In a softer tone, he adds, "Don't worry, baby. I'm going to make it so fucking good for you."

At that, all my defenses melt.

He drops his forehead to my belly. His hands caress my hips for a moment before helping me shove my pants off. My panties go next.

"*Shiiiit*, Noli." His tone is reverent as he gazes down at me.

"Come here." I pull him down to kiss me. His hands are restless, molding over my curves, kneading and grabbing like he can't get enough.

When I'm wriggling again, he pulls back and sticks his index and middle fingers in his mouth, wetting them. I bite my lip when I realize what he's going to do. Parting my thighs, I let out a ragged moan when he glides over my folds, searching, and then . . .

"Oh *god*!"

My head falls back and my eyes flutter shut as two thick digits press into me. The sound of his groan imprints itself in my memory.

"Fuck, you're so . . . Is this okay?"

I sigh. "It's *perfect*."

He emits something like a growl and kisses my stomach as his fingers begin to pump. His other hand joins in, rubbing circles over my clit. I buck my hips in time with his thrusts, giving myself over to the mounting pleasure. He touches me like he knows my body inside and out, like we've done this a thousand times.

I can barely believe this is happening. That this is *David* touching me. David, the object of all my fantasies. David with his kind eyes and heart-melting grin, his strong body and sure hands.

David, who has given me a safe space to land when I needed it most.

"David."

I don't realize I've said it out loud until he groans in response and rubs his face against my inner thigh. The rasp of his facial hair feels intimate and delicious.

"Yeah, Noli?"

"I'm close."

"Good. Come for me, baby. Let me see you fall apart. I've been dreaming of this for so fucking long."

This isn't dirty talk. It's better than that. And it pushes me right over the edge.

I . . . fucking . . . *shatter*.

When I finally come back to myself, he's trailing kisses up and down my hip.

"Please tell me you have condoms," I wheeze.

"I definitely have condoms."

I exhale in relief. "Merry Christmas to *me*."

Exhibit D.

Further proof that David Fonseca is annoying?

He edges me until I agree to scale back the decorations.

"Get rid of the place mats."

I shake my head back and forth on the pillow. "*Nooo.* I love them."

When I clench around him, he grunts but doesn't move.

"The reindeer, then."

"You want me to evict Blitzen?" My tone is scandalized.

"Blitzen's an asshole. If you'd named it Comet or Prancer, we could talk."

I frown up at him. "How do you know Blitzen's an asshole?"

"With a name like that? Besides, they're all assholes. You know the song."

My giggle turns into a moan when his cock pulses inside me. "Fair point."

"Do we have a deal?" His thumb circles my clit again and he resumes the short, shallow thrusts that make my whole body quake.

I dig my nails into his hard thighs. "Fine, I'll get rid of the fucking reindeer. Just let me come!"

This time, he does.

I guess he's not so annoying after all.

I have no idea how long it is before we're lying in his bed, sweat drying on our skin, our limbs entwined, and his fingers threading gently through the ends of my hair. The postcoital haze following the best sex of my life feels like a space where I can say anything without emotional consequences.

So I do.

"Can I ask you a question?"

"Anything."

"Why do you hate Christmas?"

He huffs out a laugh. "I don't hate Christmas, Noelia."

"Then why have you been acting like such a Scrooge?"

He shrugs. "Nando said you'd been feeling stressed, and you seemed to enjoy tormenting me. Besides, it's fun getting you all riled up. Reminds me of when we were young."

"You say that like we're old now."

He grunts. "I *feel* old."

"You're only thirty-six."

"Tell that to my knees."

"Oh, was that the creaking sound I heard? I thought it was the bed."

"Brat." He kisses the tip of my nose.

Since we're confessing, I say, "You know I don't actually need all these decorations, right? I only did it to annoy you. I would've been fine with the tiny fake tree."

"I'm flattered you went to such lengths to get my attention."

"Shut up."

"I'm serious. But I'm glad to hear that." His brow creases, and his gaze drifts away from mine. "I don't know if you knew, but . . . my parents were basically hoarders. It's part of why I was over at your house all the time. After my dad died and my mom got sick, I had to deal with all their stuff, so clutter is kind of stressful for me."

My stomach sinks. I'm a bigger asshole than Blitzen. "Shit, I'm so sorry. I've taken over your home with a stupid prank. We can pack everything up and donate it back to the thrift store tomorrow."

He pulls me closer. "Don't apologize. You were right, it's festive. And you've made this place feel more like a home than it ever did before. Just tell me you don't intend to leave it all up until Valentine's Day."

"Not a second past Three Kings Day. I promise."

"Thank you." His expression turns serious, and I stay quiet, waiting for him to gather his thoughts. Finally, he says, "Look, this wasn't a onetime, heat-of-the-moment thing for me."

"Me either," I say quietly, but I'm not ready to go there yet, so I deflect with humor. "After all, I've only been dreaming of this for fifteen years."

He ducks his head like I've embarrassed him, so of course, I go on.

"Seriously, I had the biggest crush on you in high school."

He gives me an indulgent look. "You weren't exactly subtle."

"Yeah, that's never been my strong suit."

"Lucky for us, self-control is *my* strong suit. You were incredibly difficult to resist."

My brows draw together, partly in confusion, partly because I'm looking into the past, remembering who we used to be. "So why did you?"

"Because you were *seventeen*."

"You were twenty-one. Hardly a dirty old man."

"Maybe not, but those four years felt significant. I was going to be a senior in college, and you were only a senior in high school."

"I overheard you talking to Nando about it."

David groans. "What did I say?"

"Nothing bad. Nando said, 'You know my sister likes you, right?' And you shook your head and said, 'It doesn't matter.'"

"Shit. I'm sorry."

"Why? It's not like you made fun of me."

"No, but . . . Look, I wasn't saying *you* didn't matter. It was more to put *him* at ease, and let him know I wasn't going to take advantage of you."

What will Nando say about us now? I wonder, but I don't voice my concern. Instead, I say, "I always wished you would make a move. But I *was* young. Emotionally. I would've made you my whole personality."

"I would've done the same with you."

I roll my eyes. "Don't feel like you have to flatter me now."

"It's true. I used to reason with myself. Like if I'd been nineteen, it would've been okay to be obsessed with you. Two years wasn't so much. But four? So I told myself to wait. To back off. Let you get through college."

"I didn't see you much during that time."

"You were too tempting."

"Even during my grunge phase?" I tease, and he grins.

"You're sexy in anything. Even flannel."

"Right answer." I pillow my head on his chest and peer into his face. "But I graduated college ten years ago. Why did it take us so long to get here?"

He blows out a breath and gazes up at the ceiling. "Life. Work. Everything with my parents. Helping my sister with her kids when they were little. It's like I blinked and was suddenly in my mid-thirties—no wife, no kids. I had a business, an apartment, but not a home. And then . . . you showed up." He slides his fingers into my hair and sends me a fond smile. "In case it's not clear, you being here has been really good for me."

I lean into his touch. "For me too. With you, I don't feel like I have to hide the annoying parts of myself. Not like I usually do. And I feel at home here."

"You wouldn't believe how happy it makes me to hear you say that."

My cheeks warm at the sincerity in his tone, but all I say is, "One more question."

"Shoot."

"Why'd you come back early today?"

"The gym was closed because of an electrical problem, and Mom was tired." His expression turns sheepish. "Also . . . I was hoping you'd be here and we could watch another movie."

I purse my lips like I'm thinking about it. "We still could."

His gaze softens. "I'd love that."

CHAPTER FOUR

We spend the rest of the week getting freaky all over the apartment. I'm on winter break, and David puts up an out-of-office reply on his email a few days early. It's like years of pent-up lust has taken over, and we can't keep our hands off each other. When we're not screwing? We're cooking, eating, watching movies, and running errands. I even join him at the gym, because I like seeing him all sweaty.

Actually, I just like being around him, period. And luckily, David seems equally as enamored with me.

It's two days until Christmas Eve, and we're in the middle of a double feature: *Reindeer Games*—his choice—and *The Best Man Holiday*—my choice.

We're cuddling under a fleece throw blanket, but I get a little handsy, and he starts kissing my neck. Before you can say "Rudolph the Red-Nosed Reindeer," we're naked and I'm straddling his lap. I grab a condom from my purse and moments later, he's inside me. Our arms band around each other as we rock in a slow, measured pace, kissing lazily.

I come with a quiet, shuddering gasp, my eyes captured by his steady amber gaze. Pleasure floods my system, but it's a thick, rolling tide as opposed to the crash of a tsunami. I'm still on the tail end when he follows me into the deep, hugging me tight and releasing a gravelly groan as he thrusts upward.

We hold each other, breathing hard through the aftermath of sensation and emotion.

David speaks first.

"Don't leave."

The words are low, but clear. Still, I whisper, "What?"

His expression is soft, yet serious. "Don't move out. Stay here. *Live* here. With me."

I sputter. "It's not even my room." As if I haven't been sleeping in David's room every night.

"You know Nando's not coming back. And it wouldn't matter if he were."

I shake my head. "I don't want to come between you two."

"You won't."

"You don't know that. And it's only been a few weeks. What if you get sick of me?"

"I love having you around. You're sweet, funny, sexy as

hell in your tight little shirts, and you don't put up with my bullshit moods."

I quirk a brow. "You mean I force you to have fun instead of working all the time."

"I need more fun in my life. I need *you*, Noelia."

I clear my throat. "It's a little hard to take this seriously when we're both naked."

He ignores my attempt to deflect. "I want you to stay, Noli. Just think about it. Okay?"

I drape my arms around his shoulders and press my forehead to his. "I will. But how are we going to tell Nando about us?"

"Let me worry about that."

"He's *my* brother."

"And he's *my* best friend. It'll be fine." He sounds way more confident than I feel, but before I can say so, his expression darkens. "There is one other thing you and I have to talk about."

His stern tone makes me tense. "What's that?"

"The birds. In the Christmas tree. They're really creeping me out."

I don't stop laughing until his kisses shut me up.

But as happy as I am, the nagging fear over my brother's reaction just won't leave me alone.

CHAPTER FIVE

The morning of December twenty-third, my parents' boiler breaks. Since they typically host our extended families for Christmas Eve, this is a catastrophe of epic proportions.

And when I get pressured to host instead, Nando is forced to come clean about living with Iris, and I have to admit I'm staying with David.

I *don't,* however, tell anyone that David and I are together. David insists that we need to tell my brother, although I'm still worried about what it'll do to their friendship.

The potential for disaster is overwhelmingly high, and it's not improved by the presence of my mother cooking up a storm in David's kitchen all day. I've been conscripted into service, of course, so I'm in there with her, making enough pernil, arroz con gandules, bacalaítos, alcapurrias, and tostones to feed an army. The saving grace is that Titi Concha is bringing the pasteles this year.

I've apologized to David for the inconvenience at least twenty times, but he just gives me an easy smile and says it's a good thing I've already decorated.

My mother is *thrilled* that the birds are being used. Dad shuddered when he saw them and has avoided the living room every time he's dropped off more supplies.

That night, David kisses me sweetly and assures me that he doesn't mind having all my relatives descend on his home. He says he's always thought of my family as his own, and he's happy to have the opportunity to host them.

But in the event that he's just being nice, I wake him up on the morning of Christmas Eve with a blow job that leaves him shaking. After he's spent, I crawl up his body and press a light kiss to his cheek.

"Feliz Nochebuena, cariño," I whisper.

He gives me a dreamy smile and twines his fingers in my hair. "God, I fuckin' love you."

The breath backs up in my lungs and I go still. "You're just saying that."

He shakes his head, his eyes never leaving mine. "Come on, Noli. Don't tell me it's not obvious."

For once, I don't know what to say. I snuggle into his chest, and he holds me until my phone rings with the first of many calls from my parents.

Despite the chaos of the day, I find moments to mull over what he said. I *do* believe him. I see it in the way he looks at me, the way he offers support, and the way he touches me when no one's looking. Touches that comfort, soothe, and inflame. When my uncle comments on my weight, David shoots Tío a forbidding look and says, "Not in my house." When one of my aunts has a meltdown over the consistency of the coquito, David runs a soothing hand down my back. That simple gesture does more to regulate my nervous system than ten minutes of cyclic breathing ever could.

But nothing can resolve the dread I feel about spilling the beans to Nando.

I've been avoiding my brother all night, but he finally catches me as everyone's digging into the wide array of dessert dishes.

"Got anything you want to tell me?" he says, casting a meaningful glance in David's direction.

David comes over to us, his expression serious. "Let's talk in my room. Slightly lower chance of interruption."

Nando gives me an unreadable look as we follow David down the hallway. Once we're in David's room, the awkwardness of the situation grabs me in a choke hold.

"Maybe we should sit down," I tell Nando. If I don't get off my feet, I'm going to start pacing.

Nando narrows his eyes but sits on the edge of David's bed. I plop down next to him, and David settles into his armchair.

This is it. Nando is going to make us choose. Will he cut me out of his life if I stay with David? Or will he force David to leave me alone to preserve their friendship? Worst-case scenarios spiral through my mind, and my eyes fall on the angel in the snow globe on David's dresser. I just know Abuela's nosy ass is watching us.

"Listen," David begins. "We have something to tell you, and it might come as a surprise, but—"

"Quit stalling," Nando cuts in. "Did you two finally get together or what?"

Silence falls, thick and heavy as a stage curtain.

I stare at my brother as realization dawns. "Fernando Anthony Hernández, *you set us up*!"

The corners of Nando's mouth tilt upward and I want to smash that smug smile off his face with a pillow. He shrugs, utterly unrepentant. "Look, aside from Iris, the woman of my dreams, you two are the people I love most in the world." He points a finger at me. "But don't you dare tell our parents, because I'll be forced to say *they're* at the top of the list, which'll be awkward for my future wife."

I roll my eyes. "Your secret is safe."

David waves his hand at Nando impatiently. "You were saying?"

"Right. I knew you were both harboring a torch for each other, or whatever the hell the phrase is, and this seemed like the perfect opportunity to give you both a kick in the ass toward everlasting happiness."

I gape at him. Who needs Santa when you have a meddling older brother? Still, this seems too good to be true, and I narrow my eyes. "You're not . . . mad? You're not going to make one or both of us choose between you and true love?"

David's head jerks in my direction. "Love?"

"Why would I be mad when this was *my* idea?" Nando asks, bewildered.

"Noelia." David gets to his feet and stalks toward me. "Did you just say *love*?"

"That's my cue to leave." Nando jumps up and heads for the door. "I'd say you have about two and a half minutes before someone comes looking for you." And then he slips out, shutting the door behind him.

David drops onto the bed beside me and takes my hands in his. His eyes burn with intensity.

I squeeze his fingers and find the strength to put his mind, and his heart, at ease.

"I did say *love*." I smile, seeing him as he is now, but also seeing the little boy he once was, and the teenager, and the young man. I've loved him, in some form or another, at all of those phases.

And I love him now.

"I had to make sure," I explain, "that what I'm feeling isn't just a lingering crush. That this is real and true and *now*."

"And is it?" There's trepidation in his voice, but also hope.

"Yes," I say simply. "I love you. Now, as I am, and now, as you are."

He strokes my cheek with his thumb. "I was worried it would take you longer. I was all set to convince you, even before we . . ." He glances at the bed. "You know."

"Oh, I know." But my grin fades. "I'm still scared you'll think I'm too annoying."

"I promise that won't happen."

"You can't know that."

"It hasn't happened yet, and we've known each other for twenty-five years."

"This is different."

"Exactly." He kisses my forehead. "This is better."

And he's right. It is.

Then he gets to his feet and pulls me with him. "Come on. Unless you want your entire family finding out about us today, we'd better get out of here."

"Would it be so bad?" I muse as we head toward the door.

He stops. "What do you mean?"

"If they all knew. My parents were shockingly cool about Nando and Iris living in sin. Why not us?"

A blinding smile breaks over David's face. He kisses me soundly, then pulls back just enough to ask, "I don't suppose you have any mistletoe?"

My grin is as devious as the Grinch's when he gets a wonderful, awful idea. "You bet your ass I do."

He smirks. "Then let's go put on a show."

I picture my grandmother looking through the eyes of the snow globe angel, watching us like we're her favorite telenovela, and clapping.

She always loved a happy ending.

And so do I.

3

I'LL BE HOME FOR EX-MAS

Alexandria Bellefleur

"Attention, passengers of flight UA 831 with service to Park Falls, Wisconsin," a voice that was much too chipper for the hour announced over the crackling PA system. Francesca held her breath, praying that after three flight delays, boarding might finally be about to begin. "Due to worsening weather conditions, we regret to inform you that this flight has been canceled."

A collective groan rose from the gate area and Francesca's heart sank.

"All passengers have been rebooked on the next available flight departing tomorrow at 6:20 a.m., weather permitting. For more information, please see a gate agent or visit the *My trips* tab on the United app. We apologize for any inconvenience this may have caused and wish you safe and happy holidays."

"Inconvenience?" A frazzled-looking woman holding a sleeping toddler approached the desk. "It's Christmas Eve. There has to be something you can do, some earlier flight you can put us on."

Rather than join the long line of tired, travel-weary, would-be passengers, Francesca wheeled her carry-on over to the only open restaurant Dane County Regional Airport boasted and took a seat at the bar decorated with vintage Packers memorabilia and colorful string lights. She was no more thrilled at the prospect of spending Christmas Eve stuck in an airport than the next person, but there was nothing the gate agent or anyone else could do about the bomb cyclone working its way across the northern US, blasting the Midwest with blizzard conditions. Complaining wouldn't get her home any sooner, but a strong drink might at least help pass the time.

My flight's officially been canceled, she texted the family group chat after thanking the bartender for the hot buttered rum he'd set down in front of her. He was wearing a Santa hat and an ostentatious Christmas sweater covered in silver tinsel and flashing LED lights. They've rebooked me on the first flight out tomorrow.

Her little brother, Mike, sent back, bummer. Dad, never much one for texting, replied with a single thumbs-down emoji, and Mom with several broken hearts and a promise that they would wait to open presents until after she arrived. Not thirty seconds later, she sent Francesca a photo; Mom, Dad, and Mike were wearing red-and-green plaid pajamas, pajamas Francesca would also be wearing right now if she were at home instead of stranded on the opposite end of the state, missing out on all of her favorite Christmas Eve traditions.

Francesca hearted the photo before setting her phone screen-side-down atop the bar with a resigned sigh.

"And that was the reigning Queen of Christmas herself, Mariah Carey, with the perennial favorite 'All I Want for Christmas Is You,'" the radio jockey rasped through the speakers. "Don't go anywhere, folks. After a brief commercial break, we'll be right back with the song topping the Billboard Mainstream Rock Airplay chart this week, 'Please Come Home for Christmas' by Apollo's Child."

The bartender changed the station and Francesca frowned.

"Wait, sorry, could you—would you mind switching it back? Just for the next song."

He looked at her sideways, Santa hat sitting askew atop his head, then shrugged, changing the station. "Sure. You a fan?"

"Sorry?"

"The band?" he asked. "Apollo's Child. I heard the lead singer's from around here. Benjamin Donnelly? Not here, like, Madison. But you know. Wisconsin."

"Oh. Right." She smiled. "I heard that too," she said, because it was easier than saying that before he was Benjamin Donnelly, the famous front man of Apollo's Child, the hottest rock band to grace the scene in a decade, she'd known him as Benji. And long before he was performing in front of sold-out crowds to thousands of screaming fans, he used to sing for her. Because Francesca wasn't just a fan, she was his *first* fan. And Benji Donnelly was her first *everything*.

Not for the first time, she was struck with an almost irresistible urge to pick up the phone and call him. To hear his voice, not over the radio. Not that hearing him on the radio wasn't nice, but it wasn't the same. Not even close. But just like complaining wouldn't get her home any faster, wishing wouldn't help her now. Benji had changed his number years ago. And even if he hadn't, she wasn't certain he'd pick up. Not when he saw that it was her calling.

"*I* heard that guy's a real loser."

Francesca's hackles rose, the old urge to snap back at the good-for-nothing assholes who used to pick on Benji for daring to care about music more than football, rearing its head. She set her drink down with a dull thud and turned in her seat.

"I'm sorry," she said, voice acerbic. "I must have missed the part where I asked for your op—"

The retort died on her lips, a familiar face staring back at her from the nearest booth. The nondescript ball cap pulled low over his brow flattened his golden curls and cast shadows over his slate-gray eyes, and the dark navy hoodie he wore hid most of his tattoos. She wasn't sure she could call it a disguise—it might have worked on most people, but Francesca *wasn't* most people. She would have recognized him anywhere.

"*Benji?*" she said, exhaling a tiny squeak of disbelief.

A grin spread across his face, his eyes crinkling at the corners. "Hey, Frankie."

Frankie. Her heart beat double time. The only person to ever call her that was him. "What are you doing here?"

His smile faltered, and she felt a swift stab of regret that her first words to him in three and a half years weren't something better, something more sincere.

It's good to see you.

How have you been?

I missed you.

I'm sorry.

"I mean . . ." She cleared her throat. "I didn't expect to run into you here of all places."

Somewhere else, maybe. Countless hours she'd lost to daydreams of bumping into him inside a crowded bar in

Camden, of turning a corner on her walk home from class and seeing him standing there. But *Dane County Regional Airport*? Never.

"I was supposed to fly into O'Hare, but my flight got rerouted."

"Were you flying from LAX?"

If the tabloids were to be believed, he had purchased a house in the Pacific Palisades last spring.

He nodded. "You?"

"Newark."

"Ah. Headed home for Christmas?" He winced. "Jesus, sorry. Dumb question."

"Trying to, at least." She looked down at the empty seat across from him. "Can I sit?" *Shit.* "I mean, unless you're with someone and they're—"

"Frankie." He pressed his lips together like he was trying not to laugh. "Sit."

She grabbed her drink and took a seat opposite him in the small booth, the vinyl squeaking as she shifted her weight, casting about in the ensuing silence for something better to say than *Some weather we're having, huh?* What did you even begin to say to someone with whom you hadn't spoken in three and a half years, someone you used to tell everything?

"You look really beautiful," he said, breaking the silence before it broke her, sparing Francesca the mortification of putting her foot in her mouth twice in as many minutes. "Can I say that?" he asked, eyes roving anxiously over her face. "Is that allowed?"

Heat filled her cheeks. She *looked* like she'd been traveling for the last six hours and was jet-lagged on top of it.

Embarrassed, she pivoted the topic. "You changed

your number," she said, praying it didn't sound like an accusation.

"Yeah, I . . ." His head cocked to the side, and he was probably wondering how she knew that. *Maybe* wondering. It once had been so easy to guess what he was thinking. Now she wasn't sure. "Someone leaked it. Sold it, maybe. I don't know." His eyes dropped to the peeling label of his Heineken. "I thought about messaging you, but I wasn't sure if you wanted me to."

Because *she* had broken up with him. Because this stiltedness that existed between them was her fault. Because she had turned what had once felt as easy as breathing into something confusing and hard, a puzzle with missing pieces.

Francesca hated herself for it, for breaking his heart and hers. She really did. And yet she couldn't bring herself to regret it when it meant watching him live his dream, even if she had to do it from afar. Even if she had to do it as a stranger.

Her parents didn't understand—well, they pretended they did, but they didn't. No one did. She and Benji had been high school sweethearts, joined at the hip from the moment Benji, the sweet, shy transfer kid from Texas had asked if he could sit with her, inseparable during senior year and throughout all of college. Where Francesca went, everyone knew Benji was bound to follow. Which was precisely why when his band had been asked to open for The Masqueraders on tour, Francesca had known she didn't have a choice.

She'd been accepted to the Courtauld Institute of Art's MA Conservation of Easel Paintings, a rigorous three-year, full-time program. In the five years that they had been together, Francesca could have counted on two hands the number of days they'd spent apart. And suddenly they were supposed to go months without seeing each other?

No, the distance would have been too great, and missing her was a distraction Benji didn't need. It would have only been a matter of time before one of them caved and quit, and Benji's dreams were too big, too important to sacrifice for her. She loved him too much to be the thing that held him back. A clean break—not that there was anything *clean* about heartbreak—hadn't been easy, but it was for the best. *Still*, she told herself when she needed the reminder, when the grief crept in, when she found herself missing Benji so much it hurt to breathe.

"I saw you perform at Wembley," she said, an answer to a question he'd only sort of asked. He could have messaged her and she'd have welcomed it. Even if it would have muddied the waters. "I was there."

Benji's eyes flashed to her face, his lips parting in surprise. "You were?"

"It was a great show. You were amazing." She smiled and hoped it wasn't too wistful. "You always are."

Amazing was too mundane a word. Francesca understood beauty, she knew art, and she was acutely qualified in her appreciation of both. Watching Benji perform never failed to snatch the air from her lungs and make her ache in ways words couldn't fully hold, humbling her and filling her with the same awe she felt when faced with any other precious, priceless piece of art, paintings by Caravaggio and sculptures carved by Bernini. Benji was one of the greats and she hoped he knew it, hoped he understood now why she'd had to let him go, had to set him free.

"You should've said something." He frowned. "I could have gotten you into the tent. Or said hi."

She swallowed hard and shrugged, feeling like her shoulders were screwed in wrong. "I didn't know if you'd want to see me."

"Frankie." Exasperation bled into his voice. "I'm not the one who—"

"Another round?"

Francesca hadn't noticed the bartender approach. Benji looked at her.

"Sure. Another would be great," she said, sliding her empty glass across the table.

Benji nodded. "Thanks."

"So I guess your parents must still live in Park Falls." Francesca waited until they were alone to speak. "Do you make it home often?"

"Not as often as they'd like. This was going to be my first Christmas home since . . . It's been three years."

"Same. My family's been coming to London. Which has been nice. Don't get me wrong. Christmas in London is . . . It's gorgeous. But I was really looking forward to being home this year."

To opening matching pajamas on Christmas Eve and driving around the neighborhood to see the lights before returning home to decorate gingerbread houses while *A Christmas Story* played on the television in the background. She was sure she could still do most of that, but her first holiday home in years wasn't exactly off to an auspicious start.

"Don't lie." Whether it was intentional or not, Benji's foot nudged hers under the table. "We both know what you were really looking forward to was Mrs. Leibovitz's Christmas Snow Salad."

"*Gah.*" Francesca stuck out her tongue, pretending to gag. "Gross." She laughed. "Don't even joke."

Maybe it made her a bad Midwesterner, but she'd never understood the logic, let alone the appeal, of a Jell-O salad.

Benji wasn't laughing, instead staring softly at her.

"What?"

"Nothing. Just . . . your laugh," he said. "I missed it."

Francesca's throat was tight and aching, her chest, too, her heart throbbing inside her breast. "Benji, I—"

"One hot buttered rum," the bartender, who had, quite possibly, the *worst* timing, said, setting a fresh mug down in front of her. "And another Heineken. Cheers."

He left and Francesca was about to open her mouth, to say what, she wasn't entirely sure, when Benji spared her the trouble and said, "So tell me about London."

She blew out a breath. "You've been to London. In fact, you've been all sorts of places I've never been before. You should tell me about being on a world tour. Hell, you've been on *two* world tours now. Tell me about that, Mr. Headliner."

He snorted and reached for his beer. After a moment, when she didn't speak, he lowered the bottle from his lips and wiped his mouth with his thumb.

"Oh, you're—you're serious. Okay, uh, let's see. World tour . . . It involved a lot of buses. Hotels. Planes. More airports than you could imagine."

Francesca rolled her eyes. "Better airports than Dane County Regional."

"Eh, I don't know," he said, foot bumping hers beneath the table, and this time she knew it was on purpose. "I kind of think this one has its charm."

"Charm?" She snorted. "Okay, let's hear it. What exactly do you find charming about this place?"

As far as small, regional airports went, it wasn't bad, but it was a small, regional airport. Enough said.

Benji shrugged, the dimple in his left cheek deepening when he smiled. "Might just be the company."

Her face burned, and she knew she was blushing. He was an even more terrible flirt than she remembered. "You've played at Wembley! *And* Madison Square Garden. For Christ's sake, Benji, you played at the Olympia. Come on."

His smile didn't quite fall as much as it flattened by small measures until he was left wearing a pensive frown.

"Yeah, it's . . ." He paused like he was choosing his words carefully. "It's been the stuff dreams are made of."

She leaned back in the booth, her stomach a sudden jumble of knots. "But you're happy, though. Right?"

"Most of the time," he said quietly, and Francesca exhaled, unclenching her stomach.

Most of the time was better than *none of the time.* "I'm glad."

"And you?" he asked. "Are you happy?"

"I'm—"

Francesca didn't know what to say. Was she?

She stared at the table, at Benji's hands resting atop it, the fingertips of his left hand calloused from years of fretting the strings of his guitar. She knew that she had taken too long to reply already, but she couldn't recall the last time anyone had asked her that question. She was living her dream, doing what she'd always wanted, so everyone probably just assumed . . .

"Frankie?"

Benji was staring at her, gaze piercing, his eyes searching hers. He looked concerned.

"Most of the time," she said, and they shared a smile.

"You're really not going to tell me about London?" he prodded. "Come on. I want to hear about the Courtauld."

"The program was great. I graduated in June, and I've been interning at the Tate for the last six months."

As of last Monday, her internship was officially over, and her new job didn't start until after the new year.

Benji grinned. "That's awesome. You love the Tate."

"I do." And she loved that he remembered. Not that she should be surprised. She'd never kept her love of the museum to herself, and unlike a lot of people, Benji paid attention.

"You know, I actually went the day after the concert. We had a day off before we had to leave for Paris."

"To the Tate?"

"Mm. I remembered you telling me about *The Lament for Icarus*. How it was your favorite. I wanted to see it."

Feelings Francesca had tried to repress a long time ago stirred inside her chest. "That's how you spent your free day in London? Going to see my favorite painting?"

"To be fair, I went to the Tower of London and Buckingham Palace too."

"Good choices."

"I do have a question." He leaned forward, elbows resting on the table, and dropped his voice. "Spotted dick."

Francesca laughed, glad she hadn't taken a sip of buttered rum because she'd have likely choked. "I'm no expert, but I'd say you should probably talk to your doctor."

Benji groaned out a laugh and hung his head. "I walked right into that one, didn't I?"

"You really did." She grinned. "It's pudding, by the way. Steamed, with raisins. Don't ask me how it got its name. I didn't ask."

"Heeey." The bartender sidled up to the table and set down both her check and Benji's, looking almost sheepish.

"So, no rush, but I wanted to tell you we're going to be closing soon. We're normally open until eleven or the last flight leaves, but we thought we'd stay open a little later given the circumstances."

She followed his gaze as it flitted to the clock on the wall showing it was nearly quarter till.

"Oh my gosh." She dug inside the front pocket of her bag, searching for her wallet. "It's Christmas Eve. You probably want to get home."

"Hey, don't worry about it. I've got it." Benji tossed a stack of bills down on the table. "You can keep the change."

The bartender stared at Benji, gobsmacked. "You sure, man? That's, like, really generous."

Benji ducked his head, fingers fiddling with the strings of his hoodie. The slightest flush dusted the bridge of his nose and spread across his cheeks. "Yeah. I'm sure."

"Thanks." The bartender swept the cash off the table. "Happy holidays, you two. Safe travels."

"You didn't have to pay for me," she said, reaching for her drink. "But thank you. That was really nice of—" She yawned into her palm. "Oh, geez. Sorry."

Benji smiled and slid from the booth. "Tired?"

"Jet lag." She grabbed her bag. "Finally catching up to me, I guess."

"It's . . . what, coming up on six in London?"

"Something like that."

"You think this airport has a hotel?"

"Fingers crossed?"

The gate area was practically deserted. There was a woman clicking away on a laptop that was plugged into the wall, someone else stretched out across a whole row of seats, beanie pulled down over their head, and three girls who looked like sisters huddled together on the floor playing cards.

Francesca approached the smiling gate agent standing behind the service counter. "Hi. We were both supposed to be on the flight leaving from this gate. UA—

"Eight thirty-one," the gate agent, who looked to be around her mom's age, said. "Your new flight is still on schedule. Weather permitting."

"Small favors." Francesca smiled wearily. "Is there a hotel nearby or . . . ?"

Heather, her name tag read, winced. "There is, but unfortunately they're all booked up for the night. The rooms got snatched up real quick."

Francesca swallowed a groan. Of course they did. "Okay, I guess we'll just—"

"The airport installed a few of those new napcabs earlier this year. I can't make any promises, but there might still be one or two vacant."

"Napcabs?" Benji asked, his shoulder brushing hers.

"You know, a sleeping pod? It's no hotel suite, but you can lie down and get a little shuteye. Just make sure to set an alarm," Heather cautioned. "Don't want to miss your flight."

Francesca didn't even want to think about how awful that would be. "And these nap cabins are—"

"Napcabs. They're down the hall at the end of the terminal." Heather pointed. "Big white boxes that look like—well, to be honest, they look a little like a cross between a porta potty and a giant vending machine." She laughed. "You won't be able to miss 'em."

Francesca turned to Benji and shrugged. "I guess we should probably check out the napcabs, then."

"Couldn't hurt," he agreed.

When they were a few feet away from the desk and no longer in earshot, Benji leaned his head toward hers, dropping his voice. "A cross between a porta potty and a vending machine? She really sold it."

Francesca laughed. "Don't tell me you're not the least bit curious."

"Yeah." He chuckled. "Morbidly."

Heather was right about one thing: the sleeping pods, whatever they were called, were impossible to miss. And, weirdly enough, thanks to their glossy glass touch screens, they did look a little like giant vending machines. Though Francesca would argue they more closely resembled fancy, high-tech photo booths than honey buckets.

"So, how exactly do these things work?"

"I think . . . Hold on." She circled the cluster of napcabs, each a separate cubicle that butted up against the next, creating a big blocky rectangle at the far end of the terminal. There were six sleeping pods total, five of their screens lit up red. Upon closer inspection, those screens said, *Occupied.*

"You take it," Benji said, realizing at the same time she did that there was only one vacant napcab, its screen lit green.

"No, you should—"

"Frankie." He pinned her with a look that said he wasn't going to back down.

She looked away, nibbling on her bottom lip as she eyed the sleeping pod. There was another option staring them straight in the face. "We could . . . we could just share it."

She could feel Benji's eyes on her, could feel him staring. Without looking at him, she shrugged.

It didn't have to be a big deal. It was just sleep, and it wasn't like they hadn't shared a bed before.

"We . . . could," he said haltingly. "If . . . I mean, if that's okay with you."

It was her suggestion. "Are you okay with it?"

Benji reached out and tapped the touch screen.

Renting the napcab cost fifty dollars for the first hour and thirty for each hour after that. Six hours in the napcab was going to run them two hundred bucks. It wasn't cheap, but it was less than they would have spent on a hotel. For the second time, Benji waved her off when she reached for her wallet, holding his phone over the contactless reader and selecting his Apple Pay.

"Can I least Venmo you for my half? Please?"

"Please." Benji shook his head, chuckling under his breath. "You know what, if it'll make you feel better, sure. Knock yourself out."

The payment finished processing and Benji grabbed the door, opening it and taking a look inside before stepping back and sweeping out a hand for her to step over the threshold.

The pod was predictably cramped, but clean, everything sterile white from the sheets to the walls to the tile floor. There was a teeny-tiny desk wedged into one corner, a closet just big enough to stow their carry-ons, and a bed that reminded her of the twin XL in her dorm freshman year at Lawrence. She knew from experience that she and Benji would both fit.

"Here," he said, holding out a hand. "Let me take your bag."

While Benji tucked their belongings away in the closet, Francesca toed off her thick-soled winter boots, turned down the bed, and crawled under the crisp cotton sheets. She hated sleeping in her jeans, hated it almost as much as she hated sleeping in her bra, but she wasn't going to make this anymore awkward than it already was by stripping down to her underwear.

"Ha!" Benji laughed. "Hey, Frankie, look what I found."

In his hand was one of those car air fresheners, the retro kind that hung from the rearview mirror and smelled like pine and was shaped like an evergreen tree.

"Someone left it hanging in the closet," he said, beaming at her. He'd ditched the ball cap along with his hoodie and he looked more like himself with his golden curls unconfined and his colorful tattoos on display. "It's . . . well, it's kind of like a Christmas tree? Is that stupid?"

It wasn't stupid at all. "No, it's the perfect size tree for a napcab. Here." She held out a hand. "Let's put it here." She leaned forward, propping it on the small shelf beside the bed. "There." She settled back against the pillows. Or, well, *pillow*. There was only one. "That's a good place for it."

Benji's hand hovered over the light switched beside the door. "Are you good if I . . . ?"

"Sure."

He hit the switch and the room went dark, only the smallest sliver of weak light leaking in from under the door.

Francesca held her breath as Benji lowered himself down beside her, the mattress dipping softly beneath their combined weight. She couldn't see as much as feel his hand hovering over her, just barely skimming the sheet tucked around her.

"You can," she blurted, and god, was she glad it was dark so that he couldn't see her blush. "Put your arm around me. It's a twin bed. There's really no way to do this without touching. It's fine. I mean, it's not like we haven't . . ." She pinched her eyes shut. "You know, you could always just tell me to shut up."

Benji's chest rumbled against her back as he chuckled and curled his body around her, his knees tucked up behind hers and his arm wrapped around her waist.

"I like it when you ramble," he said, his breath tickling the back of her neck. "I always have. You know that."

"I don't know. Time changes things."

A pause followed, long enough that she'd convinced herself Benji was done talking until he whispered, "Does it?"

It took every ounce of restraint not to mold herself against him. He was so warm, and he smelled just like she remembered, like fabric softener and spice and—home. Benji had always felt more like home to her than anyplace ever had. She wanted more than to mold herself against him. She wanted to roll over and lay her head against his chest and listen to the beat of his heart. She wanted to tell him that time hadn't changed a thing for her, not where her feelings for him were concerned. She wanted to tell him how much she'd missed him, that missing Christmas wasn't so bad since it meant she'd gotten to see him, and that was a better present than any gift she could dream of finding under a tree. That, if given a choice, right now there was no place on earth she would rather be than right here, crammed into the nap cabin—sorry, nap*cab*—with him curled around her.

But she couldn't. It didn't matter how badly she ached to say the words; they wouldn't change anything. Francesca had made her bed and now she had to lie in it. Crowded though it currently was.

"You asked me what it was like?" Benji murmured. "Being on a world tour?"

She nodded.

"You want the truth?"

Francesca frowned. "Always."

"Well, then if I'm being completely truthful, most of the time it was pretty lonely."

"*Lonely?* Really?"

"You sound surprised."

"You couldn't have been *that* lonely." She cringed, realizing belatedly how harsh that sounded. "I only meant . . . Come on, Benji, I've seen the pictures."

She couldn't imagine anyone who hadn't. His face had been splashed across every tabloid in the supermarket checkout line, every gossip blog. Francesca couldn't even check her Instagram without stumbling across dozens of photos of Benji on dates with supermodels, stepping out of clubs and bars and climbing out of back seats hand in hand with some of the most beautiful men and women in Hollywood.

Clearly, Benji wasn't wanting for company.

"Keeping tabs on me, Frankie?"

Hardly. The retort was on the tip of her tongue, but it would have been a lie. Not the whole truth, at least. Yes, it was true that his exploits were inescapable, but Francesca hadn't put up much of a fight. She could've muted his name on her socials, but she hadn't. Maybe it made her a masochist, but she'd have rather had her heart broken every single time she opened Instagram and saw his face than go the rest of her life without seeing him, even if it meant seeing him with someone new.

"Maybe. Yes. I—" She took a deep breath. "I missed you."

She was tired of pretending she didn't, tired of keeping

it to herself. Maybe it wouldn't change anything, but maybe that didn't matter. She wanted him to know.

He huffed against her skin. "Then why'd you break up with me?"

His voice had an edge to it that made her stomach clench.

"You know why," she murmured. "It was—"

"So help me god, Frankie, if you're about to say that it was *for the best*, I'm going to lose my ever-loving mind."

Francesca closed her mouth.

"Who the hell was it supposed to be for the best for, anyway?" Benji went on. "Because it sure as hell wasn't me. I missed you *every day*, Frankie. *Every. Single. Day.* Losing you? Could never be for the best. It was stupid, was what it was. I thought so then, and I think so now."

"Maybe," she whispered.

Benji sucked in a stuttered breath. "Yeah?"

She nodded.

"I didn't want any of it without you," he said, voice pleading, and something twinged near her heart. "You have to know that. Tell me you get that."

"It's been three and a half years," she said. "Why are we even talking about this?"

"Can you look at me?"

She huffed out a wry laugh. "I can't see a damn thing, Benji."

"I don't need you to see. I just need you to . . . Will you just roll over? Please?"

Francesca wiggled in his arms until she was facing him. Lying like this, she couldn't figure out what to do with her hands, so she tucked one under her chin and rested the other lightly on his chest. "Okay."

"You said time changes things." Benji shifted beneath her. She couldn't see, not really, but her eyes had adjusted enough that she could make out vague shapes and outlines. Benji tugged on the collar of his shirt. A moment later his hand wrapped around hers, and then he was pressing something solid and smooth against her skin.

Her fingers closed around the skin-warmed metal, and her breath caught in the back of her throat. "Is this—"

"Time didn't change anything for me, Frankie."

They had only been dating a few weeks before their first Christmas together, but she'd still wanted to get him something nice, something she had hoped he'd really like. She hadn't had much money, but she'd spent practically all of it having matching key chains engraved with their names on each, his on hers and hers on his. They had been shaped like puzzle pieces, and when you set them side by side, they clicked together. A perfect fit.

Benji had it. In fact, he'd loved it so much he'd taken it off the split ring and put it on a sturdy silver chain, choosing to wear it as a necklace instead. That way, he'd said, he'd always have her close to his heart.

Getting rid of it after the breakup had been out of the question, but keeping it on her key chain would have prompted too many questions that Francesca didn't want to answer. She kept her half of the matching set tucked safely away inside her jewelry box, away from prying eyes. If she sometimes took it out at night and ran her finger over Benji's etched name, that was no one's business but hers.

Three and a half years had passed, and Benji was still wearing it, her name tucked right against his heart.

She didn't let herself think about what she was doing. She reached up and cupped the back of Benji's neck, her fingers sliding into his soft curls as she leaned in and pressed their mouths together, kissing him with all the pent-up longing she'd harbored for the last three and a half years.

A moment passed and then another, Benji frozen beneath her. Her heart seized, terrified she'd gotten this all wrong, that she had ruined what she wasn't even aware she could wreck further, and then—

Then he groaned, a broken sound that came from deep inside his chest, and he was kissing her back with a desperation that rivaled her own. His hand squeezed her hip, his fingers curling around her thigh, and Francesca arched against him, wanting, *needing*, to be closer. Her hand traveled down his back to the hem of his T-shirt and then slid beneath, wanting to feel his skin against her fingertips.

Benji broke the kiss and pressed his forehead against hers, breathing hard. "What are we doing, Frankie?"

She was breathing just as hard. "Well, I *was* kissing you."

"That's not what I—" He made a frustrated sound, and even though she couldn't see his face, she could picture the crease between his brows growing deeper. "I can't do this and then watch you walk away again. I can't."

Francesca's heart thudded against her ribs.

He was right. What did it matter if they still had feelings for each other? Their circumstances weren't any different now than they had been three and a half years ago, not really. As much as she ached to spend the night showing Benji just how much she'd missed him, doing so would only make saying goodbye that much harder.

"You're right," she said, sliding back as far as she could in a bed this small. "We shouldn't."

Benji sighed. "I've hated this, you know? Not being

able to talk to you whenever I wanted. You were my best friend, Frankie. I've missed you. Can we please not go another three and a half years without talking? I think this time it might kill me."

Francesca sniffed, blinking hard a few times, her eyes burning, her throat too. "Would you . . . would you maybe want to get dinner together while we're both in town? Or we could do coffee. Something."

Anything.

Benji's hand found hers on the pillow between them, and he gave her fingers a squeeze. "I'd like that. How long are you in town for?"

"Through the first," she said. "I'm starting a new job on the fourth."

"At the Tate?"

"At the Frick, actually."

"The Frick?" She could hear him swallow. "But that's in New York."

It was. "I love London, and interning at the Tate was a dream come true, don't get me wrong, but I wanted to be a little closer to my parents. One of my teachers at the Courtauld Institute told me they'd heard from an old colleague that the Frick was looking for a new associate conservator, and, well . . . I got the job. That's why my flight here was out of Newark. They wanted me to come in and sign some onboarding paperwork in person, and I needed to pick up the keys to my new apartment."

"New York," he repeated. "You're serious."

"Yes?"

He exhaled long and slow and said, "We're getting back in the studio to start working on a new album."

"That's great, Benji."

"No." He laughed. "I mean, yeah, it is, but we're not recording in LA this time. The studio's in New York. I've already got a trip booked to look at apartments."

Her heart beat wildly inside her chest, her breath stuttering from between her lips. "You're moving to New York? As in, New York *City*?"

"I am."

"We're *both* going to be in New York."

In the same city, at the same time, and not just for one night before he had to leave for the next stop on tour. This could be their second chance, not only as friends, but more. So much more.

"Sounds like it." She could hear the smile in his voice.

"Would you maybe want to—"

"Yes," he blurted, his enthusiasm making her laugh.

"You don't even know what the question is."

"I don't care." With a hand cradling the back of her head, Benji pulled her down until their foreheads touched. "Whatever it is, my answer is still going to be yes."

Warmth flooded her chest. "Would it be weird if I said this has been the best Christmas I've ever had?"

His thumb swept an arc across her cheek. "This one's going to be hard to top, but what do you say next year we try?"

Francesca grinned. She liked the sound of that. Loved it, even. "Merry Christmas, Benji."

"Merry Christmas, Frankie," he said.

And it really, *really* was.

4

SOMEONE TO HOLD ON TO

Elise Bryant

As I crouch down in a patch of dirt behind a plastic snowman and a camellia bush covered in glowing rainbow lights, I'm struck by how much my life has changed in the past year. Before that call from Mom that changed everything, when it was unspoken but still blaring loud that I needed to come home to Long Beach right away, every day was a new adventure: walking on trails through poppy-covered hills in the Antelope Valley, finding secret swimming holes in Big Sur, waking up to blankets of snow in Yosemite. And every night I parked Fanny, the van(ny) I converted into a camper after saving up and studying YouTube videos for years, and watched the stars through the skylight I installed in the roof, dreaming of where I'd explore next. As long as I had an internet connection to respond to client emails and show my face on an occasional Zoom, I could follow my excitement. My world felt limitless.

But now it's very much *limited* to the two city blocks that make up Jacaranda Senior Living. Instead of Half

Dome, I look up to three stories of salmon-colored apartments. Instead of bright, clear stars, there's the blurry haze of LA smog. And currently following my excitement means hiding in the bushes at 6:43 on a Tuesday night, spying on the over-fifty-fives of Jacaranda, so I can catch whoever has been stealing from me.

At the sound of shuffling footsteps, I sink back farther into the darkness, my muscles tensing as I prepare to pounce on the culprit. But just as quickly, my shoulders release as I recognize the grunts and snorts of Emily Brontë the pug. Seconds later, she appears around the corner, tongue out in a smile, even though her labored, wet breathing sounds like she can barely find the will to go on. Her owner following behind her, Mr. Walter, definitely isn't the one stealing from my bakery stand. He was the fiercest opponent against giving me permission to start the stand at the HOA meeting three months ago—inspecting my Class A Cottage Food Operation permit like it was forged and curling his lip when I said everything was gluten free, like I'd admitted I injected each pastry with rat poison.

Unless . . . maybe he's too stubborn to admit that he actually likes my gluten-free cookies? And he wants to avoid the paper trail of paying for them with Zelle, or leaving fingerprint-covered dollar bills as evidence?

But no, he keeps walking, shaking his head at my stand across the courtyard by the mailboxes, letting out a grunt that rivals Emily Brontë's. I cross him off the suspect list.

My cheeks heat in embarrassment. I'm being ridiculous, compiling a suspect list in the first place, having a whole goddamn stakeout over some missing cookies. And really it's only *one* cookie each Tuesday and Thursday evening I set up the stand. So minor, I didn't even notice until last month, when Mom had a bad flare-up after insisting on making Thanksgiving dinner by herself and I spent all night checking and rechecking my numbers as I stayed up monitoring her. It's probably someone's innocent grandma, confused by the QR code, and here I am making it a whole thing. Because I'm bored. Because my life of work and caregiving and repeat is *boring*.

Still, it's the principle of it all. I can't just let this go . . .

"Are—are you okay?"

The small LEDs tucked into the garden suddenly seem like floodlights, illuminating the man standing on the path, peering into the bushes. He's *under* fifty-five—no wrinkles on his honey-brown skin or salt and pepper in his close-cropped curls. It doesn't seem like he was planning on seeing anyone, dressed in a faded Paramore shirt and sweatpants, with socked feet in Adidas slides. And the furrowing of his thick eyebrows, the narrowing of his dark eyes rimmed with even darker lashes, make it clear that he *definitely* didn't expect to see anyone hiding in the planter. And apparently not hiding very well.

"Do you need help? I can call someone?"

"No, just—shhh," I whisper, looking around to see if he's blown my cover. Or really, to make sure that no one else is witnessing this mortifying moment, because evidently I didn't really have much of a cover at all.

He cups a hand behind his ear. "What's that?"

"It's nothing. Can you just . . ." I wave my hand, which obviously signifies *Move along; I no longer wish to be perceived*. But he takes it as an invitation to perceive me even further. He steps carefully over the milkweed lining the path and crouches in the dirt next to me. If I weren't already sure that he was closer to my age than the rest of the residents of Jacaranda, the silence of his knees seals the deal.

"Wait, are you sitting here on purpose? Are you trying to prank someone?" The Christmas lights hanging on the plants around us reflect in his eyes, making them sparkle with his curiosity. "I'm not judging or anything, but you're just asking for trouble, with the number of pacemakers around here."

"I'm not pranking anyone. I'm on a st . . ." I stop myself. "I'm—I'm watching for something."

He whips his head around, and I catch the scent of something spicy and sweet mixed with the earthy smell around us. His gaze lands on my stand.

"The dessert table? Is something shady going down at the dessert table? I was just heading over there to get some Neapolitan cookies for my nana. Oh, and the ginger molasses tea cakes. She's hyped for the new Christmas menu."

"The Neapolitan cookies?" I repeat, arching an eyebrow. Those are the exact cookies that have been going missing. "Who's your nana? Do you have money to pay for those?"

"Lily Anne Watson. And she said she prepaid." The confusion on his face quickly shifts to amusement. "Wait—are you the baker? Nana said it was someone's daughter, but I wasn't expecting . . ." He shakes his head and then keeps talking before I can properly digest if that was an insult or not. "So, you're watching your stand. Why? Is this, like, a . . . what is it called? Oh, a honey trap!"

I wrinkle my nose as he blinks back at me. I can't tell if his cheeks are reddening in the dark, but they should be.

"The cookies are the honey. Obviously. I wasn't trying to say that—"

"Someone has been stealing cookies. *Neapolitan* cookies."

"Shit, well, yeah—those cookies are good. I must have eaten at least a dozen in the week I've been here. Hey, how do you get the strawberry section to be so . . . strawberry-y? Because it's the same texture as the other parts, and . . ." He stops rambling when he sees how I'm looking at him and puts his hands up. "It's not us. Nana is *not* a thief."

"Sure." I know it's not sweet Ms. Lily Anne, with her floral embroidered cardigans and always slightly askew blond wigs, stealing my cookies. But still, maybe if I make him feel uncomfortable enough, he'll leave. Because he's still just crouching next to me in the bushes, showing no sign of leaving. I sit down in the dirt and pointedly scoot away a few inches. "Well, this is kind of a one-person job, so . . ."

"Why not just set up a camera?"

"I—I . . . What?"

He shrugs. "It would be more efficient than staying out here all evening."

And that's . . . true. Infuriatingly. Why didn't I just go pick up a cheap camera? I know almost immediately the reason why: I wanted—no, *needed*—to leave the apartment. And out here, close enough to get to Mom in seconds if she needed me, felt safe.

"And what are you gonna do when you catch them?" he asks.

"I don't know . . . appeal to their better nature?"

"That's all? All this effort . . . They may see you coming, though, in this spot. Frosty, here, might as well be a neon arrow pointing you out." He laughs as he claps the snowman on the shoulder, and it makes me feel ridiculous again.

"Okay, well, I didn't ask for your feedback."

He puts his hands up again, and I fight the urge to slap them back down.

"Hey, I'm just trying to help the cause. What about over there behind the mailboxes? There's no lights, so—"

"Simone Jackson? Is that you?"

Ms. Earlene, my mom's upstairs neighbor comes around the opposite corner, where Emily Brontë and Mr. Walter disappeared a few minutes ago. She's wearing one of the extra-festive outfits she's been rocking since the day after Thanksgiving—tonight it's a green velvet swing dress with red polka-dot tights and a rhinestone-covered Santa hat. There's a large tree in the middle of the dress, and she must have a battery pack tucked somewhere because it's lit up and twinkling. She runs the theater society in Jacaranda, and I swear it's just to put her extensive closet of costumes to good use.

Behind her is her grandson, who seems to have sprouted up overnight. I see him often when he comes to visit his grandma after school, and I swear he wasn't her height last week. He's less festive in a *Minecraft* hoodie and an expression that seems like he'd rather be anywhere else—though that may just come standard on ten-year-olds nowadays.

Ms. Earlene was one of the deciding votes approving my bakery stand . . . mostly because she seemed to forget what they were even voting on by the time her turn came around. Still, I brought her a tin full of my greatest hits as a thank-you. And I hope finding me in the bushes isn't going to make her call up Mr. Walter and get a recall going.

"Um, hi! Hi, Ms. Earlene."

"Hi, ma'am," the man next to me echoes.

"Oh!" Ms. Earlene's hand flies to chest, jingling the bracelets of bells on her wrist, and that's quickly followed by knowing laughter. "Simone, you have a male suitor."

"No. No, no, *no*!"

"And in the foliage, *well*. Now, I sure understand needing a little time for the, uh, amorous congress." She shimmies her shoulders and then throws in a single hip thrust, just in case I wasn't picking up what she was putting down. Her grandson's eyes go wide in horror. "You probably don't get much privacy with your mom always home, and all that you've had to take on . . . You know what? *Here.*" She digs into the pockets of her dress and pulls out a heavy ring of keys. "Why don't I give you the keys to the pool room, so you can go there next time you and this handsome fellow need somewhere quiet to . . . explore? I'm not supposed to—you know Walter would probably call the Feds if he knew I was breaking the rules. But it could be our little secret."

"I'm not—I'd never—" I sputter as she maneuvers a key off the ring. "I don't even know who this is!"

"Oh, honey, I'm not judging. But maybe be more discreet next time."

Next to me, the man laughs, big and booming, but I can hardly hear it over the thundering in my ears. I jump up, knocking Frosty over in the process, and run back to Mom's apartment.

❄

"Are you gonna hand sell your desserts again today?" Mom asks from the couch when I unlock the front door. I thought she was dozing in front of the Hallmark Christmas movie she's had some version of on all day (stressed-out woman from the big city meets small-town doctor/contractor/barista and leaves her problems and pesky job behind), so I could sneak out without her noticing.

"Um, yeah. Just for a little while." After the disaster that was last Tuesday, I didn't want to risk a chance to embarrass myself further by attempting another stakeout on Thursday. But when I checked the inventory that night, there it was: a single Neapolitan cookie missing again. So I spent all weekend alternating between insisting it didn't matter, scrolling through nanny-cam reviews on Reddit, and feeling so stupid and silly that I almost vowed to give up on the whole stand altogether. But I found myself baking again Monday after work, when Mom's afternoon meds make her sleepy, and in the hours since I set up the stand, I've been finding myself peeking out the front bay window, trying to see if I can spot a missing cookie from here. And now here I am at the door, ignoring all my better judgment to try to catch the thief again.

"Oh, I meant to tell you, Earlene came down here on Saturday when you were at the store, talking 'bout 'Simone was doing the hanky-panky with some hunk in the garden.'"

My body freezes until Mom's raspy laugh fills the room.

"She said *what* now?"

"Can you believe that?" Mom slaps a pillow, melting away my remaining anxiety. "But I shouldn't even be laughing. There've been a lot of signs lately that she's, well . . . having some troubles. Did I tell you how I found her in the parking lot last week when I was on my walk? She was looking for a car, but she hasn't had a car for years, not since she lost her license. I've been meaning to call her daughter to check in . . ."

Mom is always helping others. It's what made her so good at her job as a pediatric nurse, before she had to take the leave of absence that eventually turned into an early retirement. She never even considered that the tables could ever be turned, and she'd need some of that help for herself. It's why it took her so long to finally call me when her lupus flare-ups went from bad to debilitating.

"Mom, I don't want you to worry about that. Let me check on Earlene. You need to rest."

"Okay, baby. Thank you."

I'm surprised that she agrees. It's usually a fight, gently reminding Mom of her own needs, suggesting she shouldn't do something. But I can hear the pain in her voice, see the delicate way she's readjusting herself on the couch, as if each small movement takes something much bigger out of her.

I was hoping that Christmas approaching, her favorite holiday, would bring some magic, or at least a little distraction. I got a tree from the lot on Ximeno December first and decorated it just like she would have, if her swollen hands didn't make holding the ornaments so hard.

Still, she's getting better, I remind myself. She's nowhere near as bad as she was in February, when something in her voice over the phone told me I needed to abandon my plans to head for Joshua Tree and go home. I'll never forget what it felt like, finding her in bed—the butterfly rash stark against her golden-brown skin, her hair matted in the back from many days in that same position, hands too inflamed to braid her graying curls.

And so, the same job that gave me the freedom to go to Joshua Tree, to live the limitless life I always dreamed of, also made me perfectly suited to come home for good.

Because no matter how exciting it was to explore somewhere new whenever I wanted, how could I not show up for her in the way she always had for me? As a single mom, she'd poured all that she had into my happiness, my education, my everything, keeping only the tiniest amount for herself, barely above empty. It's probably the reason she got so sick, only a few years after I graduated college . . . I owe that back to her now.

That's why the only thing I do for myself anymore, in the slim margins between fulfilling my work responsibilities and taking care of her, is baking. But even that started as experimenting with gluten-free recipes for Mom, to fulfill her incorrigible sweet tooth but still adhere to the anti-inflammatory diet her rheumatologist recommended. It quickly became a reprieve for me, though—browning butter, rolling out dough, precisely measuring each ingredient. It quieted the wanderlust and what-ifs. It gave me a small sense of control in this life, which feels like it's tossing me in the waves, pulling me under and washing me up somewhere I didn't choose. Baking has become my only anchor.

Which is why, no matter how silly it is, no matter how much I embarrassed myself last Tuesday, I need to figure out who's trying to ruin this for me.

"I'm going to head out, but I won't be gone for long. And I'll be right out there if you need me."

"I know, baby. Don't you worry about me. Have fun."

As I quietly close the door behind me, I check to make sure no one's around or snooping from their balconies and then dash over to a new stakeout spot behind the mailboxes. *Not* because that guy told me to, but because it does offer more coverage, with even bigger camellia bushes and also some lily of the Nile and miniature palm trees. And I wait . . . for a while. There are a few customers at first—Ms. Gladys and her much younger boyfriend pick up an aluminum tray of my cranberry crumble, and Mr. Clarence buys out all of my sprinkle cookies. But then it's slow and my eyes start drooping, even though it's not even seven yet. I'm about to give up, maybe even clean up the stand earlier than its official closing time of eight, when I hear . . . my name?

"Simone." The whisper feels like a shout, the way it sends a jolt through my body. "Pssst, Simone? Are you there?"

Before I whisper back, *No, I am not here*, or run away or, like, spontaneously combust—all of which are more preferrable options—the man is clambering into the planter next to me. He's dressed nicer than he was last week—in a tartan button-down, jeans, and real shoes. He has a tote bag slung over his shoulder, with *Read Banned Books* written in bright white letters that seem to glow in the dark.

"This is a *much* better stakeout spot. I only knew you were here because I suggested it."

"How—what—*why* are you here?"

"I'm here to help," he whispers, as if that's perfectly reasonable. "And I came prepared." He pulls the tote bag from his arm and holds it open to reveal . . . craft supplies?

"I went through my nana's stash," he explains, and then, only partially reading my *what the hell* expression, adds, "With permission. I'm not a thief."

"Who even *are* you?"

"Oh! Henry Watson." He puts out a hand, and when I just stare at it, he pulls it back and starts digging in his bag. "Okay, let me preface this by saying, I was watching *Home*

Alone. So first, ornaments." Three jewel-toned spheres appear in his hands. "I don't think we should break them because that seems kind of aggressive considering the crime. But maybe we could roll them like marbles in, I think—the third one? Maybe the fourth. It was actually a *Home Alone* marathon."

I have a lot of questions spinning in my mind. But for some reason the one that makes it out of my mouth is: "So, making the thief break a hip *isn't* aggressive in your mind?"

"Right. Never mind." He returns the ornaments to his bag and pulls out some tubes of acrylic paint. "You know the scene with the paint cans? I didn't have actual cans, but we could . . . toss these at their head?" Again, my expression speaks for itself, and the paint is quickly replaced by rainbow feathers. "Or these? I was thinking we could . . ." He throws a couple into the air and blows, making them fly toward my face. "Or, oh, if we *squirt* the paint first, they'll stick."

He starts to dig into his bag again, but I cut him off with a voice that's admittedly too loud for a stakeout. "Why are you doing this? Why do you *care*?"

He cocks his head to the side and his eyebrows furrow, as if he doesn't understand the question. Finally, he shrugs. "I mean, it's not right, someone messing with your livelihood."

"This isn't my livelihood. I have a job. This is what I do for—for fun."

I can see myself as he must see me, hiding in the bushes, stalking my cookies. So much fun!

But luckily, he doesn't call me on it. "So . . . um, what's your job, then?"

"I'm a digital marketing strategist—hey, why'd you make that face?"

"I wasn't. Well, I was, but not like that. It's just—digital marketing strategist. It's one of those jobs I don't understand. Like, I feel like I missed how real adult jobs work, which sucks because, yeah . . . I'm trying to get one now."

"You're unemployed." I leave the *That explains a lot* unspoken, but he must hear it anyway.

"I mean, only recently. Just this school year. I was steadily employed before as a teacher, for the record, and it's only because—"

"Shhh." I slap a hand onto his chest and nod toward the path, where Mr. Walter and Emily Brontë are grunting and snorting along. Mr. Walter shakes his head at my stand again, and Emily Brontë pauses to pee in the milkweed a respectful yard away.

Only when they're out of sight do I realize that I'm still touching something warm and solid. I snatch my hand back, and Henry clears his throat.

"So did you have to find a new job when you moved here to help your mom?"

I arch a suspicious eyebrow at him.

"My nana told me. I asked her after what Ms. Earlene said."

I feel my cheeks flush, thinking about what *else* Ms. Earlene said and how close we are right now, hidden away again. I scoot over a few inches.

"I didn't have to quit my job. It's remote. And I didn't move from anywhere, or I guess I moved from . . . everywhere? I traveled with Fanny—my, uh, van. I went all around the state before I needed to, well, come back."

"Your van is named Fanny?"

Why did I say that? Why did I say *anything*? God, am I really so starved for communication that's not my mom or my clients?

"Fanny the van . . . ny." He laughs. "That's dope."

I keep my face neutral and just nod, because there's no way I'm admitting to this virtual stranger that I also call her that.

"So what's your handle?"

"Huh?"

"For the van and your traveling. That's the thing to do, right? Make content. Like, hashtag van life." He laughs again. "Shit, did I really just say *hashtag* out loud? A couple weeks with my nana and apparently I start talking like an old person."

I wasn't planning on laughing, or giving him any sort of validation, but a small one escapes on its own. "No hashtags for me. I don't have a handle or any content. At least not anything I post online. I just do that stuff for work, not myself."

"You mean, you were living the most TikTok-able existence probably ever, and not monetizing it? Wow, you are . . . much cooler than I am." He smiles. "So, why do it, then? Traveling like that couldn't have been easy."

And I don't know if it's the false intimacy of this moment—sitting close in the dark, a whispered conversation—but I actually tell him the truth.

"Because I could. Because I felt almost, like, like . . . a *duty* to choose the most exciting path that I could. To take control of my life before anything else—my body, my health—could make that decision for me."

I feel a familiar rush of guilt. Mom's had flare-ups for as long as I could remember, and I knew she always would—lupus is incurable. Maybe that gives context to my decisions, but it also makes me selfish, that I chose to grab for my own happiness when I could have been looking after her.

"That's really—" Henry starts, but then his eyes go wide and he points past me. I turn and see a figure in a huge red velvet coat, red sparkly pants, and a Santa hat sprinting toward us. Before I can even process what's happening (and what the person has on their face—is that a red light mask?), the figure has grabbed a cookie and is running away.

"Hey!" I jump up to chase after them, but my foot catches on the strap of his tote bag and then I'm flying through the air. My body falls onto something warm and solid, but soft too . . . something that smells spicy and sweet . . . like gingerbread?

"Oh my god!" I clamber backward and off Henry, hoping there's nothing giving away the tug I was feeling in my belly. Because I shouldn't be feeling something there or anywhere else. Except I trip on an ornament—several are rolling out of his bag now—and he catches me again in his strong grip. Shocks of pleasure shoot up my arms from where he's touching me. My cheeks burn in embarrassment, but with the adrenaline rushing, that quickly grows into flames erupting in my chest, smoke shooting out of my ears, because I'm angry at myself for feeling this way. But even more so, I'm angry at *him* for putting me in this position, for messing up my stakeout, for making me feel things I don't have time to feel.

"I'm sorry, but was that *Santa*?" he asks.

"Can you just—can you leave me alone? I didn't ask for this." I fling my hands at him, stepping backward. "For you."

He winces, confused. "Sorry, Simone, I was just trying—"

"I don't *care* what you were trying. Just leave me alone," I repeat. "I know you have a lot of time on your hands, but *I* don't. So—so you need to find some other entertainment. Okay?"

He lets out a short exhale of surprise and then shakes his head. "Okay."

I go to my stand and start closing up, ignoring him as he walks away.

❄

By the time I'm walking into the pharmacy the next evening to pick up Mom's prescription, I feel like shit. And the too-bright lights only seem to make that feeling worse, like I'm a cockroach being suddenly revealed by a flipped switch. Even my favorite Christmas song, the Temptations' "Silent Night" playing over the store's speakers doesn't help.

I know I overreacted with Henry, was mean to him when he was a little goofy but mostly kind, and that my embarrassment and guilt and anger and whatever was going on with my stomach weren't his fault. It's all I thought about as I worked on the third draft of a newsletter layout for a client in the morning or rolled out the dough for sugar cookies after I did the laundry and made dinner. So, when I hear his voice halfway down the hair dye aisle, I think I must be imagining it, my conscience haunting me like the ghost of Christmas past.

"Can you check again? Please?"

I reach the back of the store, where the pharmacy counter is, though, and see a very real Henry, wearing the same Paramore shirt from last week. In the bright light, I notice things I didn't before: the definition of his strong shoulders under that thin shirt, the dusting of dark hair on his forearms, the fullness of his lips . . . pulled into a frown.

Henry clutches his hands together, leaning toward the red-haired man in a white coat. "I'm not trying to be difficult, or act like you don't know how to do your job. You look very, very good at your job, but . . . I need that medication. Please can you look again?"

"I'm sorry, sir," the pharmacist says, gesturing toward his computer screen. "But it says that you no longer have that insurance coverage. Have you looked into a manufacturer coupon?"

Henry shakes his head. "Yeah, but it's still hundreds, even with that. And my insurance wasn't supposed to stop until the end of the year. Could it be because I'm at a different pharmacy than usual?"

"I'm sorry, sir," the pharmacist repeats, and at least it seems like he really means it. "The pharmacy location shouldn't affect things, but if you'd like to call your insurance again, we're open until ten." His gaze darts to the long line behind Henry, and as Henry turns to look, too, his eyes catch on me. I see him wince, just like he did last night.

"Sorry. And thank you," Henry says, and then walks down another aisle, purposefully and with his head down. I want to follow him, but I don't think he'd want that. So I step in line instead to pick up the medication I came here for. On my way out, though, I hear his voice again.

"Yeah, I'll tell them that. Thank you." He hangs up his phone, and then looks up, eyes widening when he sees me. He smiles sheepishly this time. "How much of a scene did I make in there?" he asks, nodding toward the automatic doors.

"No more than the one I made last night," I say with a sheepish smile of my own. "I'm sorry. You didn't deserve all that from me."

He shrugs like it was no big deal, but I know it was.

"I figured it was part of something bigger."

"Well, I appreciate the grace. And yeah . . . life is just a lot right now." I let out a small laugh. "That's why I'm hiding in bushes and launching myself at Santa."

"Okay, so you saw Santa too? I wasn't hallucinating that?"

"It was definitely someone . . . Santa adjacent."

"Maybe he was testing your generosity and, I don't know, levels of Christmas spirit?"

"Santa doesn't give tests! He isn't Jesus!"

"Yeah, well, with *that* attitude, someone's going to get a lump of coal."

We both fall into easy laughter, and it feels good, being loud and loose, when most of our talking has been whispered and tense.

"And, look, I get it. I'm going through it too, as you probably gathered," he says. He sighs and shakes his head. "Unemployed, insurance issues—I guess I can see why you weren't trying to mess with me."

"No, no. We already established I was being a jerk. And you shouldn't have to explain your situation to me. But, um . . . if it would help to talk about it, I can listen."

His brown eyes widen in surprise and then curve into crescents as he grins graciously.

"Well, like I told you, I was a teacher." He pauses, pressing his lips together. "Still *am* a teacher—or at least want to be. It wasn't my choice, to leave. I had just moved to San Francisco to start at this new charter school whose mission

I was really excited about. But then something shady happened with their funding, and they had to close the whole place down one week into the school year. I was looking for other jobs, doing a lot of subbing—but I finally accepted last month that I could barely make it there on a teacher salary, and definitely not as a sub. Nana offered to let me come stay with her until I figured it out."

"Wow, Henry, that's—that's awful. I'm really sorry."

"Thank you." He sighs again and runs his hands over his short curls. The headlights of a car driving by in the parking lot cast across his face, a spotlight on his sad smile. "I think the worst part is . . . that I did nothing wrong? I feel like it would be easier to accept my life getting blown up if I'd fucked up somehow, you know? But, like, I followed the path I was supposed to, got my degree and my credential, did student teaching. I spent all this time preparing for one specific job—so much so that I don't even know how those skills apply, like, anywhere else or what other jobs are out there. And still . . . I couldn't stop this. I have no control." He looks like he's just lifted and tossed away something heavy, and now he's tired from the effort. "I don't know . . . it's like a tsunami just came and washed over the whole life I planned for myself. And if I don't find some way to float along with the waves, I'll sink. Does that . . . make any sense?"

"That makes *perfect* sense." It's like he plucked the thought, and that overwhelming feeling of out-of-controlness, right out of my own head.

"Sorry, I know I'm rambling."

"No, you're not. I get it. Like, I really, really get it."

We're both being tossed around by forces outside of our control, and it can make me feel so tiny and insignificant and powerless. But what if instead of treading water and thrashing against the current . . . we reach for someone else in that same ocean? What if we could help each other through?

"Anyway, thanks for listening, Simone. I need to go talk to the pharmacist again—the insurance guy insisted it would work this time. But maybe . . . we could hang out sometime? I know you're busy, so, like, no pressure. Maybe after Christmas—"

"How about tomorrow?"

"Meet you behind the mailboxes?" His whole face lights up with a smile when I nod. "Okay, good, because I've got a plan with a brick. *Home Alone 2*. Only it's my nana's brick *phone*—"

"Yeah, I don't think we'll need to do all that."

"I still don't understand why you have your stand open until eight," Henry whispers. We're sitting in our spot, hidden in the bushes. "Like, who is even coming out of their houses that late? I feel like the average bedtime around here is six."

"Because D&D gets out at seven thirty, and they're usually my biggest customers."

"They got D&D here? I need to see about joining. And yeah, that makes sense. They're probably hitting the . . ." He presses his thumb and forefinger together and raises them up to his lips. His lips that are full and look especially soft from where I'm sitting, much closer than we were the past two stakeouts . . .

I shake that thought away and laugh softly. "Honestly, you're probably right. Mr. Joseph, their dungeon master, does look like the type."

"Is he on your suspect list? The munchies could be his motive."

"No, it's not him. He hates chocolate."

"Ah, got it." Is it just my imagination, or is he leaning in closer? "What about Ms. Earlene? I feel like she's the only one in this complex who would have all those clothing pieces we saw."

"Ms. Earlene? No way could she run that fast. Plus, I just can't see her planning a heist like this."

"A heist, huh? Well, maybe someone else in the theater society pulled a heist on her costumes first. Oh, oh—maybe they're trying to frame her." Yeah, he's definitely closer. His spicy, sweet smell feels like it's encircling me, warming me up.

I swallow and try to will all of my nerve endings to calm down, to stop reaching toward him like a plant to the sun.

He swallows, too, and I study the bobbing of his Adam's apple closely, if only to stop looking at his lips. "Hey, after tonight?" he whispers, and it feels softer, like he *wants* me to lean in. "After we catch this person, because I know we're going to catch this person, maybe we could . . . find some other mission? So we could keep, uh . . . spending time together."

"I'd like that." I let my body move the way it wants to.

"Yeah?"

"Yeah. Because I like—"

My hushed words are drowned out by the clattering of footsteps, racing toward us. Henry nods at me, I nod back, and we both leap out of the bushes toward the thief wearing green velvet pants, a leopard-print coat, and a Grinch mask. We grab them around the waist, trapping them in between us.

That's it. That was the plan.

And it *worked.* I pull off the Grinch mask to reveal who's been taking the Neapolitan cookies from my stand, trying to ruin one of the few things I control in my life, and find . . . Ms. Earlene's grandson?

I'm speechless, and when I look over at Henry, he seems to be the same. But the boy starts hollering enough for all three of us.

"I'm so sorry! Please, please don't tell my grandma! I was getting them for her, I swear!" He sniffles and fat tears begin to fall down his face. Henry and I let go of him.

"You were stealing Neapolitan cookies for Ms. Earlene?" I ask. "If it's a money thing, I would have given them to her . . . She just had to say."

"My grandma, she doesn't know I've been stealing them. It's just, she doesn't know a lot of things lately. She keeps forgetting that my grandpa died, or even who I am sometimes." He drags a sleeve of the leopard-print coat across his wet face. "But the cookies, they make her happy, at least for a little while. And when she's happy, she remembers more. I didn't have money for them because my mom doesn't even give me an allowance for my chores, even though I told her that *everyone* gets an allowance for their chores." He gulps for air, his confession spilling out faster. "And I couldn't ask her for the money because then she might not let me come to Grandma's house after school anymore on the days she has night shift and make me stay with Gracie the babysitter instead. And Gracie is the worst. So, so—I *had* to take the cookies! And I'm really sorry! I can pay you back when I get my birthday money next month, I promise!"

"Wow." I let out a long exhale. Over the boy's head, I can see that Henry is just as surprised as I am.

“I’m so, so sorry,” Ms. Earlene’s grandson continues. “I knew it was wrong. But I just felt like—”

“Like you had no control over your life,” Henry finishes for him.

“So you had to snatch it any way you could,” I add.

I smile at Henry, feeling even more sure than I did last night that I’ve found someone I want to hold on to in this unpredictable ocean.

“Yeah! Yeah, that,” the boy says.

“Well, we understand, little man,” Henry says.

The boy looks between us with pleading, hopeful eyes. “Does that mean you won’t tell my grandma?”

“No, I’m going to tell your grandma. And your mom too,” I say, making his shoulders slump in defeat. “But I’m also going to help you out.”

❄

As I put the freeze-dried strawberries in the food processor, I’m struck again by how much my life has changed in the past few weeks. At the beginning of December, Mom and I planned to spend Christmas Eve alone—eating my gluten-free cookies and watching another Hallmark movie (the one with the stressed-out woman from the big city and the small-town *bookstore owner*).

That movie is still on the TV, and those cookies are still being made, but we’re not alone. Ms. Earlene and Ms. Lily Anne are on the couch next to Mom, laughing along with her and resting after the big meal they all made together. Sherry, Ms. Earlene’s daughter and August’s mom, is sitting at the kitchen table with Henry, going over a part-time after-school enrichment program he wants to start for August and some of the other visiting grandchildren at

Jacaranda, until he can find a teaching position next school year. And August is here with me in the kitchen, learning how to make the Neapolitan cookies his grandma loves. Because now that his mom, and his community, know what he's been holding, he doesn't have to hold it alone.

"Does that look right to you?" he asks, holding up a small ball of dough mixed with cocoa powder. "Silent Night" by the Temptations plays softly in the background, harmonizing with the sounds of this community that's here to hold me too.

"That's perfect."

Sometimes life can feel like you're being tossed around by cold, unrelenting waves, that what happens to you and the ones you love is completely outside of your control. And that ocean may never calm.

But you can choose who you reach a hand out to in those times, to lift them out of the water or be pulled up yourself. You can choose to look for small glimmers of excitement in the ordinary everyday—like cookie stake-outs or cheesy movie marathons or making out in the pool room (I took that key after all).

That may not be what I wanted or expected for my life of adventure. But still, for now, it feels pretty limitless to me.

5

HO HO OH NO

M.A. Wardell

CHAPTER ONE

THE WORST SANTA IN RECORDED HISTORY

I should not be here.

That's the first, clearest thought I have as I stare at myself in the narrow mirror propped against a stack of folding chairs in the back room of Day's Bookstore. The glass is warped just enough to make me appear wider than I already am, the red suit stretching tight across my shoulders, mocking me. I shake my head, and the beard, itchy as hell, rubs even more against my skin.

This is not my department.

This is not my skill set.

This is not—under any circumstances—me.

Martin Howard is Santa.

Martin Howard, who works in HR. Martin Howard, who sends reminder emails about benefits enrollment and brings a slow cooker of something aggressively bland to every potluck. Martin Howard, who has played Santa at the Little Falls Christmas Eve Festival for the last nine years without incident. Martin Howard, who enjoys being perceived.

I do not.

I work in the Little Falls logistics department. I track inventory. Manage permits and timelines. I create contingency plans.

I'm not Santa.

If I were meant to play anyone it would be the Grinch, but I don't even have the spirit for that. I prefer holidays alone. My sister and her family live in California, which means a very long plane ride, only to deal with my niece and nephew crawling all over me and asking me what presents I've brought them. No thank you.

I never expected to need a contingency plan that involves being Santa. But Martin Howard "had to do something silly," which is how Trina Darlow from the licenses department phrased it when she called me, in a whisper that suggested both scandal and delight. Something involving a selfie, hanging decorations on a ladder, and a very unfortunate angle. He's currently stuck at home with a broken wrist and a town-wide text chain filled with offers of sympathy casseroles. Lucky bastard.

And now I'm Santa.

The worst part? I volunteered. No one forced me. No one cornered me or assigned me or even officially asked. I did this to myself because I made the mistake of walking past Brad Lee Levi's office at the wrong moment.

Brad Lee Levi, who has three first names. Maybe four—I've never asked his middle name. Brad Lee Levi, who makes my breath hitch every time he glides by my cubicle with a smile plastered on his face. Brad Lee Levi, the town events and community programs coordinator, who is effortlessly likable and way out of my league—always joyful, everyone's friend, and his title literally has the word *community* in it—while I haunt the town hall offices like the ghost of Christmas present.

Brad Lee Levi was on the verge of tears.

Not actually crying, but his eyes were glassy, lower lip pressed tight, shoulders squared a little too carefully—like if he relaxed for even a second, the tears might spill over. The man was trying desperately to be fine. He absolutely was not.

"I don't have a Santa," he said through a sniffle, when he noticed me standing there like a reindeer in headlights. "Phillip, I don't have a Santa."

I should have kept walking. I should have offered to help find a replacement. I could have pulled up the town's volunteer list, flagged the risk, documented the failure point, and gone home.

But then Brad Lee looked at me with those big brown eyes—wide and earnest. It was the same look he'd had at last year's festival, when we'd both had a little too much punch and he'd admitted he wished he had someone to kiss under the mistletoe. "The kids are looking forward to seeing Santa," he said. "I can't cancel, Phillip. I can't." He glanced at the suit draped over the back of his chair. The one Martin always used. The one that smelled faintly of peppermint and old storage.

"I guess I could do it," he said, voice wobbling. "I mean, I know I'm not really . . ." He paused, staring at his beanpole body with a surprised expression, as though he was noticing his size for the first time. He's too small. Too thin to play Santa. All elbows and enthusiasm. Clearly someone whose metabolism never caught up to adulthood. Brad Lee Levi is a certified twink. "Plus, I'm Jewish," he added, as if it was the final nail in the coffin.

"No offense," I said. "But you won't work."

He exhaled a laugh, equal parts embarrassment and relief.

After a beat, I glanced down at my decidedly un-twink stomach. In July, when I hit forty, my metabolism took a vacation, and my body seemed to agree. My stomach is round. Soft. I'm what you'd call a certified bear.

Brad Lee looked up with those puppy-dog eyes again, and the words came out of my mouth before I could stop them.

"I can do it."

So now here I am.

In the back room of Day's Bookstore, which has been repurposed into a makeshift dressing room with a folding screen, empty boxes that look to have held ornaments, and exactly one chair that looks like it might collapse out of spite.

The suit does not fit. The pants are too short. The jacket is too tight. The belt digs into my stomach like it's teasing me. The beard itches. The hat itches. Everything itches. Was I supposed to pop a Benadryl before this? If I had any hair on my head, it might provide a buffer. Something between my scalp and the relentless scratch of polyester cheer.

I adjust the beard for the fifth time and immediately regret it when glitter comes off on my hands. This is how the holiday spirit spreads. This is how they get you.

I take a breath. In through my nose. Out through my mouth. Systems. Processes. Steps.

Put on suit. Walk out. Sit down. Say hello. Ask what they want for Christmas.

How hard can that be?

The bell above the bookstore door jingles as I lumber out into the town square, and the noise hits me all at once. Laughter. Music. The hum of conversation layered over the tinny sound of a recorded carol looping from somewhere near the tree.

Twinkle lights are strung everywhere—across storefronts, around lampposts, zigzagging overhead. Clearly, Hugh from the parks department got overly ambitious. The tree stands in the center of the square, hauled in from Anderson's Farm like it is every year. It's a little skimpy on one side, branches sparse enough to notice if you're looking for it.

Basic tree.

Basic Santa.

Kids are everywhere. Bundled up in coats two sizes too big, hats pulled down over their ears, mittens dangling from strings. They clutch candy canes and cups of cocoa like lifelines.

Lord help me. There's a line.

A long one.

I swallow.

I sit and the makeshift throne creaks ominously.

Trina approaches, all smiles and sparkles, in an elf costume that suggests she has been waiting all year for this. Her cheeks are flushed, her ears pointy, and there are bells on her shoes. She looks ridiculous.

And then I realize, so do I.

"Santa!" she says, like she hasn't known me for twelve years. "We're so glad you're here."

That makes one of us.

She escorts the first child up—a little girl in a purple coat, her face mostly hidden behind her scarf. She takes one look at me and freezes. Her eyes widen. And then she bursts into tears.

I don't know if it's the suit or my face or the fact that I forgot to smile, but the sound hits me like a punch to the stomach.

"Oh," I say brilliantly. "It's okay."

It's most certainly not.

Trina swoops in, murmuring reassurances, and whisks the girl away before I can make it worse. The next child steps forward. Then the next. And the next.

I forget names. I say the wrong thing. I call one boy by his sister's name and don't realize until she corrects me, arms crossed, insulted for life. After that, it's a blur of names all starting with *N*—Nathan, Nolan, Noah, Nora, Nick, Naomi, the festive Noelle, and possibly a Nevaeh—and I lose the thread entirely. At some point, I call a child *champ* with so much enthusiasm I cringe.

I nod so much my neck starts to get tired, but nodding seems to soothe them. At least a little.

One child breaks down sobbing when I accidentally tell him he's on the nice list without checking the clipboard Trina hands me. Apparently, that matters.

By the time the ninth kid cries, I'm sweating under the suit and considering faking a medical emergency. I'm about to weep myself when Brad Lee appears at my side.

He's dressed as an elf—green tunic, striped tights, the

whole shebang—and seeing him in this getup, it hits me. He was made for this. Unlike me, he belongs here.

"Hey," he says softly, crouching down to the kid's level. "What's wrong, friend?"

His voice is gentle. Steady. The kind of voice that makes you want to listen.

Of course he'd be good at this. Of course he'd kneel down and make a weepy child feel like the only person in the square.

He's good with everyone. I don't know why I ever thought I might be an exception.

Last year, under the same twinkling lights, when he mentioned longing for a festive kiss, I thought maybe it was a hint. Turns out, he wasn't interested in locking lips. He only wanted to ask if I had any nieces or nephews.

The kid sniffles. Brad Lee listens. Nods. Smiles. Offers a tissue and a candy cane. Fixes everything in about thirty seconds.

Then he leans in close to me.

He smells like cocoa and peppermint and his lips shine with some balm that sparkles under the lights.

"Okay," he whispers. "Let's try something different."

And just like that, Brad Lee assigns himself as Santa's Helper.

He stays right next to me, whispering prompts.

"Okay," he murmurs, close enough that I can feel the warmth of his sweet breath. "Ask her how old she is. Then say that sounds like a very important age."

"Try his name again," Brad Lee hints. "Slowly. You've got this."

"Maybe don't promise a pony," he says under his breath. "We don't have the paperwork for that."

The line shows no sign of dwindling, and my ass has gone numb. He slides me a cup of cocoa when my hands shake. Adjusts the beard when it slips. Fixes the hat. Fixes me, really, without ever making it obvious.

"You can say 'Ho ho ho,'" he murmurs.

"Ho ho—oh no," I reply, aborting a *hell* at the last second when I remember I'm surrounded by children.

"Close." He grins.

It dawns on me how damn kind he is. Not loudly. Not for show. Just . . . constantly. How he thanks volunteers by name. How he kneels to talk to kids like they matter. How he never once makes me feel like a failure, even though I clearly am.

The line still snakes back when the sky darkens. Snow starts falling—thick, sudden flakes that stick immediately. I hear the distant grind of snowplows, and a familiar knot of concern twists in my chest.

"This is going to get bad," I mutter.

Brad Lee looks up at the sky, unfazed. "It's a squall," he says. "We'll wrap up and get everyone home."

The snow thickens as the square empties in stages—parents hustling, kids protesting, strollers turned into snowplows. By the time the last few children come through, cheeks pink and eyes bright, the crowd is mostly gone. Thankfully, nobody cries. When it's over, I stand carefully, my joints protesting.

"I should get going," I say. "Before the roads—"

"That ship's already sailed." Trina's voice cuts in from behind the chair. She's shrugging into her coat, phone pressed to her ear and brow furrowed in a way I recognize from other storms.

"They've closed the outer roads," she says, pulling the phone away just long enough to look at me. "County says anything past Miller Ridge is a no go. Your road is already flagged."

The ground seems to tilt. "Already?" I ask.

She nods. "The temperature dropped quickly, and they're not messing around with ice out there."

Snow comes down heavier now, the streetlights blurring into halos. The roads I take home are narrow, unlit, and absolutely not plowed with any kind of urgency.

Brad Lee clears his throat. "Well," he says carefully, "if you need somewhere to stay . . ."

I turn to him.

"I live upstairs." He points. "Above the bookstore. It's nothing fancy, but it's warm. And close. And you're welcome." He smiles, small and apologetic, like he's already bracing for me to say no.

Trina, traitor that she is, brightens immediately. "Perfect," she says. "Problem solved."

I hesitate, then glance up at the sky. Snow is coming down even harder now, swallowing the lights, the square, the whole night.

Last Christmas, I misread the moment. Pulled back fast enough to pretend I hadn't and made an ass of myself.

This year, it looks like he's stuck with me.

I don't detest the thought nearly as much as I should—and that's what worries me.

CHAPTER TWO

SNOWED IN ABOVE THE BOOKSTORE

The night ends the way winter events always do—quickly.

Someone unplugs the speaker playing tinny carols. The twinkle lights stay on, stubborn as ever, but the square empties fast.

Brad Lee locks up the bookstore, keys jingling, checks the door twice, then nods toward the narrow staircase tucked between the shop and the bakery next door.

"Home sweet home." He flicks on the light at the top of the stairs and steps aside to let me in.

The apartment is small—smaller than I expected—but it's warm in a way that isn't just temperature. Christmas has exploded in here, but gently, thoughtfully, like someone who loves the season but knows restraint is a myth.

There's a tree in the corner, not much taller than me, decorated with mismatched ornaments: a felt snowman, a tiny ceramic lighthouse, something glittery shaped like a pickle. White lights only. No blinking. A strand of garland is draped over the single window, fragrant pine overtaking the small room. There's a wreath on the inside of the door, because of course there is. A red throw blanket is folded neatly on the bed. Stockings—plural—hang along a shelf above a narrow kitchenette, one embroidered with *Brad Lee* and one that simply says *Guest*.

"I thought you were Jewish?" I ask before I can stop myself.

Brad Lee smiles, bright as the moon. "I am," he says easily. "But my parents divorced when I was seven, my mom remarried, and somewhere between the tree and 'All I Want for Christmas Is You,' I was completely hooked."

As if that explains everything.

I take in his apartment more slowly now. The furniture—or lack of it. A small table with two chairs that don't quite match off the barely there kitchen. A dresser that looks like it's been with him since college. A single armchair pushed near the window. And the bed.

One bed.

No sofa.

Heat creeps up my neck, but I keep my face neutral. I am very good at that.

Maybe I could sleep on the armchair.

"Bathroom's through there," he says, gesturing. "I'll go change. You okay out here?"

"Yeah. Sure. All good." The words come out, but my stomach's doing this strange thing, like when an unexpected snowstorm comes out of nowhere. Yeah, exactly like that.

He nods and disappears into the bathroom.

I'm left alone with Santa.

Getting out of the costume is like shedding a second skin, one that has been aggressively itchy. The beard comes off first, leaving glitter on my hands again. The hat, the coat, the pants. I fold them as neatly as I can, like that will somehow apologize for how badly I wore them or for shaking glitter everywhere.

All I have with me are my work clothes. Dress shirt.

Khakis. Sensible belt. The uniform of a man who did not expect to be snowed in overnight. I end up in my white undershirt and khakis and sit on the edge of the bed.

When Brad Lee comes back out, I almost don't recognize him.

No elf. No forced cheer. No work clothes I'm used to seeing at the office. Just a soft gray T-shirt and dark sweatpants, sandy brown hair slightly damp like he rinsed his face. He looks . . . real. Approachable in a way that makes my chest tighten.

"Sorry," he says. "I should've offered you something to change into."

"It's fine."

He looks at me. Really looks. "That does not look fine."

Before I can protest, he's at the dresser, pulling open drawers. "I think I've got something." He holds up a pair of red-and-green plaid pajama pants, the kind that scream *Christmas morning*. "My aunt bought these for me a few years ago," he says. "Said I'd grow into them someday. Then immediately handed me a full plate and said, 'Now eat.'"

I snort despite myself. "You don't have to—" I start.

"I want to," he says simply. "Please."

I take them, turn my back to him, keep my boxers on like a gentleman, and change. The fabric is soft. Warm. Absurdly comfortable. When I turn around, he smiles like he's won something.

"See?" he says. "Much better."

I look down at myself and shrug.

Brad Lee nods. "They look handsome on you."

We sit at the small table, cocoa steaming between us, snowflakes slanting sideways past the window.

"So tell me. Why did you volunteer?" he asks, never breaking eye contact.

I stare into my mug. "You looked . . . sad."

"I was. Worried. Disappointed. Panicked."

"And the holidays are . . . complicated," I add. "My family's on the West Coast. It's just my sister and her kids now." I mentioned my family at the party last year, but with me making a fool of myself leaning in for an unwanted kiss, he probably doesn't remember. "And the idea of traveling at this time of year makes my skin crawl."

"Why?"

"Because the airports are loud. And crowded. And everyone's emotional." I glance at him. "And once I arrive at my sister's, it's also . . . loud and crowded and everyone's emotional. I prefer quiet. Like . . . this."

He smiles. Not wide. Real.

"What about you?" I ask, suddenly aware I'm probably ruining his holiday plans.

"Oh, my family's up north. Just my folks and younger brother. I never go up until Christmas dinner. Sometimes not until the next day. I like being in my own place for Christmas—creating my own traditions. Even if I'm alone." He smiles at me. "Which, thanks to you, I'm not."

"Sorry I ruined the whole Santa thing." I take a sip of cocoa. It's sweet, with real, deep flavor. Not from a mix. He melted the damn chocolate himself.

"You didn't ruin anything." He does this adorable half smile and something in my stomach flips. "You showed up."

The power flickers.

We both look up and the lights go out.

"Well, I guess that means it's bedtime," he says casually. "I can take the floor."

"No," I say immediately. "Absolutely not."

We stare at each other, lit only by moonlight and the pale glow of snow through the window.

"We're grown men," I say, squaring my shoulders. "We can share a bed for one night."

He nods. "Okay."

We lie down, careful at first, like there are rules we haven't been handed. Brad Lee leaves the shade open, and the snow-bright light seeps into the room, turning everything pale and quiet. I can make out his face beside me, the curve of his cheek, the shadow of his lashes. I know he's at least a few years younger, but he looks even more youthful like this. Unarmored.

My stomach does that strange, unsettled flip again, like I've stepped somewhere I wasn't invited but nobody's asked me to leave.

"So," I say. "How is it having three first names?"

He laughs. "Actually, it's four. My middle name's Robert."

I turn my head. "Wait. Your full name is Brad Lee Robert Levi?"

"Yup."

I laugh, really laugh, and something in my chest loosens.

His hand brushes my face. Probably by accident.

"Merry Christmas Eve, Phillip," he says.

It happens again. His fingers are on my cheek. Soft. Warm.

"Merry Christmas Eve."

And for the first time in a long while, I actually mean it.

CHAPTER THREE

CHRISTMAS MORNING UNDER THE MISTLETOE

I wake up disoriented.

Not the bad kind. Not the cold, panicked inventory-taking kind. The other kind. The kind where my body feels heavy in a way that's pleasant, where my brain lags a few seconds behind.

Light spills in through the window—soft, pale, almost blue. Snow light. The light that makes everything outside feel muted, like the world has agreed to lower its voice.

I breathe in.

Pine. Coffee, faint but there. Clean cotton. Something warm and human.

Then I realize I'm not home.

I'm not alone.

My arm drapes across a solid chest, my leg thrown over a thigh like it's always belonged there. My face tucks against the back of Brad Lee's neck. His warmth surrounds me, anchoring me, and my entire body wraps around him like I reached for him during the night and didn't dare let go.

Oh.

Oh.

No.

Panic flickers, instinctive and sharp—but it doesn't catch. It simply . . . fizzles out, like a match struck in the wind.

He's still asleep. Breathing slow and even. And I kind of love this.

The realization lands gently, terrifying and quiet all at once.

I try to pull back without waking him, easing my arm away, inch by careful inch. I almost succeed.

Brad Lee stirs, a faint sound leaving his throat—half sigh, half protest—and his hand tightens around my forearm, pulling me closer. My palm presses more firmly against his chest, warm and taut beneath his thin T-shirt.

"Mmm," he murmurs, voice thick with sleep. "Merry Christmas."

The words are barely formed, but they hit me square in the chest.

"Merry Christmas," I whisper back, my voice rough with things I'm not sure how to name.

He rolls over, slow and unhurried, until we're face-to-face. Nose to nose. Close enough that I can see the faint crease between his brows, a few pale freckles dotting his cheekbones, the curve of his mouth. His eyes flutter open, still hazy, and when they focus on me, something bright sparks in my core, like all the twinkle lights in town flashing in unison.

I become acutely aware of my own existence. Of my breath. Of the fact that I have not brushed my teeth. Of the way he doesn't seem to care.

Brad Lee just looks at me and smiles. It's slight, sweet, and just for me. Damn if that smile couldn't solve most of the world's problems.

My stomach growls, loud and traitorous.

He blinks, then laughs, soft and delighted. "Oops."

"I—sorry," I say automatically.

"Hungry?" He pushes himself up on one elbow. "Gosh, where are my manners? I should've offered you a snack before bed."

He's so damn thoughtful.

"I'm fine," I say, even as my stomach betrays me again.

He grins. "Come on." He nods toward the tree, lights glowing. "Power's back, and I've got breakfast ready to go."

He moves through the small kitchen, opening cabinets, pulling things from the fridge. I sit at the small table, in borrowed pajama pants, and watch him like this is something I'm allowed to have. He pulls out a tray of cinnamon buns from the fridge.

"I prepped yesterday," he says, catching me watching. "Habit."

"They smell . . . incredible."

"Wait until they're baked."

He cooks sausage on the stove, cracks eggs, and chops an onion. Watching him cook like this feels like witnessing a version of Christmas I stopped believing was possible.

The apartment smells amazing. Sweet. Savory. Like home.

"Don't you want to be with your family?" I ask. "I mean, after the roads clear."

He shrugs, stirring the sausage-and-onion mixture. "I'll head up once it's safe. Probably tomorrow. Already texted my mom."

There's no heaviness in it.

"I assumed you'd have a whole thing today," I admit. "I figured you wouldn't want to spend it with . . . me."

He turns, leans back against the counter, studying me. "Why wouldn't I?"

I don't have a good answer. "I'm not exactly . . . festive," I say finally.

He smiles. "You showed up. You stayed. You wore the suit. I'd say that's festive."

"Barely competently."

"Still counts." He winks.

Heat flushes my face, and I feel like Rudolph on Christmas Eve—nose and all.

Breakfast is absurdly good. We eat too much. Laugh. Sit longer than necessary.

Afterward, I'm at the counter drying dishes while he washes. The window above us is fogged with steam, mistletoe hanging crookedly from the frame.

The last time we stood under mistletoe, I was foolish enough to hope.

He glances at it. Then at me.

I dry the same fork twice.

"Feels wrong not to kiss under the mistletoe." He pulls his lips in and waits for my reply. "It's Christmas, after all."

My throat tightens. My chest blooms, and I close my eyes and nod.

"You know, I've always thought you were cute, Phillip Jones. Grumpy pout and all." He stares up at me with those giant brown eyes. "Are you sure?" he asks.

My entire body hums, and I nod again.

He steps closer, slow enough that I could stop him if I wanted to. But I don't.

And then Brad Lee's lips are on mine.

His mouth is warm, soft, careful. My heart races, and I can't tell if it's nerves, surprise, or both. My hands hover, unsure where to rest—on his shoulders? His chest?

My brain is already a muddle of heat and snow light and breakfast smells lingering in the kitchen.

His body presses gently against mine, steady, grounding, and I'm keenly aware of something new. Being wanted. Being allowed to exist here without pretense. Brad Lee's hand brushes my forehead, whether by accident or intention I can't tell, and it's enough to make my stomach clench and relax all at once.

I open my eyes for a moment and glimpse the Santa suit on top of my work bag. My mind wanders back to the long night of children, glitter, and cocoa. Of my embarrassment last year. Every awkward moment and every small disaster that led to this—and it's like all of it was necessary, like it was the prelude to a single, perfect moment of stillness under the mistletoe.

I inhale, caught between wanting to pull back and wanting to sink further into the warmth of him, into the quiet certainty of this small apartment, snow muffling the world outside. My pulse races in a way that's uncomfortably perfect. I notice his eyelashes, the slight rise and fall of his chest, the way he's on his toes, and the way his presence presses into me.

When he pulls back, it's barely an inch. Just enough to rest his forehead on my chin. My heart is still thrumming, my mind whirring. I could stay like this forever. Or at least until the roads clear. And I hope he knows that without me saying it.

His phone buzzes on the counter, interrupting the quiet of the moment.

He checks it, then looks at me with raised eyebrows. "Trina says the roads are still bad."

I open my mouth to respond, but he's already tugging me gently toward the bed.

"Looks like you're stuck for a while," he says, smiling.

Somehow, being snowed in with Brad Lee Robert Levi doesn't feel like trouble at all. More like an unexpected Christmas miracle.

CHAPTER FOUR

UNWRAPPED

The snow outside hasn't stopped. Light filters through the window, dusting the room in a gentle glow. The apartment is warm. Cozy, even. It's bright. Maybe too bright, but nothing like the sparkle in Brad Lee's brown eyes.

I sit on the edge of the bed, hands resting on my knees, watching him. His movements are slight, intimate gestures—adjusting a pillow, brushing lint off the comforter, folding the throw neatly.

I feel exposed. Not in the usual way I do when someone sizes me up. Which, let's be honest, doesn't happen very often. Brad Lee's gaze doesn't do that. It's warm, steady, intent. He sees me—surly, stubborn, reserved, the world's worst Santa—and still wants me. That thought makes my pulse quicken.

"You okay?"

"I—I think so," I say, though my voice sounds foreign to my own ears.

"You know," he says, sitting beside me close enough that his shoulder brushes mine, "maybe it was the punch, but I was really hoping you'd kiss me at the festival last year."

"Excuse me?" I stare at him. "I leaned in."

He blinks. "You—what?"

"You mentioned mistletoe. I stepped closer and you asked if had any nieces or nephews."

His entire face falls. "Oh my god."

"Exactly."

"Phillip, I panicked. You moved in and I thought I was imagining the whole thing, so I changed the subject."

"To children."

"I know." He lifts his hand to rub my smooth head. "I'm sorry. Truly."

I close my eyes, and lean into his touch.

"Do you forgive me?" His voice is gentle, even as his fingers are firm on my scalp.

"Yeah. I guess."

"I want you to know, you're safe here," he whispers. "Even the parts you think are . . . grinchy."

I want to tell him he doesn't know what he's signing up for. But the warmth in his eyes stops me. My hands tighten in my lap before loosening again.

"Trust me," he says, leaning closer.

And I do.

He reaches for my T-shirt, fingers catching the hem. He lifts it slowly, giving me time to breathe, to steady myself. When it clears my head, the room feels cooler, quieter. Then he peels his shirt off with the same unhurried care, and Merry Christmas to me. He's got more hair on his chest than I expected. It's clipped. Neat. But my fingers twitch, wanting to touch it. I notice the heat of him—the sharp lines of his shoulders, the subtle rise and fall of his breath. How did I get so damn lucky?

The bed is small, but it doesn't matter. There's room enough for warmth and closeness. The blankets smell faintly of our sleep, mixed with breakfast. I'm aware of everything and nothing at once—the sound of his breathing, the weight of him leaning in, the nearness of his face.

I finally let myself exhale, letting him take the lead. His lips brush mine again, slower this time, soft, teasing contact.

"There," he says, mouth still brushing mine.

My stomach does that strange fluttering thing. My hands hover, once again unsure where to rest. Lord, I want to feel him.

He takes my hands in his. "Do you want to touch me?"

I swallow past the lump in my throat and nod.

He guides my hands to his chest. The instant I make contact, my eyes go wide. While his pecs are firm, the soft hair feels like a warm blanket against them. Deck the freakin' halls, I'm touching Brad Lee.

"That feels nice," he whispers. "You're getting me all worked up."

I glance down and his sweats are tented. Suddenly, I can't look away.

"You seem excited too," he murmurs, biting his lower lip, nodding at the pajama pants I borrowed. My stomach drops, the instinct to be embarrassed creeping in until Brad Lee stands.

"You okay if I take these off?" His fingers brush the top of his sweats, waiting.

I nod quickly. They come off and there's his cock, pointing right at me. He's naked. Hard. Beautiful. Every hair on his body matches the sandy brown waves on his head. My mouth opens, just slightly, and I feel my tongue run over my bottom lip.

I take a deep breath. Not sure who I should thank for this, but it's probably Santa.

"Go ahead." He steps closer. "Touch me."

I reach out, his heat warming my fingers the moment I begin stroking. He settles between my legs, hands on my shoulders, head back, and I'm suddenly thrilled about the storm still churning outside.

"Oh, PJ."

I pause.

Brad Lee looks at me, abashed. "Sorry, it slipped out."

"PJ?" My brow furrows.

"Yeah, Phillip Jones. PJ. Nobody's ever called you that?"

My mind races, thinking of all the nicknames I've had hurled at me over the years. Phil. Philly. Phil-dog. Flip. But never PJ. It feels . . . different. Unique. Brad Lee coded.

"No, but . . . you can."

"Are you sure?"

"So sure."

"Okay, PJ. How about you get these . . . pj's off." A laugh bubbles out.

I stand to remove them, but before my hands reach the waistband, Brad Lee yanks them—and my boxers—down. My aching cock springs free.

I'm completely naked. And . . . proud. Always have been, and now that my stomach is a little rounder, there's even more to admire. Apparently, Brad Lee agrees, because his hands find my belly first, tracing gentle circles.

"Such a sexy Santa."

I huff a laugh, and he pushes gently.

"Sit, please."

I do as I'm told.

"Can you toss me a pillow?"

And just like that, I'm naked, hard, with Brad Lee kneeling between my spread legs. Consider me thoroughly jingled.

He takes my dick in his hands. "Tell me if anything doesn't feel good, okay?"

"Okay."

He holds me, eyes glassing over. I'm so damn hard, pulsing in his grip.

Brad Lee licks his lips, gives me a few slow strokes, then swallows me almost to the base. Every nerve in my body jolts to attention.

Not only does he know how to plan an event, handle a crowd on Christmas Eve, and coach me through it, but Brad Lee Levi also clearly knows how to suck dick.

He's bobbing up and down. Using his hands to add friction. And then pulls back and slaps the wet head against his cheek. I watch in awe. That we're doing this. Here. Now. That he's so into it. It's a side of him I didn't expect. And it's amazing.

"Brad Lee, you. You're . . ." I'm not sure how to say it. "C'mere." I grab under his arms, pulling him up, and he pushes me back, lying on top of me.

"Hey." His lips ghost over mine.

"Hey." I tilt my head up and kiss him. Soft. Gentle.

"Did that not feel good?" he asks.

I clear my throat, and it comes out indecently loud.

"No. Oh gosh, no. I mean yes. It did. Feel good. Fantastic. I just . . . I don't know. I wanted to kiss you," I admit, reaching back, hands landing on his ass. It's covered in soft fuzz and feels incredible. "And maybe . . . wanted more."

"Oh." His eyes go wide. "Am I on the naughty or nice list?"

My fingers dig into his beautiful butt. "Both."

Brad Lee's eyebrows wiggle. "I like this side of you."

"Must be the new nickname."

"Okay, PJ. What do you want? You tell me."

I chuckle. "Gosh, you're cute. Do you know that?"

"I've been told."

"How are you single?"

He shrugs. "I'm not into the scene. The apps. I prefer someone . . ." He pushes himself up, kissing my forehead. "Real."

My lips catch his as he moves down and I make an amendment to my long-standing position on Christmas.

"I was wondering . . . if you might like to . . ." I tug at his ass, spreading his cheeks, licking my lips.

"Oh, my cinnamon buns weren't enough for you? You want more? With pleasure." He moves onto his knees. "Stay right there. You good if I sit on your face? This way I can still play with your gorgeous cock."

"Gorgeous?"

"PJ, don't you know how glorious it is?"

He's on his knees, facing away from me, holding my erection up.

"Truly. A stunning specimen. Anyway." He lets go for a moment, reaching back to spread his cheeks wide.

A little soft brown hair frames his entrance. My cock strains at the sight. "Fuck, Brad Lee. Your hole is beautiful."

He responds by leaning forward, stroking me, then spitting lightly on my dick.

I pull the pillow behind me, prop my head up, and press a soft kiss to his ass cheek. He smells like cocoa, cinnamon, and absolute heaven. My fingers stretch him wide, and my tongue follows.

I never considered how our bodies might fit together, but here we are, like a candy cane curved perfectly into someone's hand. My hands land on his waist, yanking him back, and Brad Lee sits up.

"You want more, PJ?"

He grinds into my mouth, my tongue plunging deeper, his sweetness overwhelming in the best possible way. His hips find a rhythm, fucking my face, while his hands stroke me in unison. I moan into him. It's absolutely perfect, and I'm fairly sure I'm not going to last long this way.

"There we go," he says, jerking faster. "Come for me, Phillip."

My hips shake, lifting off the bed, and my orgasm arrives like the snowstorm—sudden, intense, and relentless. I can't see it, but I can feel every pulse. Strong, long spurts I know must be landing somewhere—on Brad Lee, the bed, or both.

"Fuck." His hands don't stop, draining every last drop, and I don't stop rimming him like I'm chasing the last gift under the tree.

When I finally finish, he lets go. "Now . . . just keep doing that with your mouth, and I'll come in no time."

I obey, and within a minute, I feel him contract around my tongue. Pulsing as he unloads on my chest. Stomach. A few drops hit my thighs. It's magnificent.

When he's done, neither of us moves for a moment. In the stillness, all I can think is, *What the hell just happened? And, Dear Santa, can you please make it happen again?*

Brad Lee climbs off, grabs a snowman dish towel from

the kitchen, and carefully cleans us both up, methodical and unbothered by the mess, while I just lie there, admiring him.

"You're quite smiley." He wraps the towel around my dick, making sure it's spotless.

I shrug. "Can't help it. That might be the best Christmas morning . . . ever."

The room goes quiet. Just us, the apartment, and the snow pressing softly against the window.

He lies against me, forehead resting on my chest. My pulse slows, warm and heavy. I could stay here forever. The room smells like . . . us. Soap, sweat, sex, and a hint of cinnamon—and it makes me ache in the best possible way.

Brad Lee's arms tighten around me, not possessive, not demanding, simply claiming me gently. I notice how natural it feels, how easy it is to let myself melt against him. The part that usually keeps walls around everything that matters, shrinks a little. All because of him.

He hums a carol softly—low and contented—and I pull him closer. Every small movement he makes, brushing a hand across my shoulder, the gentle curve of his fingers along my arm, reassures me I'm exactly where I belong. I've never felt this seen, this wanted, this . . . safe.

"I could get used to this," I murmur.

He smiles, tilts his head, and kisses my chin. "Careful. That's how habits form."

I can't help the small laugh that percolates out. Comfort spreads from my chest to my toes. The snow outside is falling again, but I don't care. I've never felt warmer.

We shift together under the blankets, tangled, lazy, perfectly comfortable. He brushes his hand along my jaw again, and I hope he does it a million times more.

For the first time in a long time, I feel like the world

isn't pressing against me or demanding I be anyone other than myself. Brad Lee wants me just as I am. The thought makes me dizzy with relief, with disbelief, with something dangerously close to hope.

And so we stay in his bed, cuddling, kissing, the room quiet except for our breathing, and the occasional soft hum or shift. I close my eyes, letting myself sink into the warmth, the safety, the undeniable joy of being with him. We're wrapped in a blanket of lights and snow, the world hushed around us. Santa really outdid himself this year.

CHAPTER FIVE

NEW BEGINNINGS

One week later, I'm back in the town square, but this time it doesn't feel like a punishment.

The Christmas lights are still up—Little Falls never misses a chance to linger in the holiday glow—but now they're joined by silver streamers and paper clocks taped into storefront windows. Someone has hung a banner between lampposts that reads HAPPY NEW YEAR! in slightly crooked letters. The tree from Anderson's Farm is still standing too, a little drier now, a little more hunched, but lit all the same. Stubborn. Relatable.

There's a crowd, but it's thinner than Christmas Eve. Families drift in and out, kids bundled up in coats that are still too big, hats still slipping down over their eyes. A few of them look at me like they're trying to place my face.

I try a smile on one of them—a boy with a red scarf and matching hat.

"Hey there," I say, immediately regretting opening my mouth. "Uh. Happy . . . almost New Year."

He squints at me.

I nod, like that'll help.

Brad Lee presses closer to my side, his shoulder warm through my coat. "Hi, Oliver," he says easily. "Did you have a good Christmas?"

The kid lights up. "I got a drone!"

"That's awesome," Brad Lee says. "Just what you asked for." He knocks his shoulder against mine. "Santa really delivered."

The boy nods, suddenly chatty, and I stand there, useless but smiling anyway. When he runs back to his parents, Brad Lee looks up at me, eyes bright.

"You did great," he says.

I snort. "I said three words."

"Exactly."

And the thing is—I'm laughing. Actually laughing. Not the tight, careful version I usually offer to be polite. Genuine laughter that comes from my belly and booms out.

I didn't know I had it in me. I guess I needed Brad Lee Robert Levi (and Santa) to coax it out of me.

Christmas feels both a lifetime and ten minutes ago. I stayed. All of Christmas Day. And the night. We couldn't keep our hands off each other. It was . . . unexpected, yet completely correct. I went with Brad Lee up north the next morning to see his family—warm, loud people who hugged me like they'd been waiting for me without knowing it.

We've been inseparable all week.

We only had to work one day between holidays, and

Brad Lee brought me lunch like it was the most natural thing in the world. Hot butternut squash soup from the deli next to the bookstore. He sat across from me while I ate, feet hooked around my legs, telling me about an idea he had for a spring festival.

I didn't tell him how much the soup meant. I just wiped my face and kissed him softly.

The night stretches on. The children disappear one by one, herded home by parents who keep checking their watches and the sky. Snow drifts down again, light and lazy this time, like it's got nowhere urgent to be. And neither do we.

We end up near the clock tower, tucked slightly out of the wind. Brad Lee's hand finds mine, and my fingers lace through his without thinking. One week and we're a couple. And when I let my mind ruminate on it, that scares me.

"I need to say something," I tell him quietly.

He turns toward me, patient. Always patient. "Okay."

"I'm not good at . . . this," I say, gesturing vaguely between us. "Wanting things. Letting myself have them."

"I know," he says.

"I'm scared," I admit. The words feel heavy, but also lighter once they're out. "Because I want this. You. And I don't want it to be a holiday thing. Or a snowstorm thing."

Brad Lee smiles, and my entire world lightens. "Then let's not call it that."

"What do we call it?"

He shrugs, squeezing my hand. "We don't have to name it yet."

The clock tower chimes, drawing the crowd's attention. People start counting down together, voices overlapping, messy and joyful.

Ten.

Nine.

Brad Lee turns fully toward me.

Eight.

Seven.

I can smell him—clean, familiar, with a hint of pine from the tree.

Six.

Five.

My chest expands, like a million stars exploding.

Four.

Three.

He leans in.

Two.

One.

"Happy New Year," he says, and then he's on his toes, kissing me—warm and sure and perfect.

Cheers erupt around us. Someone lights a handful of sparklers. Snow keeps falling, like it's reminding us of its role in all this.

When we pull back, he rests his forehead against my chin.

"Maybe we call this"—he motions between us—"new beginnings."

I nod, holding him close, the town glowing around us, the future stretching ahead of us like a promise I'm finally ready to keep. This must be what all the holiday magic fuss is about.

I've never been very good at asking, but somehow Santa still got me exactly what I wanted—for Christmas and beyond.

6

TWELVE SECONDS TO FOREVER

Rebecca Jenshak

CHAPTER ONE

LAINEY

Jess takes both of my hands in hers with an intense look of a panicked bride on the eve of her wedding. “I have a favor.”

“Whatever it is, yes.” I smile at my best friend. For nearly twenty years I’ve been doing her favors, and asking for my own in return, but this week in particular I’d do anything for her.

“Can you check on Alex?” she pleads. The twinkle lights strung around the old barn-turned-event space dance in her eyes.

“Your brother?” I ask, doing my best to ignore the prickle of irritation every time I think of my best friend’s older brother. “Why? I thought he was flying in late tonight.”

That's the story she's been telling everyone. Alex, her extremely busy, superstar football player, is flying in late tonight after playing a game across the country yesterday, just in time for his little sister's wedding. He's a groomsman, so there was a noticeable gap at the rehearsal tonight, but Jess reassured everyone he'd be here tomorrow. I think people were more disappointed they didn't get to see and talk to him than they were about him missing the actual rehearsal. He's a big deal. The hometown hero. Star high school running back–turned–professional football player.

Jess bites the corner of her lip—an unmistakable sign that she's not telling me something.

"Jessica Renee?" I prompt in my best imitation of her mother.

She lowers her voice. "I lied. I have no idea where he is." She looks around nervously. "He flew in this morning. He said he might go snowboarding this afternoon but then be here for the rehearsal."

"Seriously?" I let out a huff. He blew off his sister's rehearsal to go snowboarding? I pull out my cell phone, prepared to call the man I haven't spoken to in nearly three years.

"It's no use. His phone is off," she says before I can pull up his contact. "I've been trying for the past hour."

"Are you sure he's here? Maybe his flight was delayed because of the storms on the East Coast."

"Maybe." Her tone tells me she doesn't think that's the case.

I grind my back molars.

"I know what you're thinking," she says, shaking her head. "But it isn't like him to flake. Not today. Something is wrong."

I don't know what he's like—not anymore. But he better have a damn good reason to not be checking in. I take a deep, cleansing breath.

The whole wedding was planned around Alex, or rather, his team schedule. He couldn't make it for Christmas last week, but a New Year's Eve wedding fit perfectly between games. Jess and her brother have always been close, and I know how much it means to her to have him here. So like it or not, I will do whatever I can to make sure he doesn't ruin this for her.

"Okay. What can I do? Do you want me to see if I can find out his flight information and see if he landed?" I have no idea if I can pull that off, but I'm not about to tell the bride-to-be no, no matter how difficult the task.

"Jessica!" her mother calls from across the room, where friends and family are waiting to go to the rehearsal dinner.

My best friend flashes her mother a smile while holding up a finger to indicate she'll be there in a moment.

"Just find him," she says. "Please? He's staying at my grandparents' cabin."

I nod, swallowing the lump forming in my throat.

"I know you two aren't on the best terms, but there's no one else I can ask. My parents would freak if they knew he was MIA, and you're the smartest, most determined person I know."

"You don't have to butter me up." I let out a small laugh. "I already said I'd do it."

"I mean it, though. You're the best. I don't know what I'd do without you."

"Yeah. Same." The smile that pulls at my lips is filled with a bittersweet sort of happiness. "I can't believe you're getting married tomorrow."

Things will be different. She's entering a whole new era. She's going to be someone's wife, and I haven't been someone's girlfriend in so long I've forgotten how long it's been.

"Me either." Her grip on my hands tightens. "Promise we'll always be best friends?"

My heart squeezes in my chest. "I promise."

"Okay. I better go. My mom will have a meltdown if we don't get to the restaurant soon." She rolls her eyes. "You'll meet us there as soon as you find Alex?"

"Yep. Save me a margarita." I'm going to need it.

"You got it." She backs away a step. "Try not to kill him."

"I will find him and deliver him unscathed."

She lunges forward, hugging me around the neck. "Thank you. I love you."

"I love you too," I tell her. "Now go enjoy your rehearsal dinner."

She pulls away and hurries toward the door. She looks back and waves one last time before she steps outside with her fiancé and their families.

I grab my coat and purse and follow them out, then get into my SUV and crank up the heat. While I wait for my vehicle to warm up, I send a text to Alex—something I thought I'd never do again. I stare at the screen for a beat to see if he'll respond. After two full minutes have passed, I close out of the message and then pull up his social media page. It's a sucker punch to see his last post. It's from the very last time I saw him. It was the holiday break, just like now, and we were both home from college. It feels like a lifetime ago.

"In the past three years he couldn't have posted anything else?" I ask absolutely no one as a prick of something needles my skin. I can't even begin to wonder why. There's plenty of content out there of him posted by other people. Alex getting drafted to the NFL, Alex at practices with the team, Alex at games and in media photos, not to mention plenty of fan edits. Alex is well loved by both the football fans and women, who have no idea what he does but think he looks great in tight pants and a jersey that shows off his biceps.

Ignoring the pang in my chest, I open my search browser and navigate to the local airport website. I scan all the arrivals from Denver. A few early morning flights were delayed, but everything else looks like it was on schedule, and the planes have arrived. Which means he should be here.

Despite our issues, I can't believe he'd just flake, at least not on something this big. And not on Jess. I know they're still close. She doesn't mention him much to me lately except in passing, but they've always been the kind of siblings that made me wish for my own brother or sister. Even when they were yelling or fighting and pretending to hate each other, it was obvious how much they cared deep down.

I stare out the windshield, debating my next move. Light snow drops onto the glass and melts. I put my SUV in gear and decide to look for him. Jess said he was staying at the cabin, but I drive through town first. I don't really expect to spot him. I don't even know what he's driving, and there aren't a lot of people walking around, but I check anyway. Gas stations, hotels, the grocery mart, the local bar.

There's no sign of Alex and no one has seen him.

It leaves only one last place to look, and I really, really don't want to check there.

My phone pings with a text from Jess. Any luck?

Not yet, but I'll find him, I type back.

The drive out to the ski lodge is beautiful. The mountains are covered in fresh snow, and the entire property is lit up with lights for the holidays. As I navigate my SUV up and around the winding road, I feel a pang of melancholy. How long has it been since I was here?

I know the answer before I've even finished the question.

More than three years.

Once I reach the lodge, I make a right down a private road. It's been a long time, but I could never forget this place. Jess and Alex's family ski cabin was a constant in my childhood. Jess and I would hang out here when everyone else was skiing, and we preferred to read or play board games, and then in high school Alex and his football buddies threw parties here all the time.

It's only once I've driven more than two miles and still don't see the cabin that I start to second-guess myself. The snow is a little thicker up here, and the gravel road quickly becomes hard to see. I breathe a sigh of relief when I turn a corner and see it. That relief is short-lived, though, because the lights are on and there's a shiny black sports car in the driveway.

I don't allow myself time to think as I park and get out of my SUV. It takes some effort to walk across the gravel in my heels. The snow makes it hard to see any sort of path, and the only light is from inside the house. I focus on staying upright and doing my best not to ruin my favorite shoes. But once I'm standing in front of the door, I panic.

If he's in there, it'll be the first time I've seen him in years. What will I say? What will he do?

I shake off the runaway thoughts. If he's here, then I'm simply going to tell him to stop being a jerk and get to his sister's rehearsal dinner. And perhaps remind him that there's this amazing technology that allows you to alert people when you're unable to attend an event when you previously said you would.

Alex, meet the telephone. Telephone, Alex. Charmed, I'm sure.

I steel myself and then knock on the front door. I'm poised, ready for action. Thirty seconds or less, and then I'm out of here and we can both go on pretending that the other doesn't exist.

The cold air stings my cheeks and whips around my bare legs. I start counting to myself. One, two, three, four.

Ten seconds pass and there's no answer. Some of my nerve wobbles. I knock again, louder this time. Someone calls out from inside, but I can't make out the words. Only the tone. Deep, clipped, undoubtedly Alex.

I let out an exasperated sigh while heavy footsteps stomp closer. I keep counting in my head. Eleven. I steel myself for coming face-to-face with my first love. My only love, if I'm perfectly honest. Twelve.

The door opens and there he is. The glower on my face falls as I get my first look at him. Dark, messy hair, gray eyes, square jaw, and a scar along his chin from a bicycle accident when he was a kid.

All the perfect things I planned to say go right out the window. Alex is standing in the doorway. Shirtless. Towel around his waist. Wet hair. And just as handsome as I remember.

CHAPTER TWO

ALEX

"Brainy Lainey." My words come out in a whisper. Of all the people I expected to be on the opposite side of this door, she was at the very bottom of the list.

Lainey squeaks out a small noise of surprise and puts both hands over her eyes like I flashed her my bare ass. "Sorry . . . I . . ."

My lips twitch with a smile. The first one in days. "What are you doing here?"

She drops her hands and aims a scowl at me. My smile widens in return, which I can tell pisses her off, but damn, it's good to see her.

"Why aren't you at your sister's wedding rehearsal?" she asks.

A pang of guilt slams into me. "Something came up."

Her brows lift and she stomps into the house past me.

"Please, come in," I say dryly as I shut the door and try not to flash her.

She comes to a stop in the middle of the cabin's living room. She looks good. Great. Even better than I remembered, and I remembered her pretty well. Her honey-blond hair is longer now. It hangs in big curls falling over one shoulder. The coat she's wearing is unbuttoned, revealing a dark green dress that molds to her body like a second skin. Lainey's all grown-up and just as stunning as I knew she'd be.

"Don't just stand there. Get ready." She waves at my bare chest, but her stare lingers a little too long, like she's taking me in, the same way I am her.

"I was working on it, but then someone started pounding on my front door."

We face off. My heart pounds in my chest like I just sprinted down the football field. Only the pain in my quad reminds me that isn't possible right now, so I guess this reaction is all her. I've often thought about Lainey over the years. I started to text her dozens of times, thought about dropping by to see her every time I visited my family. Now that I see her, I'm glad I didn't.

"Brainy Lainey," I say again, mostly to myself. I can't believe she's here.

"Don't call me that. And put some clothes on."

"I don't remember you being so bossy," I tease, trying to alleviate some of the tension radiating off her.

"Yes, well, a lot can change in three years."

My gut clenches, but I chuckle softly for her benefit. "Shots fired."

"This is the most important day of your sister's life."

"Tomorrow."

"Excuse me?" She crosses her hands over her chest.

"Tomorrow is the most important day of her life. And besides, do you really think we should be putting so much pressure on a wedding? I've been to a lot of them, and they're all sort of the same."

"So help me, if you don't make it to Jess's wedding I will . . ." She falters. "Upload all your terrible childhood photos. The world of Alex Carrington fans would loooove to see your seventh-grade school photo. Or the Halloween you dressed up like Edward from *Twilight*."

"I wasn't Edward. I was just a vampire."

"Who looked suspiciously like Edward Cullen."

I fight a laugh. Fuck, I've missed her. No one has ever gotten under my skin like Lainey. Even when we were kids. Before I knew what it was to want a woman, I understood that she was someone who intrigued me endlessly.

"You can't just flake because you're too busy snowboarding or staring at yourself in the mirror."

"Can you blame me?" I run a hand over my jaw and smirk at her.

Frustration bleeds out of her.

"I'm not going to miss the wedding." I swallow down the truth. "You don't need to worry your pretty little head about me."

Her eyes turn to little green slits and her lips purse. "Why weren't you at the rehearsal?"

"I thought we already established that I was a selfish asshole with my own agenda and no regard for other people." I flash her another grin, though it takes a little more effort. The longer I stand here, the more my leg throbs with pain.

Lainey lets out an exasperated groan, flinging her arms up in the air and then whirling around and marching back to the door.

Which is the same moment my quad decides to give out on me. I stutter-step to the closest surface—the dining room table—and grab onto the side. My weight pushes it across the wood floor with a screech.

"Fuck. Shit. Fuuuuck." I can't hold back the string of curses as pain radiates up my leg. I somehow manage to shuffle around the table and collapse into one of the chairs—and keep my towel (and dignity) intact.

"What's wrong with you?" I look up to find her hovering a few steps away with wide eyes.

I wince. It was too much to hope she'd already made it outside before I collapsed dramatically.

"Just a flesh wound," I joke as I blink back the stars exploding in front of my eyes and work my fingers over the tight muscles of my left thigh.

She squats down to inspect it herself. When she sees the myriad of colors splashed across my skin, she sucks in a breath.

"I'm fine." I tuck my leg back, hiding the worst of it from view.

"That does not look fine." She stands, brows pulled together as she studies me. "This is from your game against Kansas City?"

"Keeping tabs on me?"

She rolls her eyes. "Jess mentioned it." Her face softens. "I'm sorry about not making the playoffs."

"We made it pretty far, and there's always next year." It's a bullshit response, and from the look she gives me, she knows it.

"You weren't snowboarding at all," she says, more to herself than to me, but I nod anyway. "Does Jess know?"

"She knows I took a bad hit."

"And that you can't walk?"

Did I play it off like it wasn't as bad as it is? Of course I did. My baby sister only gets married once, and she doesn't need to worry about me. I'll be fine in a week or two.

"I can walk," I insist.

"Yeah, obviously." She snorts. "Are you even cleared to be on your feet?"

I glare at her.

She hums and smirks in a very *I knew it* type of way, then pulls out her phone.

"What are you doing?" I ask and simultaneously try to adjust the position of my leg so the pain eases.

"Letting Jess know you're alive."

"Don't tell her about my leg," I say quickly.

She glances up at me, pausing her typing.

"Please? I'll tell her myself tomorrow, but not tonight." The last thing I want to do is worry my sister the day before her wedding.

"Don't you think she'll notice when you walk into the rehearsal dinner?"

"I'm not going." I thought I could but after seeing the look on Lainey's face I know now that there's no way I'll be able to fool Jess. "I'll text her and let her know I'm jetlagged or something."

"Alex, I swear, if you miss the wedding—"

"I know. I know. Public humiliation. Got it."

Sexy Lainey continues to glare at me like she can see way more than I want to show her.

"You should head to the rehearsal dinner. Jess would rather you be there than me anyway." I check the time on the oven. I'm not even sure it's accurate, but it feels close enough.

"That isn't true, and you know it."

"It is, and besides, isn't the maid of honor mandatory at all wedding festivities?"

"Only when there aren't more pressing matters." She puts her phone away and glares. "Like dealing with the idiot brother."

"You always were the smart one."

Her stare bores into me, silently calling bullshit. I bet

she's a great teacher. The kids probably love her and know they can't get anything past her either.

"Don't worry. I'm not going to miss my baby sister's wedding." Even if I have to call my dad to come help me get dressed. I shudder at the thought. What a way to end the year.

She nods, seemingly placated by my answer. She hesitates, watching me another few seconds, before she heads to the front door. I get to my feet and hobble behind her. Now that the jig is up, there's no use pretending that it doesn't take great difficulty for me to walk normally.

"I guess I'll see you tomorrow, then," she says. Her stare drops to my chest and abs then flicks up quickly, and her face flushes. I fight a smile. It's good to know that after all these years, she still finds me attractive.

Before she can leave, I do my own appreciative appraisal of her, not lingering nearly as long as I want. "You look great, Lainey." She was always gorgeous, but seeing her tonight is a reminder that I never wanted. "It was really good to see you."

"Thanks," she says flatly.

She pulls open the door, letting in a gust of cold air so strong it forces her back a step.

"Whoa," I say, steadying her with a hand on her waist. Outside, the snow is coming down so hard the night sky is basically just a sheet of white.

My sister was hoping for snow. I'm pleased it'll be the perfect New Year's Eve wedding she dreamed about. The girl in front of me, however, does not look nearly as happy.

Lainey sucks in an audible breath. "Oh no."

"I don't think you're going anywhere."

"My SUV will be fine," she insists as she leans away from my touch.

"It'll take you twenty minutes just to clear it off." Several inches of snow already cover her vehicle, and it's coming down so fast it'll be a lot more soon.

"I am familiar with snow." She takes a step out onto the porch, and I reach for her hand so she doesn't slip. "Come on, Lainey, I'm not letting you drive in this."

"Funny, I don't remember asking for permission."

I tug her hand slightly. "Come inside. It'll likely stop soon, but until then you're safer here."

I like the idea of her staying more than I'd like to admit, and the thought of her stranded on the side of the road makes my gut twist. If I'm perfectly honest, the thought of letting her go again *at all* hurts more than my injured leg.

"I can't stay here with you," she blurts, still hesitating in the doorway. "We aren't friends. Not anymore. So you don't get to care or swoop in and save me."

Ouch. I deserve that, but it still stings.

"You're not doing it for me. You're doing it for Jess. She'd never forgive me if I let you out in this."

She acquiesces, and I pull her back inside and shut the door.

"But, Lainey? I'm always going to care."

CHAPTER THREE

LAINEY

Outside, the snow continues to come down, blanketing everything in a sheet of white. I let the curtain fall into place and chew on my thumbnail as I run through scenarios to get out of here.

"Would you stop pacing? You're making me nervous."

I don't bother responding. I can't sit still. If I sit still, I'm going to think way too hard about this situation and the things he's said. And how I'm stuck in this small cabin with the only guy I've ever really loved, who kissed me three years ago and then said it was a mistake.

I texted Jess to let her know I found Alex at the cabin and that I was going to stay with him until the snow stopped. Her reply was a screaming face emoji. Which, coincidentally, is exactly how I feel.

"Lainey." Alex's voice is part command and part plea.

I stop and look at him. He's no longer in a towel, thankfully, but unfortunately the T-shirt and sweatpants don't hide his handsome face. Those gray eyes like storm clouds and his stubble-covered jaw. That's new—the stubble. It's a good look for him.

Alex's sitting on the couch, looking as comfortable in this situation as out on the football field. Meanwhile I'm a mess.

I grab a bag of frozen peas from the freezer and take it

to him. I hold it out and he stares at me like he's going to resist.

"Are you going to sit?" he asks.

There's absolutely no way I'm sitting on the couch with him. It's barely big enough for three people, and Alex takes up half of that with his broad frame and long legs.

I drop the makeshift ice pack in his lap, and he grunts. Then I head to the dining room table, grab a chair, and bring it into the living area. I sit as far away as I can. Which, unfortunately, is still too close to him.

Alex adjusts until his left leg is elevated on the coffee table in front of him and he holds the peas in place.

He smirks. "You look like you're five seconds from running out into the snow."

I hum my agreement. I would if I'd worn better shoes.

"How've you been?" he asks.

I arch a brow. We haven't spoken in years, and he wants to make small talk?

"C'mon, time will pass faster if we don't sit in silence," he adds.

"Great," I deadpan. "I've been great."

He nods slowly, studying me. When it's clear I'm not going to reciprocate, he chuckles softly. "This is where you ask me how I've been," he whispers like he's helping me out.

I roll my eyes. "Everyone knows how you are. You're Alex Carrington. Dating celebrities, splashed across headlines, winning awards."

Both dark brows lift, and he points toward his injured leg.

A pang of guilt hits me. "That does suck. I'm sorry. Are you going to be okay?"

"Yeah, I'll heal."

"But?"

"We still lost." His jaw clenches.

I forgot how personally he takes each loss, as if he himself is responsible. I guess at least that hasn't changed about him.

"I don't understand why you didn't tell your family." I look pointedly at his injured leg.

He tries to shrug it off and sighs. "Jess has always been supportive of me and my career, but the last couple years, when I've come back for family events, I don't know, it just feels like . . ."

"All the attention is on you instead?" I ask, suddenly getting a very clear picture of it. I've heard about his visits. The whole town talks about it every single time. Even my second graders.

He nods.

It's hard to wrap my head around this version of Alex, who's just like the guy I used to know. But he isn't. He can't be. This Alex broke my heart.

The wind blows against the cabin windows, and a quick glance confirms what I already know—it's still snowing. I won't be leaving anytime soon.

I clear my throat. "Where is your girlfriend?"

"I don't have a girlfriend."

"I thought you were dating the jewelry designer," I say as casually as possible, like I have not consumed every photo and article about his dating life. "What's her name, Brenda? Bethany?"

"Brianna. And she's just a friend."

I snort.

"It isn't like that," he insists, squirming a little.

"Mm-hmm." I nod, grinning. I don't know why he's so uncomfortable admitting it.

"I swear."

The more he protests, the less I believe him.

He sighs. "She's a friend of a friend. I contacted her to help Brad out with the rings."

My smile falls. "What?"

He winces and presses the bag of peas into his thigh.

"She's a great designer, and Brad wanted to do something special for Jess. It was all his idea. I just put him in contact." He's quiet for a beat then follows it up with a quiet plea. "Please don't mention it to Jess."

"I won't. I just . . ." I get back to my feet. I need a distraction. In the kitchen, I open cupboards until I find a bottle of Malibu that's likely been here since the last time Alex or Jess threw a party. It's dusty but unopened. In another cabinet I find an assortment of old mugs. I recognize some of them, but there's a noticeable addition of Denver mugs. I can picture Jess and Alex's dad buying these. Mr. and Mrs. Carrington are the loud, supportive kind of parents. I was always a little jealous of that. My dad was never in the picture, and my mom spent so much time working that her support was much quieter.

I grab a Garfield mug and fill it with Malibu.

"Want any?" I ask without looking back at Alex.

"No thanks," he answers from the couch.

I cap the bottle and take my mug back to the living room. I eye the chair. I swear it's moved a foot closer to Alex than it was before, but he's still in the same position. My skin pricks under his gaze as I take my seat. The alcohol is strong, with a hint of sweet coconut. I cough as soon as I swallow it down.

Alex smirks. "Good?"

"Great." My voice is hoarse.

He laughs. "I forgot how stubborn you are."

"Me?" I scoff. "You're one to talk."

We're smiling at each other when I remember I'm still mad at him. I clear my throat and take another, much smaller sip.

"If you're not dating the jewelry designer, then which gorgeous, famous woman are you seeing these days?" I ask. I should let it go, but I want him to know that I don't care. Even if my stomach is currently working itself into knots. I set the Malibu down on the end table. It isn't helping.

"I'm not dating anyone. Famous or not."

"How come?" I stand again, needing to put distance between us. I walk to the far wall in front of the low-burning fire. On the mantel are pictures of Alex and Jess from preschool through college during the holidays, along with a few leftover decorations from Christmas. I pick up a snow globe and shake it.

"Lots of reasons."

I roll my eyes where he can't see, then set the globe back on the mantel. "Hard to pick just one?"

"Yeah, something like that."

"Well, if you didn't bring a plus-one, then I'm sure you'll have your pick of single women at the wedding."

He huffs a small, quiet laugh. "My pick, huh?"

I shrug and go to the bookcase next. Someone strung garland with lights along the top, and a copy of *A Christmas Carol* faces out.

"Even you?"

My heart stutters and my stomach clenches. I don't

turn around, though I'm curious if he's got one of those cocky grins aimed at me. "Don't joke around."

"I'm not joking. If I can have my pick, then I choose you."

"Ha. Ha," I mock in a dry, sarcastic tone.

"Lainey." The way he says my name is soft and intimate, and I make the mistake of looking at him. His gray eyes are filled with sincerity. "I never even considered bringing a date. Not when I knew my favorite person was going to be there. Then imagine my surprise when she shows up on my doorstep the night before."

I whirl around so fast I nearly make myself dizzy. "But we haven't talked in years."

"Doesn't mean I stopped thinking about you," he confesses.

"You kissed me and said it was a mistake."

His face scrunches up. "I'm sorry about that." He gets to his feet and walks over to me.

If I weren't aware of his injury, I might not even be able to tell he's favoring the left side.

"I messed up, but not a single day has gone by where I didn't think about you."

"You have a funny way of showing it."

"I wasn't sure you wanted to hear from me. Or that if I saw you again, I'd be able to walk away."

"I don't get you."

"Yes, you do." He reaches up and cups my face with one hand. His thumb glides along my skin slowly.

I shake my head. Insistent.

"I was six months away from the draft."

"And you didn't want to be tied down, yadda yadda." I try to pull away, but he circles one arm around my waist.

His gaze is hard. "No. Fuck no."

"Then why?" I swore I'd never ask him, but maybe if I finally get the answers, I can move on.

"I didn't want to start something when I didn't know where I was going or if and when I'd be able to see you. I've always known that if we crossed that line, it'd be end-game for me, and you still had a year left of college and big dreams of your own to chase. I couldn't ask you to drop everything and be with me. I wasn't even sure I'd make it at that point, and then what?" He shakes his head.

A new kind of frustration seeps into me, and tears pool in my eyes. "You could have given me a choice. You made me think that you wanted nothing to do with me." I'm so mad I want to pound my fists on his stupid, broad chest.

"You would have tried to change my mind, and I would have caved. And maybe it all would have worked out, or maybe in six months or a year you would have been miserable. I couldn't take that chance."

"You still could have said something." A tear betrays me by leaking from the corner of my right eye.

Alex swipes it away with a finger and leans closer. "It killed me to walk away. I was a dumb kid who didn't handle it well. I know that. But I'm telling you now: It was never about not wanting you. I needed to prove myself and become the guy who could give you everything instead of taking away your dreams."

I stare at his chest as I process his words.

"I'm sorry," he says again.

My throat burns as I swallow and try to hold back more tears.

He tips my chin up. "Say you forgive me," he says softly.

"I forgive you," I whisper, finally looking up into his eyes. "But I'm still mad."

His lips pull up on one side. "I can work with that."

His stare bounces from my eyes to my lips and back. Then, finally dropping all hesitation, he brings his mouth down to mine slowly, like he's giving me time to decide I don't want this.

I close the last few inches, pressing my lips to his. Alex lets out a soft hum. Both of his big hands frame my face, but the gentleness turns to something more insistent. He walks me back to the couch and sits, pulling me on top of him.

"What about your leg?" I freeze.

"Doesn't hurt at all." He kisses me again.

He's lying, I know it, but as I try to shift my weight off him, he holds me tighter.

Alex pulls back and meets my gaze. "I promise, I'm fine, but if you stop kissing me again, I might die."

We both laugh, and then his mouth is back on mine. I still move so that less weight is on his bruised leg, but I don't stop kissing him. His hands drop to my waist, leisurely exploring my curves and then finally moving to my bare thighs. The feel of his calloused hands along my smooth skin has heat coursing through me.

"I missed you so damn much."

I don't respond except to kiss him harder. There are so many more things to say, but his touch is laced with apology and desire, and for right now that's enough.

My body melts into his until I'm nuzzled as close as I can get. My chest brushes against his, and I revel in his warmth and the hard expanse of him. My hips rock of their own accord, and Alex lets out a low growl. He nips at my bottom lip and then drives up into me from below. Stars dot my vision. I want—no, I *need* more of him.

"Do you have any condoms?" I ask as I slide my hands under his shirt and let my fingers explore the hard ridges of his muscles.

"Lainey." His gray eyes search mine. "God, I . . ." He trails off and his stare moves past me.

I turn to see what has his attention. Headlights stream through the window at the same time a heavy knock sounds on the front door.

And then my best friend yells from the other side. "Alex! Lainey! Open up!"

CHAPTER FOUR

ALEX

"Congratulations." I wrap my sister in a hug. "Brad's a lucky guy."

Her head rests against my chest, veil falling down her back, as she circles her arms around me. "Thank you for being here."

"I wouldn't have missed it for anything."

She pulls back and looks at me. "Not even a playoff game?"

I glance up like I'm considering it. "Ehhh . . ."

She swats at my arm and steps back.

It was the perfect day, and the wedding went exactly

as planned, complete with snow on the ground outside. The venue twinkles with fairy lights overhead, tables are decorated with candles and flower displays, and there's a merriment in the air. Love, happiness, and the countdown to the new year.

My gaze snags on Lainey dancing with one of Brad's friends in the middle of the dance floor. She's smiling at him and he's smiling at her. Something twists in my gut.

As soon as Jess and Brad showed up last night to rescue Lainey, something shifted between us again. She's no longer pretending I don't exist, but she's acting like nothing's changed, either—like that kiss didn't happen and we weren't minutes away from crossing another big line.

"So, you and Lainey?"

I pull my stare away from my sister's best friend. Jess pins me with a serious look. "Are you going to screw things up again?"

I bark out a surprised laugh. We've never really talked about Lainey. Until now I wasn't even sure how much she knew. I always suspected Lainey had confided in her, but Jess has kept that to herself.

"You've been in love with her since high school, and everyone knows it but her," Jess says.

I shake my head.

"I know you. And I know Lainey," she continues. "Whatever happened between you two, I know it can be fixed."

"My baby sister, the eternal optimist."

"Yes, well, I'm married now, which also makes me wiser than you when it comes to relationships." She nudges me with an elbow. "Go talk to her."

"I'm not sure it'll make a difference." Last night, I could

see how much I hurt Lainey. I can't change what I did, no matter how badly I wish otherwise.

"Just . . . go." She nudges me a little more.

"Easy on the shoving," I joke as I hobble forward.

Jess grins as she watches me go, shooing me with both hands to keep going.

I take a deep breath as I walk slowly. My leg feels a little better today, but I'm almost regretting leaving my crutches at the cabin.

Lainey glances up when I'm a few feet away. Her hair is swept back from her face, and her lips are painted a red that matches her dress.

"Can I cut in?" I ask, sliding my gaze from her to her partner.

The guy's smile falls, but he recovers quickly. "Yeah, of course, man." He gives Lainey one more smile, then backs away.

I step in front of her.

"Are you in any condition to dance?" she asks.

"Probably not," I admit. "You may have to hold me up."

She places her hands lightly on my shoulders. Mine glide around her waist, caressing her and the warmth radiating through the smooth satin material.

We sway to the music for several minutes in silence, me staring at her and her pretending not to notice.

"Sooo . . . about last night," I start.

Immediately her cheeks flush.

She's so damn gorgeous. "Too soon? Do we need to wait three years to talk about it?"

She narrows her gaze.

"Just kidding."

She squares her shoulders. "I thought a lot about it, and

thank you," she says evenly. "I appreciate what you said last night."

"You appreciate it?" That is not the reaction I expected.

"Yeah. I've been holding on to what happened between us, trying to hate you but unable to move on. I think I finally got the closure I needed."

My leg twinges with pain, but it's nothing compared to the knife slicing through my chest. "Closure?"

"Well, yeah, I can't be in love with you forever." She gives me a small smile.

I stop pretending to dance. "Why not?"

Her brows pull together. "I thought you'd be happy. Now we can go back to being friends and not avoiding each other when you visit. I can't promise that I won't be a little jealous if or when you bring other women here, though, at least in the beginning. But it's about to be a new year, and I think we should start it with a clean slate."

I can't help it, I chuckle. "Brainy Lainey." I hold her tighter.

"I hate it when you call me that."

"No, you don't."

"No." She shakes her head. "I don't."

"Didn't you hear anything I said last night?" I bend down to look directly in her eyes. "I am in love with you. I plan on being in love with you for a very long time. So hopefully when I come visit, the only woman I'm hanging out with is you."

Her red lips part and form an O then close.

In the background, the countdown to the New Year starts up and everyone around us joins in.

I raise my voice so she can hear me over the noise. "Now that the season is over, I was thinking I could stick around or you could come see me in Denver while school is on break. Once the season starts back up, it'll be a little trickier, but you have the summer free and—"

She cuts me off and kisses me before I can finish telling her my grand plans. I kiss her back and relish this perfect moment. As long as my plans include her, the rest doesn't matter.

7

A SOLSTICE KISS

Olivia Dade

On a snowy winter solstice afternoon in Stockholm, Ellie was staring at an odd painting.

It wasn't overly large or especially complicated. Against a dark gray sky and above what might have been a quiet teal sea, one ladder stretched toward a pink cloud, while another climbed to a bright crescent moon. The mysterious landscape defied both reality and easy explanation, which made it a fitting inclusion for the modern art museum's surrealism exhibit.

And her reaction to the image was even odder than the painting itself.

Based on the previous forty-three years of her existence, she'd have sworn that she only appreciated simple representational artwork. Flowers that looked like actual flowers. Portraits of people with recognizably human features. But here she was, standing in a crowd of Swedish strangers, gaping at a ladder to the moon and—inexplicably—tearing up a little.

When her phone vibrated from inside her jeans pocket,

she almost welcomed the interruption . . . until she saw her older sister's text.

Permission to murder your ex?

Heather had followed the question with several knife and skull emojis.

Ellie sighed.

Denied.

Just this once? As a treat?

Nope. I'm worried you'll get a taste for homicide.

Her older sister wasn't exactly the forgiving sort, especially when it came to anyone who'd wronged her loved ones.

Dean's at the holiday luncheon, huh?

Ellie's ex worked in the IT department at the Maryland high school where her sister taught. Heather had made the introduction after last year's luncheon and still felt guilty about it.

Unfortunately, yes.

Ellie took her best guess.

You overheard him talking about me to his IT buddies?

No response. Which was as good as a *yes*.

What did he say this time?

She waited a minute, then added,

Heather, it's fine. I've been over him for months.

Her sister finally, begrudgingly, gave the shortest possible answer.

The usual.

Ellie could practically hear Dean's booming baritone, could probably quote exactly what he'd said. Goodness knew she'd listened to his favorite diatribe countless times over their final, terrible days together. No doubt he'd informed his cronies that she was boring and staid and unadventurous, the sort of woman who preferred a cozy evening indoors to a raucous bar crawl, hesitated to try unfamiliar restaurants, and refused to go parasailing with her boyfriend. The sort of woman any self-respecting man would leave without regret—which was exactly what he'd done during their summer vacation in Florida, after his solo parasailing expedition.

And while she genuinely didn't care about him anymore, something about that particular criticism continued to sting, even now. Even after she'd traveled solo to another darn continent on a lengthy business trip and rousted herself from her comfortable hotel room to explore more of Stockholm. Sure, the museum was within easy walking distance of said hotel room, but darkness fell early on the shortest day of the year, so this *felt* like a late-night jaunt. And she didn't usually understand or enjoy modern art, so wasn't her outing an adventure of sorts?

It counted, dammit!

He's looking at your travel photos on social media.

Why he'd bother, Ellie had no clue. But he definitely wouldn't consider a museum visit interesting, even though it was.

Why did his criticism bother her so much?

Winter solstice was supposed to represent the rebirth of the sun on the darkest day of the year. But Ellie didn't feel reborn. She felt . . . mired.

You know what would show that bastard?

Heather had apparently interpreted her sister's silence as hurt feelings, which wasn't quite right. But not entirely wrong either.

You should post a pic of you kissing some sexy Swedish dude. Let him see it in front of all his braying bros.

Ellie snorted out loud.

Yeah, no.

Even if she were the sort of person who'd smooch a total stranger for the sake of social media pettiness—and she wasn't—there were no reasonable kissing candidates nearby. The earlier crowds of tall people in seemingly identical dark coats conducting hushed conversations in Swedish had left a while back. And the two men near the Dalí painting were holding hands and sweetly preoccupied with each other.

There *was* still a guided tour occurring behind her. The jeans-clad docent had led his small group to a raised pit of bubbling mud that was apparently supposed to represent sin or nature or maybe the subconscious itself? Ellie genuinely couldn't say, and eavesdropping didn't help, because his presentation was in Swedish too.

Actually, the docent was kind of hot. Tall and solidly built, with dark blond hair flopping over his broad, pale forehead and a strong, scruff-covered jaw. At first glance, he even appeared to be roughly her age.

She squinted, straining to see his hand as he gestured at the mud pit.

No ring. But she still couldn't walk up to a total stranger and ask him to kiss her.

Could she?

No. No, she really couldn't. If she *could*, though, he'd definitely be her first choice.

Someone spiked the sherbert-ginger ale punch.

I need to drink my fill before Assistant Principal Killjoy finds out and dumps it down the sink. Love you. I'm sorry I even mentioned that asshole ex of yours.

Love you too.

Don't worry about it.

And you're definitely against some minor, recreational ax-murdering?

Ellie had to smile.

Go drink your punch, Lizzie Borden.

As she slipped her phone back into her jeans pocket, she glanced again at the docent leading the tour group.

He'd shifted to face her direction and was pointing toward the painting with the two ladders. She moved several steps to the side, giving him and everyone else a clearer view of the artwork, and he smiled at her in thanks before returning his attention to the group.

His eyes were blue. Blue and warm.

Ellie's heart wobbled.

Instead of moving to another room, she lingered and listened. She might have no clue what the man was saying, but she liked how he was saying it. His voice was low and calm and infused with enthusiasm. Whenever someone in his group asked him a question, he listened intently and thought for a moment before answering. Graceful swoops of his long-fingered hands punctuated his remarks, and every flash of that same sincere smile hitched Ellie's breathing.

After a minute, though, he led the group across the expansive gallery, away from Ellie. With an odd ache in her chest, she turned her attention back to Gertrude Abercrombie's *Two Ladders*.

One route to the fluffy pink cloud. One route to the bright, sharp-tipped moon.

Most of the time, life proceeded along a single, orderly path. Sometimes, though . . . Sometimes that path forked before you, and you had a choice to make.

She'd been invited to visit the Stockholm branch of the bank where she worked in hopes she might relocate to Sweden—at least for a year or two—and improve international cooperation within the company. She'd gently told her supervisor that wasn't going to happen, but both he and Heather had encouraged Ellie to take the trip anyway. It was free travel to Europe, after all, during the height of the festive holiday season.

"No matter what, you can strengthen your ties with your Swedish colleagues," Ellie's boss had said. "Who knows? You might even love it there. So don't give me an answer now. I don't want your final decision until the twenty-second."

Which was . . . tomorrow.

In the end, she'd agreed to the trip and even decided to stay through New Year's. And she'd genuinely adored what she'd seen of the city thus far and liked her Swedish colleagues. But she was still going to say no to an international move, because all that uncertainty and disruption to her daily routine would only make her miserable.

Wouldn't it?

Two ladders stood before her.

Her ex would probably bet his life savings that she'd climb toward the familiar, cozy cloud. But did she truly love it there? Or did she simply find it comfortable and predictable?

Behind Ellie, the guided museum tour ended with an enthusiastic round of applause as her phone vibrated against her thigh once more. Maybe with a social media notification. Maybe with another text from Heather, urging Ellie to kiss a stranger because Dean was still perusing her posts with his obnoxious buddies.

The butter-yellow moon shone against the gray sky, curved like a beckoning finger.

If only for tonight, she intended to answer its call.

Ellie turned around. Saw that the last members of the tour group had exited the exhibit, leaving only the guide, and he seemed poised to follow them.

"Excuse me," she called to the docent. "Do you have a moment?"

As she'd discovered, most Swedes in Stockholm spoke at least some English. Apparently, this man did, too, since he strode in her direction without hesitation.

"Hello." When he halted in front of her, she almost swayed under the knee-melting impact of those soft blue eyes. "How may I help you?"

From his accent, she could have sworn—"You're American?"

"Guilty." When he smiled at her, his cheeks creased beguilingly under his golden-brown scruff. "I was born and raised in Colorado, although I've lived in Sweden for the past decade. Lovely to meet you . . ."

He paused expectantly, but she was still focused on those dimples. After a moment, he cleared his throat, and she jumped a little.

"Uh, sorry." She forced her eyes back up to his, her cheeks warm. "I'm Ellie. From Maryland. And you're"—she peered at his badge, which indicated that he was a curator at the museum—"Felix?"

"Felix Kent." His handshake was firm but gentle. "How can I assist you, Ellie from Maryland?"

Now that the moment was here, she couldn't seem to form the words. "Umm . . . this is going to sound a little odd and extremely *forward* of me, and please feel free to say no, but I noticed you leading the tour earlier, and you were very . . . very . . ."

He waited patiently, broad chest rising and falling slowly beneath his charcoal-gray sweater, intently focused on her and her alone. Goodness help her, having this man's undivided attention was intoxicating.

"I was . . ." he prompted, his voice husky.

"You were *perfect*," she finished, to her utter dismay.

His eyebrows rose, and she wanted to smother herself in her own sweatshirt.

"I—wow." He paused. Leaned infinitesimally closer to her. "Thank you."

He must think she was unhinged, but it was too late to back out now. She sucked in a deep breath and said, "I was wondering whether you'd be willing to—"

Just then, an announcement in Swedish crackled over the loudspeaker, followed by its English translation. The museum was closing, a female voice crisply informed them. All visitors were asked to gather their belongings and leave for the evening, although they were cordially invited to return the following morning.

When the loudspeaker fell silent once more, Felix offered Ellie another encouraging smile. "You were saying?"

Ellie's sudden courage had failed her, however, and all her rule-follower instincts were urging her to exit the museum posthaste.

"Never mind." She shifted her weight. "I guess I need to leave. You do, too, I suppose."

His smile faded. Did he look *disappointed*? Or was that just her imagination?

"Yes." He cast a glance over his shoulder, toward the hallway outside the exhibit. "But I'd be happy to answer your question before I go. Delighted, in fact."

She thought fast. "Will you be here tomorrow?"

Because she could regather her nerve overnight, put on something more flattering than her oldest jeans and her thickest sweatshirt, and walk back over again in the morning.

"Unfortunately, no." His brow creased. "After today, I'm off until the second week of January."

She wouldn't see him again before her flight home.

Why did that make her sinuses prickle with incipient tears for the second time that evening? He was a total stranger.

Although she could change that, couldn't she? If she was brave enough.

"You don't know me, of course." He was still speaking, his tone cautious. Unfortunately, Ellie was too caught up in her inner turmoil to pay attention. "But I'll be done here in about fifteen minutes. Maybe you'd like to have di—"

"Kiss me," she heard herself blurt out, as if in a fever dream. "Please."

This time, his brows rose all the way to his hairline. Before he could say *Hell no, you sweatshirt-clad weirdo*, though, she kept rambling, because maybe she'd sound slightly less disturbed if she clarified the situation.

"I want to post a picture of us kissing on social media." She gestured helplessly, the tips of her ears aflame. "My sister told me that my ex is looking through my posts with his horrible buddies and saying rude things about how boring I am, and I thought . . ."

Heavens, it sounded so *juvenile* when she said it out loud.

"You thought you could prove him wrong and show him up in front of his bros," Felix said slowly, finishing her thought for her. "I see."

That wasn't the only reason she wanted to kiss him. It wasn't even the main reason.

Sure, she wanted to prove something to Dean. More than that, though, she wanted to prove something to herself. She couldn't possibly move to Sweden—could she?—but in her own modest way, she could still climb a ladder to bright joy through gray skies, despite her fear of heights. On this darkest day of the year, she needed that reminder more than ever.

Also, she simply wanted to kiss Felix. Because he was, in fact, ridiculously perfect.

Saying all that would only make her sound *more* unhinged, however, so she just nodded and waited for his answer.

He stood in front of her, still and silent and unsmiling. He didn't turn her down, but he certainly wasn't agreeing to her cockamamie plan either. And after another lengthy interval of fraught silence, Ellie figured she had the disappointing but predictable answer to her question.

She was embarrassed, of course. But even more than that, she was sad that she wouldn't get to kiss Felix. Surprisingly so, given how briefly she'd been acquainted with him.

"I get why you don't want to kiss a random tourist, and I apologize if I've made you uncomfortable." Clearly, he was too polite to refuse her outright, so she'd make this awkward situation as easy on him as possible. "I hope you have a lovely vacation, Felix. Happy holidays."

When she turned for the exit, though, his strong fingers lightly wrapped around her forearm.

"Ellie, wait." His low voice rang with urgency. "I'm not saying no. I just needed to think."

Even through the thick fleece of her sweatshirt, goose bumps bloomed on her skin where he touched her. Not from chill. From anticipation. She waited and held her breath, worried that even the slightest movement might puncture the fragile bubble of hope growing within her.

"I'll do it." He gave a decisive nod. "But not in my

workplace. I'll meet you outside the main entrance in fifteen minutes, if you're willing to wait for me."

In that moment, she would have sworn that the sparkling mineral water from her hotel's minibar was coursing through her veins.

"Of course." She beamed up at him, giddy with joy and pride in her own daring. "It's a date, then."

Under his breath, he muttered something that sounded very much like *That's what I'm hoping*, then guided her to the museum's exit.

Barely ten minutes later, the crunch of Felix's boots on the gravel pathway announced his arrival at the wooden bench where she sat waiting. Her breaths formed clouds of smoke in the chilly winter air, and darkness had fallen hours ago, even though it was barely dinnertime.

Now clad in the same black puffer coat seemingly every Swede was issued, he looked like any other stranger she might walk past on the Stockholm streets, and she momentarily quailed at the prospect of kissing someone entirely unfamiliar to her.

Then his gaze locked with hers under the buttery light of a nearby streetlamp, and his sweet smile crinkled the corners of his eyes.

Bathed in such bright warmth, the shadows of her doubt simply couldn't survive. "You haven't changed your mind, then?"

"Definitely not. I'm honored to be your social media kissee, Ellie from Maryland." He gave an endearingly dorky little bow. "Shall we set the scene for maximum romance?"

Honestly, she'd never contemplated the optimal aesthetics for announcing a fake European fling. "What were you thinking?"

"I have some ideas, but . . ." His gaze searched hers. "I'd like to hear yours first. What feels most special to you? A historic building, snow-covered trees in a park, a holiday light display . . ."

When he trailed off, her brain supplied the answer with surprising ease. "The waterfront."

"That would've been my choice too." He looked pleased. "Luckily, waterfront views aren't hard to find here."

He offered a hand to help her up from the bench. She took it for the effervescent thrill of touching him, even through his gloves and her mittens, and released it slowly, with an embarrassing degree of reluctance.

They now stood only inches away from each other. The breath he blew out billowed like fog between them, and the hand she'd briefly held curled into a loose fist at his side.

"I live close to the Chesapeake Bay," she found herself explaining. "Looking at the water has always sort of . . . settled me."

He thought about that. "Because it reminds you that there's a world out there larger than whatever problems you might be struggling with?"

"Yeah, actually." She blinked, startled by the insight. "Is that true for you too?"

He nodded. "If I'm restless or anxious, I walk to the water if I can. It soothes me, just like you said."

She offered him a wry smile. "Also, it's just very pretty."

His face turned soft, and his head tipped as he studied her. "It truly is."

Something about that expression had her blushing, and she couldn't even say why. They were talking about *scenery*, for heaven's sake.

She cleared her throat. "Is there a particular spot near the water that would work well for a photo?"

"There's a place not far from here where you can see the amusement park in the background." His brows drew together as he considered the matter. "Their holiday lights will reflect off the water. Off your dark hair as well."

His gloved fingertip lightly brushed the end of a curl resting against her shoulder, and she would have sworn—in contradiction to all known science—that the strand contained a million nerve endings, all attuned to his touch.

"That sounds perfect." Felt perfect too. "Shall we?"

They set off into the solstice night, walking toward the water. Once they left the protective bulwark of the buildings, the brisk, frigid wind stole her breath, even as the slick cobblestones and gravel-studded, snowy sidewalks tested her balance. He offered her his arm, wordlessly and with zero self-congratulatory fuss. She accepted with a shy smile of thanks, moving close enough that their jackets swished against each other with every step.

"How long have you been visiting Sweden?" His hip bumped hers, once and then again. Neither of them moved farther apart. "Do you plan to stay through the holidays? Because if you've never been here on New Year's Eve, I can tell you that it's pretty spectacular. Swedes are very enthusiastic about their amateur fireworks displays. Like, *alarmingly* enthusiastic. But it's a fun experience." He paused. "Unless you work in the ER, I imagine."

She snorted. "I arrived a week ago and leave on January second, so I look forward to dodging wayward rockets and admiring the explosive fruits of all those lost Swedish fingers."

His laugh echoed in the night, husky and low. The sound warmed Ellie down to her half-numb toes and caused the handful of other people walking nearby to briefly glance his way.

She looked over at him, too, admiring how the streetlight gilded the edge of his face. "You moved here ten years ago, you said?"

His head dipped in affirmation. "For my position at the museum. I was fresh from earning my doctorate in art history and jumped at the opportunity. I was incredibly lucky, and I know it."

She was about to ask how difficult his transition had been—out of idle curiosity, she told herself, rather than any particular applicability to her own situation—when they reached their destination. Both the museum and her hotel were located on the same relatively compact island, one of thousands that comprised Stockholm's archipelago. The shoreline was never far away, and she could actually see the front entrance to her hotel from where they stood.

From neighboring Djurgården, the amusement park's holiday lights glowed in the dark sky and—as Felix had predicted—reflected on the rippling water. And just as the two of them halted, a few fat snowflakes began drifting from the sky to swirl at their feet.

"Perfect timing. Everyone will think you used a filter." Lifting his free hand, he caught a fluffy white flake on his gloved palm. "Do you want to take the picture? Or shall I?"

Any photo she took in these conditions would undoubtedly suck. "I'm no good at selfies, especially at night."

"Photography is one of my interests, so if you're willing . . ." When she handed over her phone, he removed his gloves and fiddled with its settings for a minute or two. "All right. Should we . . . ?"

"Uh, yeah." Awkwardly, she shuffled closer to the edge of the waterfront, then lifted her arms in an invitation he promptly accepted. *"Oh."*

His body was large and sturdy and entirely unfamiliar. Pressed lightly against hers, it blocked out the wintry chill and erased every coherent thought from her brain.

"Is this okay?" His eyes searched hers. "We don't have to do anything you don't want, Ellie."

"I really, really want this," she whispered, too pole-axed by the *rightness* of the embrace to feign nonchalance. Only—wait. "Do you have a significant other? A spouse, a girlfriend or boyfriend, or . . . ?"

"None of the above." Gently, he guided her arms to loop around his neck, extended his own arm to capture the embrace in her phone's display, then cupped her chilled cheek in his other bare, warm hand. "You?"

"I'm extremely single." And apparently incapable of summoning even an ounce of chill, despite the current outdoor temperature.

His smile widened, and he edged even closer to her. So deliciously close, she couldn't see or feel anything but Felix.

Felix, who wasn't quite a total stranger anymore. Felix, whose thumb was coasting so softly over her cheek as his head lowered inch by inch. Felix, whose lips met hers with such tender care and lingered sweetly, as if he was savoring the feel and taste of her.

The thrill of it stole her breath. Made her tingle down to her fuzzy-socked toes.

After another suspended, breathless moment, his head tipped farther. His mouth played over hers in slow, teasing brushes of heat and sparking excitement. She shifted restlessly, stretching upward on her tiptoes, tightening her arms to get closer, to bring their bodies more firmly together. Then, in a heady rush, her mouth was open and so was his, and their tongues tangled as her head buzzed with shocked excitement. He tasted like mint, smelled like the woods, and felt like absolute glory against her.

The palm cradling her cheek slipped away, then pressed firmly in the center of her back, hitching her against him as her quiet sound of pleasure drifted on the waterfront breeze.

There were other people nearby; vaguely, she registered the footsteps and quiet conversations of passersby, but she didn't care what they thought or what they might be saying. Her entire being was focused on one thing. One man. One kiss, spinning into dozens.

When he lifted his head untold minutes later, they were both panting and flushed. His dark blond hair was rumpled from her fingers, which were unexpectedly bare. Apparently, she'd flung her mittens to the snowy ground for more skin-to-skin contact at some point.

She smoothed a fallen strand of his hair away from his forehead before dropping her arms to her sides, unable to muster the right words for the moment. Afraid of severing the new, fragile connection between them with a careless phrase.

His eyes had closed at her affectionate gesture. When he opened them again, the blazing blue heat in their depths nearly incinerated her on the spot.

"Post your picture, Ellie." He dropped another brief,

hard kiss on her parted mouth before pressing her phone into her trembling hand and taking a step back. "I assume your sister will tell you how your ex reacts?"

She nodded and peered down at her phone, wondering at the sudden crease in his brow. "I'm sure she will."

Felix had taken several snow-speckled photos, ranging from an image almost chaste enough for the cover of an Amish romance novel to a shot that should have singed her eyebrows. She chose a pic that fell somewhere in the middle, full of passionate intensity but only a discreet glimpse of tongue, and posted the image with emojis of the Swedish flag and a yellow heart as her only caption.

Then she slipped her cell back in her pocket and turned expectantly to Felix.

His gaze was searching. "You're not going to wait for his reaction?"

She shook her head. "Nah."

That deep crease in the center of his forehead promptly disappeared. He retrieved her mittens from the ground and began easing her frozen fingers into them.

"In that case . . ." The corners of his mouth indented in a small, private smile. "How convincing do you want your story to be?"

She blinked up at him, dazzled. "What do you mean?"

"To truly sell your story, you need more than a single romantic photo. You need a *series* of romantic photos." He scritched his scruff consideringly. "One from the Skeppsholm Bridge, maybe, and another from the Gamla Stan Julmarknad."

At her questioning look, he clarified, "The Old Town's Christmas market. It's about a thirty-minute walk away, if that's okay with you."

"That sounds perfect. And then . . ." Since he was apparently suggesting an entire evening spent at her side, she wasn't even nervous about her intended proposal. Just excited and hopeful. "Could we post a picture from a cozy café dinner together?"

"An excellent idea." He put back on his own gloves, then held out a hand. When she unhesitatingly took it, his dimples reappeared. "Do you need to get anything from your hotel before we head out?"

Since she didn't, they set off in the direction of the Skeppsholm Bridge—and she finally got the chance to ask one of the hundreds of questions she'd been mentally compiling since their first moment together. "What was your dissertation about?"

"Latin American and Caribbean surrealists." Enthusiasm rang from every word of his answer. "Specifically, the various personal and artistic connections between Frida Kahlo and Wifredo Lam, who was a Cuban artist of Chinese, African, and Spanish descent."

She would love to say something smart about that topic, but she had nada. "Why surrealism? What attracts you to that style of art?"

"Good question." He took a minute to consider his answer. "Surrealism's origins as a response to the horrors of World War I fascinate me. As someone who resists easy answers, probably to a fault, I also appreciate how surrealistic artwork raises questions instead of reassuring viewers that their daily reality is absolute and immutable. I have to believe there's more to our world and our existence than the obvious and the practical." He paused to guide them safely past an ice patch, then added, "And as a human being living in the twenty-first century, I find surrealistic works emotionally evocative. The last few years have underlined how lives and institutions that once felt solid and predictable can abruptly *twist* and turn unrecognizable."

Apparently, thoughtful, intelligent answers that took her questions seriously were her sexual kryptonite. Good to know.

"They can melt away." She cast him a sidelong glance of understanding. "Like a clock."

Like her certainty about what her future could and should encompass.

He tugged her closer, his lips quirking. "A Dalí reference. Well done."

The sordid things she would do for that smile didn't bear thinking about.

She ducked her head, her cheeks warm with flustered pleasure. "Thank you."

"We have paintings by Lam and Dalí on display right now, but you seemed especially focused on a different work." He squeezed her hand. "What about the Abercrombie painting drew your attention?"

She couldn't see any good reason not to tell him. "I have a decision to make before tomorrow. I've been offered a temporary position in my bank's Stockholm branch, and I was certain I'd say no." Her chest rose and fell on a small sigh. "Until I wasn't."

"Ah. I think I see." His lips pursed as he thought it over. "Two futures, two ladders?"

"Exactly." She laughed weakly. "Here's the thing, though: Uncertainty makes me uncomfortable. I'm very much a creature of habit, so I shouldn't be debating which ladder to take. I'm not nearly as adventurous or curious about the wider world as you are."

His voice was mild. Nonjudgmental. “You don’t think so?”

She shook her head, and he only gave a noncommittal hum in response.

While they’d been talking, they’d entered one of the pedestrian walkways that bracketed the relatively short but charmingly historic Skeppsholm Bridge. Halfway across that iron expanse, each walkway’s railing boasted a gilded crown, and Felix stopped beside theirs.

“That’s Old Town to the west and Östermalm and Djurgården to the east.” He waved with his free hand, indicating the beautifully lit islands that lay across the water, then tapped the crown. “And *this* is occasionally stolen by tourists looking for a royalty-themed souvenir.”

Inspiration struck. “For our picture, we should pretend that we’re trying to take it!”

So that’s what they did, pantomiming for the camera that Ellie was attempting to shove the crown into her capacious handbag while Felix served as her trusty lookout and photographer, both of them trying very hard not to laugh. After she posted that pic, too—while studiously ignoring the string of recent texts from her sister and various social media reactions to her earlier photo—they kept moving toward Old Town, hand in hand.

“I know it’s been ten years, but I’d love to hear more about what your move here was like.” She couldn’t even imagine how it must have felt to rip himself, roots and all, from the familiar soil where he’d grown. “What was good about it? What was hard?”

As he mulled over his answer, they neared another bridge.

“So many things about Sweden and Stockholm suit

me," he finally said. "The pace of life and cultural opportunities. The way Swedes prioritize families and personal lives over work. The diversity of the city's population and all the incredible restaurants."

All of which was lovely, of course, but . . . "Are you happy here?"

It was the central question, as far as she was concerned.

"Yes. Mostly." He hesitated. "Any life contains difficulties, Ellie, no matter where you live. I can't say there haven't been hard days or even hard months in the past decade, and I can't say I never miss Colorado and my family. I don't know that I'll ever feel fully and completely at home here, and whenever I visit the United States, I no longer feel fully and completely at home there either."

That sounded incredibly lonely. "So you're a man without a country?"

"No." His headshake was immediate. "Sweden is my country now, even on its darkest winter days. I have a home here. I have good friends. I have a job I love and an existence that's as full and beautiful as I want it to be. I have the life I want, with only one real exception."

"What's that?" She thought—hoped—she knew, but she needed to hear him say it.

"I . . ." He spoke slowly. Cautiously. "I guess I always thought I'd be in love and married by now. I've met and dated some wonderful people. But I haven't met the *right* person."

Boy, did she know that feeling. Although, to be honest, Dean hadn't been especially wonderful. "I understand."

"So that's my life, Ellie from Maryland." They were crossing the next bridge now, and without making a fuss about it, he helped steady her in the spots where the sidewalk turned slick. "What kind of life do *you* want?"

The hell of it was, she couldn't answer the question. Not for him. Not even for herself. Not with any confidence.

But somehow, she had the feeling that her uncertainty might change. Sooner rather than later.

The Christmas market—Sweden's oldest, dating back to the Middle Ages—somehow managed to be even more charming than Ellie had imagined.

Located in an open, central square of gravel-studded, snowy cobblestones, the Gamla Stan Julmarknad was surrounded by centuries-old colorful town houses and official buildings with gorgeously curved rooflines, unique sculptural features, and holiday decorations in every window. Each of the market's several dozen deep red wooden stalls was adorned with lush, bristly garlands and the same creamy yellow lights that hung from nearby roof overhangs and trees.

As Felix and Ellie approached the area, clusters of people in black coats, beanies, and gloves visited the vendors, perused the uniquely Swedish offerings, and handed over credit cards in exchange for hand-painted ornaments dangling from strings, gnome figurines carrying blue-and-yellow flags, palm-sized straw goats, small wooden houses with heart-shaped windows, stuffed mice wearing sweaters and red-and-white–striped scarves, homemade woolen stockings, artisanal teas, and carved reindeer, among other treasures.

She drew to a halt by the first wide row of stalls, let go

of Felix's gloved hand, and circled in place, giving herself time to take everything in. To memorize the beauty of what she saw, in hopes that the recollection would remind her: Even on the darkest day of the year, the world contained loveliness beyond her imagination. Loveliness she'd only experience if she took a chance and looked for it.

Felix didn't rush her. Instead, he simply watched her with soft blue eyes and the calm patience of a man who could fully appreciate a moment without rushing to the next one.

After a minute, her attention drifted toward several vendors in particular. Her stomach faintly growled at the sight of stalls offering freshly baked bread, jams, cheeses, and roasted almonds next to another selling mulled wine, which Swedes apparently called glögg.

She and Felix were having dinner together, though, so she resolutely looked away from the food vendors and returned to his side. "I'd like to pick up some presents for my family and friends, if that's okay?"

"Of course it's okay." He lifted an arm, and she happily accepted the unspoken invitation to cuddle close. "Are you warm enough?"

"Now I am." His arm over her shoulders and the heat radiating from his solid body served as her blanket, even though her breaths emerged as clouds in the chill. "What should we do for our next photo?"

His lips rested at the crown on her head. "You tell me."

At the sight of the charcuterie stall nearby, another burst of inspiration struck, and they used a large heart-shaped sausage—reindeer meat; poor Rudolph!—as a prop for their photo, with the vendor's permission. As Felix dramatically offered it to her with the hand not holding her phone, she had both her own hands clasped over her jacket-clad chest in exaggerated shock and delight.

Afterward, she browsed at various stalls, and both of them picked up a few holiday handicrafts. At one point, while she finished paying for a box of tiny marzipan fruits and then visited a stall selling wreaths and other greenery, he vanished for several minutes—only to reappear with two steaming mugs of hot chocolate and raisin-studded saffron buns, as well as a white knitted hat with colorful yarn trim.

"Handmade in Swedish Lappland," he told her, and had her hold their snacks while he carefully tugged the beanie over her head. "You were shivering, and I thought the white would look nice against your hair."

"I . . ." She stalled out, her eyes prickling at the thoughtfulness of his gift. Blinking rapidly, she smiled up at him. "That was very kind of you, Felix."

"It was my pleasure." Dimples peeking through his scruff, he adjusted the hat to cover the tips of her ears. "Also, I didn't want to explain your Little Match Girl–esque death to Swedish authorities."

"Thank you." Rising on tiptoe, she kissed his cold-pinkened cheek. "I'll wear it for the rest of my visit, if only to save you from criminal charges."

"Much appreciated," he said, before taking another photo of them under a sign reading God Jul. Swedish for *Merry Christmas*, as she'd learned.

As they browsed the stalls together for the next hour, they sipped their cocoa and talked through their lives and interests. What she enjoyed about her work, what sort of music he liked, where they'd both gone to school.

When she spoke, he listened and asked follow-up questions. When she asked her own questions, he answered them—as he'd warned—with charmingly pedantic thoroughness and a teasing wit that invited mutual amusement instead of wounding her.

Maybe, she thought, *if I knew I had someone there to help steady me, I wouldn't mind uncertain, slippery paths so much.*

At the top of the hour, just as the snow-laden clouds scuttered away and faint stars began to appear around their edges, the market closed. One by one, the stalls' awnings drew shut as the crowds dissipated into the night.

It was time for her to move on, too, and she was ready.

Felix lightly squeezed her hand. "Dinner?"

"Yes, please, but first . . ." She swiveled to face him, the American-turned-Swede whose kind smile had melted her heart from their first shared glance. The man who'd become closer and more precious to her than a mere stranger over the course of a single winter evening. "Back at the museum, why did you agree to kiss me, Felix? I was just a random tourist."

As was his custom, he thought for a few seconds before answering.

"At the very beginning, that was true." He reached for her other hand, too, and she gladly gave it to him. "But you were a random tourist who chose to spend a dark winter afternoon in an art museum. You were a random tourist who took time to study and think about a painting that interested you and cared enough about others to move so that a tour group could appreciate the painting too. And you were a random tourist with the sweetest, warmest brown eyes I'd ever seen."

Her vision blurred, and she ducked her head until she could blink the tears away.

"Ellie . . ." He freed a hand to cradle her cheek, guiding her eyes back to his. "By the time you called me over, you weren't random anymore. You were specific to me. You were *special*, and when you asked to kiss me, I didn't intend to quibble with my unexpected good fortune. Even though I didn't want to be just a means of revenge on another man you still had feelings for."

There was a flicker of uncertainty in that steady blue gaze. A request for reassurance that she'd gladly offer, even if doing so would reveal a raw expanse of her heart.

"I was wondering why what he said stung so much, when I genuinely don't give a flip about him anymore." She held Felix's stare, willing him to believe the truth. "I finally figured it out earlier. His words didn't hurt because I care what he thinks about me. They hurt because they're what I think about myself."

Understanding softened his expression. "Ellie . . ."

"If my life truly made me happy, what he or anyone else thought wouldn't matter to me. If they considered me boring, fine. But I no longer found *myself* interesting." Even though her words shook, she powered through her emotion to say the rest. "So when I asked you to kiss me, it wasn't about him. Not really. It was about me and whether I had the strength and courage to take chances. And it was about you, Felix, because from the moment I saw you leading that tour, I wanted to climb you like a . . ."

She trailed off, her mind supplying all the pleasurable things that could happen if she were draped over him like a blanket.

"A tree?" he suggested, his face flushed in a way the

chill couldn't quite explain. "I'm flattered to hear it. Actually, more than that. I'm *thrilled*."

"Not like a tree," she corrected. "Like a ladder."

Two of those ladders stood before her. At long last, she knew which one she was taking.

His dimples flashed again. "Even better."

"You asked me earlier what kind of life I wanted, and I didn't have an answer then. I do now." Her newfound certainty steadied her voice. "I'll never be an adrenaline junkie. But I do need a life that feels like I consciously chose it—and made that decision through hope, rather than fear or simple inertia."

He took that in, letting the declaration settle between them.

"All right, then." He traced the curve of her cheek with his gloved thumb. "What's your first choice, Ellie from Maryland?"

"I have two ready to go, actually." She took a deep breath and climbed the first rung toward the unknown. "First, I'm moving to Sweden in the spring. I'll agree to work for a year in our Stockholm branch, with an option to stay longer, as desired."

Was she scared? Of course. But she needed to see what lay beyond the cozy confines of her pink cloud, and the view required some risk-taking. Hopefully, Felix would be at her side to help ease her path, and she could do the same for him. Even if not, though, she still didn't intend to turn back.

"I can't tell you how happy I am to hear that." His face alight with joy, he beamed down at her. "What's choice number two?"

With her unoccupied hand, she reached down into the reusable cloth bag she'd procured that night. It took some digging, but she eventually unearthed what she'd found while he was buying her snacks and a hat. The stall selling evergreen wreaths had featured a few other items, too . . . one of which she'd promptly and discreetly purchased before Felix could return.

She brandished the sprig of mistletoe, lifting it high overhead. The lush red velvet ribbon securing its stems fairly glowed with warmth, and its white berries glinted in the light of the newly revealed crescent moon above.

That moon was a bright, thin sliver of yellow, just wide enough to hang her hopes on.

"I intend to kiss you again," she told him. "If that's something you want too."

He was already drawing her closer, his nose a hair's breadth from hers. "To post on social media?"

His voice was husky, his body warm and firm.

She shook her head. "Nope."

She rose on booted toes, chin tipped to the sky. And this time, when she kissed him—once, and then dozens of times more over the course of a long, dark Swedish solstice night—it was only for the two of them.

No one else.

8

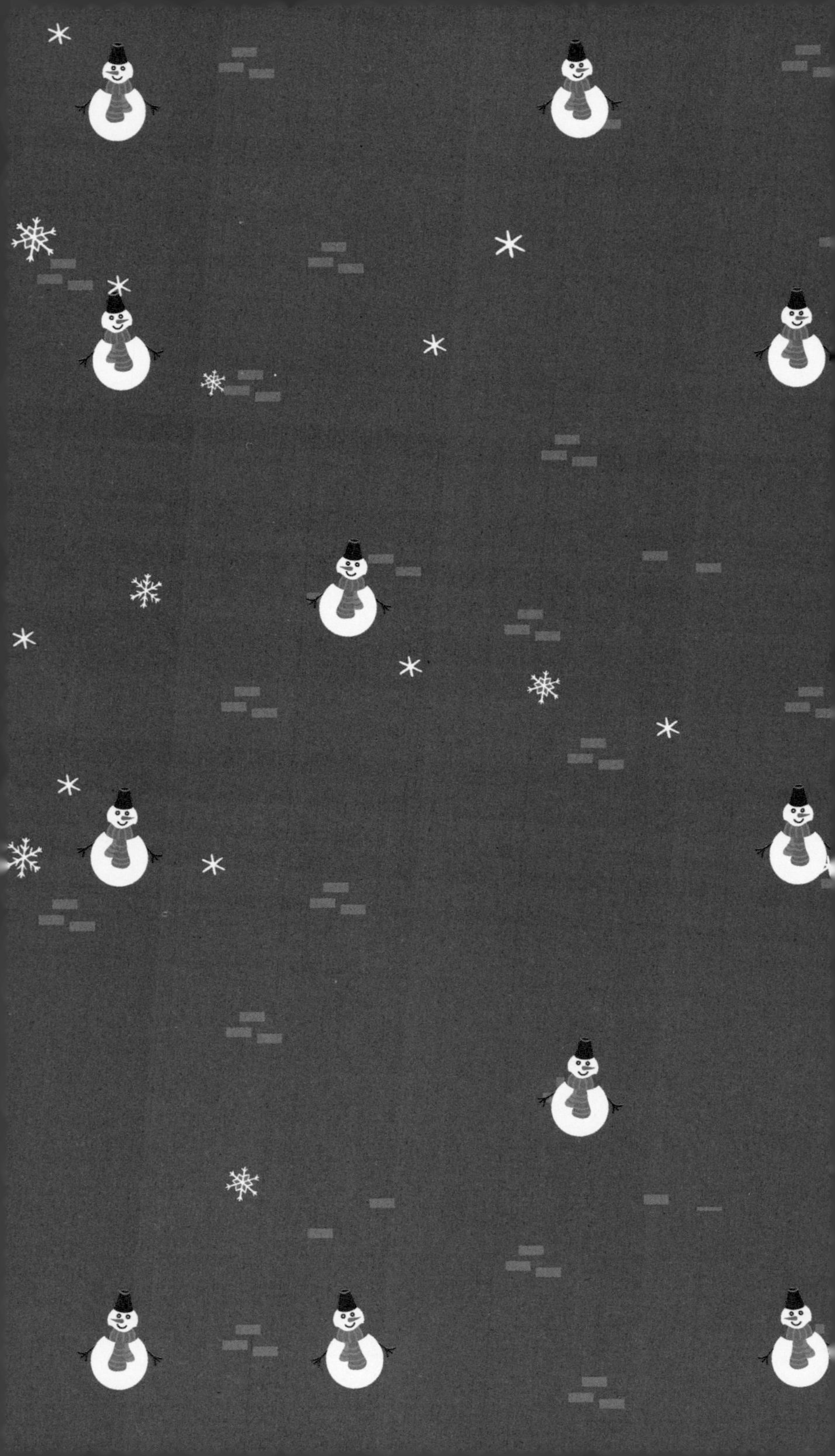

ALL ROADS LEAD HOME

Joss Richard

It's a lot colder than I remember. I would have assumed the opposite given global warming. Perhaps my threshold for the East Coast winter is lower than when I was seventeen. Now, at twenty-six, I can appreciate how picturesque my hometown is.

Beacon, New York, is about an hour and a half train ride out of the city, up the Hudson River. I don't remember the last time I saw blankets of snow—I certainly don't see it living in Florida. This is not like the snow you see in the city; once you leave Manhattan it's thick, pillowy, and covering every surface within eyesight. Outside the window is a winter wonderland. It's beautiful.

"We are now approaching Beacon," the voice on the announcement says. "Beacon station."

Despite it being Christmas Eve, there are more people on the train than I expected. It's already 5:30 p.m., and I assumed everyone would already be at home with their families. When the train stops, a few people around me gather their belongings and I reach overhead and grab my carry-on suitcase.

Once I get to the platform, I pinch the top of my jacket, bracing myself for the December air's harsh bite. I pull a beanie out from my purse and wrap a scarf around my neck. It's not by any means freezing, but my ass is used to Orlando weather now. Anything below sixty feels cold.

I thank my past self for booking an earlier train; the anxiousness I have about seeing my dad hasn't dissipated. I'm not quite ready to show up for dinner just yet. Instead, I take a short walk over to Main Street. It feels familiar; the bones of the town haven't changed, but stores have been swapped out and repainted. My gaze flickers between holiday decorations on store-front windows, Christmas lights wrapped along the snow-dusted trees, and festive wreaths stationed above every lamppost. I spot a café up on the corner, and my heart lifts when I see a "Come on in, we're open" sign.

There's a subtle chime from the bell above the door, and I feel like I just walked into a cozy holiday movie. I take in the smell of coffee beans and nutmeg and the twinkly sound of the first few bars of "The Christmas Song." There's a warm glow throughout the café, a fire crackles in a brick fireplace in the back, and a Christmas tree with red and gold ornaments glimmers by the front window.

The complete lack of customers makes me feel a little foolish walking into a coffee shop at almost 6 p.m. on Christmas Eve. I'm sure whatever part-time student is being forced to work over the holidays is just dying to get a home-cooked meal.

Taking another step, I scan the seasonal options written in chalk on the wall: eggnog latte, hot buttered rum, caramel apple spiced chai, and dark peppermint mocha. There's also a case of mouthwatering pastries off to the side, reminding me all I've had to eat today were plane nuts and a cup of black coffee.

"Hi, so sorry about that," a voice says. A man comes out of the back area, distracted and wiping his hands with a towel. He's tall, around six feet if I had to guess, with a head of light brown hair and a thick beard. He has a strong nose, a deep voice, and crystal-blue eyes. I've only ever seen eyes that blue once before. "How can I help—"

"Ryan?" I pinch my brows together, studying the familiar but almost unrecognizable face in front of me.

He glances up and for a moment looks utterly confused. Like he doesn't know where he is or *when* he is. "Elle?" he says slowly and not confidently. "Is that you?"

"Holy shit." A breathless laugh escapes me. "How are you?!"

"I'm good . . ." he replies, but he's looking at me like he doesn't quite understand how I'm in front of him. "How are *you*? Are you here visiting or—"

"Yeah," I say, still processing that Ryan is here in front of me. What would I call Ryan? My childhood best friend? My crush? The person who consumed all the days of my youth? "I'm just here for a few days," I elaborate. "I'm visiting my dad."

Ryan's brows raise. "He still lives here?"

"Mm-hmm. Same house."

"Wow." He drags a hand through his hair. "Well, uh, welcome home. It's been, like, what? Ten years?"

"Yeah," I say. The last time I saw Ryan we were just teenagers, although at the time we felt wise beyond our years. "Right after graduation."

"Fuck," he breathes out. "Yeah, I remember, it's just . . . time goes by fast, doesn't it?"

"God." I laugh. "It feels like a lifetime ago," I say, and then there's a moment of silence between us as we look at each other. Almost taking in how different we are. Perhaps I've grown an inch or two, but I was most likely still five four when Ryan saw me last. My dark hair is longer, highlighted, and I'm more filled out than what I was in high school. I wear probably half the amount of makeup I used to, and I like to think I carry myself with a confidence I could have only dreamed of at the tough age of seventeen.

My eyes travel across Ryan, taking in every single detail. His eyebrows are thicker than I remember, and I'm still wrapping my head around the fact that he has facial hair. He's wearing a forest-green fisherman's sweater with a red shirt peeking out from under the collar. His blue jeans are faded, and his dark brown Blundstone boots are worn in. He's a *man*.

"You look great," he says, and then looks like he almost regrets it.

If I weren't still cold from the winter air outside, my cheeks flushing would be a lot more noticeable.

I instinctively take off my beanie. "Oh, thanks . . . so do you," I say, and it's not a lie. Ryan was always cute; he was the cutest guy in our school. *Cute* could not be more of an inaccurate way to describe him now. *Muscular*, *handsome*, *sexy*, or *hot* feel more fitting.

"So, uh." He pats the sides of his thighs. "What can I get you?"

"Oh." I quickly scan the menu again. "I'll, um, take the dark peppermint mocha and a cinnamon bun, please."

"You got it." He pauses for a moment like he's disoriented, then spins on his heels, reaching for the espresso beans. "For here or to go?"

I bite my lip. I've only *just* seen Ryan. I'm not ready to leave. "What time are you open until?"

"Seven," he says.

"For here," I say, and he grabs a speckled red-and-white mug from the shelf. I shrug off my jacket and take off my scarf. Running a hand through my hair, I choose a seat at the bar area and watch Ryan.

He pushes his sleeves up, revealing strong forearms. These aren't the forearms of the kid I used to ride my bike around town with, the kid who used to make me laugh in the middle of class during silent reading time, or the kid who hugged me, saying everything was going to be okay when I was positive it wouldn't. In Ryan's presence, so many memories come sweeping back like a heavy tide. I think of our junior prom and how Noah Klein bailed the morning of because he'd rather go with Madison Bennett. I cried in my room and Ryan stepped in to be my date. I remember going on vacation to Montreal with my parents and Ryan texting me the entire trip to take my mind off my parents fighting. Every single memory from my childhood and teenage years includes Ryan.

"So," I say over the sound of milk steaming. "What have you been up to?"

A corner of his mouth pulls up, revealing a trace of a smile. "Up to?" he repeats, concentrating on the white liquid in the stainless-steel pitcher. "Same old."

"Same old? Since graduation?" I look at him evenly. "Are you married? Kids? I assume you still live around here—"

"No." He shakes his head.

"No, you don't live around here?"

"No wife. No kids," he says.

"Girlfriend?"

"Just single." He looks at me and when he does, I begin to feel a little warmer. "What about you?" he throws to me.

"Same." I pull at the sleeves of my sweater. I opted in for a thick red cardigan with a white shirt underneath and am aware how alarmingly *Christmasy* we look combined. "After my ex, I kind of swore off dating."

"I hear you." He lets out a heavy sigh that tells me all I need to know about his last relationship. He squeezes a tube of rich, dark brown mocha filling into the cup and then places a small piece of chocolate at the bottom. "But yeah, I'm still here. I got a place across the bridge in Balmville."

"That's crazy," I breathe out. The thought of Ryan having his own place just feels so grown-up of him. But I guess we are adults now.

He pours the frothed milk over the espresso, creating a subtle Christmas tree outline. "Are you still in Florida?" he asks.

"Yeah." I take the warm cup that he slides in my direction. "Orlando."

I don't say much more because there isn't much to say about my life there. Yes, I had a tight group of girlfriends, but that wasn't enough to make me love it. I lived in a shitty studio apartment and I hated my job. I'm ready for a change.

Ryan's gaze stays focused on me, like he wants to say something but is treading lightly. "Do you come back often?"

"No," I say almost immediately. Maybe because I want

him to know that if I had come back years ago, I would've reached out. "It's my first time back."

"Seriously? Since you left?"

"Mm-hmm." I take a sip of the peppermint liquid. The velvety chocolate and rich espresso flavor warm me up. It's delicious. "I got a job in the city . . ." I say.

"Oh." Ryan's brows shoot up. "You, uh, don't sound excited."

"No, *I am*," I redact. "It's an amazing job. It's on the marketing team for one of my favorite publishers."

"No shit." Ryan smiles. "So you're still reading at every waking moment?" he says, and I reach for my purse and pull out my Kindle.

"Even more than I used to."

"Congratulations, Elle."

"It's been a long time coming," I confess. "I used to work at this auto insurance company . . ." I make a tired face. "There are just no jobs in publishing in Orlando, so I took the leap to move to the city."

"So what's the problem?" Ryan asks.

"I haven't found a place just *yet*, so after New Year's I'm moving in with my dad until I get situated."

"And you haven't been back since you left . . ." Ryan leans back against the counter, filling in the blanks. "I miss your dad. He's the best."

Ryan's not wrong. My dad *is* the best. He's an Amtrak engineer, and I remember on weekends he would let me sit up with him in the locomotive cabin and we'd go down to the city for a few hours, just us. He'd either take me to his favorite soup dumpling place in Chinatown or what he deemed the best hot dog cart in Central Park. I could talk to him about anything. He taught me how to play baseball and would help make sense of my math homework. Then in my junior year of high school my parents divorced. My mom had plans to move to Florida to be closer to her family and she encouraged me to apply for colleges down there. Cut to me moving almost eleven hundred miles away to be close to her—and eleven hundred miles away from my dad.

"My mom painted him out to be this bad guy, and I never really knew the full story," I say. "I didn't realize she was sort of keeping me from him. So I'm kind of seeing this job as a sign that I should rebuild that relationship."

"Elle," Ryan breathes out. "I'm sorry."

"It's fine. Really." I wave him off. I already made my peace with the reality of my parents' divorce. "I've seen him over the years," I explain. "He would visit, but just being back here, I don't know . . . I'm a little nervous."

"Of course," he says.

There's a pang in my chest that isn't necessarily pain, it's more the urge to open up. It's hard not confiding in someone who just knows you. Ryan and I became friends when were in preschool and were attached at the hip ever since. He was my person through prepubescent acne, frizzy hair, and braces. Ryan would spend weekday dinners with me and my parents, and vice versa. He wasn't just my friend; he was my family.

Then one day things just . . . changed. In sophomore year of high school, I started looking at him differently, noticing how attractive he was. I'd notice his eyes linger on my lips; I'd feel an electric spark if ever we brushed shoulders in the school hallways. Suddenly, hanging out in his basement watching movies after school felt a little too intimate and silence was no longer comfortable but charged. By senior year, I could hardly focus on anything other than my physical attraction to Ryan.

"What if things aren't the same?" I ask him.

Ryan's mouth opens and then presses tight. "I'm sure things might be different . . . You're an adult now," he says. "I don't think you can just pick up from where you left off all those years ago, but things can still be good . . . maybe even better." His words sit with me. I oddly feel like they don't necessarily apply to just my dad and me. "When is dinner?" he asks.

"Around seven thirty," I say, and glance at my phone. Less than an hour. "My dad told me to call him when I get in . . ." I trail off, and Ryan clearly understands that I haven't done that yet.

"You got this," he says with a nod. When he says it, I almost believe it. I trust him.

"So, uh . . ." I change the subject. "Do you still talk to anyone from school?"

"Nah." He shakes his head. "Not really. I see Connor and Danielle sometimes, but most people moved away."

"Oh my god." I adjust in my seat, feeling invested in people I haven't thought of since I left. "What are they up to now?"

"Connor has like three kids," Ryan says.

"Shut up." I lean in. "That doesn't sound like Connor."

"Three different women."

"*That* sounds like Connor." I snort.

"He's a good dad, though," Ryan adds. "And Danielle's a hairdresser in town. She gives me a discount." He smiles.

A customer comes in and orders an eggnog latte to go.

He and Ryan make a little bit of small talk about the recent snowstorm, and I observe like my favorite television show is on.

When the man leaves, I give Ryan an apologetic look. "I'm sorry you're stuck working the holidays."

He shrugs. "I like to give the staff the holidays off."

I take a bite of my cinnamon roll, the warm, pillowy dough tasting sweet and buttery. "Are you the manager?" I ask, my mouth still full.

"I own this place," he says.

"You . . ." I look at our surroundings: the intentional holiday décor, the homey vibe that you're thrust into immediately when entering, and the sense of comfort that sweeps the entire space. On the chalkboard menu I notice impressive drawings of gingerbread men and wrapped gifts. There's no doubt Ryan drew those himself. He always loved doodling. "You *own* this place?"

"Mm-hmm." He pushes himself off from the counter and takes a sip from a mug sitting by the pastry case.

"That's amazing," I say in disbelief. "How did that happen?"

"It was closing down, and I wanted to preserve it," he explains. "Two years now."

"Wow," I say under my breath. I don't know what I thought Ryan would grow up to be, but of course it's something with meaning, something he's passionate about.

Ryan's gaze stays fixated on me, and all it takes is a small crinkle in my brow for him to shake his head like he's snapped out of a trance.

"Sorry." He takes in a sharp inhale. "It's just, uh, nice to see you again." There's something about the way he says it that makes my heart twist. There's weight to his words.

"You too," I agree. "Really. And you look . . . good," I say, and kick myself for not moving past his appearance.

"As you've said." He laughs.

"No, seriously," I hone in. "I don't know, you look different, but the same."

"Well, I'm not seventeen anymore," he says.

I sit up straighter. "Do *I* look different?"

"No," he says.

"No?" My face collapses.

"You're still just as beautiful."

My cheeks heat up, and I smile.

The next thirty minutes go by far too quickly. Ryan and I reminisce about our old teachers, inside jokes, and milestones in our lives that I didn't realize I've been holding on to.

Spending time with him doesn't feel like I'm with an old friend who I haven't seen in a decade, but more like catching up with my best friend after going weeks without talking.

Ryan still manages to make me laugh so hard my cheeks feel sore, and I haven't lost the ability to expose his playful side that he likes to conceal. We were always like this growing up, but is it normal to still have this effortless dynamic as adults?

"Do you remember when we drove up to Woodstock before I left?" I finish the final bite of my cinnamon roll as Ryan refills coffee beans.

"Are you kidding?" He eyes me. "That was the day I got the truck. You were my first passenger."

The day before I left for Florida, I told Ryan I wanted to do something fun, so he suggested we drive up along the Hudson River.

"It was *the most* perfect summer day." I reminisce about

having the sun on my face and the wind in my hair from the passenger side of his truck.

"We found that venue playing live music, but we weren't allowed in because we weren't old enough," Ryan says with disbelief.

"So we listened from your parked car." I laugh.

Ryan runs a hand through his hair, reliving the memory. "God, do you remember that?"

I don't think there's a world in which I could forget. It was the night we almost kissed.

Before I can respond, a woman walks in picking up an order for two dozen gingerbread cookies. Ryan runs to the back and brings over a box.

"Merry Christmas," he calls out as she leaves, and then turns to me. "We close in fifteen."

I take a final sip of my drink, which has given me just the right amount of caffeine and a sugar spike that I needed. "I guess I better call my dad."

"You said your dad's at the same place?" Ryan asks, and I nod. "I'll drive you," he offers, and I don't want to say no. I want to spend as much time with him as I can.

"Are you sure?"

"You live an eight-minute bike ride away," he deadpans. "I'm sure."

Once Ryan starts the engine, the radio instantly starts playing a classic Christmas tune that makes me smile. "You ready?" he asks, and I nod.

My heart starts to beat a little faster being so close to him in such a confined space. Sitting in the passenger's side feels all too familiar, except now we're not in some beaten-up old truck—Ryan's upgraded to an impressive SUV, and it's so clear that he's not the boy I once knew. He's a man. A man who's over six feet, with hands that could cover my entire waist and stomach . . . not like that's what I'm thinking about. Except it's almost impossible not to. The last time we were driving together, he had my hand in his. He had my heart.

I think about that night in Woodstock; we were sitting in his parked truck. Holding hands is something we never used to do, but that night it felt right. He grazed my knuckles, and I leaned in closer, wanting nothing more than to feel his lips on mine. We were *so close* until another car pulled in beside us. I've replayed that moment in my head over and over again, wondering what would've happened if we'd just kissed.

"What?" Ryan looks over, feeling my eyes on his profile.

"Nothing." I look away.

"Tell me," he demands playfully.

"I'm remembering the last time I sat in the front seat of your truck."

He smiles, keeping his focus ahead. "I guess a few things are different."

"Yeah." I chuckle. "You're a lot bigger."

He peels his eyes off the road and looks at me. His eyes are a cool blue, almost like the snow around us. The look he gives me causes my internal temperature to shoot up like a thermometer dropped in boiling water.

"That I am" is all he says.

We drive past streets that I remember like an old movie. All have quaint Christmas decorations, and everything feels so comforting. There's one house on the corner of Oak that is completely decked out with multicolor lights, a twelve-foot blow-up Santa Claus, and nine inflatable reindeer on the front lawn.

"Are you kidding?!" I beam, remembering that I always loved seeing this house decorated as a kid. "They still go all out for Christmas?"

"Every year," Ryan confirms.

"That's awesome." I admire the view in passing. I find myself wondering how my life would have turned out if I'd stayed.

"How does it feel being back?" Ryan lowers the volume on "I'll Be Home for Christmas."

"Well, on one hand it feels like I'm taking a step backward," I say, but then hear how it sounds. "I'm sorry, that sounds awful—"

"No," Ryan says. "I get it. That's how I felt when I came back after college. I went to Columbia, and I felt like I was a failure or something coming back to Beacon. Like *this* is the place that people work so hard to leave, so why would I come back?"

"Why *did* you come back?" I ask.

"I like it here." He shrugs a shoulder. "I was able to afford a house before the town got popular . . . Everyone and their mother is starting to move up here from the city for the *Upstate New York* vibe," he says, and I giggle. "But I don't know, there's something special about Beacon. Maybe I'm just holding on to certain memories." Ryan's eyes briefly land on me and then look away when I notice.

I don't ask what memories he's referring to . . . but I have a feeling they're shared ones.

"I never realized how pretty everything is." I look out the window.

Ryan slows down once we turn onto my old street. I see my childhood home up ahead, and my heart feels warm for so many different reasons. The red brick, green shutters, and white window trim are exactly how I remember them. There are two cars in the driveway and a light on in the living room.

Ryan turns off the car. "Here we are."

I give him a nervous smile and notice his hands gripping the wheel. "Thanks again for the ride, Ryan." Even though I'm not ready to leave, I must. I reach for the door handle when I feel Ryan's hand on my arm.

"Look, can I just say something?" Ryan's touch begs me to stay. "It's going to sound stupid because I know we were just *kids*, but I always felt like if you never moved maybe we could've . . ." He drags his hand through his hair and lets out a heavy sigh. "I always had feelings for you, Elle. And I think about that night a lot . . . the night we almost kissed."

My breath staggers and the car suddenly feels much smaller than it is. Ryan pauses and looks out the window, like he's looking for an answer. The Ryan I know, who grew into a man big enough to protect me from anything, looks helpless right now.

"I don't just think about the kiss; I think about *you*," he continues. "Whenever I cross that bridge we used to play under or if a certain song comes on. I know there's no point in me saying it now, but I just didn't want another ten years or even our whole lives to go past us without me telling you," he says, and his eyes stay locked on me like he wants to say more but just doesn't know how. "I used to think if I'd told you when we were younger, you would've stayed—

which I know doesn't make sense, but I just wish you knew. And you coming here out of nowhere, into *my* shop, felt like a sign, you know?"

I would be lying if I said I didn't feel the same way. *God*, of course I feel the same way. Ryan Mills was my whole entire world. It devastated me to move away from him. I've thought about him over the years. When I had my first kiss, I closed my eyes and thought what it would be like to kiss Ryan instead. The first time I had sex, I wondered afterward if he'd experienced the same firsts that I did. He wasn't consuming my thoughts, and the memory of him eventually faded, but I did miss him, and I did have feelings for him. I think maybe I still do.

"I . . ." I stumble, not sure what to say. "I felt the same way, Ryan."

His gaze snaps up to mine, a glint in his eyes. "Really?"

"Of course I did." I let out a soft laugh. "You weren't just my best friend . . . You were *everything* to me." I feel a release saying it out loud. Like it's a secret I held all these years.

"What happened to us?" He looks at me, his eyes bigger than I've ever seen them before.

"I don't know." I look down. For the first month or so after I moved, Ryan and I talked on the phone and texted as much as we could. Until one day we didn't. "I guess life," I say softly.

"I should've tried harder, Elle," Ryan says, a pang of regret in his voice.

"What?" I rear back. "Ryan, we both know it wasn't just you. I mean, I was in a different state! We were both starting college, and we were *seventeen* . . . It would've been impossible."

Ryan's jaw muscle tenses. "Do you think we would've . . . been something if you'd stayed?"

"I'm positive," I say, and he lets out a low hum. "We could've gone to the same college," I muse.

The corners of Ryan's mouth curl up into a smile. "We would've lived in the city. Gotten a tiny studio apartment."

"I would be able to have your mom's fettucine alfredo every Saturday." My eyes go wide at the memory of Mrs. Mills always cooking.

"We could've seen the new *Star Wars* together."

"I thought of you when it came out!" I turn in my seat. "What did you think?!"

"I loved it," he says. "The second movie, not so much."

"Oh, hard disagree. I loved *The Last Jedi*."

A puff of air escapes from his nose. "You would."

"What's that supposed to mean?" I gape.

"This coming from the same person who thinks *Problem Child 2* is better than the original."

"It is!" I laugh, not believing we're actually having this conversation again. Ryan shakes his head, and we let a moment of silence linger between the two of us. "You would've been my first kiss," I say just loud enough for him to hear me.

"I always regretted not kissing you, Elle."

My stomach flutters. I swallow and my extremities become warm despite the snow outside. "Why didn't you?" I hear myself asking.

He sighs. "I didn't know what I felt for you. I just knew it was confusing. You were my best friend, but you were also so much more . . . and it wasn't until you were gone that I realized I should have."

I understand what he means. Your teens are a rare and confusing time. I know people who have difficulties expressing their feelings at our age. It's scary to tell someone how you feel about them . . . no matter how old you are.

My teeth scrape my bottom lip. "Would it be crazy if you kissed me—finally?" I smirk.

Ryan's gaze sticks to me. His throat bobs, and he takes a deep inhale. His tongue quickly wets his lips as he stares at mine. I didn't know it was possible to feel this way, to feel like you're losing air supply but at the same time feeling so protected, so safe, like your whole life has been leading up to this very moment.

Slowly, Ryan's hand gently cups my jaw. We both tremble slightly at the touch. His thumb grazes my skin and lingers on my lip. The taste of him makes me shut my eyes. A simple touch shouldn't feel this good. It's not possible. He moves in closer until I have no sense of space or time, I just know that he's in front of me, the smell of peppermint and pine filling my senses.

"Elle," he rasps. His voice is low, even deeper than normal. "Can I kiss you?"

"Please," I whisper.

He leans in, and before I know it, our lips are touching. It's not awkward or unfamiliar. Quite the opposite. I let out an embarrassing moan, to which I feel Ryan's mouth curve upward. He kisses me deeper, and I instinctively arch my back. His tongue asks permission to enter my mouth, which I enthusiastically accept. I don't know what to focus on—the fact that he softly bites my lower lip, or that he's gently massaging my earlobe between his thumb and his knuckle.

"Ryan, don't . . ." I breathe out in between kisses. "Stop . . ."

He pulls away with a deep inhale.

"Sorry," he grunts.

"No." I grip his collar. "I said *don't stop*."

I pull him back in, and now the two of us can't control our sounds. We're back to being two teenagers who have never touched another human being before. It's like we're making up for lost time. I feel giddy around him, but I also feel more sexy, confident, and sure of myself than I ever have.

We explore each other the best that we can in this space. I don't want this to end. Kissing him alone I think I could do for hours. I feel drunk off the way his hands squeeze my hips and the low gruff that comes from him when I let out the faintest moan. Everything feels electric, and I can't believe we haven't been doing this our whole lives.

My hands reach underneath his jacket, desperate to feel his skin, but Ryan stops me.

"Wait," he huffs.

"What?" I look up at him.

"Not like this," he says, a strain in his voice.

I inhale and look around us. My childhood home is just up the street, and it's 7:20 p.m. on Christmas Eve.

"You're right." I sigh.

"It's not that I don't want to, Elle." Ryan holds my hand. "*Fuck*, I want to. More than you know . . ."

"No, I know," I say, my fingers intertwining with his and the fog in my head beginning to clear.

"I just, uh, I don't know, Elle. It was really hard to say goodbye to you, and I'm afraid if we do something we can't take back . . ." He wipes a palm over his face. "I wouldn't know how to get over it this time."

Ryan studies me, waiting for me to continue, but I don't want to say out loud what I'm thinking. That this has been wonderful, but I can't make a promise that we'll pick up from where we left off. That I missed him, but maybe this is the nostalgia talking . . . What happens next week or next month when the realities of our lives come into play? Can things be that easy?

"If that's how you feel," I say.

"How do *you* feel?" he asks.

"I . . ." I begin, but then stop when I see Ryan's attention shift.

"Is that your dad?" He nods to the distance.

"What?" I frown and look up the street. Ryan's right. That's my dad.

My heart instantly melts as I see him wearing a brown sweater with a dress shirt underneath. He's halfway out the door, carrying a garbage bag. He makes his way swiftly to the end of the driveway and stuffs it in the trash can then heads back inside.

I haven't seen him in person in over two years.

"That's him." I chew the side of my tongue.

Ryan turns to me. "Well, uh, I guess you better get going. He's probably waiting for you."

"Right." I sling a smile. "Text me?"

Ryan hesitates and my heart instantly plummets. "I don't know if that's a good idea," he says slowly, and I hate the way it sounds.

"You know what . . ." As if on reaction, I recoil. "You're right. Stupid idea."

"It's not stupid," he says earnestly. "It's just this evening felt *too* good, Elle. I so badly wish I could say, *Yeah, let's be friends and hang out like old times . . .*" His voice trails off. "But losing you was too painful, and if I can't have all of you, I'm not strong enough to have any of you."

My throat tightens, and it feels like my chest is about to burst. I don't *want* to say goodbye, but I don't know what else to say in this moment. I suppose Ryan and I already got more time than we were ever meant to have.

Ryan pulls his keys from the ignition and dips his chin lower. "You ready?"

"I think so." I reach for the door handle.

Everything suddenly feels *so* cold. Ryan gets out and then meets me by the hood of his car. We linger for a moment as he wraps his arms around me, pulling me in. I bury my face into the crook of his neck, underneath his jacket, and it feels so warm. His embrace is strong, firm.

My gaze lifts to Ryan, and the warmth of his lips already feels like a distant memory. *He* feels like a distant memory.

"Good luck," Ryan huffs into my hair, and I give him another squeeze.

"Thank you for everything," I say.

"That's what I'm here for, right?" He gives me a crooked smile that makes me feel like we're kids again. "Remember, you got this," he says.

It's then I'm pulled back to ten years ago. Us saying goodbye to each other on this very street before my flight to Florida. A sheen of tears across my cheeks and Ryan giving me a smile that everything was going to be okay. That I would make new friends; I'd have fun and go to Disney World every weekend and college wouldn't be scary. *Remember, you got this*, he told me.

He was right. He's still right.

I grip the handle of my carry-on suitcase. "Tell your mom I say hi."

He slowly reveals a smile, and I picture that left dimple of his underneath his beard. "Tell your dad hi too."

"I will," I say, and head toward my childhood home.

"Elle," Ryan calls out, and I spin on my heels. He's halfway into his car and the light snowfall softens my view. He almost looks like a sketch from here. "For what it's worth, seeing you was probably the best Christmas gift."

My face beams into a smile. "For me too," I say loud enough that he can hear me. He tips his forehead in my direction and then gets inside his car.

As I walk toward my dad's, that dull ache in my chest no longer exists. I'm not scared of being back home, I'm not anxious to see him. There's a sense of safety and comfort being back here. Perhaps I needed to reunite with Ryan. Maybe he was sort of a holiday miracle to help me through tonight. I look back over my shoulder, and he's patiently waiting for me to safely get inside.

I ring the bell and when the door opens, I'm immediately greeted by a symphony of delicious smells: honey-baked ham, spiced cider, and gingerbread. My dad stands in the doorway, wearing that same brown sweater I saw him in five minutes ago, with a nervous smile on his face. I can hear *Home Alone*, my favorite Christmas movie, playing in the living room.

"Hi, Dad." I take a step forward and wrap my arms around him.

"Hi," he says, surprised, but then immediately returns the gesture, squeezing me like I'm a little kid again. It feels nice. "Elle, Merry Christmas."

I quickly check behind me and see that Ryan's now gone.

"Merry Christmas," I say, and then pull back to look at my dad. I've only seen him a handful of times since I moved. All of which were when he came to Florida to visit, and all have been for less than twenty-four hours.

"How was your flight?" He takes my coat, hanging it in the closet.

My eyes scan the rest of the house. It's exactly how it looked the last time I saw it. Oddly, it feels so much smaller than before. I can hear faint voices down the hallway, and I already know it's my Aunt Cami and grandma Traci.

"It was good, I slept," I say, and my dad's gaze lingers on me. "What?" I ask.

"You just look so grown-up." After a beat, he adds, "You look like your mom."

A puff of air escapes my nostrils. "She always says I look like you."

"Be thankful you don't." He rolls his eyes.

My dad's a big, tall man. My friends used to joke and say he looked like a giant when we were younger. I think he's right, though, I do look like my mom, but my eyes are all his.

We make our way to the living room, and my aunt and grandma squeal with excitement and give me hugs and kisses. I adore my Aunt Cami. She was someone who always got me the most personal gifts on my birthday and came to every dance recital growing up. The two of them force-feed me so much baked Brie and pigs in a blanket before dinner that I can barely eat any of the ham my dad made. As we sit at the table, Bing Crosby plays in the background, and the view out the window is a perfect contrast of the black night sky and the white blanket of snow on the ground. Everything feels so easy.

"So, Elle." My aunt grabs another dinner roll and smothers butter on it. "Are you excited for the new job?"

"I am," I answer. "It's only two days in office, which is *so* nice."

"Oh, I bet," she says. "And the train is only an hour and a half. That'll be a breeze commuting from here."

"I promise it won't be here that long." I turn to my dad, reminding him. "Just a few weeks until I find a place."

"Elle." He takes a sip of his mulled wine. "You know you have a place here for as long as you want."

He's said as much *many* times before.

"I know," I say. "But I don't want to impose—"

"Enough of that." He clicks his tongue. "Your room will always be your room."

"Are you going to catch up with any friends while you're here?" my grandma asks.

Truthfully, the only person I would want to catch up with just had his tongue down my throat a few hours ago.

"Well, I ran into Ryan Mills just before I got here," I say. "Dad, you remember Ryan, right?"

"Remember him?" My dad laughs. "He practically lived here." He looks at my aunt and my grandma. "Remember, Elle and Ryan were attached at the hip? Your mom and I thought you two were going to get married."

The joke causes my heart to lodge in my stomach.

"He was such a nice boy, Elle," my grandma adds.

"What's he doing now?" my dad asks.

"He actually owns that café on Main," I say, realizing I didn't catch the name of it. "There's a fireplace inside, and it's all decorated for Christmas . . ."

"No shit." He sits back in his seat. "Good for him. I didn't know he was still in town. I've got to say hi." The timer for the oven goes off, and my dad stands up. "How about some dessert?"

He heads to the kitchen and pulls out a pecan pie from the oven. He places it on a rack to cool, and I eye the glistening toasted pecans. My mouth begins to water.

"Oh man, I've missed this," I say.

"There's also a Yule log cake in the fridge," he says. "Mind grabbing it, Elle?"

"Of course." I stand up, and when I get to the fridge door my heart stops at the sight. "Where did you find this?"

I stay fixated on a drawing of a younger version of myself. I'm in front of this very house with a book in my hand, my bike beside me, and a giant smile on my face. It's a silly drawing, but I thought I lost it. When I moved to Florida, I looked everywhere for it and remember crying thinking I'd never see it again.

My dad looks over his shoulder. "Oh, that was always there," he says. "I remember you loved that drawing. I couldn't take it down."

The piece of art is a representation of me. It's me in front of the place I felt safest, with my favorite things in the world. It's this home without the drama of my parents, the sound of voices being raised through the walls. It's my happy place.

"I thought I lost this." My fingertips gently graze the colored pencil.

"It's the only thing you ever drew," my dad says from the kitchen table. "Didn't know you were an artist."

"I didn't draw it . . ." I say softly.

In fifth grade when my parents started fighting, Ryan

came over and started drawing me a picture. He asked if I could go anywhere in the world, where would I want to go? I told him I'd want to stay right here.

My throat starts to close in, and my heart flutters. A smile creeps up on the corner of my mouth, and I touch the drawing again. Twenty-four hours ago, I had no idea what to expect being here. I was scared and anxious. Maybe on some level I felt bad for my dad. I felt bad that I'd left him. He was my best friend, and I loved Aunt Cami and my grandma, and suddenly they became strangers. It's not that I don't love my mom, but I find it unfair that I was used as a pawn in their relationship. That whatever problems they were having in their lives were reflected onto me. Just because my mom hated my father meant that by proxy, I had to hate him too. Even though I had no reason to.

Being within these walls again and with these people, I'm reminded that I'm with *family*.

I look at my dad in the kitchen, cutting slices of pie, humming along to the Christmas music playlist. I missed him.

"Hey, Dad." I walk over to him.

"What's up?"

"I was thinking . . . Since I'm only in the office two days a week, maybe I don't *need* to find a place in the city."

My dad looks up and his brows rise. There's so much hope in his eyes, but also pain, like he doesn't want to believe something that won't happen.

"Really?" he barely gets out.

My eyes land past him to the drawing on the fridge.

"Really." I smile. "At least for now."

My dad pulls me into a hug, and it just feels *right*. Everything feels right, except there's one thing that's missing.

"Dad," I say. "Would I be able to borrow your car? I just need to do something super quick."

"Now?" He looks at me.

"Yeah," I say. "Now."

I wish I could say it was as simple as me getting in my dad's truck and flying down the small streets of Beacon. The reality is that in the time I've been inside, there has been significant snowfall. Thankfully, the size of our driveway is modest, and my dad loves shoveling. Eventually, I'm able to get out, but only after ten minutes of heating up the truck and scraping the snow off it. East Coast winters are fun.

"Shit." I hit the brakes at a stop sign, not sure whether I make a left or a right. I've never driven in Beacon. I left before I got my license. Instead, I let my muscle memory take over and remember my bike path.

The streets are quiet and magically illuminated by all the homes with Christmas lights. It looks like a dream. How can a town be so perfect?

I get to Willow Street, and that's when I see the house. The house that practically makes me feel just as nostalgic as when I entered my childhood home. I park on the street, clutch my jacket close, and run to the front door.

I can see the lights on inside and a few cars in the driveway—one of which I remember from earlier. As I wait for someone to answer I can practically feel my heart beating through my chest, an overwhelming burst of joy and hope flowing through me.

The door opens, and I see a familiar face, just as pretty as I remember, with a few more lines around the eyes.

"Elle?!" Ryan's mom says. "Elle, is that you?"

"Hi, Mrs. Mills," I say awkwardly.

"Oh my goodness, honey!" She steps out onto the front porch and gives me the biggest hug. "My god, look at you! You're beautiful."

"I'm so sorry to intrude," I say, "but—"

"Elle?" Ryan appears behind his mom, wiping his hands on a dish towel. He looks confused. Worried. Like I might be in trouble. "Is everything okay?" He rushes toward us.

"It's fine," I assure him. "I just—"

"Lord, come inside, Elle." Mrs. Mills pulls me in. "It's freezing out there."

"Mom," Ryan says. "Could you just give us a second?"

"Oh yes, of course," she says. "Wow, look at you two. It's like you're just a couple of kids again, huh?"

"Mom," Ryan says pointedly.

"Sorry, yes, I'm going. I'm going." She heads down the hallway but calls back, "Elle, don't you leave now until I pack you some food to go, okay? Your dad's doing good?"

"I won't and he's great." I smile.

When his mom is out of view, Ryan turns to me, grabbing my hands. "Are you all right?"

"I'm fine, I swear I just . . . I needed to talk to you. Is that okay?"

Ryan grabs his coat hanging by the door and shoves his feet into a pair of boots. "Here, let's step outside."

We settle on the porch, and there's a warm glow cast around Ryan from the Christmas lights.

"I don't want to move to the city," I say, and Ryan's brows rise. "I know it sounds silly, but . . ." I continue, voice now shaky. "But I've never opened up to anyone the way I do with you . . . and I haven't kissed anyone the way I kiss you." I stop and take a breath. "I know what happened between us, Ryan, and it was *me*. I missed you so much, and with me losing my relationship with my dad it was too hard knowing you were here. That all the things I cared about were somewhere I wasn't. So I stopped responding. I stopped updating you, and I'm sorry. It's my fault. But I always hoped that maybe one day we would reunite . . . and I'd have the courage to tell you how I really feel."

The muscle in Ryan's jaw leaps. "How do you feel?"

"I feel like I've always loved you," I say, hearing how crazy it sounds. "And I know it's not possible . . . or maybe it is. Is it crazy to love someone your whole life?"

"Elle," Ryan interrupts me before I can continue a tangent that most certainly won't make sense. "I think I've always loved you too."

An incredulous laugh escapes me. "Really?"

"Yeah." Ryan looks up. "It's like no matter how many years go by, I think about you. I *care* about you. I miss you. And I don't know, I thought it was a memory I was holding on to, but being with you today, kissing you . . . it's real."

"I thought coming back here would feel scary, like I didn't belong anymore," I admit. "But it felt like coming home."

Ryan's expression flickers as he takes a staggered breath in. His eyes are searching mine for an answer, but I don't know what his question is.

"It's funny you say that," he says softly. "Because this place never felt like home after you left."

A warm tear escapes the corner of my eye and falls down the side of my cheek.

"Ryan," I say. "I don't want to leave you again."

He takes a step forward, placing both of his hands on my arms. The contact makes me shiver, and he starts to gently rub, warming me up.

"Are you sure? Because I can't say goodbye one more time, Elle."

I think of my dad, Aunt Cami, my grandma Traci, this beautiful town sitting on the edge of the Hudson River . . . Ryan. Why would I ever want to leave something so special?

"I can't either," I say, and then Ryan's lips crash into mine.

It's a tender yet hungry kiss. I almost fall apart right here, right now, knowing that I'm finally where I belong. There is nobody else for me other than Ryan. He showed me what it means to care for someone, to protect someone, to be protected by someone. He imprinted on my heart long before I knew what to do with it. He was always with me, and after today, always will be.

"So, what now?" I say as he pulls me in for a hug.

"Well," he says, "I think my mom is definitely watching us through the window."

I let out a laugh and press my forehead against his chest. "Of course."

"Do you want to come inside? Have some food?" he asks.

"I'd love that," I answer. "And then do *you* want to possibly come over and hang out with my dad?"

Ryan zips my jacket up a little higher. "I would want nothing more."

I can't help but beam. Maybe this is all happening too fast, and perhaps it's crazy to jump into something with someone I haven't seen since I was a teenager . . . but it doesn't feel like that at all. If anything, it feels like I'm with the only person who really knows me, in the only place I ever felt like myself.

"Oh." Ryan stops before turning the doorknob. "In case I didn't say it yet, Merry Christmas, Elle."

I pull him in for another kiss, something I will be doing at every chance I get. "Merry Christmas, Ryan."

9

SKIPPING CHRISTMAS

Rebekah Weatherspoon

As the final notes of "Sleigh Ride" play through my speakers, I shut off my car with a groan, thankful as Kris Kringle that no one decided to let their friend or their girl just "borrow" my parking spot—which I pay for—overnight. My neck, my hands, and my back protest as I climb out of the driver's seat, the cool California night air reminding me that the day is definitely over and there is nothing but a stop by the mailboxes between me and at least two Christmas cookies, some fresh, hot cocoa, and an even hotter shower.

Every season is a busy season for me. Girls' nights, baby showers, graduation parties, new jobs, first dates, not to mention the routine fill and the inevitable repair. There is no rest for professional nail techs, but with Christmas right around the corner, my schedule is booked solid. Holiday parties, office parties, pictures with the local mall Santa, and don't get me started on all the Christmas Day proposals around the tree. I have to keep my clients' hands looking good for those hard launch moments.

After pulling up the zipper of my oversized pink hoodie, I grab my stuff, triple-checking that I have everything, before my phone vibrates in the back pocket of my jeans. I know exactly who it is: the same person who's been blowing up my phone all day. I tuck my keys into my bag and pull out my phone.

Mommy said I can use her car.

I'll get you from the airport.

I shake my head, stopping in my tracks. It's time to end this once and for all.

Yeah, but how she say it? 😂

I try to keep it light 'cause I know my sister is upset, even though middleman is the job she hired herself for.

She just said I can use her car.

Yeah, and Mom probably rolled her eyes and called me everything including ungrateful, I think to myself. My fingers hover over my phone. I don't need to give my sister a hard time. Amaya is not the problem; our mama is. Amaya knows that better than anyone, but I still need to remind her *why* I moved three thousand miles away. As soon as I got a little bit of my own grown folks' money, I realized pretty quickly I needed to put as much distance between myself and Angelica Wallace as possible. Call it eldest daughter's trauma, but I deserve to spend my Christmas in peace—as well as all three hundred and sixty-four days that come before and after it. I think about what skipping going home would mean and how much I still love my little sister.

What if I fly you out here?

We can do Sister Christmas all cutesy like.

I'll take you to the beach and the mall.

My stomach swoops a little as I hit send, and I know that there's a pretty good chance I might cry, so I should probably get inside. I swap my phone for my keys and let myself into the building. The lobby is empty, but there's someone shuffling around in the mail room, muttering to themselves. I slap on a polite smile, ready to greet whichever of my neighbors is clearly over this day too. I round the corner, then almost swoon and die right on the spot.

It's 2A, aka Girl Dad, aka Pretty Teeth, aka the finest man I've ever seen in my life. He's bent over rearranging a stack of packages against the wall, looking good as always in dark jeans and a black hoodie. Not that he didn't look good all the times I've bumped into him in his brown delivery uniform. He'd look good in rags and even better wrapped in nothing but a bow under my Christmas tree. He spots me and does a double take before he stands to his full height. He flashes me a blinding smile, his perfectly straight teeth gleaming white against his perfectly trimmed facial hair, and I remind myself for the hundredth time that this man is taken and he has a child.

"Hey. How you doing?" he says, his voice silky and deep.

I want to close the distance between us and cup his cheek as I explain just how good we could be together. As soon as I learn his actual name.

"Hey! They got you stacking boxes on your day off?" A safe, corny reply.

He laughs and adjusts the last two boxes carelessly dropped on the floor. "Nah. Quit that gig, but I still can't stand when buddy comes in here and just tosses things everywhere."

"I don't think it's him, actually," I say, easing toward my mailbox. "It's those kids in 3D. I've caught them knocking stuff all over the place in here before."

"Ah, makes sense." He stands again, gripping a box this time, the relief on his face clear. Those little punks didn't steal his stuff.

"Christmas present for little miss mamas?" I say, nodding toward the box in his hand.

The smile on his face drops for just a second before he clears his throat and smiles at me again. It's different, though. A little tighter, like he's embarrassed.

"Nah—um—her mother and I aren't together anymore," he says.

"Ah, I'm sorry." I see him with his little girl all the time, and she adores him. "Stuck splitting the holidays now? Mom gets Christmas, you get her for the Rose Parade?"

"Uh, no. Jaeda's not mine. Bria got back with Jaeda's dad right before Halloween. They moved out."

Two months? Have I really not seen his girlfriend—his ex—or the baby in almost two months?

"And that's what I get for minding *your* business." I shift uncomfortably.

He laughs, a warm, genuine sound. "It's okay."

"I'm really sorry."

He lifts one shoulder in a sexy shrug. "Better now, while Jaeda's young, than years from now, when she has solid memories."

"Oh man, that's bleak. Too bleak for Christmastime."

"It is what is," he says before he leans down. I watch him as he reaches for another box and try not to freak out when he hands the box to me. "Ashley, right?"

"Yeah, that's me." I take the box, ignoring the way my cheeks feel all hot suddenly. "I have to admit, I don't know your name."

My friends and I have mostly been calling him 2A or Sexual Chocolate, which I don't think is appropriate for this current conversation.

"Micah." He smiles a bit wider, and suddenly all I want to do is sing *Ashley and Micah, sittin' in a tree . . .*

"Nice to meet you, Micah."

"You're friends with Kendra in 3J, right? She told me your name after you let me know my tire was flat." That was over a year ago. "I meant to thank you properly; I was busy with the kid and work."

"Oh, no worries. Nothing worse than being in a hurry and coming out to a flat," I reply, and then I realize we've breached the small-talk bubble. I'm about to give him the ole *weeelp* when he speaks.

"You got plans for Christmas?"

"Not much, just gonna chill," I say.

"I like that." He nods, and I think we should make out right here, right now, since he's single and all.

"Actually, I'm lying," I confess. "I'm gonna bake and get real cozy and watch Christmas movies." I do keep the part where I already bought pink footy pajamas to wear through it all to myself.

"Not spending it with family?" he asks.

"No. I'm from Boston, and I'm only taking a few days off. Doesn't make sense to fly there and back." I also don't tell him that my mom and I can't go more than five minutes without having an argument and that's no way to spend the most wonderful time of the year. "What about you? You're from here, right?"

"Nah, I'm from the Bay. My dad and I don't really see eye to eye on anything, so there's no need for me to get into all that."

"Well, if you're around and you want some cookies, you know where to find me," I reply, realizing immediately that I definitely just offered this man my cookies.

"Actually, I don't. You're on three, but—"

"Oh. 3C."

"I might take you up on that," he says. I know he's just being polite, so it's definitely time to go. I'll check my mailbox later.

"All right, well, night." I'm really calm and cool as I turn around and practically sprint up the stairs to my apartment. I kick my shoes off at the door, toss my stuff on the couch, and pull out my phone. Amaya hasn't responded to my text yet, so I text Kendra instead.

I just ran into 2A!

He's single!

I repeat! He's single!

Kendra's already in Tulum with her parents and her man for the holidays, but family trips have never stopped her from texting me back.

Girl! Now's your chance!

Go sit on his face!

I did invite him to drop by for some of my cookies.

I give him an hour before he's breaking down your door.

Your cookies are delicious and I'm sure he'll like your baking too.

You're nasty and correct. 😂

It's all jokes and wishful thinking. Still, Kendra and I spend a little too much time joking about how Micah and I belong together, speculating on a scientific level as to why he and Jaeda's mom broke up, and then joking again about how I should show up at his door Christmas morning in nothing but a smile and a mistletoe headband. He's so nice to look at, and from the little I know about him he does seem like a good boyfriend and a good father figure, but I've been burned by a good-looking man before, and for all we know his ex ran for the hills because he's secretly a bum, or worse, a creepy weirdo. I'll keep it cute and casual, and let him stay right where he belongs: in my box of fantasies.

When I finally say good night to Kendra, the high from my run-in with 2A has worn off. I get ready for bed, taking one last look at my first client's request for tomorrow morning. Fresh full set, switching from coffin tips to almond with snowflakes and candy canes. I got this.

Just as I'm about to shut things down for the night, I swear I hear something at my door. My heart slams against my ribs, and all I can think about is Kendra's dad raging about how we both need to get pit bulls. I grab the baseball bat I keep near my bed and creep toward the door. There's definitely someone out there, lingering. I swallow, waiting for the knob to turn so I can really practice my swing. I suck in a breath, my fingers tightening on the handle. I brace myself for the jump scare of a lifetime and look through the peephole.

"The hell?" I whisper to myself. "Micah?!" I say a little louder. Loud enough for him to hear me. He freezes and takes a step back. Of course he's wearing a tight black tank top that's hugging his pecs and showing off his perfect arms. The plaid pajama pants are slung low on his hips. It's a sinful look, but it doesn't change the fact that he's lurking outside my door, possibly planning to eat my skin with his Christmas dinner.

"Ashley. Sorry. Hey. I thought you might be asleep."

"Yeah, that's— What are you doing?"

He holds up a folded piece of paper with a little piece of tape on it. "I realized I didn't have your number."

I freeze. "You want my number?"

He relaxes, that damned smile spreading across his face. I appreciate that he's looking down and not staring into my soul through the peephole. "I know it's kinda late, but I'm gonna go grab a tree tomorrow, and I wanted to see if you had one already. But I don't have your number. So I was gonna leave you a note." He laughs, embarrassed.

"Well, as long as you weren't planning on breaking and entering," I joke. "Your number is in the note?" I ask.

"Yeah."

"Okay. I'll grab it in the morning."

"All right. Good night."

"Night." I watch as he successfully tapes the note up and I try not to giggle as he waves his goodbye before heading down the hall. I listen for his footsteps heading down the stairs, then wait another full minute before I open the door, clutching the bat in my other hand. The hall is empty, and the note is still hanging there. I snatch it and dart back inside. With the door locked behind me, I flick on the kitchen light. I scan the note like it's holding the key to life.

I was thinking about picking up a tree tomorrow.
Wanna come? Or I can grab you one and help you put it up.
—Micah 2A

I look at his number scrawled in his blessedly legible handwriting before I scurry back to my bedroom like a squirrel with the freshest peanut. Grabbing my phone, I dive under my covers. I can't believe this is happening. 2A, sexy father of one, is now Micah, sexy single man with no children who has just given me his phone number and wants to do cute stuff like run holiday errands together. Do I text him now or wait until tomorrow? Do I hit up Kendra and dissect every millisecond of what just happened at my door? I decide to go the cool, logical route. I text Micah because I cannot go to sleep horny and curious.

U up?

It's Ashley.

He responds right away.

My bad. Again.

Daylight approach next time.

I promise.

I'd appreciate it.

I don't have a tree and I'd like one.

Can I ask, though, why did you guys break up?

Short version, we wanted different things.

Different things, like more kids and a move to Oregon

Or different things like you cheated?

Damn. Do I come off like that?!

I don't know!

I'm asking! 😩😂

Suddenly, my phone rings in my hand. I panic and almost drop it. I know hitting decline is an option. A voice call requires an appointment or at the very least an engagement ring. Still, I hit accept and put the call on speaker.

"Hey." God, his voice is sexy. I can't help but wonder if he's lying in bed, like I am. "I wanna answer your question, but it's a lot to type."

"Sure. Go ahead," I reply, bracing myself for an elaborate bullshit excuse. He's too fine to be a good guy. The universe just isn't that generous, even during the holiday season.

"We met when Jaeda was just six months old. I thought Bria was just going through a rough time, so I was cool with the ups and downs. Things started to get better, for both of us, but she starts picking weird fights when nothing is going on. Yelling at me for getting the wrong diapers and formula when I got the exact kind she wanted. Meeting me at my truck when I'm out on my route, but just to watch me, like I'm cheating. Shit like that. Again, I'm trying to just understand what's going on with her. But I start saving up, getting ready to get us a house, get her a ring, to prove to her I'm serious. That's when she tells me she's been talking to Bria's dad and she's moving back in with him. I realized she just liked drama, so I didn't fight it. They left, and now I'm taking the money I saved up to go to veterinary school. I start in January. I've always wanted to work with animals. She hates animals, so that should have been the first sign we weren't gonna make it."

"Wow," I say, trying to rerun his words through my head, searching for red flags, but it sounds pretty cut-and-dried. People don't work out all the time, and vet school seems like a great idea.

"Yeah."

"That sounds awful. I didn't mean to dig that up. I'm sure you miss Jaeda a lot. She's a sweetie."

"I do, but there's nothing I can do. She's not my kid."

"Still, I'm sorry you went through that," I say, staring down at the phone screen.

After a beat, he continues, "I was thinking about drowning my Christmas day sorrows in back-to-back NBA coverage, but then I ran into you and I figured I don't have to give up on Christmas 'cause I ain't got nobody."

"I *did* offer you cookies." I laugh and Micah's warm chuckle joins mine through the speaker. "I don't have a tree yet, but I have to work all day tomorrow. My last client is at seven."

"What do you do?"

"I'm a nail tech. NailsByAshleyLove," I say, bragging a little. I'm really good at my job.

"Oh, all right." He sounds impressed. "Well, I'll grab you a tree and you let me know when you're back from work. I'll come set it up for you."

I search my gut for more red flags, but none pop up. "Okay." *Why not?*

We talk for a few more minutes then say our goodbyes, and I'm left wondering what the hell just happened—again. I plug my phone into the charger before I fall asleep with this completely goofy smile on my face.

With the time difference, it's too late for me to call Amaya when I get off the next day, but her last text was enough to end the conversation.

Mommy would kill me if I skipped Christmas to come chill with you.

I'll fly out for St Patrick's Day.

It's the answer I was expecting, still I find myself wishing things were different. I never want to argue with my mom again, but I miss my sister. I let myself into the building and actually grab my mail this time. Up in my apartment I look at the texts Micah sent earlier in the day.

Tree secured.

I can bring it by tonight.

Or tomorrow.

LMK.

I sent a thumbs-up and a smiley face back hours ago, and now I need to decide if I want this man in my apartment right now or if I really should wait. If the answer is tonight, I need to decide if I answer the door in a thong and a crop top or if he gets to see the more relaxed version of me who has been waiting all week to get into my new footy pajamas. I quickly wash up, because I definitely feel like I've been at work all day, and then I send the text, my mind made up.

I'm home.

You can bring it up now if you're around.

Micah responds before I can even lock my phone.

On my way.

I do the normal things when you're expecting company at 10 p.m.—turn on the TV and make it look like I was already relaxing in my pink snowflake jammies, pull out the rest of the decorated sugar cookies I made the other day and put them on a cute little plate. Try not to rethink the thong idea. And definitely try not to freak out when I hear a knock at the door. It was fine when Micah was just 2A, taken and completely untouchable. But now he has a name, he's single, and he's bought me a tree. Who knows, he might ask me to marry him tonight. It's a lot of change all at once. A lot of pressure.

I open the door, instantly confused by what's waiting for me in the hallway. It's Micah with a really big box.

"I like the getup," he says, looking me up and down with a smile.

"I like to be cute and cozy. What is that?"

"Your tree. Can I come in?" Right, it's LA freezing and he's in jeans and T-shirt.

"Oh, right."

I move out of the way and try not to stare too hard at the way his back muscles look as he lugs the thing inside. He sets the box on my living room floor, face up so I can see the label. A fake tree was not what I had in mind.

"I thought you were gonna go all rustic. Drive up to Big Bear and cut me down the real thing," I tease, kinda.

"I thought about it, but then I got to the tree lot. Shit was picked over. I got this sad-looking Charlie Brown looking thing for my place. Here." Micah pulls up his phone and shows me the saddest-looking piece of evergreen draped in lights and like three bulb ornaments next to his TV.

"Oh, that is pathetic." I laugh.

"I—uh—looked you up on Instagram last night, and sad and shabby didn't seem like it fit your vibe. I might be wrong, but I think you like pink."

I look down at my footy pajamas and then around at the rest of my apartment. Pink and white everywhere. My nail studio is exactly the same, and I'm wearing pink in almost all of my posts. I glance down at the artificial pink tree that comes with its own twinkling white lights.

"Plus, you don't have to keep it alive."

"Micah, it's been like an hour, and I don't appreciate how well you're getting to know me."

"My bad." He laughs and taps the box. "I can take it back to the store or you can have a seat and let me set it up for you."

"I mean, I guess." I playfully roll my eyes before I fall back on the couch and enjoy the show.

He works in efficient silence and has the tree up and

shining in no time. It looks perfect in the corner by my windows, and so does he as he steps back and looks at his handiwork.

"There. What do you think?"

"I love it. How much do I owe you?"

"Nothing. Unless you still have some of those cookies you mentioned."

"I do." I hop off the couch and ignore the way it feels to have Micah following close behind me as we move into the kitchen. He doesn't hesitate to wash his hands, which I appreciate. I grab the plate of cookies and show off *my* handiwork.

"You decorated these, didn't you?" he asks as he grabs one of the elaborate snow globe cookies I spent way too much time on.

"I did, and I made the dough from scratch."

He takes a bite and I feel that thrill of pride 'cause he's clearly fighting a moan.

"Damn, these are good. *You're* good," he adds before he takes another bite.

I feel my face go hot. I'm happy to accept the compliment, but I need some clarity. "What do you mean?"

"I was on your account for a while last night. You're talented. It's impressive. I kept going back to all the Halloween nails you posted. For real. You're *good*."

"My mom thinks I'm wasting my time. Part of the reason I'm not going home. I'm doing pretty well for myself and I don't need her trying to convince me I'm not."

"What does she think you should be doing?"

"Taking over her salon back home. I moved out here to do hair for movies. She thought I was gonna meet some celebrity and become their main stylist, and she'd really have something to brag about. I just wanted to do hair, but I've always done nails and lashes as a side hustle. It was hard to break into the industry, so I did nails to support myself while I looked for movie work."

"It looks like it's working out so far," he adds, reaching for another cookie. It's cute as hell the way he studies the plate before snatching up a frosted wreath.

"It is, and I do have celebrity clients. I just don't tell her that."

"My dad is still pissed that I didn't make it to the league. I got one good concussion and decided I was done, but he thinks the paycheck was worth getting my brains scrambled. He wasn't impressed when I started delivering packages."

"Do you miss playing?" I ask, my mind making more sense of his amazing physique.

Micah shakes his head. "I needed time to figure out something I could be good at and something I actually want to do. I was good at football. I didn't care about playing. It's why I'm excited about vet school. Treating animals, being there for their owners, that's something I *want* and something I think I'd be good at."

"I think you will be too." I think about stepping into a vet's office with my injured dog or sick cat and coming face-to-face with Micah's fine self. Animal and human would instantly feel better. I try to cover my snort of laughter, but it melts into a yawn. "Sorry."

He leans over the sink and dusts a few crumbs from his fingertips. "Let me get out of here."

"You're good. I always take Mondays off. I don't have to be up early."

"What are you gonna do with your day off?" he asks.

You, I hope. "I'm definitely going to sleep in, and then I'm gonna take my Christmas tips from my clients and do some shopping for myself. There's this bag I've been eyeing at the mall. You wanna come?" I say before I can stop myself.

"If you'll let me take you out to dinner after."

My whole body goes hot. There's neighborly behavior, there's even a little flirting, but I have to be sure *this* is what I think it is.

"Like a date?"

"Yeah, like a date."

My cheeks get even hotter. "We can do that."

"Cool. I'll let you get some sleep and we can reconnect tomorrow."

"Okay." My voice sounds all light and giggly. Micah gathers all the trash from the tree packing, and I send him off with two more cookies in packaging. His arms are full, so we can't dry hump or anything before he heads out the door, but he does lean down and kiss me on the cheek before he leaves me with a soft and sexy "good night." Skipping the Christmas trip home might be my best move yet.

By the time we make it into the mall parking deck, it's clear letting Micah drive was the way to go. He's clearly learned how to whip around heavy machinery after all those years and it's kinda sexy watching as he smoothly navigates through all the holiday traffic. I get to see that he keeps his truck clean and it smells so good, just like him. He has good taste in music. He's easy to talk to, and I can tell he's okay with a comfortable silence too. Nothing worse than a guy who can't stop talking. But he also has the patience of a saint and I tell him so.

"You're better than me," I say as we wait for an elderly couple to back out of a parking space, going exactly one millimeter an hour.

"Got a little road rage?" he says with a warm laugh. He swings into the vacant spot near the top of the parking lot. There's so much traffic and the place is packed.

"I would have lost it back on Fairfax. Maybe the mall two days before Christmas was a bad idea."

"Nah, we gotta get your bag."

"Just so we're clear. You're along for the emotional support and your distractingly good looks. Not to buy me anything."

His eyebrows shoot up. "Distracting?"

"I mean, I plan on pulling a Christmas heist. I need a sexy accomplice."

"Is that right? How can I help with your heist if I'm too busy looking at you?" he replies.

On the inside, I melt. "Well, I guess we'll rob the place another time."

Micah shakes his head, the corner of his mouth tipping up in a sexy smile. "Come on, kingpin."

Micah comes around to the passenger side of the truck and opens my door. I take his hand as he helps me down and decide to roll with it when he doesn't let go until we make it to the crowded escalators. He guides me in front of him, hands off but still close. He sticks right behind me as we make our way through the mob-filled mall. The whole place is decorated, string lights above leading from the parking structure to the Santa and reindeer that look like they are going to fly right into the marquee on the front of the movie theater. The singing fountain is in full swing and spray, and Stevie Wonder's voice fills the air. I spot Santa's

Workshop set up about halfway down the outdoor mall. The line is massive. Why wouldn't it be? It's a little bit of chaos, but I still love it. I almost turn to Micah to let him know, but we have to keep moving.

When we finally make it into the store, Micah follows me over to the first display. "Is it weird that I love this?" I say.

"The world of handbags? No, I think a lot of women like handbags." He looks around like he's seriously considering their choice of light fixtures.

"No." I laugh. "I mean the holiday crush. The madness. I've been working so much, the baking is really the only Christmasy thing I've done. I miss the thrill of almost getting trampled while listening to 'Jingle Bells.'"

"Good thing I made reservations for us to see Santa himself. You can tell him all about your holiday-themed *step on me* kink," he says.

"You did?"

"I thought it was worth a try. I checked before we left and there was a spot available." He double-checks the time on his phone. "In thirty minutes. You need more time to shop?"

"No," I say, feeling a little breathless. My friends can be sweet and spontaneous, but this feels different. "I see the bag I want; it's over there."

"Okay. Well, we have time. Show me what's good here. I'm used to diaper bags. Give me a fashion lesson."

"Okay." We make it two feet before a sales associate swoops in and offers their assistance. I stake my claim on the caramel-brown pebbled leather shoulder bag that's been calling my name for the last few months. My new best friend, Jeffrey, has a fresh one brought down for me. While we wait, I show Micah all the wallets and wristlets I've been eyeing as well.

"These are so cute, but a little pricey," I say, showing him one of their most expensive bag charms, cute gold-plated teddy bear. I want it, I definitely deserve it, but I want to save some money for my sister's St. Patrick's Day trip.

Micah takes the bag charm out of my hand, testing the weight and looking at the price tag. "That's a lot of gas money," he says before he winks at me and gently hangs it back on the rack.

"Yup. I don't need it. It's just cute," I say, just as the man who disappeared upstairs returns with my fresh, untouched, gorgeous new handbag. We follow Jeffrey to the register kiosk, and Micah checks twice to make sure that I don't want him to pay for my bag. He doesn't give me a hard time as we walk toward the exit, and I can't stop smiling at the large shopping bag in my hand.

"Feel good?" he says.

I look up at him, grinning even wider. "I do. I worked hard for this."

"I could see. The proof's all over your Instagram. Come on." He takes my hand again and leads me back outside. He doesn't let go this time, and I think it's for the best, considering that I'm practically floating. I got my bag, and I'm with a real sexy—and, I'm starting to see, real thoughtful—man, and we're on our way to see Santa. Things are pretty good.

The line moves quickly and I can't help but cackle when Micah greets the mall Santa like they're good friends and this old white man dressed like North Pole's finest stands and daps Micah up like they are old football buddies.

"This beautiful lady must be Ashley." The reservations really help keep the magic alive.

"That's me."

"Old neighbor, new friend," Micah says, like he's about to tell Santa that the only thing he wants for Christmas is for us to be more.

"Hmmm," Santa says with an impressed nod. "I'm a happily married man, but if I were you, I'd upgrade this to more than friends before New Year's Eve." He taps his watch.

"Dang, Santa!" I burst out laughing. "It's our first date!"

Mall Santa shrugs. "I calls 'em like I sees 'em. Now you two crazy kids get in here and let's make some first date memories."

I have no idea who this guy really is, but I hope they are paying him one million dollars.

I think I like Micah. We stop at my door, this pretty perfect night coming to an end, and I know I want a second date. And I definitely want him to kiss me. Dinner was perfect. Our pictures with Santa turned out hilarious and adorable, and Micah made me feel comfortable and like he's interested in really getting to know me. I can feel his eyes on me as I dig out my keys.

"How many clients you have tomorrow?" he asks, his voice all sexy and low.

"More than I should for Christmas Eve. I should be done around six."

"Oh, all right. Well, Christmas Eve or Christmas Day might be a little heavy for a second date, but I'll be around and I would like to see you."

"Mmmm. Well, since we'll both be around and I'd like to see you, too, maybe we can grab something real fancy like pizza and watch a Christmas movie. We can even do a little gift exchange. Ten-dollar limit."

"That's like two dozen eggs." Micah laughs.

"Hey, I'll take free eggs. Just a little something so it'll still feel like Christmas around my little pink tree."

"We can do that," Micah says, his voice dropping even lower. I watch his gaze as it drops to my mouth, and, like a desperate invitation, my tongue peeks out and wets my lower lip. It's all the hint he needs, and he takes it.

Micah leans closer and then we're kissing. His lips are perfect, full and soft. I feel the trimmed hairs of his mustache, and it makes me want to kiss him deeper, so I do. My tongue slips out again, and he meets me where I'm at immediately, his relaxed but focused mouth playing with mine. He's good in bed, I just know. I want to find out for sure and at the same time, I don't want to rush it. It's fresh. He's my neighbor. I'll take a slow burn any day if there's a chance that this all just gets better and better, if there's a chance I can keep him.

A moan slips out of me, muffled by his mouth as he gently backs me against the door frame. Suddenly, I'm picturing what his tongue would feel like between my legs and I know we need to stop. I press my hand to his chest, meaning to push him away, but my fingers grip his T-shirt, pulling him closer, and then his knee is between my thighs, pressing the denim of my jeans and the cotton of my panties against my soaking, swollen center. I pull back with a gasp, letting my forehead drop to his shoulder. He kisses my temple, my cheek, and I know we need to stop because the rest of our neighbors are just as nosy as I am and the whole third floor doesn't need to hear me come on his leg.

"I'm gonna wait," he whispers, his lips brushing my ear, making me shiver. "But if you think about us tonight while you're touching yourself . . ." He lets the words hang in the breath between us. I. Am. In trouble. I look at his dark eyes and I'm so close to inviting him inside, so close to begging him to come with me. Instead, I just nod, letting him know that touching myself is exactly what I'm going to do.

"Go on," he says.

I hate being ordered around, but this time I'll allow it. I kiss him one more time before I turn and let myself into my apartment.

❄

It's been a while since I had *someone* to look forward to, and this time, it's Christmas! I lock up my studio space and like I'm starring in my very own holiday rom-com, I practically skip back to my car, humming the tune to Frosty's magical journey through small-town life. I have Kendra's and Amaya's blessings. My best friend desperately wants me to sleep with Micah. She needs to know if he lives up to the legends we've created about the man in 2A. I can't lie: So far, he's exceeding them.

Once I send Amaya a picture of the pictures we took with Santa, she's convinced the universe left us both alone and without a friend on Christmas so we could smooch each other. I think the universe is busy with more important things, but maybe she's onto something.

I blast my Christmas playlist all the way to the store where I scoop up Micah's gift, and then I blast it even louder as I make my way home, thinking of the perfect thing to wear for our night in. I pull into my parking space, then send Micah a text.

I'm back.

Gonna freshen up and throw in a batch of cookies.

I'll teach you about royal icing this time.

He's pretty quick with texting back, so I'm sure I'll hear from him by the time I get up to my place. I drop my phone into the center pocket of my new caramel-brown pebbled leather shoulder bag and make my way inside. A quick stop at the mail room and then I head upstairs. I'm showered and almost done getting dressed when Micah responds.

Ordering dinner now.

I'll be up in a few.

I do the most: fresh makeup and a skintight sleep romper with long sleeves that does absolutely nothing to hide my curves, especially the cleft between my legs. After I step into my fuzzy slippers and put on the mistletoe headband I found at the checkout, I head into the kitchen to preheat the oven and get my sugar cookie dough ready for rolling. I'm putting Micah to work icing and decorating. Right on time, just after I've turned on my perfect pink Christmas tree, there's a knock on the door. I stop myself from ripping it off its hinges as I move to let him in. I slide a seductive hand to my hip, but as soon as I see the look on Micah's face, the *HO HO HO* dies on my lips.

"Hey," I say cautiously.

"Hey. You look good. Damn." Micah leans down and lightly kisses me on the lips. Things are still fresh and new, but I like it. I'd like it a lot more if something weren't clearly bothering him.

"Come on in. What's going on?"

"Nothing," he groans. Clearly, it's not nothing. He steps out of his sneakers and scrubs his hand over his face. "Actually, it's something. I want to talk to you about it, but I don't want it to kill the mood or Christmas."

"Are you dying? Did you cheat on me already?"

"No," he says with a dry chuckle.

"Here, come sit down." We move to the living room and I notice then that he has a small gift bag in his hand. Setting it down on the coffee table, he takes a seat, dwarfing my pink couch. I sit down beside him, sliding into his personal space, where the cushions dip under our weight. I can feel the warmth and the stress coming off him. "What's going on?" I try again.

He sighs then turns to face me. "I had to block Bria today."

"Okay," I say with a cringe. "What happened?"

"She just sent me a video from Jaeda, saying that she misses me. It was weird and it pissed me off."

"Ugh, I'm sorry."

"I'm sure Jaeda misses me on some level, but I'm not her dad and it's better if she has space to forget about me. I do not want to have any relationship with her mom."

"Yeah, I can't imagine how tricky that is," I reply. There's a small siren sounding in the back of my mind, and I'm praying it doesn't get louder as this conversation goes on. "I have to be honest."

"Yeah?"

"I don't—I don't want drama with Bria. I like you. I'm starting to like you a lot, but I'm not a drama girl. I like to keep things cute, light, and breezy. That's why I don't want to live near my mom. Her middle name is drama."

"No, that's why I like you. I don't want that either. And that's why I blocked her. I was having a good day. Got back from scooping up your gift for eight dollars and seventy-eight cents after taxes. I want to eat you and your cookies," he says, a little smile finally peeking out.

"Micah," I tease, pressing a scandalized hand to my cleavage. "Please. Santa can probably hear you."

"He knows what I'm about. I want to say something, and I don't want it to sound fucked-up."

"Go for it."

"The last two years have been . . . not good, but something shifted, like right when you admitted that you didn't know my name. I never wanted to step out on Bria, but that didn't stop me from noticing you. Noticing your smile every time I saw you. When I ran into you the other day, it felt like there was a reason I didn't move out right when Bria left and I should have. I don't need a two bedroom, but something told me to stick around. I know it's big talk for date two, but that's just how I feel. I'm moving on in all the other important ways and it was important for me to move on and meet someone like you."

I swallow, sudden raw emotion clogging my voice. He's said everything I've been thinking. It's new, but it's been two years, really. For two years I've been wishing I could find someone kind and thoughtful like him, someone who wants to know me and take care of me in all the ways I'll let him.

"Me or someone like me?" I ask.

"You. The cookies are really good and I want to know about the chemistry of acrylic and adhesive glue, and I still wanna see the sketchbooks you mentioned last night at dinner. I don't want *Bria* to mess that up, no matter how much I miss the kid."

"Okay," I reply. "So we won't." I stand from the couch and go to grab his gift off the kitchen counter, shutting off the oven on my way back. Those cookies will have to wait. I hand him the gift bag, then sit back down, closer this time, so my knee is pressed against his thigh. With his strong grip, he shifts me so my legs are draped over his lap. "It was seven dollars and thirty-eight cents after tax."

I watch Micah's face as he pulls a cheap stethoscope out of the bag. "I don't think that thing is truly medical grade, but I think vets use them. You can keep it as a reminder of where you're trying to go while you're in school."

His brows pull together as he nods. "Thank you."

"Sure," I say.

He reaches toward the table and hands me the gift he brought. "It's nothing much."

I take it, shocked at how heavy it is. Reaching inside, I freeze as soon as my hand brushes the cool metal. I pull out the gold-plated teddy bear bag charm and cradle it in my palm.

"Um, I think this is over the ten-dollar limit. You went *back* to the mall?"

Micah shrugs. "I think you're worth it."

I shift my weight until I'm straddling his lap. I lean in to kiss him, slowly, sinfully, shivering as Micah wraps his hands around my waist. This is definitely not where I thought a trip to the mailboxes would lead me, but I have to thank Santa with all my heart, and all the sprinkles still waiting in my pantry, for bringing this man to me. I may never go home for Christmas again.

10

HOLIDAY BLACKOUT

Susan Lee

CHAPTER ONE

"Tell me you're not still at work."

"Are you asking me to lie to you, Mom?"

Yoona could hear the concern and exasperation in her mom's voice. It was no secret to her family she was a workaholic, usually the first to come into the office and the last to leave. Which often meant she'd show up late to family events, if at all.

But this was Christmas Eve and she had used up her can't-make-it hall pass on Thanksgiving when her boss called her with an emergency that required Yoona in the office to run some data analysis. That night, she settled for eating a turkey dinner plate, delivered from the local diner, alone at her desk.

"Yoona, need I remind you that there is an extreme weather warning? The snow is already really coming down over here. What's it like in the city?"

"It's fine. I'm fine. I only have a little left to do and then I'll be on my way. Don't worry," Yoona said. "I'll call you when I get to the station. And don't send Dad to pick me up. I'll grab a taxi." If the snow was already coming down in Jersey, she did not want her parents driving on slicked roads. "Love you, see you soon."

Yoona had been so consumed with work she hadn't bothered to check the updated weather forecast. She'd heard on the morning news as she was getting ready for the day that "The Big One" was going to hit the tristate area. But morning weather reporters always overreacted. And it sounded like they didn't think it would hit until after the evening commute anyway.

She looked at her phone. 8:22 p.m. Okay, so, everyone was likely gone already.

Yoona, however, had a mountain of work to do before year-end reports were published. If she didn't do it now, she'd be stressing about it every day, likely ruining not only her own, but everyone else's holidays too.

She took out her earphones and turned her desk chair around to look out the window. It was dark other than the streetlights and a few warmly lit apartments of those who stayed in town. How had she not noticed the sky turning to black? And the streets—they were blanketed in snow. When did that happen? Yoona looked down the road to the left and then to the right. The snow was falling hard and fast, and she could see the wind blowing the flakes every which direction from the rays of the streetlights.

It would have felt idyllically peaceful, a scene from a painting, if it weren't so eerie. Something was off about its stillness. It was completely empty. No one was walking. No one was driving. The streets were void of people, cars, taxis, or plows. The snow on the ground untouched on both the sidewalks and roads. She'd never seen the absence of life and movement in all the years she'd lived in New York.

It was either the zombie apocalypse, or everyone except Yoona had heeded the warning and gotten out of town to hunker down somewhere before it was too late.

Maybe she should pack up and go just to be safe.

She just needed to check one thing.

She walked to the door of her office and opened it, peeking her head out. No one. The lights were all off, except for one.

He was still here. And that settled it.

If Ian Young was staying, so was Yoona.

Of course he was working late. Nights that Yoona stayed until she couldn't keep her eyes open any longer, he'd still be around. She wouldn't say it was a competition. But she wouldn't not say it either.

She'd met Ian during the new hire orientation at Wire One Technology, Yoona's first job out of grad school. She clocked him right away despite being the most nervous she'd been in her whole life starting a new job. Tall, lean, dressed in a slightly ill-fitted navy suit, which, at the time to Yoona, seemed like overkill for their first day. He was stone-faced, serious, furiously taking notes, and she could see that he was angling to be the most successful of them all. She was intrigued, endeared even, and if she was being honest with herself, smitten. Yes, he was handsome. But he was also a challenge.

Because Yoona, herself, had determined to be the most likely to succeed.

But Ian didn't show any interest in Yoona. In fact, he seemed to have no interest in anything other than work. He quickly became one of the hardest and smartest workers at the company.

It had been three years since, and both Yoona's and Ian's

careers were on the rise. Each had been awarded multiple promotions, led their own respective teams, and moved from the land of cubicles into coveted private offices. She barely spoke to him other than the occasional awkward greeting when getting into the same elevator or simultaneously reaching for a mug in the employee kitchen.

Except for that one time.

But Yoona tried very hard to forget that particular night.

For a brief moment, Yoona wondered if she should go to his office and warn him about the weather. Instead, she crept back to her desk and dove back into the mountain of data in front of her, promising herself she'd stay for just one more hour. Ian Young be damned.

❄

Ian rubbed his eyes trying to clear away the blur. He'd been staring at this same report on his screen for hours now, examining and reexamining every line of data to find any errors. If he had known managing a team of direct reports basically meant his job would become checking and fixing their work, he might have considered passing up the role.

But being promoted to management after just three years with the company was a big deal. If only he hadn't had to share that moment with Yoona Cho. In fact, every win he'd had professionally in his short career since moving to New York from Korea seemed to be alongside her. He wouldn't call her a nemesis, or a competitor either. More just a nuisance.

One he'd tried hard to forget—especially after that night.

Ian set his glasses down and looked out the window. The snow was coming down hard, and the streets were quieter than he'd ever seen. People with lives outside of work, holiday traditions and families and friends to celebrate with, were likely all tucked in their homes enjoying Christmas Eve.

Ian didn't have any of that waiting for him. His whole family lived on the other side of the world, and he'd only gone back once since he moved here by himself ten years ago for school. So, no, he was not in a rush to leave the office. In fact, holidays were the perfect time for Ian to get a head start on his colleagues who took time off. It's how he got ahead—no rest, no distractions. Just work.

If only Yoona would get the memo and finally go home. How long did she plan to be here?

It didn't matter. Because however late she stayed at work, he would stay later.

CHAPTER TWO

It was well after 9 p.m. when Yoona decided to finally give in, finish for the night, and make the trek across the bridge to visit her family, excuses and apologies at the ready. She pressed save on all her work and started to pack up her things. She stood up, her back protesting after being hunched at her desk for hours. Just as she stretched her arms in the air to relieve some of the tension, the harsh overhead lighting flickered once, then twice, and suddenly everything shut off, the echo of a loud electrical zap ringing in her ears. Yoona was enveloped in complete darkness.

Shit.

She reached for her phone and turned on the flashlight.

Yoona heard another loud sound, like something heavy dropping, from somewhere outside her office. She knew it was likely Ian. They were the only two here, weren't they? But what if they weren't?

Nope, she would not let her imagination run wild. She would just go and investigate.

She pointed her phone in front of her, hand shaking slightly, and followed the beam of light out into the open space, slowly moving toward Ian's office. She knocked on the door.

"Ian?" she called out. It came out louder than she expected. The darkness seemed to amplify everything—the sound of her voice, the beating of her heart, the echo of silence in the empty office.

She heard a curse and what sounded like the scrape of a chair from the other side of the door. Well, that was confirmation he was in there.

Yoona turned the knob and peeked her head in. "Ian, are you okay? I heard something fall." She didn't know why she thought she'd be able to see anything, it was so dark.

"You scared the shit out of me," he said. "I'm okay. I knocked the paperweight off my desk when I was looking for my phone."

A paperweight? What was he, sixty?

She couldn't place Ian's voice. She scanned his office and found him sitting on the floor next to his desk, back to the window. He squinted at the bright light of her phone and lifted his hand to shield his eyes.

"Sorry," Yoona said, moving the beam off to the side. "You're not hurt or anything, are you? Why are you sitting down there?" Even in shadow, she could see his face looked piqued, scared. His hands were balled in fists by his sides.

"I'm . . ." He hesitated. "Fuck, I just don't do well in the dark."

The admission surprised her. Ian Young was an imposing figure, bigger than most of the other men in the office. He had a take-no-prisoners aura about him. She never would have guessed he was afraid of the dark.

"Okay, well, it looks like the power is out on this entire part of the grid. There's nothing on outside either. I doubt you can get any more work done. Maybe we should leave?"

Ian lowered his head between his knees, wrapping his arms around them, trying to make himself as small as possible.

Yoona had never seen him like this. She rushed over and sat down next to him. "Hey, hey, it's all right. Let's just both call it a night and get out of here. We can use our phones to direct us." She rubbed her hand along his arm, trying to soothe him.

He nodded, then lifted his head and turned to look at her, as if just now realizing it was Yoona in the room with him. She stood up and offered him her free hand. He took it, palm clammy, and rose to standing. He looked over his shoulder out the window. "Shit, you're right, it's off everywhere."

"Where's your phone? It'll be brighter with both of our flashlights on. I don't have a lot of juice left, though." Yoona's phone battery only had twelve percent charge remaining.

Ian felt around all the papers and coffee mugs cluttering his desk. He found his phone and with a couple taps illuminated his light. "Got it," he said, releasing a sigh. "Let's get out of here."

"Okay, let me go get my stuff . . ."

"No." Ian grabbed Yoona's arm. "I mean, I'll come with you. In case, um, your phone dies." Yoona looked down to where he held her. The touch, the pressure, the heat familiar.

She should have forgotten about it by now. She'd wanted to. But sometimes, in the privacy of her own room, when the voices in her head quieted and all she wanted to do was feel, Yoona would think back to the night, two years ago almost to the day, when she had sex with Ian Young.

Ian didn't tell anyone about his night terrors and how in the black of night he'd often wake up in a cold sweat, praying to go back to sleep, to forget the fear. He didn't even know the origin of the terrors or why he was so afraid of the dark. There was just the random panic of an existential void of light. He had various night-lights plugged in around his apartment. His alarm clock was one of the digital ones with huge LED numbers. He even had battery-operated candles he could turn on if all else failed, like the electricity. He should have brought some of those candles to work to keep in his desk. But he never thought he'd get stuck in his office during a blackout, here only with Yoona no less.

He followed her eyes' focus down to where his hand closed almost entirely around her thin arm. It was the first time in two years since he'd touched her. But he remembered, and he thought about it more often than he cared to admit—how soft her skin had been, and how incredible she'd smelled. How her body had formed to his so perfectly. The gasp she'd made when he kissed just below her ear played on repeat in his head.

He loosened his grip now, dropped his hand, and let her go.

"Okay, yeah, we'll go to my office together on the way to the elevator," she said calmly. Of course she'd be calm in a situation like this. Yoona did everything well. She probably wasn't afraid of anything at all. Not like Ian. It felt like he was scared of almost everything—the dark, rats, pimple-popping videos . . . failure.

She led the way, and he followed closely, maybe too closely, behind her.

CHAPTER THREE

The elevators, of course, did not work. The call buttons did not light up, and the display screens were black. Even so, Yoona watched as Ian pressed the button again and again, as if he could will it to work.

She put her hand over his and pushed it away. "Let's take the stairs. It won't be too bad." They were sixteen floors up. They'd have to move carefully with their limited lighting, but they'd be fine.

Except when they got to the stairwell door marked Emergency Exit, it wouldn't open. The locks were supposed to release automatically in an emergency. That should have included a power outage.

"What the heck?" Yoona asked aloud, pulling on the handle one more time. "How come the locks didn't disarm?"

"Old building and new systems don't always work well together. Same reason the air-conditioning always turns off on the hottest day of the summer. Or why the sprinklers randomly spewed water on the finance team last month."

Yoona had forgotten about that. She let out a laugh, remembering their controller in his completely soaked dress shirt, surprising everyone who had seen them—nipple piercings.

"Did you just snort?" Ian asked, a laugh in his own voice, as if remembering the exact same thing.

"This building has always had its own sense of humor, I guess," Yoona said.

Being stuck in the dark notwithstanding.

Ian looked around the hallway searching for another option. "Shit, how long do you think the power will be out?" he asked.

"If we're lucky, there's a fellow workaholic at the power company who handles issues during a weather emergency on Christmas Eve," Yoona said. "But if it's out all over, who knows when they'll get to our block or our building."

The odds seemed stacked against them.

"Yeah, that doesn't sound too likely." Ian sighed. "Looks like we're stuck." He let out a nervous laugh. "No power, no way out, no cell service, even."

"My parents are going to freak out," Yoona said. It all hit her at once, their impossible situation and the ripple effect it would cause. She could imagine the look of panic on her mom's face. The worry in the lines between her dad's eyes. "I have no way of letting them know I'm not coming. What if they go out into the storm to come looking for me? What if they try to drive in these conditions to find me somehow? What if they think the worst happened? What if . . ."

Ian reached his arm out to Yoona and pulled her into him, wrapping his other around her. He laid his chin on her head and held her close. She felt his breath release into her hair.

She froze for a second before melting into his embrace. It should have felt weird. But she couldn't help but let herself go and receive comfort from him.

"Shhhh . . . don't worry," he soothed. "They might freak out for a bit, but they likely have access to more information than we do, and they'll assume you're stuck somewhere safe to ride out the storm. They know you wouldn't take unnecessary risks, so they won't either."

Ian had no idea what her parents would or would not do. And yet his words comforted her. She rested her head against his chest and listened, letting his strong heartbeat calm her own. When she felt more herself and the panic had subsided, she finally pulled away. His arms fell to his sides.

"What about you? Do you have family waiting? Any holiday plans?"

The silence lasted a little too long, and Yoona regretted asking, worried that she'd overstepped.

"We should wait it out in your office," he said. The abrupt change of subject did not go unnoticed. "We'll close the door, try to save as much heat as possible, just in case. I noticed you have a throw blanket on your sofa, which could come in handy. We should also save what little battery power we have left in our phones." His voice shook a little, and Yoona could tell the suggestion had cost him. He was nervous about being back in the dark.

Yoona hadn't even thought about the heat cutting off without the power. Or what a dead phone battery might do to Ian's fears, for that matter. "I think there's an extra flashlight under the sink in the kitchen too. Should we stop there on the way?" she suggested.

"That's a good idea. We can grab some waters and see if there are any snacks left. There also should be an emergency kit under the sink just in case we need it," Ian said.

Ian had moved into manager mode, making plans and giving direction. His voice stronger in this role, more certain. It was incredibly attractive, and Yoona remembered what it was that had drawn her to him in the first place. This Ian, who was both vulnerable with his fear of the dark but competent and capable in a difficult situation despite it.

"Yeah, a kitchen raid sounds like a great plan," she said.

Ian looked down into Yoona's eyes, searching for what, she couldn't tell. She smiled and nodded, letting him know she was ready. He grabbed her hand and led her down the hallway to the kitchen to grab the supplies.

❄

It may not have been entirely necessary, but holding Yoona's hand seemed to steady Ian. They had a plan, and that helped him stop freaking out from the dark. He'd just have to face his fears while in the presence of someone he did not want seeing him at his weakest.

He opened the refrigerator and shined his phone inside. The company regularly stocked drinks and snacks for its employees. He grabbed two water bottles and some juice boxes. He also grabbed the last apple in the bin. He heard Yoona rustle through the snack drawer.

"I'm grabbing this tin of leftover holiday cookies and whatever this is." She looked at the package closer in the limited light. "Goldfish, I think."

"Sounds good," Ian said. "I haven't had those in forever."

"Yeah, you look like you only eat protein and leafy greens," Yoona joked.

"What's that supposed to mean?" Ian couldn't tell if that was a judgment or a jab or both.

"Just that it's obvious you take really good care of your body."

So, she'd noticed his body. He shouldn't like that as much as he did.

Ian had clocked Yoona immediately on their first day of work. Her smile lit up the room, and everyone seemed drawn to her. They'd danced around each other that year, both always the last to leave the office, working long hours and being singularly committed to success. In the beginning, Yoona would often ask if he wanted to order anything for dinner when she was having something delivered. She'd stop by his cubicle on her way out and ask if he was staying much longer. She would bring him coffee from the cart downstairs first thing in the morning.

He was exhilarated by her attention. He was distracted by her affection. But he couldn't afford to lose focus, not with him trying to make it on his own. It had been a scary and lonely time, and he often felt completely overwhelmed. So he lost himself in the work.

And though there was no stopping that one night years ago, Ian saw what would follow, and he knew what he had to do to keep it from going any further.

He shouldn't be surprised, however, that somehow, years later, he found himself once again alone with Yoona.

He was beginning to feel they were inevitable.

CHAPTER FOUR

She didn't have to do it.

In fact, if she could see his face clearly, she was certain Ian would be staring at her in confusion.

But it was Christmas Eve, after all. And at Yoona's house, that meant a family dinner and laughter and love. So even though she was sitting in the dark of a blackout, with a coworker she'd spent a good part of the past two years trying to avoid, only a small beam of a flashlight found in the kitchen between them, she set the table.

She used the pocketknife she carried on her key chain and did her best to cut up the apple. Her mom would have designed it into a flower and arranged a variety of fruit onto a platter. Apple slices on a paper napkin would have to do. She tore open the bag of Goldfish and sprinkled them out onto the coffee table. The leftover holiday cookies stacked into a pyramid was as close to a Christmas tree as she could make it. She placed the bendy straws into the juice boxes, then sat back onto her haunches, taking in the effort.

As good as it was gonna get.

She got up and took a seat next to Ian on the couch.

They sat shoulder to shoulder on the sofa in her office. They were close, but not touching, and yet Yoona swore she felt the heat radiate from Ian's body. He stared down at the makeshift feast she'd put together on the coffee table, not saying a word.

"Look, I know it's silly, but . . . my family always does Christmas Eve dinner, so . . ."

"It's not silly," he said. "I'm sorry you're missing it."

She hadn't expected the sincerity and the kindness in his voice. It made her surprisingly emotional.

"I almost chose to miss it because of work. And now that I can't be there, I guess I'm kicking myself for all the times I didn't make those moments a priority." She took a sip of the juice and put it back down. "I think I'm gonna miss our midnight toast most of all. We always cheers the love we all share just as we ring in Christmas." She cleared her throat and pushed back the regret. "It's cheesy, but it's ours, you know? Anyway, does your family have any holiday traditions?"

"Not really. I don't see my family much. I've been on my own for holidays most of my adult life." Ian's voice was even, steady. Maybe too much so. A simple delivery of information rather than an admission. Yoona didn't want to push. She was so curious about this man she worked with, respected, had crushed on, given herself to, but been ultimately rejected by and tried to avoid since.

"But . . ."

She held her breath, wondering if he was actually going to open up, to share something. A Christmas miracle?

"When I was a kid, we got to open one present at midnight. Which, when you think about it, is wild, making your kid stay awake that late, right? Then, when I was like ten maybe, I caught my dad turning the clocks in the house forward. I guess they made it so midnight could come early for us."

"That's so . . . lovely," she whispered. Yoona looked away. She was surprised to feel a teardrop slide down her cheek. She quickly wiped it, not wanting Ian to know that she cared as much as she did.

❄

Ian saw the tears pool in her eyes as Yoona talked about her family. It surprised him how it brought about his own longing, memories of the family traditions he hadn't been a part of in years. He didn't know why he spoke the memory out loud to Yoona; he just knew he wanted to.

Ian tracked the first tear as it escaped from her eye. His hand itched to reach out, to touch her face, to be the one to wipe it away. Yoona turned from him to hide the emotion. But she'd never been good at that.

From the moment he'd met her, he could see everything she felt on her face. Her steely determination to do well at her new job. Her curiosity in him as they went through orientation together. Her need to challenge him and prove herself every night the two of them worked late. The amusement in her eyes the first time they allowed themselves to flirt with each other at their company holiday party. The desire she felt as they took the elevator up to the hotel room gifted by the company to each of their management team members that night. The ecstasy as she came with him inside her. The confusion when he iced her out because of his own fear of how he felt about her afterward.

Ian looked down at his watch and turned its face toward the glow of the flashlight. 10:27 p.m. He didn't know how much longer they'd be stuck here. But he could try to not make it so terrible for Yoona.

"I have an idea," he said. "Let's do our own midnight toast. I know it's not the same without family, but we should at least keep the tradition for you if we can." He pulled out the small knob on the side of his watch and twisted it forward until the arms landed at 11:59. He turned it toward

Yoona so she could see the time. He passed a juice box to her and grabbed one of his own.

She looked up to him with a smile so warm, he had trouble catching his next breath.

"Wait, before we toast, can you turn it back a few more minutes? We have to keep your tradition too." She looked behind her and then around her office. "What if we each grab something to gift the other person from our offices. Just something silly. Something we can receive and open at midnight."

Ian looked at the door that led to the darkened floor. He wanted to do this for her, but he hesitated. It wasn't just the fear of the dark. It was his fear of allowing himself to want something, someone, beyond the lonely bubble he'd sheltered himself in. Making memories with Yoona would most definitely make it harder to shut her out.

But he nodded and the corner of his mouth curved up. "Okay." He could face his fears and go for it. For her.

"You take the flashlight and your phone," Yoona suggested.

"Meet you back here in ten minutes," he said, and he took off into the dark.

CHAPTER FIVE

It had taken no more than a few minutes before the two met back together in her office, gifts in hand. Yoona noticed that this time, they'd sat down much closer together, thighs and shoulders touching.

Ian held his watch up to the flashlight, showing Yoona

the time. He'd set it back so both the long and short hands of the watch pointed to twelve.

"Ready?" he asked, once more passing her a juice box. "Cheers," he said as he held his up to hers.

"Cheers, Ian." She raised her box to meet his. They each took a sip out of the small straws. "Thank you for this."

He looked at her and held her gaze for what felt like an eternity. Yoona forced herself to look away. She put her drink down on the table and reached for the small package she'd placed beside her.

"Here."

Yoona offered the small gift she'd hastily wrapped in a sheet of printer paper. She'd drawn a holly leaf and berries on the front and written *To Ian* beside them.

He held out both hands as if receiving a most precious present, and something about the gesture was so dear to Yoona.

"It's silly," she said.

He unwrapped it carefully. Inside was the pocketknife she'd used to cut the apples.

"I've had this since I first moved to the city. I almost never use it, but knowing it was on my key chain gave me a sense of security. I thought, well, I thought you might like to keep it . . . to protect you from the things in the dark."

"I . . ." He swallowed. "I can't take this from you."

"I don't need it anymore. I realized a long time ago that I'm working on my own sense of security from within."

The light reflected in his eyes as he stared at her. The intensity of his gaze bore deep into hers, and she wondered what he was trying to find, what he read when he looked at her. "Thank you," he said.

"Plus, I carry pepper spray with me now."

Ian threw his head back and laughed. She had once watched this man come during sex, but this, this still might have been the sexiest thing she'd ever seen.

A smile lingered on his lips as he stood to get the brown lunch sack he'd placed on her desk. He looked back over his shoulder at her and hesitated.

"Um, now I'm not so sure I want to give this to you. There weren't a lot of options in my office. It's pretty boring." Ian so rarely seemed unsure about anything. Yoona quickly stood and walked to him.

"Oh no, I showed you mine, now you show me yours," she teased.

He held out the gift to her. "Sorry about the wrapping job. I may have been scared shitless the whole time and just wanted to get back here as quickly as I could." He let out an uncomfortable laugh.

She squeezed his arm before clapping her hands excitedly and took the bag from him. It was heavier than she'd expected. She quickly unfolded the top. "Is it safe for me to reach inside?" she teased.

"You didn't need that hand of yours, did you?"

God, she was obsessed with this playful side of Ian.

She reached in and pulled out a round globe, not quite a sphere, with a felt-lined flat bottom. "Um . . . pretty?" She wasn't sure what it was.

"It's a paperweight," he said, a smile dancing around the corners of his mouth.

"Oh," she said. He'd mentioned the paperweight earlier. It had fallen off his desk when the lights first went out. Yoona didn't use many papers. She couldn't see a need to weigh them down at least. So . . . "This is amazing. Thank you."

Ian reached for Yoona's hand that held the gift. "It was already on my desk when I first moved into that office. Someone must have left it behind."

"Wow, a regift. Even better," she said flatly.

He tugged on her hand and pulled her forward, a small smile playing at the corner of his mouth. She took a step closer to him. Despite the snow falling outside and the blackout cutting off the heat in the building, she swore she felt the temperature rise as their bodies came close to touching.

"I don't keep anything in my office remotely worthy of giving to you," he whispered. "But this, this random paperweight, decided to fall off my desk when the lights went out. And the sound brought you to me. It brought you to my office and now we're here. I might just believe it has magical powers."

Her breath caught as Ian leaned in, lowering his head. She kept her eyes open till the very last moment as he drew even nearer. And then she finally closed them as his lips met hers in a kiss.

❄

No matter how many times he told himself to stay away from her, that he had too much at stake to risk a distraction, Ian had been able to control himself physically. But his mind? It never forgot. It never kept Yoona far from him.

He was tired of trying. He wanted her. He wanted her more than he wanted anything else. He kissed her and her lips immediately softened to welcome him. She wrapped her arms around his neck and pulled him closer. He slipped his tongue into her mouth, exploring, piercing, giving. She moaned and he thought he would lose his mind.

She was so responsive, pliant, melding her body to his, holding him tighter, making it clear what she wanted. He lifted her up so she could wrap her legs around him and walked them to the couch, not separating from their kiss. He turned slightly so he could sit first, letting her straddle him as they went down.

Yoona ground herself against him and Ian felt out of control with desire. He moved from her mouth down to her neck, sucking, nipping, licking. He pulled at her ear with his lips and then kissed down her jaw. His hands moved up her back, wrapped around her neck, and then came up to cradle her face. He wanted to touch her everywhere.

He crashed their lips back together.

"Ian," she said through ragged breaths. "I want you." The words were heady, but it was the look she gave him when she said them, fire and desire and determination in her eyes, that snapped any last sense of control.

They moved frantically. Her fingers quickly undid his belt and the top hook of his slacks. She pulled down the zipper and reached in, working around his boxer briefs until she found what she was desperate for. She wrapped her hand around his shaft and tightened her grip.

He hissed at the contact, wanting the warmth of her hold, but wishing for more. She pumped her fist once, twice, dragging down to the base with just the right amount of pressure, then back up to the tip. Her thumb rubbed over his slit and spread the wetness of his precum over the head.

Ian needed to get closer. "Baby, stand up for me so I can get your pants off." She quickly got to her feet and stepped back. She looked down at him with hunger in her eyes as he unbuttoned her pants and dragged the fabric down her legs till it hit the ground. She had on red cotton underwear patterned in snowmen. He looked up at her, raising an eyebrow.

"They're festive," she said, a smile spreading across her face.

He nodded in agreement, then grabbed her ass, pulling her close, lifting her blouse as he placed wet kisses down her stomach to the top of her panties. He hooked a finger into each side and slowly pulled them down, kissing each bit of skin revealed along the way. She dragged her fingers through his hair and held on as he teased with gentle pecks all around her sensitive parts.

"Ian," she begged. She pulled back and stepped out of her underwear. She unbuttoned her blouse, unsnapped her bra, and let them both drop to the ground. Yoona stood before him completely, and gloriously, naked.

"Next time, Yoona, I will be the one to take off your bra," he said, voice as steady as he could keep it. And he'd do it with his teeth, he thought. "Now come here." He reached for her.

She straddled him again, this time hovering on her knees, taking him back in her hand. She lined his tip up along her pussy and pulled it along her folds. She was wet, and the heat radiating from her, along with this slight pressure, was good enough to almost make him come.

"We don't have a condom," she said.

"Lots of fun things we can do without one," he replied. She whined, and he whispered promises of the other stuff for next time. Because he would make sure there was a next time. Many more next times to come.

He wrapped his hand over hers and continued to work his cock against her, dragging along her slit, letting the tip of his head touch and tease her opening. When her moans grew louder and her movements more erratic, when he knew she was close, he pressed his thumb against her clit, moving in circles with unrelenting pressure until he felt it begin to pulsate.

"Ian," she called out. "Oh god, I'm coming, I'm coming, yes . . ."

He pushed one finger inside her, thrusting in and out as her walls tightened in pulses. When she finished riding the wave, he pulled his finger out and wrapped his hand back over hers around his shaft. He guided her to speed up the pace, gripping him a little tighter, and after a few more pumps he covered the head and emptied himself into his hand, some spilling onto his lower stomach.

Their foreheads met as they recovered and caught their breath. After a few more moments, Yoona placed a kiss on Ian's mouth and scrambled off, grabbing some Kleenex from her desk for both of them.

Ian shifted to lie down, head against the arm of the couch. He reached for Yoona, who lay down alongside him with a contented sigh and snuggled up against him. She was half on him, half off, legs tangled, and his arm wrapped around her back to keep her close. He pulled the blanket off the back of the couch and covered them.

He held her tightly—never wanting to let go.

CHAPTER SIX

"How am I ever gonna get work done in this office again?" Yoona teased. She could feel the rumble of his laugh as her head lay on his chest.

"People are gonna wonder why I keep coming over here and sitting on your couch with a stupid grin on my face," he said.

This was good. Joking around was good. Yoona waited a few minutes to see if Ian would freak out, would regret this happening. She needed to read the situation. Which made her very aware that she, alone, was completely naked, while Ian lay in his shirt and boxers. She sat up, taking the blanket with her to cover herself.

"I should get dressed," she said.

"One more kiss first," he said, giving her arm a gentle tug. She leaned down and met his lips.

"Thank you," he said. She wasn't sure for what, but she smiled and kissed him once more before getting up to get her clothes.

While buttoning her blouse, Yoona snuck a glance over her shoulder at Ian. They'd both gotten up to dress themselves. He was turned away from her, tucking his shirt into his slacks. She thought he might be almost as gorgeous from the back as he was from the front.

As she adjusted her clothes, and he stayed silent behind her, she couldn't help but worry how he would react now that they'd come down from the high. Would it be like last time—him ignoring her, barely speaking to her, hardly looking at her afterward? She'd come to accept that he'd pretty much ghosted her, but it hurt and confused her nonetheless.

Despite how much she still wanted him, yearned for him and for something real, she was determined not to expect anything after tonight either. What happened in the darkness of a blackout and the emotions of a missed holiday, could stay there.

She let out a resigned breath just as the lights of her office turned back on.

Ian squinted as the harsh overhead lighting of their offices blinked on. Various beeping and buzzing filled the once-silent air as equipment reset itself. He found Yoona looking out the windows. He joined her there, standing shoulder to shoulder, taking in the outside world. The streetlights once again illuminated the block, looking almost too bright compared to what had just been a completely black night. Various windows of neighboring buildings glowed, and the sound of people cheering even reached up to them on the sixteenth floor.

The world outside looked untouched, a moment of blissful peace in a usually busy city that wouldn't last long. But the storm and the blackout made it feel like a fresh start.

"It's a Christmas miracle," Yoona said wistfully.

He reached for her hand, interlocked his fingers with hers, and squeezed.

"Yoona," he started. He turned to face her, but she kept her gaze forward, out the window. Her shoulders were pulled back like she was preparing for bad news. Ian knew he had to get this right. He cleared his throat and continued, picking his words carefully. "Last time we were together, my life had been really complicated. I was on my own and scared and stressed and I"—he hesitated—"well, happiness was a luxury I didn't think I could afford—or deserve."

She finally turned to face him, not letting go of his hand. She peered up at him with softness. He was grateful she was giving him a chance to explain.

"Being with you ignited something inside me that scared the shit out of me. I couldn't allow myself to feel it again. I had to focus on work, nothing else. Maybe it wasn't fair, to either of us. But, I'm sorry I never talked to you about it. I'm sorry I pushed you away. Shit . . . I'm so, so sorry if I hurt you."

Yoona stepped closer to Ian, taking his hands and wrapping them around her waist. She put both hers on his chest and met his eyes. He knew she could probably feel his heart beating wildly.

"It's okay," she said at last. "I was confused and, yes, a little hurt. But I wasn't expecting declarations or promises from you. I just, well, I liked you and hoped you liked me too. So maybe just a little bummed we couldn't explore that."

Ian closed his eyes and dropped his head, shame and regret weighing down on him for how he'd handled the past.

Yoona reached out and lifted his chin, forcing him to face her. He opened his eyes and was met with the warmth of a small smile.

"But I'm gonna be honest with you, Ian. This time, I want more. I want to give us a try. So I need to know, are you willing to do that now?"

Ian bent down till he was a hair's breadth away from her. "I am," he whispered without hesitation against her lips, and kissed her. He felt her mouth stretch into a smile under his.

He placed tender kisses on each of her eyes, her cheeks, her nose, and back to her mouth.

She let out a contented sigh.

"Merry Christmas, Ian," Yoona murmured against his lips.

"Merry Christmas," Ian replied, kissing her again.

She pulled back a tiny fraction. "You ready to get out of here?" she asked.

Ian was more than ready. For once, he was excited to see what would come next. He nodded, rubbed his thumb against her cheek, grabbed her hand, and led the way.

11

HOPE THIS HELPS

Sarah Hogle

Dear Mr. Gladwin,

Hello! This is Kaylee Jamison's mom. I was wondering if it would be okay if Kaylee retakes the test from last Friday? She wasn't feeling well, so she wasn't at the top of her game. But she definitely knows the material better than that and would like another chance! She thinks you won't allow a retake for some reason, but I wanted to go ahead and ask anyway because Ms. Levitt and Mr. Ortiz have allowed retakes in the past with no problem. Thanks in advance!

Audrey Thorn

Dear Mrs. Thorn,

Indeed, Kaylee is correct! I do not allow test retakes unless a student missed school on the day of the test. I agree that Kaylee knows the material better than her grade reflects; she seemed tired on Friday morning, and I heard her telling her friends that she went to a concert on Thursday night. A good night's sleep is extremely important for students! There will be another test this Friday to cover chapters four through seven, so hopefully Kaylee won't be attending any concerts beforehand.

Best regards,
Joel Gladwin

Dear Mr. Gladwin,

My sincerest apologies about Kaylee's tiredness! Trust me when I say that going to concerts on a weeknight is NOT common in our household, lol. We had tickets to see Sabrina Carpenter, which were expensive and hard to get. I'm sorry that Kaylee was tired on Friday, but I can assure you that the once-in-a-lifetime memories were worth it! I actually have another question. This one is about Kaylee's research paper that was handed back yesterday. I'll admit I'm scratching my head a bit here because the paper's very well written, I think, and I don't understand why she got an F? She is doing her best in your class but is still averaging an F somehow, which puts her in danger of not being able to attend the Snowfall Dance. She'll be devastated if she misses it.

Miss Audrey Thorn

Dear Miss Audrey Thorn,

I appreciate your advocacy for your child. I assure you that I do not wish for any of my students to fail, and have given them every opportunity to succeed. The rubric sent home with Kaylee for the research paper three weeks ago explained my expectations and how the points were divided. Kaylee only used one source in her works cited page. She was supposed to use seven. The source she used was Wikipedia, which I do not consider to be a credible source. It takes effort on the parts of both the teacher and the parents to provide a nourishing education. I can only assure you that I am doing my part.

Best regards,
Joel Gladwin

Mr. Gladwin,

I am doing my part as well. One of the questions on the worksheet you sent home today is factually inaccurate: You stated that F. Scott Fitzgerald was born in 1869, but he was born in 1896. I hope this helps.

PS: I did some research, and according to Common Sense Media, *The Great Gatsby* is recommended for readers fourteen-plus due to mature themes. Another source, The Center for Learning, says that *The Great Gatsby* should be read by students in grades eleven and twelve. Don't you think this book is a little too mature for thirteen-year-olds?

Miss Thorn

Dear Miss Audrey Thorn,

Thank you for your concern, which helps me a great deal. One can only wonder how much time was spent Googling the questions from my assignments in efforts to find an error. You are the savior of public education, Miss Audrey Thorn.

PS: Isn't Sabrina Carpenter's music a little too mature for a thirteen-year-old?

Best regards,
Joel Gladwin

"You horse's ass," I mutter.

Kaylee flounces into the living room, dropping her backpack in the middle of the floor. Her long curls are in a French braid now, which means her friend Emma did her hair at school. I take a moment to grieve the lovely long spirals I had when I was her age, as well, and which I flat-ironed to death for some unholy reason. My hair is still the same honey brown as Kaylee's, but these days it demands a ton of products to curl properly and won't grow past my shoulders.

"What about a horse?" she asks.

I minimize my email before she can snoop. "Nothing. Your backpack doesn't go there."

She kicks it under the Christmas tree, which responds by shedding tufts of fake snow. I loathe that tree. It looks gorgeous, but if you so much as breathe while you walk past it, the flocking goes everywhere.

"Thank you so much, dear."

Kaylee laughs and puts her backpack in the closet, then inspects the living room for any new baubles I might have added while she was at school. I have perhaps gone a tiny bit overboard with the holiday decorating, trying to make Kaylee's world as magical as I possibly can. I'm talking string lights on big red bows on garland on red-and-green table runners. I'm talking a battalion of snow globes, a legion of reindeer figurines, a city of Christmas village buildings. We live in a small two-bedroom Craftsman, and our living room is barely big enough to accommodate a sofa and an armchair, but that has not stopped me from shopping as if I need to furnish the entire North Pole. From where I sit, I can count eleven different wall hangings bearing messages like FA LA LA LA LA, MERRY & BRIGHT, and HAPPY HOLIDAYS in loopy cursive. I am not proud of this. Rustic wooden signs are my weakness.

Kaylee helps herself to my plate of carrot sticks. "Dad texted me," she says as she chomps away. "He asked if I want to stay over tonight"—I abruptly turn to look at her—"because he and Aubrey need me to babysit Breighdynn while they go out."

Few things are more annoying than my ex's girlfriend having almost the same name as me. It does provide great relish, however, to know there is a ninety-five percent chance that Dustin has called her Audrey at least once by accident, which I'm sure enrages her. It's somewhat more annoying that she used to be my best friend (and was the maid of honor in my wedding to Dustin). And you know, the whole "she's living in what used to be my house with what used to be my husband" thing, but whatever. She'll be looking over her shoulder for the rest of her life for an Aujrey or an Auvrey just waiting to usurp her position, and frankly that sounds like hell. Good luck!

I take a deep breath and say to myself all of the things I cannot say out loud to Kaylee. Dustin is supposed to ask me first when he wants Kaylee on a night that isn't his. And he needs to stop using her as a babysitter for Aubrey's kid. I cannot even calculate the number of *I need more time with my daughter* texts I've gotten from him, which were all code for *I need a babysitter* or *I need someone to wash my dishes because I'm not any good at it and Aubrey's tiiiired, wahh wahh.*

"Is that something you want to do?" I ask carefully.

She shrugs. "I don't really care. He said he'll pay me."

"It's up to you, honey."

She bites her lip. "I don't wanna leave you all alone, though."

My stomach bottoms out. I have failed, and I am going to Parenting Hell. "Don't be silly," I rush to say. "I have the cats!" *Do I seem lonely to her? If so, then why does she think it's her responsibility to fix my loneliness? What am I doing with my face right now? Put your face in neutral, Audrey! Neutral!* "Plus, I don't mind being alone." *Wait a minute, she might think this means I would prefer to be alone. Or that I'm trying to get rid of her.* "Now and then. But I've got work to catch up on, I'm gonna FaceTime Kate later, I'm gonna order tacos, it'll be a grand old party." *Not party! Don't want her to think I celebrate whenever she's gone.* "A grand old boring party," I amend.

I am doing everything wrong and unknowingly instilling irreversible trauma in my poor child. She will be talking about this moment with a therapist someday.

She raises an eyebrow at me. "Are you okay?"

"I am always okay, and when I'm not, that's okay too. It is not on you to shoulder adults' emotions, all right?"

She groans, sensing I'm about to go on a tangent.

"I'm the parent; you're the child. Do not worry about me."

"Mom." She holds my face between her hands and stares me dead in the eyes. Whereas both of her parents have brown eyes, she inherited her vivid green from my mother. "Will you please chill out?"

"Sorry. Yes." *You are not chill enough! Get a grip on yourself before you damage her for life with your un-chill-ness!* I don't remember being this neurotic pre-divorce. Now that I'm living the single mom life, I find myself sliding every decision I make under a magnifying glass. My ex once made the suggestion that he was the "fun parent" and I was "just the mom," which sent me into an insecurity tailspin. *Just the mom. What does that even mean??*

"How was school?" I ask.

"Ugh. I left my phone in math and couldn't find it, and I was kinda freaking out. But then I went back later and got it. We're gonna start volleyball next week in PE. Yay!"

"Yay!" I clap enthusiastically.

Kaylee grabs the TV remote and jumps onto the couch. She can never simply sit down. She must launch herself from as far away as possible. "Okay, I'm gonna text Dad and tell him to come get me."

"Okey dokey." Then a realization hits me. "You studied for your test tomorrow, right?"

Kaylee squints. "What test?"

"In English."

"Oh, right. I'll take my book with me."

"Good idea." I want to tack on a few items: *Are you eating okay at your dad's house? Has he bought you a bed of your own yet or are you still crashing on the couch? Do they still talk badly about me in front of you?* But I do not, because I am Being Chill.

The following day, Kaylee goes straight to the fridge when she gets home from school and cracks open a can of root beer.

"Tough day, huh?" I say jokingly, but she nods. Rolls her eyes.

"Guess who didn't get any sleep last night?"

"Oh no. Couch uncomfortable?"

"Dad and Aubrey didn't get home until *twelve thirty*."

"WHAT." Instantly, I have my phone out of my pocket, ready to call Dustin. Kaylee throws her arms around my waist.

"Noooo, Mom. If you yell at him, he'll be whiny at me about it later."

I massage my temples with my thumbs. I hate that this is her reality, and I am to blame, and also Dustin is to blame, but Dustin is not trying to make her life easier. Dustin is oblivious of anyone else's feelings. I am on eggshells over here stressing out about trying to do everything right, terrified of messing my kid up, and meanwhile he just does not care. He feels no guilt, no weight of parental responsibility. He just says and does whatever! There is absolutely nothing I can do about it. If I want him to do a thing less, he will do that thing more out of contrariness. He will remind me that I am not his boss and he is just as much Kaylee's parent as I am.

"And he didn't pay me either." Kaylee makes a face. "Who could've seen that one coming? Hey, can Emma and Mackenzie spend the night?"

My mind spins a bit at the change of subject. "Yeah, sure."

"Oh, and I failed my test again, but this time it wasn't

my fault. Breighdynn dropped my book in the dog's water bowl. It's ruined."

"You're kidding!"

"He tried to throw my phone in there, too, but thankfully I grabbed it from him."

I shake my head. "I'm sorry. Did you ask your teacher for a new book?"

"Yeah, but I gotta pay a fee for losing the other one." Worry crosses her face. "Mr. Brice reminded everybody over the intercom this morning that anyone failing a class doesn't get to go to the Snowfall Dance next Saturday. I was hoping he'd forget. Literally every single one of my friends is going to be there! Even Maddie, and she never goes to anything! And they're gonna have fake snow falling from the ceiling! With GLITTER. It'll be amaaaaazing."

"Glitter?" I repeat, my voice grave. I flash back to Kaylee's science project from last year, in which a one-gallon tub of glitter spilled all over our living room. It's still in the carpet, taunting me. "Missing the dance suddenly sounds great. Wanna go see a movie that night instead?"

"Mom."

"I'm kidding! There's no way you're missing the dance," I say emphatically. "They asked me to chaperone, for crying out loud. They can't expect me to chaperone a dance my kid isn't allowed to go to."

She looks haunted. "If I can't go, my life is ruined."

I resist the impulse to invalidate this statement as dramatic, because to Kaylee, the Snowfall Dance *is* the biggest, most important event going on in her life right now. She's got a sparkly new dress hanging in her closet, and she's tried it on approximately three thousand times so that she could preview her look in the mirror. Her kitten heels are broken in. Her teeny clutch is pre-packed with Dentyne Ice Arctic Chill gum. She knows exactly how she's going to do her hair and nails.

"There's got to be a way to bring your grade back up."

"By next week?" she says dubiously.

"Yes. I'll ask your teacher about extra credit." I'm feeling confident now that I've got the shimmerings of a plan coming into focus. "There's got to be *something*."

Dear Mr. Gladwin,

Hello! Kaylee's mom here again. I would normally NEVER ask for an exception for my child regarding today's test, but please allow me to explain the extenuating circumstances. Her book was destroyed (which was completely out of her control), making it impossible for her to read/study. Could she please have another chance to take the test? It's very important that she brings her grade up so that she doesn't miss out on the dance.

Audrey Thorn

I hit send and nestle into the couch with a fluffy candy-cane–covered blanket and some pizza that was probably warm at one point, but not anymore as I spent so long tweaking my email. "Now to wait for his response on Monday morning," I say to myself, opening the Netflix app. *The Princess Switch 3* and four-cheese pizza go great with a stressful day. I turn up the volume a few notches to fight the commotion of giggling and dancing footsteps in Kaylee's bedroom, which is directly above me. She and her friends have been listening to the song "Rasputin" for seventy-three minutes straight. It sounds like some kind of cult ritual is going on up there.

Bzz bzz.

I check my phone, shocked to find a Gmail notification with the subject line Re: Hello. "Ha ha!" I crow. "At home checking your inbox on a Friday night. What a loser." I pause and decide not to self-reflect.

Dear Miss Audrey Thorn,

"I would normally NEVER ask for an exception for my child." I'm sorry, what? If you just heard a loud sound coming from far away, that was me laughing. Please feel free to scroll through this email thread for easy reminiscing of all the times you have asked for an exception for your child.

Best regards,
Joel Gladwin

I hop to my feet, pizza forgotten. "Excuse you!"

I have been nothing but polite! And he has been rude and condescending at every turn! Why did the school even hire this guy? He has no people skills. Or negotiating skills. You know who *does* have negotiating skills? Me. I've been reading a lot of "how to co-parent after divorce" books. I glance at my latest read, which sits on the coffee table, called *Your Broken Home and You*. When Kaylee saw it, she howled with laughter and called me dramatic.

I should be enjoying exactly seven things right now: mozzarella, cheddar, provolone, Parmesan, and Vanessa

Hudgens talking to another Vanessa Hudgens, who is talking to another Vanessa Hudgens. But instead I am pacing, and I am vexed.

Okay, I *know* what this looks like. I know. It looks like I think my daughter can do no wrong, and that I think she should receive special treatment. But the thing is, it isn't Kaylee's fault that she stayed up late at a concert and performed poorly on a test, it's mine, because I made the decision to take her. It isn't Kaylee's fault that her father's girlfriend's toddler drowned her copy of *The Great Gatsby* in a bowl of water. I just don't want to see Kaylee get the speeding ticket when she wasn't the one behind the wheel, so to speak.

How dare he laugh at me when I am trying to be earnest! Joel Gladwin messed with the wrong mom.

Mr. Gladwin,

Your attitude is not very pleasant. I think flexibility is a necessary skill for any teacher to have. You say that you don't want any of your students to fail, but you're also just going to watch while they sink, even when they yell for a lifeboat? It's eighth-grade English! This is not the bar exam.

Audrey Thorn

Dear Miss Audrey Thorn,

Thorn! What an apt name! Did you know that in the last month, a staggering number of my students have neglected to turn in their homework due to extenuating circumstances beyond their control? It is an epidemic. These circumstances include such classics as:

1. I wasn't feeling well, and when I'm coughing I can't read.
2. It just disappeared!
3. Someone must've stolen it!
4. No, YOU lost my homework, Mr. G!
5. My grandmother died again.

I hear everything, Miss Audrey Thorn. But I usually hear it from thirteen-year-olds, and not from a grown adult. Here's an idea: let your child make mistakes and then experience the consequences! Great learning moments abound from this, I promise.

Best regards,
Joel Gladwin

Mr. Gladwin,

I am not lying about Kaylee's book being destroyed. I think your bias against me has caused you to treat Kaylee unfairly. And I know I've probably been getting on your nerves, and I apologize for that, but all this sarcasm is not very Rhinoceros Pride of you. I suggest that you reread the school motto, "Arrive, strive, thrive," and remember that children are our future.

Audrey Thorn

Dear Miss Audrey Thorn,

I am filled TO THE BRIM with Rhinoceros Pride. I embody everything about it. I will not let others walk all over me, much like the mighty rhinoceros. But by all means, do keep trying! I've got nothing else to do with my time but grade eighty papers clumsily cobbled together by ChatGPT.

Best regards,
Joel Gladwin

How am I even supposed to respond to this?

I've had my movie paused for so long that Netflix is running the screen saver, and I resume my pacing. A furious reflection of myself in the living room window joins me, back and forth and back and forth. Snow drifts from a dark sky, frosting the branches of my sycamore trees and making the yard sparkle wherever moonlight touches. Only one more week until winter break. Only five more months until summer break. I cannot wait to be rid of middle school and Mr. Gladwin.

Mr. Gladwin,

How about extra credit? 'Tis the season to be giving!

Once again, he hits back in record time. It's as if he can somehow see my emails while I'm typing them, and has his replies ready to go zero-point-one seconds after I've pinged his inbox.

Dear Miss Audrey Thorn,

Extra credit would be much appreciated. Or any credit at all, really. You can start with this: "Thank you, Mr. Gladwin, for providing my child with an incredible education." The rest is up to you; I wouldn't want to impede your creativity by giving too many suggestions.

Thank you for finally giving me some credit!

Best regards,
Joel Gladwin

This man is drunk.

This man comes home from work every day and throws back a watermelon Four Loko to cope with the misery of being a mean-spirited, compassionless ass, and now he is drunk emailing. It is the only possibility that makes sense.

My stomach growls, so I angrily stuff cold pizza in my face as I glare at his message, mentally running through retaliation methods.

Mr. Gladwin,

We used to be a professional society. I can see that you are beyond reasoning with! I do not know why a person so insistent on not compromising would become a teacher. In my opinion, you are jaded and rude. Have the weekend you deserve.

Audrey Thorn

Dear Miss Audrey Thorn,

I offer extra credit every Monday in my class. Did you know that? It's an essay. All that students are required to do, for twenty points, is write a five-hundred-word essay about their weekend. Hope this helps.

Best regards,
Joel Gladwin

No!

NOOOOOO!

This cannot be true. I tilt my head back and yell at the ceiling: "KAAAYYYYLEEEEE!"

Above, the dancing racket falters. The music stops. "COMING, MOM."

She bounds down the stairs in short order, face pink and sweaty from jumping around. She and her friends have switched pieces of their outfits, so she's wearing Emma's *Blue Eye Samurai* hoodie and Mackenzie's "vintage" Y2K choker necklace. "Yeah?" She floats on instinct toward what's left of my pizza, even though she and her friends devoured a pizza of their own, plus a two-liter of Sprite and a party-sized bag of Flamin' Hot Cheetos. And (I suspect, based on the flecks of chocolate stuck at the corners of Kaylee's mouth) a package of Oreos that I tried to hide behind cornflakes so that I wouldn't have to share them with voracious gremlin teenagers.

"Does Mr. Gladwin offer extra credit every Monday?" I ask her point-blank. "An essay about the weekend?"

She attempts to cover her face with a triangle of pizza. "Uhhh."

"Kaylee!" I throw up my arms. My voice devolves into a pitiful whine. "You've had the solution in front of you all this time!"

"I always forget about it!" She falls to her knees, pressing her hands together. "I'm sorry, I'm sorry, I'm sorry. Are you going to send me away to an evil boarding school? Where someone will die mysteriously and it will be up to me to solve the crime?"

I half-heartedly nudge her away with a socked foot. "I can't afford any of those schools. But you *are* doing extra credit from now on. And after Mackenzie and Emma go home tomorrow, you're reading the rest of *The Great Gatsby*. I'm going to quiz you."

Her forehead wrinkles. "Have you read it?"

"Yes." (I have not. I was supposed to in high school, but I was . . . shall we say . . . an undedicated student. I *have*, however, seen the movie.)

For the remainder of the night, I alternate between pacing the living room and groaning into my hands with my head between my knees. Mr. Gladwin is still a snarky jerk, no doubt, but I've lost some ground here. I despise feeling embarrassed. And stupid. No matter what I do to try to prevent it, I keep messing up. When will this end? When will I reach the summit of Parenting Mountain and be so full of wisdom and experience that I'll finally stop making mistakes? I don't think that perfection is too much to ask of the universe.

Maybe I should be a little more stringent about boundaries and consequences too. Sometimes I go a bit easy on Kaylee because I'm trying to make up for . . . anything else in her life not being easy . . . but I should work on striking a better balance. If she can walk all over me, then how can she be receptive to learning anything from me?

"I will no longer be fighting your battles," I announce on Monday morning before Kaylee leaves for school and I leave for my job at Elkport Realty.

She licks yogurt off a spoon and slow-blinks. Ponders this. "Okay."

"Okay? Just like that?"

"I don't think I ever asked you to fight my battles to begin with?"

I cross my arms. Well! That can't be right. She must've asked at some point along the line, or else I would not have meddled quite so much. Probably.

"It's a Monday, so don't forget . . ." I let the end of my sentence tilt upward in ominous warning.

Kaylee squints. "Uhh. New episode of *MasterChef Junior*?"

"No! Extra credit. Don't forget, you're doing that essay. You can write all about how you spent your weekend reading and being a good little student."

"I was kidding! I knew that." She slings her backpack over her shoulders. "I want to buy Christmas gifts for all of my teachers before break. Can we go to Walmart today?"

"All your teachers except for Mr. Gladwin, you mean." *Suck it, Gladwin. You won't be getting a cheap coffee mug from us!*

Her eyebrows pin together. "Why? He's my favorite teacher."

I chuckle heartily at this, but she retains a straight face. Kaylee cannot keep a straight face when she's joking for the life of her. My jaw comes unhinged. "Are you nuts? You're getting an F in his class!"

She shrugs. "Yeah, because I keep failing the tests. He's still nice to me, though. And he's *really* funny. He's everybody's favorite teacher."

I gape at her. "Nice?" I repeat, voice shrill. "On what planet?"

Kaylee just looks puzzled. "Wow. You got beef with him?"

What on earth is happening in my kitchen right now. Do I have beef? Do I have *beef*? I have a whole-ass Arby's franchise.

I am bamboozled for the rest of the day. For the rest of the week. I do my last-minute Christmas shopping, and I bake cookies to donate to a school raffle raising money for field trips. I shovel my sidewalk religiously because I am terrified of being sued by the mailman for slipping on ice, and finally throw out the caved-in jack-o'-lanterns that have frozen to my porch. All the while, I think of Gladwin's smug little digs.

PS: Isn't Sabrina Carpenter's music a little too mature for a thirteen-year-old?

Thank you for finally giving me some credit!

Thorn! What an apt name!

"*You're* an apt name," I mutter viciously, flinging tinsel onto my Christmas tree at one point. "Gladwin? Pshh. More like Sadwin."

"You say something?" Kaylee asks me, cross-legged on the floor wrapping presents for her friends and teachers.

"No."

My saltiness does begin to abate upon receiving certain news on Friday, however.

"I get to go to the dance!" Kaylee sings to me when I get home from work. She pirouettes into the fridge, then hops about on one foot. "Ow. Ow. Ow."

I gasp in delight. "You brought your grade up?"

She shrugs. "I dunno."

"How do you know you're allowed to go?"

"The principal said on morning announcements that he's not going to prohibit students from going even if they have low grades."

"Huh." I prop my hands on my hips. "Good."

"Right?" She twirls and twirls.

"And you're still sure you're okay with me chaperoning?" I watch her skeptically. "I can tell them no. They can get somebody else, I don't wanna cramp your style."

"It's fiiiine, I've told you a million times. Stop asking meeeee."

"Okay, okay."

"Are you still okay with me chaperoning?" I ask her again on Saturday evening as we pile into the car on our way to the school. Kaylee's trying to hide that she's upset I've made her wear a big puffy coat over her (thin, spaghetti-strap, definitely more appropriate for summer) pink dress when it's nine degrees with a windchill of negative two. But she's also extremely excited. Her eyes are lit up, and she keeps checking herself out in the mirror. She's wearing mascara for the first time ever, and from the way she talks about it, I think Kaylee half expects that her friends won't be able to recognize her. They will surely think she is a twenty-one-year-old woman of the world.

"Mom," she groans. "Don't make me turn this car around."

When we file into the gymnasium, Kaylee immediately beelines for one of the far walls where all of the girls are awkwardly loitering, casting interested looks over at the opposite wall, where the boys are doing things like trying to stand on their heads and cheering on one another's Tik-Tok dances. I notice it's really only the boys who are exceptionally well-dressed in bow ties and gelled hair that are paying any attention to the girls, and they look so anxious that I worry they might pass out.

I spot Kaylee's former sixth-grade math teacher and ask how I can make myself useful. "We need someone over there to ladle punch," she tells me, gesturing. "And if you notice anyone getting too rowdy, threaten that you'll have the deejay play nothing but slow songs if they don't stop. That usually calms them down for a minute. These kids are *terrified* of slow songs."

I snigger in response and make my way to the refreshments table. Strobe lights scatter off of every surface, highlighting tinfoil snowflakes hanging from streamers, twisting this way and that in the reverberating howl of the speaker system they've got set up in here. Near one of the doorways they have a blue-and-white balloon arch where couples are supposed to pose for pictures, but it's been taken over by twelve-year-old boys rubbing their heads against the balloons to make their hair stand up from static.

"Punch duty, eh?" a voice asks. I glance to my left, where a man is situated similarly to me, arranging snowflake-shaped cookies onto individual Thanksgiving-themed napkins. I can almost visualize whichever parent or teacher donated those napkins as they stood in the grocery store aisle, sighing at the price of winter napkins versus the turkey ones on clearance. Whoever did this has Given Up, and you know, I respect that.

"Looks like it." I stir the pinkish-red liquid with a giant

plastic ladle, sniffing its weird fumes. The carbonation tickles my nose. “What is this, anyway? It smells like someone poured Mountain Dew into Kool-Aid.”

He lifts a scrap of tablecloth so that I can see the variety of Kool-Aid and Mountain Dew bottles hiding beneath. He whistles. “You clocked that perfectly.”

“I have a gift.”

He holds up one of the cookies. “Without coming any closer, tell me what flavor this is.”

“It’s a sugar cookie. Do they even make snowflake-looking cookies that aren’t sugar cookies? It’s practically a rule.”

He takes a bite. “Correct.” He scrutinizes me, then says, “Turn around for a second.”

“Why?”

“Humor me.”

I do so, smiling and shaking my head a little. I hear crinkling from the chip bags, and then he says, “All right. For the big prize: What flavor is *this*?”

I begin to step forward, but he holds the chip aloft. “Uh-uh-uh. No smelling.”

Biting down on a laugh, I clasp my hands behind my back and observe the chip held between his fingers. It’s dusted with a reddish-orange seasoning. “Barbecue,” I say decisively.

“Errrr!” he replies, sounding like a game show buzzer. “Wrong! It’s fruitcake. Novelty flavor.”

I wrinkle my nose. “Ew. Why?”

He cackles. “I brought ’em.”

“But *why*?”

He shrugs one shoulder, grinning crookedly. He’s cute, with wavy brown hair that curls over his forehead, and a wide, dimpled smile. His light brown eyes glitter with mischief. "They're festive." He slowly reaches for a Solo cup of punch I've prepared, and, maintaining eye contact with me, takes a sip.

"Oooh, I wanna cookie!" Kaylee approaches us, dragging her friends along. "And punch. Mmmm, punch. Thanks, Mom."

The man coughs into his drink. "Mom?" His eyes grow twice their usual size as he surveys me. "Don't tell me. Not *Miss* Audrey Thorn."

"Yes." My chin drops. "No! *You?*"

"Best regards," he says, looking both curious and amused.

I shake my head. "I can't believe it."

"What's going on here?" one of Kaylee's friends asks us, red and green strobe lights shining off her braces.

"Kaylee's mom is trying to find my devil horns." Mr. Gladwin winks. "I left them at home. They're more of a Halloween vibe."

I am speechless. I scoot away from him, down toward the end of my table. I stir the punch viciously, and thank the gods it's so dim in here, because I'm pretty sure my face has gone as red as this "punch." Before I know it, I've mindlessly prepped one hundred cups of punch that I am certain will go to waste.

Out of the corner of my eye, I see Gladwin passing out cookies to the girls. "Have fun!"

"No thanks to you," I grumble under my breath, quiet enough that no one hears.

"Cool tie, Mr. G!" Kaylee and her posse flounce away, and Gladwin turns to me, right eyebrow springing upward in an imitation of The Rock.

"'No thanks to you'?" he echoes.

Whoops. "It's true." My hands are on my hips again. My hips are getting a lot of hand action today. "You wouldn't let Kaylee retake her tests. She has an F. If it were up to you, she wouldn't be here."

"It's *because* of me that she's here," he replies mildly. "No, I didn't let Kaylee retake her tests. I didn't give her any shortcuts or change her grade undeservedly. She still has an F. But I don't think punishing students for struggling by taking away the few fun moments they get to experience in middle school will make them struggle any less. I had a talk with Mr. Brice." He swirls the liquid around in his cup, analyzing my reaction. "I made a case for letting all the kids go to the dance. Mr. Brice disagreed. We squabbled for close to an hour before he gave in purely because he wanted me to shut up." Mr. Gladwin smiles brilliantly, and I am shocked by how charming it makes his face look. That should be against the rules. "So there you have it."

I am speechless. Again.

"Well," I huff after a full minute has passed.

"Well," he parrots. He sounds quite pleased with himself.

"Excuse me. I see a . . . a child being rowdy." I walk stiffly away until I reach the gymnasium doors, and once I am on the other side of them, I begin speed-walking down the hall while trying not to hyperventilate, my brain moving a million miles an hour.

Mr. Gladwin is hot!

He's hot!

Not fair, not fair! He should look like a swamp creature. And here I am in my . . . I look down at myself, having forgotten what I'm wearing. *Okay, that's not too bad.* Black leggings and an oversized burgundy sweater with a gingerbread man on it. I don't know if leggings are "hip" anymore, but whatever, I came of fashionable age in 2004, and you'll pry my leggings from my cold, dead millennial hands. I *have* changed my hairstyle from a side part to a center part, and that is as much as I am evolving with the times.

I hustle into the girls' bathroom and dig through my purse. *Tampons, Kleenex, cough drops, where is my—* Ah, there it is. My trusty, dusty, five-year-old tube of Clinique Black Honey lipstick. I watch my reflection in the mirror apply four layers of it to her lips. Then she frowns at me and rubs it off. A little stain is left.

This is so stupid. I am not *putting on lipstick for Mr. Sadwin.*

Yes, I am. I apply more lipstick and avoid my own judgmental gaze.

I emerge from the bathroom feeling nervous and also confused, because why is a deejay in the year of our lord 2026 playing hits from when I was a youth? What is today's equivalent to Usher's "Yeah!" and why isn't that playing instead?

Also? Good grief. I can't believe they let *us* dance to this when we were kids. I find Kaylee in the crowd and become disoriented when Ludacris begins to wax lyrical about getting a woman into her birthday suit. I would be a total hypocrite to start sniffing my smelling salts over this, as my friends and I danced to *the exact same song* when I was a teen. But it was different! Somehow. I don't know how.

I am both too young and too old for all of this.

When I sidle back into my punch zone, I chance a quick peek at Gladwin and find that he is standing somewhat defensively, with his arms crossed over his chest, gazing out over the crowd, angled ever so slightly away from me. The gym floor has finally filled up, kids straying from the safety of their beloved walls. I think all the Mountain Dew has emboldened them.

I swallow and mentally yell at my hands to stop being so jittery. *I am in control here, hands! You will do as I command.*

It's too warm in this gym. I keep pulling out my phone and swiping the home screen as if expecting a new notification every thirty seconds. All I get is my Ring camera at home letting me know that some trash is blowing through my yard. This is so awkward and uncomfortable, I cannot stand it. I yearn for a wall.

The beat changes. Sabrina Carpenter's voice filters out of the speakers, blowing directly into Gladwin's face. Every girl in the room, and at least half the boys, begins singing along to "Espresso" at top volume.

An ungodly sound burbles up my throat.

I can't help it. I look at him, and he looks at me at the same time. We both burst out laughing.

"Did you request this?" he asks, voice high-pitched.

I hold up a hand. "I didn't. I swear."

Mr. Gladwin hangs his head.

"*Well*," he says with a theatrical sigh.

"Well." It's my turn to be smug.

"To be fair . . ." He can't even spit the words out without laughing. "To be fair, some of her songs are pretty explicit, you've got to admit."

"Oh? I'm sorry, Gladwin, I did not realize you were familiar with Sabrina's game."

"Hey!" He draws himself up to his full height and straightens his collar. "I know 'Juno'!"

I wolf-whistle. "Look at you."

His smile twists as he watches me laugh, his eyes dark and sparkling. "Look at *you*."

I lay a palm over my heart. *Ba-boom-ba-boom-ba-boom*. "Me?"

Gladwin nods. "You're not what I was expecting."

The opportunity to scrape compliments out of this man has me perking up like an antenna. Oh, but I am vain. "Tell me."

He shakes his head and looks away. His throat is flushed. My horrible grin is going to give me jaw problems.

"Go on." I can barely believe my own eyes when I see my hand reach toward him and tap him playfully on the arm. I know what a playful tap means. If I were one of the chaperones monitoring the balloon children and I was looking at me right now, I would *tsk-tsk-tsk* and say, *Girl, get ahold of yourself. You're in public.*

"All right," he acquiesces. "Have you ever, uh . . . Have you ever seen *Judge Judy*?"

"What!" I struggle to tamp down my squeal. "You pictured Judy?"

"You had a very no-nonsense vibe going on!" he exclaims. Then his gaze slides to mine, sidelong. "I mean, I didn't *hate* it."

I laugh again. "Wow. *Wow.*"

"And me?" he prompts once he's collected himself. "Am I what you pictured?"

I bite the corner of my lip. "Not exactly. I kind of pictured a fence post with glasses."

"Flattering."

"I was wrong about the glasses."

Not too far away from us, a kid is crab-walking while

his friends rain dollar bills onto his head, and a boy and girl are fully making out. A particularly evil-looking child is gleefully mixing all of the chip flavors together. Gladwin and I pretend we do not see it.

"You're all right," he tells me approvingly.

"Yeah?" I instruct myself not to elbow him flirtatiously, but my elbow still twitches in his direction. "You too. You're an all right teacher, I guess. Even if you don't allow test retakes."

"And you're an all right mom, according to Kaylee's extra credit essay this week."

I arch an eyebrow. "Did she say that?" My eyelashes flutter. "Me? She called *me* 'all right'? High praise!"

"She said you definitely need to get out more and start going on dates because you spend your weekends making your daughter do homework, and that you pretend you've read *The Great Gatsby* but one hundred percent have not."

"I have too!"

"But yeah. She said you're a good mom." His eyes are warm when they find mine again. "I think you can relax, Audrey. Kaylee's gonna be just fine. You're doing your best."

I let out a slow, shaky breath, and it feels like a boulder that has been pressing me down begins to ease up and away, until I can stand again for the first time in a good long while.

"Thanks," I say softly.

He nods. "You're very welcome, Miss Audrey Thorn."

Hours later, after Kaylee and I have trooped back home and kicked our shoes off, and heated up leftover Chinese food because chips and cookies were not sufficiently satisfying, I get a *bzz bzz* from my phone and I open it to find a new email.

Dear Audrey,

Care to join me for an espresso one of these days?

Yours,
Fence Post

12

IS IT NEW YEAR'S YET?

Zakiya N. Jamal

Win was twenty-five years old, and she still didn't know how to say no to her parents.

Maybe it was because she was an only child, or maybe it was because at her core, she was a people pleaser, but she could not tell her parents no, no matter how hard she tried. This was why she found herself stuck between them as they stood outside of the Jacksons' house for the Jacksons' annual New Year's Eve party.

Less than a minute after they rang the doorbell, Bria Jackson, the youngest of the two Jackson children and one of Win's oldest friends, opened the door with a flourish. Christmas music and the smell of the usual crab puffs, shrimp cocktails, and other finger foods the Jacksons always served at these things wafted out all at once.

"Winnie the Pooh!" Bria said, grinning.

Win rolled her eyes. Her real name was Wendy Campbell, but when they were kids Bria and her brother decided to call her "Windy," and over the years that got shortened to "Win," and then Bria decided Win's name in her phone should be "Winnie the Pooh." Now the name had stuck.

"Mr. and Mrs. Campbell, how are you?" Bria asked. She stepped to Win's mom first, pulling her in for a hug. Next was Win's dad, followed by Win herself. Bria smelled like she'd fallen into a tub of Bath & Body Works holiday fragrance—a mix of cinnamon and vanilla, and it was thankfully pleasant but not overpowering.

When Bria pulled back, Win took in her ensemble. The Jacksons' New Year's Eve party always had a theme, and this year it was "Black & Gold." Tonight, Bria looked stunning. She was wearing a long shimmering gold dress that hugged all her curves, with a slit that came up to her knee, and her dark curls were pulled up in two neat puffs with gold twine. Her dark brown skin was also glowing with gold body glitter.

Win had gone the black route with her outfit, wearing a short black cocktail dress with a corset-like top and tulle bottom that gave tutu vibes. Her mother scolded her for not dressing for the cold weather, but they were going from their house to the car to the Jacksons' house. Win could handle it, though she was ready to go inside now. Well, she was mostly ready. She wondered if there was any possible way she could avoid Bria's brother for the whole night. Somehow, she doubted it, but there was no going back now.

Bria grabbed Win's hand, pulling her into the house, Win's parents following close behind. Bria and her family always went all out for the holidays. Their house was tastefully decorated with Christmas lights, a Black nativity scene on one side of the lawn and a Black Santa Claus on the other. Inside, there was a gorgeously decorated Christmas tree in the living room beside the fireplace, where stockings for each member of the family hung. Guests dressed in their finest milled around, drinking and chatting, and hired staff walked around with trays of food and champagne flutes.

"May I take your coats?" a man asked Win.

"Oh yes, sorry," Win said, shrugging out of it as her parents did the same. Win held on to her wristlet, which was only big enough to hold her phone and lipstick in case she needed to reapply.

The party was like this every year, and it still threw Win off-kilter every time. Win's parents and Bria's parents had been best friends since before they had kids, and when Win was five her parents moved one neighborhood over from the Jacksons specifically so their kids could grow up together. As such, Win had practically grown up in this house, so she'd always been aware the Jacksons were wealthy, or "comfortable," as her dad once said when she asked if the Jacksons were rich. But there was a difference between sliding across the perfectly polished floors to see who could go the farthest and seeing the house filled with a catering staff and a bunch of other "comfortable" people in their best black-and-gold ensembles.

"Rob! Tyra!"

Bria's parents were making their way through the crowd to Win's parents. They looked fabulous, as always. Bria's dad wore black slacks and a black button-down shirt with a gold tie that matched his wife's gold dress, which Win guessed was the same one Bria was wearing, though there was no slit, so Bria must've had that added to hers.

Everyone exchanged hugs, and Bria's mom held Win out at arm's length.

"Oh, Win, you look beautiful," she said. "Has it really been a year since I last saw you?"

Win nodded. "I think so. I've just been really busy with work lately. It's a new job, so you know how it is."

Along with their annual New Year's Eve party, the Jacksons were always throwing some kind of event for charity or another holiday throughout the year, but Win had been dodging all their invitations. After what happened at last year's New Year's Eve party, she'd decided the only way to save herself from further embarrassment was to hide from the entire Jackson family, so other than meeting up with Bria every so often when Bria was in the city, Win had been keeping her distance, and it had been working.

Until now.

"Don't work yourself too hard, honey," Mrs. Jackson said with a soft pat to Win's cheek. "There's more to life than work."

"I know," Win said. "I won't."

"Good." Mrs. Jackson smiled before turning her attention to Win's parents. "We need to get you two a drink. Follow me."

"What about Win?" Bria asked. "She can drink too."

"Not the good stuff," Mr. Jackson said. "That's saved for the grown-ups."

"As if we don't know where the wine cellar is," Bria said with a huff once their parents walked away. "Little does he know, I already grabbed one of his bottles of The Macallan and stashed it in my room." Bria grabbed Win's elbow. "Let's go."

Bria made for the grand staircase that led to the second floor, and Win quickly followed. However, as they got closer to Bria's room, Win could hear different music and voices filtering out, and she realized her mistake. Of course Bria wouldn't be leading Win to her room so they could hang out alone. No, Bria's room had become the "kids'" party, at least for now, which meant anyone else under the age of thirty, including Bria's brother, was most likely waiting on the other side of the door.

"I'll be right back," Win said just as Bria's hand reached the knob. "Bathroom."

"Okay," Bria said with a shrug.

Win quickly scurried away to the farthest bathroom in the house, down in the basement, which doubled as the family's gym. She hoped most of the party guests wouldn't think to go down there. Win just needed a second alone before she faced Benjamin "Ben" Jackson.

Except the universe clearly hated her, because when she reached the bottom of the stairs, Ben was sitting on the weight bench, elbows on his knees, as he scrolled through his phone. Just like his dad, he was in all black with a gold tie, and he looked good, as per usual. The button-down shirt stretched tight along the muscles of his arms and chest, and his hair was freshly cut, with sharp lines around his forehead and his full beard perfectly trimmed.

She could almost feel the ghost of it against her skin, along her face and then her neck as he kissed her.

Ben looked up, and their eyes locked. Neither of them moved, and it took everything in Win not to fidget as Ben took her in. Her hands itched to run down her dress to smooth out any potential wrinkles, or pat down her hair to make sure the wavy curls she'd worked so hard on were still falling effortlessly down to her shoulders.

She didn't do either, though. Instead, she waited patiently for Ben to do or say anything. Finally, he stood.

"Win."

It was all he said. Just her name. Except it felt like so much more than that.

They hadn't seen each other or spoken since they were in this very house exactly one year ago. Or rather, Win hadn't spoken to him. Ben had texted and called, but Win had ignored it all, until Ben had finally given up and stopped reaching out altogether. Now Win didn't know what to say. What did you say to someone you used to talk to almost every day for your whole life but then ghosted for a year?

"Hi" was all she could come up with.

"How are you?" Ben asked. The question sounded unsure.

"I'm good." Win paused. "You?"

"Good," he said.

Win waited for him to say more, but nothing else came. Instead, they were enveloped by an awkward silence that neither of them seemed to know how to fill, and Win hated this for both of them. When they were kids, Win was closest to Bria, but the three of them—Win, Bria, and Ben—had always been an inseparable trio. Ben was older than them but only by a year, and even when he started making other friends and even girlfriends, he'd always make his way back to Win and Bria.

They told one another everything, joked about their ridiculous parents, helped one another study for exams, and were always there for one another. Then when Bria decided to go to college on the opposite side of the country, while Ben and Win both chose to go to school in the city, it was Ben who Win would call when she got homesick, and it was Ben she'd take the Long Island Rail Road back home with every holiday break.

In the past few years since they'd all graduated college and become real adults (allegedly), Ben and Win had remained in the city and had comfortably brought each other into their new lives with their new friends. It was almost inevitable that Win had caught feelings. She'd always had a small crush on Ben, but it was something she'd pushed to the back of her mind, hidden behind the *we're just friends* and *it's not like that* lines that kept her heart safe.

However, something had seemed to shift between them these last couple of years. Their hugs lasted longer, their gazes seemed to linger, and there were little touches that left her skin feeling like she was on fire. What was worse was her friends noticed it, too, and kept telling her to just go for it, but they didn't understand how messy it was. If Win and Ben dated and broke up, what would happen with their families and to Bria? Their moms often joked about Win and Ben ending up together, but it always felt like so much pressure.

Win remembered when she was looking for a date to senior prom and her mom and Mrs. Jackson recommended Ben take her, right in front of Ben. Win was horrified and embarrassed. Of course, she would've been thrilled to have Ben take her, but not as some kind of favor to their parents. To make matters worse, Bria had already told Win she planned to get them hotel rooms for after the prom, less because she wanted to sleep with her boyfriend but more to be totally cliché like the old teen soap dramas they watched on Netflix. It didn't take more than a glance at Bria, who was also present for the conversation, to know she absolutely did not want her big brother intruding on their prom night plans.

Needless to say, Win politely shut down the idea and ultimately ended up going with Bria's boyfriend's cousin. Anyway, the point was if Win and Ben dated it would be complicated, and Win hated being a complication.

So she'd tried to bury her feelings. She'd dated other people and put space between her and Ben. Until the New Year's Eve party last year.

The theme was "New Year, New You," in which partygoers were supposed to somehow come as their New Year's resolution. It was a needlessly complicated theme, and Win was sure that was why the Jacksons had gone for something much simpler this year. Still, Win had risen to the occasion and found a lime-green dress and shoes with tennis balls on the toes, and decided her resolution was to get a new hobby and that hobby would be tennis. She never had gotten that tennis racket out of her closet, come to think of it.

Ben had come dressed in the quintessential finance bro fit of khakis and a Patagonia vest that made him look ridiculous. She assumed his resolution had something to do with being promoted at his finance job, but she'd never gotten around to asking.

She'd thought she'd done a good job of dodging him at the party until he'd pulled her into his room and asked her what was going on.

"Nothing," she'd said.

"You're avoiding me," he'd said. It wasn't a question.

"I'm not—"

"Win, you think I can't tell when you're lying?" he'd asked.

They'd faced off in his room, a place Win had been a

thousand times, but it suddenly felt different. More intimate. Too tempting. Risky.

"We should head back downstairs before someone comes looking for us," she'd said instead of answering.

She'd made to walk around him, but he'd grabbed her wrist, stilling her.

"Talk to me, Win," Ben had said, his voice almost pained. "Why won't you talk to me?"

Win hadn't wanted to look at him, because she knew what would happen if she did. It was the touch of his hand on her bare skin that had been too much. She had *liked* it too much, and she desperately wanted more. Suddenly, all her fears about wrecking their friendship and making things weird for their families vanished. All she could think about was how it would feel to let her worries disappear and go after what she wanted, for once. So she did.

Turning, she'd pressed herself into him, wrapped a hand around his neck, and tugged him down until his mouth met hers. It was the most daring thing she'd ever done, and when he didn't move, she instantly regretted it. But then his hands were on her waist, pulling her even closer, and he returned the kiss, deepening it until Win moaned.

Ben walked them back until she was pressed against the door of his room, and he groaned as she tugged on his bottom lip with her teeth. She wanted more of him. All of him. Her hands smoothed down his chest as his mouth went to her neck, but when she touched his belt buckle, Ben froze.

"Wait, stop."

His breath was hot against her skin as he pulled back, and Win almost whimpered at the loss of contact.

"What's wrong?" she'd asked.

"I can't . . . I can't do this," Ben had said.

He removed his hands from her body and took one step then two away from her. Ben was looking everywhere but at her face, and she wanted to shake him or pull him back to her. She wanted to go back to a minute ago, when she believed she could have everything she wanted, consequences be damned.

"Why?" she'd finally asked.

"I'm seeing someone," he'd said.

At least he had the decency to meet her eyes when he said it, but it didn't make the words hurt any less.

"What?" Surely she'd misheard. Win knew everyone Ben dated, or, at the very least, she knew about them, whether she'd wanted to or not. Sure, they hadn't talked much lately, but he would've mentioned if he was seeing someone.

"It's only been a couple months," Ben had said. "But I can't . . . I can't do this with you while I'm trying to see what's possible with them. It's not right."

Win couldn't hear any more. Maybe it was cowardly, but she turned away from Ben and ran out the door even as he called after her. Win was sure she looked a mess, so she hid in Bria's room until Bria eventually found her. Win had pretended she wasn't feeling well, and Bria stayed with her the rest of the night, watching movies and counting down to midnight on their own.

It wasn't until Ben finally stopped trying to contact Win that she found the courage to ask Bria if her brother was seeing someone. When Bria had said no, Win was hardly surprised. Of course Ben had lied to protect her feelings, but it only made her feel worse.

Now, as they once again found themselves staring each other down, Win found that she was tired of hiding. She'd spent the last year keeping what happened between them a secret, and what had that gotten her? She ended up distancing herself from the Jacksons and lying to her parents over and over again about why she didn't want to go with them to the Jacksons' parties. It also meant she'd spent less time with her own family too. Despite doing all of that, the truth was, she realized nothing had changed. Seeing Ben now, she still wanted him so much it almost hurt, and she was sure, even if it was just for a second, that he had wanted her, too, that night. So she had to know why he lied. She had to know if there was really no way he could ever love her the way she loved him. Otherwise, she'd never fully move on, and she had to move on.

"Bria told me you didn't have a girlfriend," Win said, breaking the silence.

Ben blinked up in surprise. "What?"

"Last year," Win said. "Or, I guess, technically, it was early this year. After the party. I asked her if you were seeing anyone and she said you weren't."

Ben's mouth opened and closed a few times as he tried to find the words.

"Why did you lie?" Win asked, tired of waiting.

"I didn't lie," he said.

Win let out a harsh laugh and crossed her arms. "So you didn't make up some girlfriend to get me to stop kissing you?"

"No," Ben said.

"Ben—"

"I said I was seeing someone," Ben cut in. "And I was." He let out a long exhale. "A guy. I was seeing a guy." He sat back down on the weight bench, elbows on his knees again, his chin resting on his clasped hands as if in prayer.

Win stood frozen for a moment before joining him.

She wasn't sure what to say, and she felt like she should know what to say. She was queer herself. So was Bria. In fact, statistically speaking, it made total sense that Ben would be queer, too, and yet she still felt shocked, and she hated that she felt that way.

It had never occurred to her that Ben wasn't straight, and she knew it was because of all the stereotypical reasons. He was masculine; he'd played sports throughout high school; he was a Knicks, Giants, *and* Mets fan; and he'd only ever dated women.

Except, obviously, that wasn't true.

"I'm sorry," Win finally said. "I shouldn't have assumed. That was stupid of me."

Ben shrugged. "It was probably stupid of me not to just tell you the truth."

"It wasn't," Win said. She turned to face him, and when he didn't look at her, she took off her wristlet, covered his hands with hers, and gave them a little squeeze.

"You weren't ready to tell me then," Win said. "You shouldn't have told me just to . . ." Her voice trailed off as she struggled to finish the sentence. "Just so I wouldn't feel bad," Win said finally. "Besides, I don't think knowing the truth would've changed anything for me, honestly. I still would've been disappointed you were with someone that wasn't me."

The words hurt to say, but if they were being honest with each other now, Win didn't want to hold back. Not anymore.

"I wanted to tell you," Ben said, looking up at her. "If I was going to tell anyone, it was always going to be you, but you weren't just my friend anymore, Win. You were becoming more than that to me."

Win knew what she'd felt between them wasn't one-sided, but hearing Ben confirm it surprised her as much as it relieved her to know it was real.

"I kept trying to dismiss the feelings," Ben continued. "I knew if we dated and our families found out, they'd make a huge deal out of it and it would change things for all of us, especially if it didn't work out. Plus, I didn't know how you felt, and I thought the smart thing to do was to just move on. That's when I started dating Teddy."

"Teddy?"

Ben shook his head. "Don't laugh."

"I'm not," Win said, though the corners of her mouth quirked up.

"Win," Ben said.

"Sorry, sorry, I'm just trying to imagine a grown man going by 'Teddy,' like the bear," Win said.

"It is a very common nickname for guys named Theodore," Ben said, almost defensively. "Ever heard of Teddy Roosevelt?"

"In my textbook," Win said.

Ben pulled his hands away so he could flip her off, and whatever tension was left between them popped like a balloon. Above all else, Ben was Win's best friend, and it felt good to remember that.

"Teddy was the first man I ever wanted to actually try something with," Ben said. "And it was nice with him. Great, even."

Win's heart ached hearing this, but she didn't want to tell Ben to stop. She wanted to be supportive the same way he'd been when she and Bria had come out.

"The longer things went on with Teddy, the more I wanted to share it with you," Ben said. "It actually took more effort for me *not* to tell you. I just . . . Whenever I saw you, all thoughts of Teddy went out the window." Ben glanced up at her, and his face looked pained. "I think I knew on some level that if I told you about Teddy, whatever was happening between us would end, and I didn't want it to."

Win knew she probably should've felt upset that he essentially wanted to have his cake and eat it, too, but she couldn't. Hadn't she done the same thing? She'd dated people knowing how she felt about Ben, and she hadn't exactly shared all her sexcapades with him either.

All she really needed to know was if anything had changed from last year to now.

"Are you still with Teddy?"

Ben shook his head. "We broke up."

"When?" Win asked. She wasn't sure why it mattered, but she needed to know.

"About a month after you and I kissed," Ben said. "I felt guilty, and he could tell something was going on, so I finally told him the truth. Surprisingly, he wasn't mad. He just asked me if I felt guilty for kissing you or for letting you go."

"What did you say?" The question came out as a whisper.

"Both," Ben said. "If I was being honest, I wanted to kiss you long before that night, and I hated myself for not telling you."

Win's heart and mind raced as she tried to digest what Ben was saying. Meanwhile, he'd taken her hand and laced their fingers together, his thumb gently stroking the back of her hand. From upstairs the sounds of holiday music and increasingly louder chatter filtered down, but it barely registered for Win. It was like she and Ben were in their own world.

"I can't pinpoint when exactly things changed," Ben said, his gaze focused on their hands. "I think maybe the feelings have always been there, in the background. I remember when you moved into your apartment and we had to keep going up and down from the van with all your boxes and we were so exhausted that all we could do was lie on your floor with a pizza and beers. I remember looking at you. You were wearing overalls and one of my T-shirts that you must've stolen. You looked so beautiful I swear I couldn't breathe for a second."

"Ben, it was like eighty degrees that day and we'd basically done a workout," Win said, incredulous. "I did not look beautiful."

"You did," he said. "Like you do now."

He finally looked up at her, and his gaze was so piercing it was startling. It was like he could see straight through her, and maybe he could. Ben probably knew her better than anyone, and she him.

It was why she knew he was going to kiss her. In a way, it almost felt inevitable, like they were always going to end up back here in his parents' house, finishing what they'd started a year ago. Except this time, Ben was the one doing the leaning, one hand moving up to cup Win's cheek as he lowered his mouth to hers, but Win pulled back.

"I'm sorry, I thought—"

"You thought right," Win said, cutting him off. "I want this. I want you, but, Ben, it's been a year. Why didn't you reach out when you and Teddy broke up? Why didn't you tell me how you felt then? If I hadn't come tonight, would you have ever told me?"

"Yes, of course I would have," Ben said. "Win, do you know how many times I went all the way to your building, ready to knock down your door just so you would speak to me again?"

"Then why didn't you?" Win asked, almost desperate. "This whole time I thought this was all me. That I had ruined things between us by kissing you. I stayed away because I was so embarrassed."

"I kissed you too," Ben said. His hand was still on her cheek, and he tilted her head so she would meet his eyes. "I wanted you too. I'm sorry it took me this long to do anything about it. When you stopped coming by the house and your parents started showing up without you, I knew it was because I really hurt you, so I thought it would be better for me to stay away. I hoped if I gave you enough space one day you'd come back to us, to the family, and I would tell you then what I know now."

"What do you know now?" Win asked.

Ben smiled, and Win's breath caught as he brushed his thumb across her cheek.

"I love you," he said. "I think I maybe always have."

The air trapped in Win's throat released, and she almost sagged into him as she said, "I love you too."

Her words were barely out before Ben lowered his mouth to hers. There was nothing gentle about this kiss. It was as if Ben had been holding himself back, perhaps for a year, and now he fully let himself go. Ben's hand moved to her hair, holding the back of her neck and pulling her closer. He took Win's mouth like he owned it, and she opened for him.

Ben pulled at Win's hips, and she was grateful for the short dress, which let her straddle him, her knees on either side of him on the bench. Her hands went to Ben's shirt, undoing the buttons while he kissed a trail down to her collarbone and then to the tops of her breasts.

"May I?" he asked, a hand on one of the straps of her dress.

"Please," she begged.

Ben smiled a wicked grin she'd never seen on him before. It thrilled her, and she realized she was wrong. She did not know everything about him. She didn't know Ben as a lover. She was so excited to meet this version of him. He slid one strap down, then the other. He brushed his mouth over her bare shoulder and Win shivered. Win, impatient, reached behind her for the zipper of her corset, but Ben moved her hands away.

"I got it," Ben said as he pulled the zipper down slowly.

Ben tugged at the dress and groaned as he took in her bare breasts. Win gasped as Ben's mouth made contact with her nipple, his tongue swirling around it. Win gripped Ben's shoulders as he moved to her other breast, the sensation enough to make her come. Without thinking, she began to grind against him, his dick hard enough that she could feel it pressing against her middle through his pants.

"Win, fuck," he said.

He held her hips, staying her, and she whimpered.

Win had a sense of déjà vu as she reached for his buckle, but this time Ben didn't stop her. It was so incredibly risky doing this here where anyone could come down the stairs at any moment, but Win was finding it difficult to care.

Ben shifted and helped her tug down his pants and boxers until his dick was free. With his eyes on her, Win spit in her hand before grabbing hold of his shaft and stroking. Ben's eyes shuttered closed and his head fell back as a soft moan escaped him. She was grateful for the heavy bass of the music upstairs so they didn't have to worry about being quiet.

"Have you been tested recently?" Win asked as her hand continued to move. "I have. I'm good."

"I'm good too," Ben said, pushing the words out through heavy breaths. Win rubbed a thumb over his tip, catching the precum and bringing it down his shaft.

"I need to be inside you, Win," Ben said, grabbing her wrist. "Or we're both going to be a mess."

Win was sure they already were. She could see her lipstick all over his mouth and his shirt was half undone, while her tits were on full display.

She lifted her hips, reaching under the fabric of her dress, pulling her panties aside to guide Ben inside her. Win lowered herself, and they both hissed as she took him deeper. They stayed like that for a moment, Win adjusting to the feel of him. He was thick, stretching her in a way that was slightly uncomfortable but also felt so good. He cursed as she started slowly grinding her hips as she rode him. Ben's hands were in her hair again and he tugged her down to kiss her as they moved together. Win wasn't sure she'd ever felt this good before, and soon she was moving quicker, holding on to Ben's shoulders as her steady rhythm became almost frantic.

"Fuck yes. Win, shit," Ben said.

He was so close, she could feel it, and so was she. Reaching under her dress, Win pressed three fingers to her clit, the pressure exactly what she needed.

"Ben, fuck, I'm—"

Win lost all control of her speech as the orgasm ran through her like lightning. Ben gripped her hips tightly, holding her on top of him as he came inside her a moment later with a deep moan.

They were both breathing heavily, taking in this moment together that felt unreal but so right.

Finally, Win knew they had to separate before someone

came looking for them. Reluctantly, Win pushed herself up and off Ben, standing between his legs. She felt a bit wobbly and sore, so she knew she'd feel it even more tomorrow, which was perfectly fine to her. She'd relish the reminder of being thoroughly fucked by Benjamin Jackson, something she'd convinced herself would never happen.

"You okay?" Ben asked, looking up at her, taking her in.

"Yeah," she said while fixing her dress. "You?" She turned around so he could zip up her dress.

"I'm feeling better than I have in a long while," he said, his knuckles brushing her spine. She turned back to face him, and he wrapped his arms around her middle, pulling her closer.

"I meant what I said, Win," Ben said. "This isn't some one-night–stand thing for me. I love you, and I want all of you."

Win blushed and clasped her hands behind his neck.

"No running this time," Ben said with a smirk. "Got it?"

Win grinned. "Got it."

"Good." Ben kissed her so fiercely it took her much restraint to resist climbing back on top of him. When they pulled apart, they were both smiling, and Win still couldn't believe this was real.

"We should probably clean up," Ben said. "Your lipstick is smudged, and I can imagine where it went."

Win laughed as she wiped a thumb over his mouth.

"Yup, it's all right here."

Ben grabbed her wrist and took her thumb in his mouth, sucking it clean before letting it go with a soft *pop*. Win had to lock her knees to stop herself from pressing into him again.

"If you want us to actually get cleaned up, you're going

to have to stop doing things with your mouth," Win said, breathless.

"Sorry," Ben said, though he didn't look sorry at all.

Win shook her head in admonishment, but it was so forced. Even she knew she didn't mean it. Kissing him quickly, she made herself pull away. Grabbing her bag, she headed to the bathroom.

Ten minutes later, and with great effort, they went back upstairs to the party, promising to keep their hands to themselves.

It didn't take long for Bria to find them among the throng of people.

"Where have y'all been?" Bria asked, looking between them. "I have a bottle of whiskey in my room that still needs finishing, and it'll be midnight soon. You know once the clock strikes twelve I only drink champagne."

"I ran into Ben on my way to the bathroom and we ended up talking," Win said.

"Yeah, we lost track of time," Ben said.

They locked eyes and Win pressed her lips together to stop the ridiculous smile spreading on her face.

Bria looked between the two of them skeptically, eventually rolling her eyes. "Whatever, I'm just glad you two are speaking again," Bria said. "If Ben asked me one more time, 'Have you talked to Win lately?' I was going to lose it. You are both aware you live in the same city, correct?"

Win looked up at Ben. "You were asking about me?"

"Perhaps," Ben said, shuffling in place.

Win smiled. "Cute."

"Ugh, whatever this is, please stop," Bria said, her face scrunched in disgust. "Everyone's in my room. We're playing Kings."

Win was sure Bria knew exactly what was going on between Ben and Win, but if Bria wasn't going to address it directly, neither would Win. At least not tonight.

"Kings?" Win said. "Are we trying to die tonight?"

Anytime Win played the drinking game with Bria, she ended up with only vague memories of the evening.

"You can sip water," Bria said with a wave of her hand. "Now come on before the 'rents find us and try to make me network. Mom is convinced if I talk to one of the three senators here, I could become one of their assistants. As if I even want to work in politics."

Win laughed, and when she looked at Ben, the way he was looking at her made her face heat, so she quickly looked away.

"Let me grab some of those," Win said, taking a couple of the bottles of water from Bria.

"Thank you. At least *someone* is helpful," Bria said pointedly.

Ben rolled his eyes and grabbed the rest of the bottles from her.

"Perfect, let's go."

Win and Ben followed her upstairs to her room, where there was indeed a small crowd of people waiting. They literally cheered as the three of them walked in, which signaled to Win that they were already a little drunk.

Bria got to work setting up the game on the floor, and Ben and Win hovered near each other. Win could feel Ben's body heat next to hers, and every so often their hands would drift together, fingers brushing. It was torture being teased this way, and she had half a mind to ask him if he wanted to get out of here, but she knew leaving would be impossible now that Bria had gotten hold of them.

"All right, everyone gather round and grab a drink," Bria said. "Let's get wasted."

Ben and Win joined everyone else in the circle. Win tucked her legs under her dress, her knees pointed in Ben's direction. He shifted slightly until their legs were touching, and they stayed like that throughout the game.

By the time Mrs. Jackson came to get them for the countdown to midnight, Win, who decided halfway through to try the whiskey, was a bit buzzed, but in a warm happy way. Ben, who'd stuck with water, helped her stand and took a second too long letting her hands go.

"Good?" he asked.

Win nodded, and Ben placed a hand at her back as he guided her out of the room with everyone else.

"All right, party people," Mrs. Jackson said, once everyone was downstairs in the living room. "Everybody grab a glass."

A server walked around with a tray of champagne flutes, and Win took one, as did Ben and Bria.

Mrs. Jackson was standing on the bottom step of the staircase with Mr. Jackson, who had his arm around her waist. Win looked around the room and found her parents standing off to the side, in a similar pose. In fact, many couples were wrapped around each other. Win looked up at Ben, who was standing to her right. He must've felt her stare, because he turned to her with a raised brow.

He lowered his head so he could hear her over the chatter of the room. "What's up?" he asked.

"Kiss me," Win said.

It was silly and ridiculous, and everyone would see, but Win didn't care. It was New Year's Eve, and you were supposed to kiss the person you loved at midnight. So what if she'd just figured out that person was her best friend and neither of their families knew about it yet? They could deal with that later. Right now, she couldn't imagine standing around watching everyone else kiss with Ben right beside her, *not* kissing her.

"What?" Ben asked.

"Kiss me," she repeated. "At midnight."

Ben looked around the room, and over at Bria, who was talking to one of her friends. Finally, he looked back at Win.

"Are you sure?"

Win grinned. "Yes."

"Here we go, people!" Mrs. Jackson said. "Ten . . . nine . . . eight . . ."

Win stepped into Ben's arms. Everyone else faded away as he looked at her with the same goofy grin she was sure was on her face.

"Five . . . four . . . three," the crowd chanted.

She stepped even closer to him.

"Two . . . one! Happy New Year!"

"Happy New Year!" Win said to Ben.

"Happy New Year!" he murmured back, lowering his head and pressing his lips to hers.

Win breathed him in, and she swore she saw fireworks.

When they pulled apart, everyone was still hugging, kissing, or cheering, and no one seemed to notice them at all. Win laughed and Ben joined her, before pulling her in for another kiss.

By all accounts, Win's year was off to a great start.

ABOUT THE AUTHORS

Alexandria Bellefleur is an award-winning *USA Today* bestselling author of swoony contemporary romance often featuring lovable grumps and the sunshine characters who bring them to their knees. Her debut novel, *Written in the Stars,* was a 2021 Lambda Literary Award winner and a 2020 winner of The Ripped Bodice Awards for Excellence in Romantic Fiction.

Elise Bryant is the NAACP Image Award–nominated author of *Happily Ever Afters*, *One True Loves*, *Reggie and Delilah's Year of Falling*, *It's Elementary*, and *The Game Is Afoot*. For many years, Elise had the joy of working as a special education teacher, and now she spends her days reading, writing, and eating dessert. She lives with her husband and two daughters in Long Beach, California.

Lifelong nerd **Olivia Dade** has held various rewarding jobs over the years—librarian, high school teacher, Colonial Williamsburg interpreter—but is thrilled to have finally achieved her ultimate goal of wearing pajamas all day as a hermit-like writer and enthusiastic hag. She currently lives outside Stockholm with her delightful family and their ever-burgeoning collection of books.

Alexis Daria is the award-winning and *USA Today* bestselling author of *You Had Me at Hola*, *Along Came Amor*, *Take the Lead*, and more. Her books have been featured on several "best of" lists and have received starred reviews from multiple trade publications. A former visual artist, Alexis is a lifelong New Yorker who loves Broadway musicals and pizza.

Sarah Hogle is a mom of three who enjoys K-dramas and provoking her husband for attention. Her dream is to live in a falling-apart castle in a forest that is probably cursed. She is also the author of *You Deserve Each Other*, *Twice Shy*, *Just Like Magic*, *Old Flames and New Fortunes*, and *The Folklore of Forever*.

Zakiya N. Jamal was born in Queens, raised on Long Island, and currently resides in Brooklyn. In other words, she's a New Yorker through and through. When she's not writing romance novels, she's falling in love with a K-drama, watching a rom-com, or cuddling with her dog, Sammy. You can find her on social media at @ZakiyaNJamal.

Rebecca Jenshak is a *USA Today* bestselling author of new adult and sports romance. She writes sexy, feel-good stories with lots of swoon-worthy moments. Rebecca lives in Arizona. When she isn't writing, you can find her cheering on local sports teams, hanging out with friends and family, or curled up with a good book.

Jessica Joyce is the bestselling author of relatable, character-driven contemporary romance stories that feature as much yearning as she can stuff into them. When she's not working on a new book, you can find her making a playlist, watching *Sleepless in Seattle* and the 2005 version of *Pride & Prejudice* on repeat, or curled up with a book she didn't have to write.

Susan Lee is a *USA Today* bestselling author of young adult and adult romantic comedies. Her work has been featured in national outlets such as *NPR*, *Oprah*, and *Harper's Bazaar. Kirkus Reviews* calls her voice "honest, fresh and thoughtful." Susan built a career as an executive at some of today's hottest companies but now channels her energy into publishing happily ever afters for those historically underrepresented in romance. When not writing, Susan can be found in her pajamas all day cuddling with her senior diva Chihuahua, Buttercup.

Joss Richard is the international bestselling author of *It's Different This Time*, who's worked at companies such as Hello Sunshine and Reese's Book Club, The Walt Disney Company, *The Ellen DeGeneres Show*, Netflix, and Paramount. She's also the creator and host of *Three's Company, Too: A Rewatch Podcast* and has been formally recognized with a Daytime Emmy Award. Born in Toronto, Ontario, to Filipino immigrant parents, Richard currently lives and works in Los Angeles, California.

Writing as **M.A. Wardell**, Lambda Literary Award nominee Matt writes spicy, heartfelt gay romance. He's passionate about telling adult queer love stories featuring flawed, messy men who deserve big feelings, real growth, and a happily ever after. Matt grew up craving more queer representation in the media, so now he writes the stories he always wanted to experience. He's the author of the Teacher in Love series (Forever, Hachette) as well as other stories that center queer joy.

After years of meddling in her friends' love lives, **Rebekah Weatherspoon** turned to writing romance to get her fix. Many award-winning novels later, she still believes in love, the fluffier the better. Raised in southern New Hampshire, Rebekah now lives in Southern California with her dog, Lizzie. She will remain there forever because she hates moving.